CLONE WARS
TIMELINE [continued]

MONTHS
(after *Attack of the Clones*)

+2   **THE BATTLE OF KAMINO**
Clone Wars I: *The Defense of Kamino* (DH, June '03)

+3   **THE DEFENSE OF NABOO**
Clone Wars II: *Heroes and Scapegoats* (DH, September '03)

+6   **THE HARUUN KAL CRISIS**
Shatterpoint (DR, June '03)

+9   **THE DAGU REVOLT**
Escape from Dagu (DR, March '04)

+12   **THE BIO-DROID THREAT**
The Cestus Deception (DR, June '04)

+15   **THE BATTLE OF JABIIM**
Clone Wars III: *Last Stand on Jabiim* (DH, February '04)

+30   **THE PRAESITLYN CONQUEST**
Jedi Trial (DR, November '04)

KEY:
DH = *Dark Horse Comics, graphic novels*
www.darkhorse.com
DR = *Del Rey, hard cover & paperback books*
www.delreydigital.com
LEC = *LucasArts Games, games for XBox, Game Cube,*
PS2, & PC platforms www.lucasarts.com
LFL = *Lucasfilm Ltd., motion pictures* www.starwars.com
SB = *Scholastic Books, juvenile fiction* www.scholastic.com/starwars

WARS.

SHATTERPOINT

Other titles by Matthew Stover

IRON DAWN
JERICHO MOON
HEROES DIE
BLADE OF TYSHALLE
STAR WARS: THE NEW JEDI ORDER *TRAITOR*

STAR WARS

SHATTERPOINT

MATTHEW STOVER

BALLANTINE BOOKS • NEW YORK

Star Wars: Shatterpoint is a work of fiction. Names, places, and incidents either are a product of the author's imagination or are used fictitiously.

A Del Rey® Book
Published by The Random House Ballantine Publishing Group

Copyright © 2003 by Lucasfilm Ltd. & ® or ™ where indicated.
All Rights Reserved. Used Under Authorization.

All rights reserved under International and Pan-American Copyright Conventions. Published in the United States by The Random House Ballantine Publishing Group, a division of Random House, Inc., New York, and simultaneously in Canada by Random House of Canada Limited, Toronto.

Del Rey is a registered trademark and the Del Rey colophon is a trademark of Random House, Inc.

www.starwars.com
www.delreydigital.com

The Cataloging-in-Publication Data for this title is available from the Library of Congress.

ISBN 0-345-45573-8

Book Design by Susan Turner

Manufactured in the United States of America

First Edition: June 2003

10 9 8 7 6 5 4 3 2 1

For Robyn, my wife,
for making me grateful
that I am not a Jedi

and for the fans
for keeping the dream alive

SHATTERPOINT

DANGEROUSLY
SANE

FROM THE PRIVATE JOURNALS OF MACE WINDU

In my dreams, I always do it right.

In my dreams, I'm on the arena balcony. Geonosis. Orange glare slices shadow from my eyes. Below on the sand: Obi-Wan Kenobi, Anakin Skywalker, Senator Padmé Amidala. On the rough-shaped stone within reach of my arm: Nute Gunray. Within reach of my blade: Jango Fett.

And Master Dooku.

No. Master no more. *Count* Dooku.

I may never get used to calling him that. Even in dreams.

Jango Fett bristles with weapons. An instinctive killer: the deadliest man in the galaxy. Jango can kill me in less than a second. I know it. Even if I had never seen Kenobi's report from Kamino, I can feel the violence Jango radiates: in the Force, a pulsar of death.

But I do it *right*.

My blade doesn't light the underside of Fett's square jaw. I don't waste time with words. I don't hesitate.

I *believe*.

In my dreams, the purple flare of my blade sizzles the gray hairs of Dooku's beard, and in the critical semisecond it takes Jango Fett to aim and fire, I twitch that blade and take Dooku with me into death.

And save the galaxy from civil war.

I could have done it.

I *could have done it.*

Because I knew. I could *feel* it.

In the swirl of the Force around me, I could feel the connections Dooku had forged among Jango and the Trade Federation, the Geonosians, the whole Separatist movement: connections of greed and fear, of deception and bald intimidation. I did not know what they were—I did not know how Dooku had forged them, or why—but I felt their power: the power of what I now know is a web of treason he had woven to catch the galaxy.

I could feel that without him to maintain its weave, to repair its flaws and double its thinning strands, the web would rot, would shrivel and decay until a mere breath would shred it and scatter its strings into the infinite stellar winds.

Dooku was the shatterpoint.

I knew it.

That is my gift.

Imagine a Corusca gem: a mineral whose interlocking crystalline structure makes it harder than durasteel. You can strike one with a five-kilo hammer and do no more than dent the hammer's face. Yet the same cystalline structure that gives the Corusca strength also gives it shatterpoints: spots where a precise application of carefully measured force—no more than a gentle tap—will break it into pieces. But to find these shatterpoints, to use them to shape the Corusca gem into beauty and utility, requires years of study, an intimate understanding of crystal structure, and rigorous practice to train the hand in the perfect combination of strength and precision to produce the desired cut.

Unless you have a talent like mine.

I can see shatterpoints.

The sense is not sight, but *see* is the closest word Basic has for it: it is a perception, a *feel* of how what I look upon fits into the Force, and how the Force binds it to itself and to everything else. I was six or seven standard years old—well into my training in the Jedi Temple—before I realized that other students, full-grown Jedi Knights, even wise Masters, could sense such connections only with difficulty, and only with concentration and practice. The Force shows me strengths and weaknesses, hidden flaws and unexpected uses. It shows me vectors of stress that squeeze or stretch, torque or shear; it shows me how patterns of these vectors intersect to form the matrix of reality.

Put simply: when I look at you through the Force, I can see where you break.

I looked at Jango Fett on the sand in the Geonosian arena. A perfect combination of weapons, skills, and the will to use them: an interlocking crystal of killer. The Force hinted a shatterpoint, and I left a headless corpse on the sand. The deadliest man in the galaxy.

Now: just dead.

Situations have shatterpoints, like gems. But those of situations are fluid, ephemeral, appearing for a bare instant, vanishing again to leave no trace of their existence. They are always a function of timing.

There is no such thing as a second chance.

If—*when*—I next encounter Dooku, he will be the war's shatterpoint no longer. I can't stop this war with a single death.

But on that day in the Geonosian arena, I could have.

Some days after the battle, Master Yoda had found me in a meditation chamber at the Temple. "Your friend he was," the ancient Master had said, even as he limped through the door. It is a peculiar gift of Yoda's that he always seems to know what I'm thinking. "Respect you owed him. Even affection. Cut him down you could not—not for merely a *feeling*."

But I could have.

I should have.

Our Order prohibits personal attachments for precisely this reason. Had I not honored him so—even loved him—the galaxy might be at peace right now. *Merely a feeling*, Yoda said.

I am a Jedi.

I have been trained since birth to trust my feelings.

But which feelings should I trust?

When I faced the choice to kill a former Jedi Master, or to save Kenobi and young Skywalker and the Senator . . . I let the Force choose for me. I followed my instincts.

I made the Jedi choice.

And so: Dooku escaped. And so: the galaxy is at war. And so: many of my friends have been slaughtered.

There is no such thing as a second chance.

Strange: Jedi I am, yet I drown in regret for having *spared* a life.

Many survivors of Geonosis suffer from nightmares. I have heard tale after tale from the Jedi healers who have counseled them. Nightmares are inevitable; there has not been such a slaughter of Jedi since the Sith War, four thousand years ago. None of them could have imagined how it would feel to stand in that arena, surrounded by the corpses of their friends, in the blazing orange noon and the stench and the blood-soaked sand. I may be the only veteran of Geonosis who doesn't have nightmares of that place.

Because in *my* dreams, I always do it *right*.

My nightmare is what I find when I wake up.

Jedi have shatterpoints, too.

Mace Windu stopped in the doorway and tried to recover his calm. An arc of sweat darkened the cowl of his robe, and his tunic clung to his skin: he'd come straight from a training bout at the Temple without taking time to shower. And the brisk pace—almost a jog—he'd maintained through the labyrinth of the Galactic Senate had offered no chance for him to cool off.

Palpatine's private office, in the Supreme Chancellor's suite beneath the Senate's Great Rotunda, opened before him, vast and stark. An expanse of polished ebonite floor; a few simple, soft chairs; a flat trestle desk, also ebonite. No pictures, paintings, or decorations other than two lone statues; only floor-to-ceiling holographic repeaters showing real-time images of Galactic City as seen from the pinnacle of the Senate Dome. Outside, the orbital mirrors would soon turn their faces from Coruscant's sun, bringing twilight to the capital.

Within was only Yoda. Alone. Perched solemnly on his hoverchair, hands folded around the head of his stick. "On time you are," the ancient Master observed, "but barely. Take a chair; composed we must be. Serious, I fear this is."

"I wasn't expecting a party." Mace's boot heels clacked on the polished floor. He pulled one of the soft, plain chairs closer to Yoda and sat beside him, facing the desk. Tension made his jaw ache. "The courier said this is about the operation on Haruun Kal."

The fact that of all the members of the Jedi Council and the Republic High Command, only the two senior members of the Council had been summoned by the Chancellor, implied that the news was not good.

These two senior members could hardly have appeared more different. Yoda was barely two-thirds of a meter tall, with skin green as Chadian wander-kelp and great bulging eyes that could sometimes seem almost to take on a light of their own; Mace was tall for a human, less than a hand's breadth short of two meters, with shoulders broad and powerful, heavy arms, dark eyes, and a grim set to his jaw. Where Yoda had let his sparse remnants of hair straggle at random, Mace's skull was smooth-shaven, the color of polished lammas.

But their greatest difference perhaps lay in the *feel* of the two Jedi Masters. Yoda emanated a sense of mellow wisdom, combined with the impish sense of humor characteristic of the true sage; but his great age and vast experience sometimes made him seem a bit removed, even detached. Nearing nine hundred years of age led him to naturally take the long view. Mace, in contrast, had been elevated to the Jedi Council before his thirtieth birthday. His demeanor was exactly opposite. Lean. Driven. Intense. He radiated incisive intellect and unconquerable will.

As of the Battle of Geonosis, which had opened the Clone Wars, Mace had been on the Council for more than twenty standard years. It had been ten since anyone had last seen him smile.

He sometimes wondered privately if he would ever smile again.

"But it is not the planet Haruun Kal that brings you in a sweat to this office," Yoda said now. His tone was light and understanding, but his gaze was sharp. "Concerned for Depa, you are."

Mace lowered his head. "I know: the Force will bring what it will. But Republic Intelligence has reported that the Separatists have pulled back; their base outside Pelek Baw is abandoned—"

"Yet return she has not."

Mace knotted his fingers together. A breath brought his voice back to its customary deep, flat dispassion. "Haruun Kal is still nominally a Separatist planet. And she's a wanted woman. It won't be easy for her to get offworld. Or even to signal for extraction—the local militia use all kinds of signal jamming, and whatever they don't jam they triangulate; whole partisan bands have been wiped out by one incautious transmission—"

"Your friend she is." Yoda used his stick to poke Mace on the arm. "Care for her, you do."

Mace didn't meet his eyes. His feelings for Depa Billaba ran deep.

She had been onworld for four standard months. She couldn't communicate regularly; Mace had tracked her activities by sporadic Republic Intelligence reports of sabotage at the Separatist starfighter base, and the fruitless expeditions of the Balawai militias trying—and failing—to wipe out Depa's guerrillas, or even contain them. More than a month ago, Republic Intelligence had sent word that the Separatists had pulled back to the Gevarno Cluster, because they could no longer maintain and defend their base. Her success could not have been more brilliant.

But he feared to learn at what cost.

"But it can't simply be that she's missing, or . . . ," he murmured. A dark flush spread over his bare dome of skull when he realized he'd spoken his thoughts aloud. He felt Yoda's eyes on him still, and gave half an apologetic shrug. "I was only thinking: if she'd been captured or—or killed—there would be no need for such secrecy . . ."

The creases on Yoda's face deepened around his mouth, and he made that *tchk* sound of mild disapproval that any Jedi would instantly recognize. "Frivolous, speculation is, when patience will reveal all."

Mace nodded silently. One did not argue with Master Yoda; in the Jedi Temple, this was learned in infancy. No Jedi ever forgot it. "It's . . . maddening, Master. If only . . . I mean, ten years ago, we could have simply reached out—"

"Cling to the past, a Jedi can*not*," Yoda interrupted sternly. His green stare reminded Mace not to speak of the shadow that had darkened Jedi perception of the Force. This was not discussed out-side the Temple. Not even here. "Member of the Jedi Council, she is. Powerful Jedi. Brilliant warrior—"

"She'd better be." Mace tried to smile. "I trained her."

"But worry you do. Too much. Not only for Depa, but for all the Jedi. Ever since Geonosis."

The smile wasn't working. He stopped trying. "I don't want to talk about Geonosis."

"Known this for months, I have." Yoda poked him again, and Mace looked up. The ancient Master leaned toward him, ears curled forward, and his huge green eyes glimmered softly. "But when, fi-nally, to talk you want . . . listen, I will."

Mace accepted this with a silent inclination of his head. He'd never doubted it. But still, he preferred to discuss something else.

Anything else.

"Look at this place," he murmured, nodding at the expanse of the Supreme Chancellor's office. "Even after ten years, the difference between Palpatine and Valorum . . . How this office was, in those days—"

Yoda lifted his head in that reverse nod of his. "Remember Finis Valorum well, I do. Last of a great line, he was." Some vast distance drifted through his gaze: he might have been looking back along his nine hundred years as a Jedi.

It was unsettling to contemplate that the Republic, seemingly eternal in its millennium-long reign, was not much older than Yoda himself. Sometimes, in the tales Yoda told of his long-vanished younger days, a Jedi might have heard the youth of the Republic it-self: brash, confident, bursting with vitality as it expanded across the galaxy, bringing peace and justice to cluster after cluster, system af-ter system, world after world.

For Mace, it was even more unsettling to contemplate the contrast Yoda was seeing.

"Connected with the past, Valorum was. Rooted deep in tradi-tion's soil." In the wave of his hand, Yoda seemed to summon Finis Valorum's dazzling array of antique furniture gleaming with exotic oils, his artworks and sculptures and treasures from a thousand worlds. Legacies of thirty generations of House Valorum had once filled this office. "Perhaps *too* deep: a man of history, was Valorum. Palpatine . . ." Yoda's eyes drifted closed. "A man of today, Palpatine is."

"You say that as though it pains you."

"Perhaps it does. Or perhaps: my pain is only of this day, not its man."

"I prefer the office like this." Mace half nodded around the sweep of open floor. Austere. Unpretentious and uncompromising. To Mace, it was a window into Palpatine's character: the Supreme Chancellor lived entirely for the Republic. Simple in dress. Direct in speech. Unconcerned with ornamentation or physical comfort. "A shame he can't touch the Force. He might have made a fine Jedi."

"But then, another Supreme Chancellor would we need." Yoda smiled gently. "Better this way, perhaps it is."

Mace acknowledged the point with a slight bow.

"Admire him, you do."

Mace frowned. He'd never thought about it. His adult life had been spent at the orders of the Supreme Chancellor . . . but he served the office, not the man. What did he think of the Supreme Chancellor as a person? What difference could that make?

"I suppose I do." Mace vividly recalled what the Force had shown him while he watched Palpatine sworn in as Supreme Chancellor, ten years before: Palpatine was himself a shatterpoint on which the future of the Republic—perhaps even the whole galaxy—depended. "The only other person I can imagine leading the Republic through this dark hour is . . . well—" He opened a hand. "—*you*, Master Yoda."

Yoda rocked back on his hover chair and made the rustling snuffle that served him for a laugh. "No politician am I, foolish one."

He still occasionally spoke as though Mace were a student. Mace didn't mind. It made him feel young. Everything else these days made him feel old.

Yoda's laughter faded. "And no fit leader for this Republic would I be." He lowered his voice even further, to barely above a whisper. "Clouded by darkness are my eyes; the Force shows me only suffering, and destruction, and the rise of a long, long night. Better off without the Force, leaders perhaps are; able to see well enough, young Palpatine seems."

"Young" Palpatine—who had at least ten years on Mace, and looked twice that—chose that moment to enter the room, accompanied by another man. Yoda stepped down from his hoverchair. Mace rose in respect. The Jedi Masters bowed, greeting the Supreme Chancellor with their customary formality. He waved the courtesies aside. Palpatine looked tired: flesh seemed to be dissolving beneath his sagging skin, deepening his already hollowed cheeks.

The man with Palpatine was hardly larger than a boy, though clearly well past forty; lank, thinning brown hair draped a face so thoroughly undistinguished that Mace could forget it the instant he glanced away. His eyes were red-rimmed, he held a cloth handkerchief to his nose, and he looked so much like some minor bureaucratic functionary—a clerk in a dead-end government post, with job security and absolutely nothing else—that Mace automatically assumed he was a spy.

"We have news of Depa Billaba."

Despite his earlier reasoning, the simple sadness in the Chancellor's voice sent Mace's stomach plummeting.

"This man has just come from Haruun Kal. I'm afraid—well, perhaps you should simply examine the evidence for yourself."

"What is it?" Mace's mouth went dry as ash. "Has she been captured?" The treatment a captured Jedi could expect from Dooku's Separatists had been demonstrated on Geonosis.

"No, Master Windu," Palpatine said. "I'm afraid—I'm afraid it's quite a bit worse."

The agent opened a large travelcase and produced an old-fashioned holoprojector. He spent a moment fiddling with controls, and then an image bloomed above the mirror-polished ebonite that served as Palpatine's desk.

Yoda's ears flattened, and his eyes narrowed to slits.

Palpatine looked away. "I have seen too much of this already," he said.

Mace's hands became fists. He couldn't seem to get his breath.

The shimmering corpses were each the size of his finger. He counted nineteen. They looked human, or close to it. There was a scatter of prefabricated huts, blasted and burned and broken. The ruins of what must have once been a stockade wall made a ring around the scene. The jungle that surrounded them all stood four decimeters high, and covered a meter and a half of Palpatine's desk.

After a moment, the agent sniffled apologetically. "This is—er, *seems* to be—the work of Loyalist partisans, under the command of Master Billaba."

Yoda stared.

Mace stared.

There—those wounds . . . Mace needed a better view. When he reached into the jungle, his hand crawled with the bright ripples of the holoprojector's scanning-matrix lasers. "These."

He passed his hand through a group of three bodies that gaped with ragged wounds. "Enhance these."

The Republic Intelligence agent answered without taking his handkerchief away from his reddened eyes. "Uh, I'm uh—Master Windu, this recording is, er, is quite unsophisticated—almost, uh, *primitive*—" His voice vanished into a sneeze that jerked him forward as though he'd been slapped on the back of the head. "Sorry—sorry, I can't—my system won't tolerate histamine suppressors. Every time I come to Coruscant—"

Mace's hand didn't move. He didn't look up. He waited while the agent's whine trickled to silence. Nineteen corpses. And this man complained about his *allergies*.

"Enhance these," Mace repeated.

"I, ah—yes. Sir." The agent manipulated the holoprojector's controls with hands that didn't quite tremble. Not quite. The jungle flicked out of existence. It reappeared an instant later, spread across ten meters of the office's floor. The tangled upper branches of the holographic trees had become glimmering scan patterns on the ceiling; the corpses were now almost half life-sized.

The agent ducked his head, scrubbing furiously at his nose with the handkerchief. "Sorry, Master Windu. Sorry. But the system—it's—"

"Primitive. Yes." Mace waded through the light-cast images until he could squat beside the bodies. He rested his elbows on his knees, folding his hands together before his face.

Yoda walked closer, then crouched as he leaned in for a better view. After a moment, Mace looked up into his sad green eyes. "See?"

"Yes . . . yes," Yoda croaked. "But from this, no conclusion can be drawn."

"That's my *point.*"

"For those of us who are not Jedi—" Supreme Chancellor Palpatine's voice had the warm strength of a career politician's. He rounded his desk, on his face the slightly puzzled smile of a good man who faced an ugly situation with hope that everything might still turn out all right. "—perhaps you'll explain?"

"Yes, sir. The other bodies don't tell us much, between decomposition and scavenger damage. But some of the mutilation on the soft tissue here—" A curve of Mace's hand traced gaping slashes across a holographic female torso. "—isn't from claws or teeth. And they didn't come from a powered weapon. See the scoring on her ribs? A lightsaber—even a vibroblade—would have slashed right through the bone. This was done with a dead blade, sir."

Revulsion tightened the Supreme Chancellor's face. "A—dead blade? You mean just—like a piece of *metal?* Just a sharp piece of metal?"

"A very sharp piece of metal, sir." Mace cocked his head a centimeter to the right. "Or ceramic. Transparisteel. Even carbonite."

Palpatine took a deep breath as though suppressing a shudder. "It sounds . . . dreadfully crude. And painful."

"Sometimes it is, sir. Not always." He didn't bother to explain how he knew. "But these slashes are parallel, and all of nearly the same length; it's likely she was dead before the cuts were made. Or at least unconscious."

"Or—" The agent sniffled, and coughed apologetically. "—just, er, y'know, *tied up.*"

Mace stared at him. Yoda closed his eyes. Palpatine lowered his head as though in pain.

"There is, uh, a history of, uh, I guess you'd say, *recreational torture* in the Haruun Kal conflict. On both sides." The agent flushed as though he was ashamed to know such things. "Sometimes, people— people *hate* so much, that just *killing* the enemy isn't enough . . ."

A fist clenched in Mace's chest: that this soft little man—this *civilian*—could accuse Depa Billaba of such an atrocity, even by implication, grabbed his heart with sick fury. A long cold stare showed him every place on this soft man's soft body where one sharp blow would kill; the agent blanched as if he could count them all in Mace's eyes.

But Mace had been a Jedi far too long for anger to gain an easy grip. A breath or two opened that fist around his heart, and he stood. "I have seen nothing to indicate Depa was involved."

"Master Windu—" Palpatine began.

"What was the military value of this outpost?"

"Military value?" The agent looked startled. "Why, none, I suppose. These were Balawai jungle prospectors. *Jups,* they call 'em. Some jups operate as a kind of irregular militia, but irregulars are nearly always men. There were six women here. And Balawai militia units never, ah, never bring their, ah, *children . . .*"

"Children," Mace echoed.

The agent nodded reluctantly. "Three. Mm, bioscans indicate one girl about twelve, the other two possibly fraternal twins. Boy and a girl. About nine. Had to use bioscans . . ." His sickly eyes asked Mace not to make him finish.

Because a few days in the jungle hadn't left enough of them to be identified any other way.

Mace said, "I understand."

"These weren't militia, Master Windu. Just Balawai jungle prospectors in the wrong place at the wrong time."

"Jungle prospectors?" Palpatine appeared politely interested. "And what are *Balawai?*"

"Offworlders, sir," Mace said. "The jungles of Haruun Kal are the galaxy's sole source of thyssel bark, as well as portaak leaf, jinsol, tyruun, and lammas. Among others."

"Spices and exotic woods? And these are valuable enough to draw offworld emigrants? Into a *war* zone?"

"Have you priced thyssel bark lately?"

"I—" Palpatine smiled regretfully. "I don't care for it, actually. I suppose my tastes are pedestrian; you can take a boy out of the Mid Rim, but . . ."

Mace shook his head. "Not relevant, sir. My point: these were civilians. Depa wouldn't be involved in something like this. She *couldn't.*"

"Hasty, your statement is," Yoda said gravely. "Seen all evidence, I fear we have not."

Mace looked at the agent. The agent flushed again.

"Well, er, yes—Master Yoda is correct. This, uh, recording—" He twitched his head around at the ghostly corpses that filled the office. "—was made with the prospectors' own equipment; it's adapted to Haruun Kal work, where more sophisticated electronics—"

"I don't need a lesson on Haruun Kal." Mace's voice went sharp. "I need your *evidence.*"

"Yes, yes of course, Master Windu . . ." The agent fished in his travelcase for a second or two, then came up with an old-fashioned data wafer of crystal. He handed it over. "It's, uh, audio only, but— we've done voiceprint analysis. It's not exact—and there's some ambient noise, other voices, jungle sounds, that kind of thing—but we put match probability in the ninety percent range."

Mace weighed the crystal wafer in his hand. He stared down at it. There. Right there: the flick of a fingernail could crack it in two. *I should do it,* he thought. *Crush this thing. Snap it in half right now. Destroy it unheard.*

Because he knew. He could feel it. In the Force, stress lines spidered out from the wafer like frost scaling supercooled transparisteel. He could not read the pattern, but he could feel its power.

This would be ugly.

"Where did you find it?"

"It was—uh, at the scene. Of the massacre. It was . . . well, at the scene."

"Where did you *find* it?"

The agent flinched.

Again, Mace took a breath. Then another. With the third, the fist in his chest relaxed. "I am sorry."

Sometimes he forgot how intimidating some men found his height and voice. Not to mention his reputation. He did not wish to be feared.

At least, not by those loyal to the Republic.

"Please," he said. "It might be significant."

The agent mumbled something.

"I'm sorry?"

"I said, it was in her *mouth*." He waved a hand in the general direction of the holographic corpse at Mace's feet. "Someone had . . . fixed her jaw shut, so scavengers wouldn't get at it when they . . . well, y'know, scavengers prefer the, the, er, the tongue . . ."

Nausea bloomed below Mace's ribs. His fingertips tingled. He stared down at the woman's image. Those marks on her face—he had thought they were just marks. Or some kind of fungus, or a colony of mold. Now his eyes made sense of them, and he wished they hadn't: dull gold-colored lumps under her chin.

Brassvine thorns.

Someone had used them to nail her jaw shut.

He had to turn away. He realized that he had to sit down, too.

The agent continued, "Our station boss got a tip and sent me to check it out. I hired a steamcrawler from some busted-out jups, rented a handful of townies who can handle heavy weapons, and crawled up there. What we found . . . well, you can see it. That data wafer—when I found it . . ."

Mace stared at the man as though he'd never seen him before. And he hadn't: only now, finally, was he truly *seeing* him. An undistinguished little man: soft face and uncertain voice, shaky hands and allergies: an undistinguished little man who must have resources of toughness that Mace could barely imagine. To have walked into a scene that Mace could barely stomach even in a bloodless, translucent laser image; to have had to smell them—*touch* them—to pry open a dead woman's *mouth* . . .

And then to bring the recordings here, so that he could live it all again—

Mace could have done it. He thought so. Probably. He'd been some places, and seen some things.

Not like this.

The agent said, "Our sources are pretty sure the tip came from the ULF itself."

Palpatine glanced a question. Mace spoke without taking his eyes off the agent. "The Upland Liberation Front, sir. That's Depa's partisan group; 'uplanders' is a rough translation of *Korunnai*—the name the mountain tribes give themselves."

"Korunnai?" Palpatine frowned absently. "Aren't those *your* people, Master Windu?"

"My . . . kin." He made himself unclench his jaw. "Yes, Chancellor. You have a good memory."

"A politician's trick." Palpatine gave a gently self-deprecating smile and waved a dismissive hand. "Please go on."

The agent shrugged as though there was little more to tell. "There have been a lot of . . . disturbing reports. Execution of prisoners. Ambushes of civilians. On both sides. Usually they can't be verified. The jungle . . . swallows everything. So when we got this tip—"

"You found this because somebody wanted you to find it," Mace finished for him. "And now you think—"

Mace turned the data wafer over and over through his fingers, watching it catch splinters of light. "You think those people might have been killed just to deliver this message."

"What a hideous idea!" Palpatine lowered himself slowly onto the edge of his desk. He appealed to the agent. "This can't be true, can it?"

The agent only hung his head.

Yoda's ears curled backward, and his eyes narrowed. "Some messages . . . most important, is how they are framed. Secondary, their content is."

Palpatine shook his head in disbelief. "These ULF partisans—we ally ourselves with *them?* The *Jedi* ally with them? What sort of monsters *are* they?"

"I don't know." Mace handed the wafer back to the agent. "Let's find out."

He slotted it into a port on the side of the holoprojector and touched a control.

The holoprojector's phased-wave speakers brought the jungle around them to life with noise: the rush of wind-rattled leaves, skrills and clatters of insect calls, dim dopplered shrieks of passing birds, the howls and coughs of distant predators. Through the eddies and boils of sound drifted a whisper sinuous as a riversnake: a human or near-human whisper, a voice murmuring in Basic, sometimes comprehensible for a word here or phrase there, sometimes twisting below the distorting ripples of the aural surface. Mace caught the words *Jedi,* and *night*—or *knife*—and something about *look between the stars . . .*

He frowned at the agent. "You can't clean this up?"

"This *is* cleaned up." The agent produced a datapad from his travelcase, keyed it alight, and passed it to Mace. "We made a transcript. It's provisional. Best we can do."

The transcript was fragmentary, but enough to draw chills up Mace's arms: *Jedi Temple . . . taught* (or possibly *taut*) *. . . dark . . . an enemy. But . . . Jedi . . . under cover of night.*

One whisper was entirely clear. He read the words on the datapad's screen as the whisper seemed to come from just behind his shoulder.

I use the night, and the night uses me.

He forgot to breathe. This was bad.

It got worse.

The whisper strengthened to a voice. A woman's voice.

Depa's voice.

On the datapad in his hand, and murmuring in the air behind his shoulder—

I have become the darkness in the jungle.

The recording went on. And on.

Her murmur drained him: of emotion, of strength, even of thought; the longer she rambled, the emptier he got. Yet her final words still triggered a dull shock inside his chest.

She was talking to *him* . . .

I know you will come for me, Mace. You should never have sent me here. And I should never have come. But what's done can never be undone. I know you think I've gone mad. I haven't. What's happened to me is worse.

I've gone sane.

That's why you'll come, Mace. That's why you'll have to.

Because nothing is more dangerous than a Jedi who's finally sane.

Her voice trailed off into the jungle-mutter.

No one moved or spoke. Mace sat with interlocked fingers supporting his chin. Yoda leaned on his cane, eyes shut, mouth pinched with inner pain. Palpatine stared solemnly through the holographic jungle, as though he saw something real beyond its boundary.

"That's—uh, that's all there is." The agent extended a hesitant hand to the holoprojector and flicked a control. The jungle vanished like a bad dream.

They all stirred, rousing themselves, instinctively adjusting their clothing. Palpatine's office now looked unreal: as though the clean carpeted floor and crisp lines of furniture, the pure filtered air, and the view of Coruscant that filled the large windows were the holographic projection, and they all still sat in the jungle.

As though only the jungle were real.

Mace spoke first.

"She's right." He lifted his head from his hands. "I have to go after her. Alone."

Palpatine's eyebrows twitched. "That seems . . . unwise."

"Concur with Chancellor Palpatine, I do," Yoda said slowly. "Great risks there would be. Too valuable you are. Send others, we should."

"There is no one else who can do this."

"Surely, Master Windu"—Palpatine's smile was respectfully disbelieving—"a Republic Intelligence covert ops team, or even a team of Jedi—"

"No." Mace rose, and straightened his shoulders. "It has to be me."

"Please, we all understand your concern for your former student, Master Windu, but surely—"

"Reasons he must have, Supreme Chancellor," Yoda said. "Listen to them, we should."

Even Palpatine found that one did not argue with Master Yoda.

Mace struggled to put his certainty into words. This difficulty was a function of his particular gift of perception. Some things were so obvious to him that they were hard to describe: like explaining how he knew it was raining while he stood in a thunderstorm.

"If Depa has . . . gone mad—or worse, fallen to the dark side," he began, "it's vital that the Jedi know *why*. That we discover *what did it to her*. Until we know this, no more Jedi should be exposed to it than is absolutely necessary. Also, this all might be entirely false: a deliberate attempt to incriminate her. That ambient noise on the recording . . ." He glanced at the agent. "If her voice was faked—say, synthesized by computer—that noise could be there precisely to blur the evidence of trickery, couldn't it?"

The agent nodded. "But why would someone want to frame her?"

Mace waved this off. "Regardless, she must be brought in. And soon—before rumor of such massacres reaches the wider galaxy. Even if she had nothing to do with them, having a Jedi's name associated with these crimes is a threat to the public trust in the Jedi. She must answer any charges before they are ever publicly made."

"Granted, she must be brought in," Palpatine allowed. "But the question remains: why *you?*"

"Because she might not want to come."

Palpatine looked thoughtful.

Yoda's head came up, and his eyes opened, gleaming at the Supreme Chancellor. "If rogue she has gone . . . to find her, difficult it will be. To apprehend her . . ." His voice dropped, as though the words caused him pain. "Dangerous, that will be."

"Depa was my Padawan." Mace moved away from the desk and stared out the window at the shimmering twilight that slowly darkened the capital's cityscape. "The bond of Master and Padawan is . . . intense. No one knows her better—and I have more experience in those jungles than any other living Jedi. I'm the only one who can find her if she doesn't want to be found. And if she must be—"

He swallowed, and stared at the moondisk of light scattered from one of the orbital mirrors. "If she must be . . . stopped," he said at length, "I may be the only one who can do that, too."

Palpatine's eyebrows twitched polite incomprehension.

Mace took a deep breath, finding himself once more looking at his hands, *through* his hands, seeing only an image in his mind, sharp as a dream: lightsaber against lightsaber in the Temple's training halls, the green flash of Depa's blade seeming to come from everywhere at once.

He could not unmake what he had made.

There were no second chances.

Her voice echoed inside him: *Nothing is more dangerous than a Jedi who's finally sane,* but he said only—

"She is a master of Vaapad."

In the silence that followed, he studied the folds and wrinkles of his interlaced fingers, focusing his attention into his visual field to hold at bay dark dream-ghosts of Depa's blade flashing toward Jedi necks.

"Vaapad?" Palpatine repeated, eventually. Perhaps he'd grown tired of waiting for someone to explain. "Isn't that some kind of animal?"

"A predator of Sarapin," Yoda supplied gravely. "Also the nickname it is, given by students, for the seventh form of lightsaber combat."

"Hmp. I've always heard there are only six."

"Six there were, for generations of Jedi. The seventh . . . is not well known. A *powerful* form it is. Deadliest of all . . . But dangerous it is—to its master, as well as its opponent. Few have studied. One student alone to mastery has risen."

"But if she's the only master—and this style is so deadly—what makes you think—"

"She's not the only master, sir." He lifted his head to meet Palpatine's frown. "She is my only student to *become* a master."

"*Your* only student . . ." Palpatine echoed.

"I didn't study Vaapad." Mace let his hands fall to his sides. "I created it."

Palpatine's brows drew together thoughtfully. "Yes, I seem to recall now: a reference in your report on the treason of Master Sora Bulq. Didn't you train him as well? Didn't he also claim to be a master of this Vaapad of yours?"

"Sora Bulq was not my student."

"Your . . . *associate*, then?"

"And he did not master Vaapad," Mace said grimly. "Vaapad mastered him."

"Ah—ah, I see . . ."

"With respect, sir, I don't think you do."

"I see enough to worry me, just a bit." The warmth of Palpatine's smile robbed insult from his words. "The relationship of Master and Padawan is intense, you said; and I well believe it. When you faced Dooku on Geonosis . . ."

"I prefer," Mace said softly, "not to talk about Geonosis, Chancellor."

"Depa Billaba was your Padawan. And she is still perhaps your closest friend, is she not? If she must be slain, are you so certain you can strike her down?"

Mace looked at the floor, at Yoda, at the agent, and in the end he had to meet Palpatine's eyes once more. It was not merely Palpatine of Naboo who had asked; this question had come from the Supreme Chancellor. His office demanded an answer.

"May the Force grant, sir," Mace said slowly, "that I will not have to find out."

PART ONE

MEN IN THE JUNGLE

1

THE DOWNWARD SPIRAL

Through the curved transparisteel, Haruun Kal was a wall of mountain-punched clouds beside him. It looked close enough to touch. The shuttle's orbit spiraled slowly toward the surface: soon enough he would be able to touch it in truth.

The insystem shuttle was only a twenty-seater, and even so it was three-quarters empty. The shuttle line had bought it used from a tour company; the tubelike passenger fuselage was entirely transparisteel, its exterior scarred and fogged with microbody pits, its interior bare except for strips of gray no-skid laid along the aisles.

Mace Windu was the lone human. His shipmates were two Kubaz who fluted excitedly about the culinary possibilities of pinch beetles and buzzworms, and a mismatched couple who seemed to be some kind of itinerant comedy act, a Kitonak and a Pho Ph'eahian whose canned banter made Mace wish for earplugs. Or hard vacuum. Or plain old-fashioned deafness. They must have been far down on their luck, to be taking a tourist shuttle into Pelek Baw; Haruun Kal's capital city is a place lounge acts go to die. Passenger liners on the Gevarno Loop only stopped there at all because they had to drop into realspace anyway for the system transit.

Mace sat as far from the others as the shuttle's limited space allowed.

The Jedi Master wore clothing appropriate to his cover: a stained vest of Corellian sand panther leather over a loose shirt that used to be white, and skintight black pants with wear patches of gray. His boots carried a hint of polish, but only above the ankle; the uppers were scuffed almost to suede. The only parts of his ensemble that were well maintained were the supple holster belted to his right thigh, and the gleaming Merr-Sonn Power 5 it held. His lightsaber was stuffed into the kitbag beneath his seat, disguised as an old-fashioned glow rod.

The datapad on his lap was also a disguise: though it worked well enough for him to encrypt his journal on it, most of it was actually a miniature subspace transmitter, frequency-locked to the band monitored by the medium cruiser *Halleck,* onstation in the Ventran system.

The Korunnal Highland swung into view: a vast plateau of every conceivable shade of green, skirted by bottomless swirls of cloud, crisscrossed by interlocking mountain ranges. A few of the tallest peaks were capped with white; many of the shorter mountains plumed billows of smoke and gas. The eastern half of the highland had already rolled through the terminator; when the shuttle passed into the planet's shadow, gleams of dark red and orange specked the world like predators' eyes beyond the ring of a campfire's light: open calderae of the highland's many active volcanoes.

It was beautiful. Mace barely noticed.

He held the recording wand of the fake datapad and spoke very, very softly.

FROM THE PRIVATE JOURNALS OF MACE WINDU
[Initial Haruun Kal Entry]:

Depa's down there. Right now.

I shouldn't be thinking about this. I shouldn't be thinking about her. Not yet.

But—

She's down there. She's been down there for months.

I can't imagine what might have happened to her. I don't *want* to imagine.

I'll find out soon enough.

Focus. I have to focus. Concentrate on what I know is true while I wait for the mud to settle and the water to become clear . . .

A lesson of Yoda's. But sometimes you can't wait.

And sometimes the water never clears.

I can focus on what I know about Haruun Kal. I know a lot.

Here's some of it:

> **HARUUN KAL** (Al'har I): sole planet of the AL'HAR system. *Haruun Kal* is the name given to it in the language of the indigenous human population, the Korunnai (uplanders). It translates to Basic as "above the clouds." From space, the world appears to be oceanic, with only a few green-topped islands rising from a restless multicolored sea. But this is deceptive: the sea that these islands punctuate is not liquid, but an ocean of heavier-than-air toxic gases, which plume endlessly from the planet's innumerable active volcanoes. Only on the mountaintops and the high plateaus can oxygen-breathing life survive—and not on many of these; unless they rise far above the cloudsea, they are vulnerable to Haruun Kal's unpredictable winds. Especially during Haruun Kal's brief winter, when the *thakiz baw'kal*—the Downstorm—blows, the winds can whip the thick cloudsea high enough to scour lowlands free of oxygen breathers within hours. Its capital, PELEK BAW, is located on the sole inhabited landmass, the plateau known as the KORUNNAL HIGHLAND, and is the largest permanent settlement on this primarily jungle-covered planet. The indigenous humans live in small seminomadic tribal groups called ghôsh and avoid the settlements, which are maintained by offworlders of a wide variety of species. The Korunnai lump all offworlders and settled folk under the somewhat contemptuous category of Balawai ("downfolk"). There is a long history of unorganized local conflicts . . .

This doesn't help.

I can't fit what I know of Haruun Kal into a guidebook description. Too much of what I know is the color of the sunflash and the smell of the wind off Grandfather's Shoulder, the silken ripple of a grasser's undercoat through my fingers, the hot fierce sting of an akk dog's Force-touch.

I was born on Haruun Kal. Far back in the highland.

I am a full-blooded Korun.

A hundred generations of my ancestors breathed that air and drank that water, ate the fruit of that soil and were buried deep within it. I've returned only once, thirty-five standard years ago—but I have carried that world with me. The feel of it. The power of its storms. The upswelling tangle of its jungles. The thunder of its peaks.

But it is not home. Home is Coruscant. Home is the Jedi Temple.

I have no recollection of my infancy among the Korunnai; my earliest memory is of Yoda's kindly smile and enormous gentle eyes close above me. It is still vivid. I don't know how old I might have been, but I am certain I could not yet walk. Perhaps I was too young to even stand. In memory, I can see my plump infant's hands reaching up to tug at the white straggles of hair above Yoda's ears.

I recall squalling—*shrieking like a wounded glowbat,* as Yoda prefers to describe it—as some kind of toy, a rattle, it might have been, bobbed in the air just beyond my grasp. I recall how no amount of shouting, screaming, howling, or tears could draw that rattle one millimeter closer to my tiny fist. And I recall the instant I first reached for the toy without using my hands: how I could *feel* it hanging there, and I could feel how Yoda's mind supported it . . . and a whisper of the Force began to hum in my ears.

My next lesson: Yoda had come to take the rattle away, and I—with my infant's instinctive selfishness—had refused to release it, holding on with both my hands and all I could summon of the Force. The rattle broke—to my infant mind, a tragedy like the end of a world—for that had been Yoda's way of introducing the Jedi law of nonattachment: holding too tightly to what we love will destroy it.

And break our hearts as well.

That's a lesson I don't want to be thinking about right now.

But I can't help myself. Not right now.

Not while I'm up here, and Depa is down there.

Depa Billaba came into my life by accident: one of those joyous coincidences that are sometimes the gift of the galaxy. I found her after I fought and killed the pirates who had murdered her parents; these pirates had kidnapped their victims' lovely infant daughter. I never learned what they wanted to do with her. Or to her. I refuse to speculate.

An advantage of Jedi mental discipline: I can stop myself from imagining such things.

She grew to girlhood in the Temple, and to womanhood as my Padawan. The proudest moment of my life was the day I stood and directed the Jedi Council to welcome its newest member.

She is one of the youngest Jedi ever to be named to the Council. On the day of her elevation, Yoda suggested that it was my teaching that had brought her so far while still so young.

He said this, I think, more from courtesy than from honesty; she came so far while still so young because she is who she is. My teaching had little to do with it. I have never met anyone like her.

Depa is more than a friend to me. She's one of those dangerous attachments. She is the daughter I will never have.

All the Jedi discipline in the galaxy cannot entirely overpower the human heart.

I hear her voice again and again: . . . *you should never have sent me here, and I should never have come . . .*

I can't stop myself from reaching into the Force, though I know it is useless. Since shortly before Qui-Gon Jinn and Obi-Wan Kenobi stood in front of the Council to report the rebirth of the Sith, a mysterious veil of darkness has clouded the Force. Close by—in both space and time—the Force is as it has always been: guide and ally, my invisible eyes and unseen hands. But when I try to search through the Force for Depa, I find only shadows, indistinct and threatening. The crystal purity of the Force has become a thick fog of menace.

Again: . . . *but what's done can never be undone . . .*

I can shake my head till my brain rattles, but I can't seem to drive away those words. I must clear my mind; Pelek Baw is still Separatist, and I will have to be alert. I must stop thinking about her.

Instead, I think about the war.

The Republic was caught entirely unprepared. After a thousand years of peace, no one—especially not us Jedi—truly believed civil war would ever come. How could we? Not even Yoda could remember the last general war. Peace is more than a tradition. It is the bedrock of civilization itself.

This was the Confederacy's great advantage: the Separatists not only expected war, but *counted on it.*

By the time the smoldering Clone War burst into Geonosian flame, their ships were already in motion. In the weeks that followed, while we Jedi tended our wounds and mourned our dead, while the Senate scrambled to assemble a fleet—any kind of fleet—to match the power of the Confederacy of Independent Systems, while Supreme Chancellor Palpatine pleaded and bargained and sometimes had to outright threaten wavering Senators to not only stay loyal to the Republic but also support its clone army with their credits and their resources, the Separatists had fanned out across the galaxy, seeding the hyperspace lanes with their forces. The major approaches into Separatist space were picketed by droid starfighters, backed up by newly revealed capital ships: Geonosian Dreadnaughts that lumbered out from secret shipyards.

Strategically, it was a masterpiece. Any thrust into the worlds at the core of the Confederacy would be blunted, and delayed long enough for Separatist reserves to engage it; any attack with sufficient strength to swiftly overwhelm their pickets would leave hundreds or thousands of worlds open to swift Separatist reprisal. Behind their droid-walled frontier, they could gather their forces at leisure, striking out to swallow Republic systems piecemeal.

Even before the Republic was ready to fight, we had lost.

Yoda is the master strategist of the Jedi Council. A life as vast as his predisposes one to see the big picture, and take the long view. He developed our current strategy of limited engagement on multiple fronts; our goal is to harass the Separatists, wear them down in a war of attrition, chip away at them and prevent them from consolidating their position. In this way, we hope to gain time for the titanic manufacturing base of the Republic to be converted to the production of ships, weapons, and other war matériel.

And time to train our troops. The Kaminoan clone troopers are not only the best soldiers we have, they are very nearly our only soldiers. We would use them to train civilian volunteers and law-enforcement personnel in weapons and tactics, but the Separatists have managed to keep nearly all 1.2 million of them fully engaged, rushing from system to system and planet to planet to meet probing attacks from the bewildering variety of war droids that the TechnoUnion, with the financial backing of the Trade Federation, turns out in seemingly unlimited quantities.

Since we need all our clones simply to defend Republic systems, we have been forced to find ways to attack without them.

The Separatists don't enjoy unalloyed popularity, even in their core systems; and in any society, there are fringe elements eager to take up arms against authority. Jedi have been covertly inserted on hundreds of worlds, with a common mission: to organize Loyalist resistance, train partisans in sabotage and guerrilla warfare, and generally do whatever possible to destabilize the Separatist governments.

This was why Depa Billaba came to Haruun Kal.

I sent her here.

The Al'Har system—of which Haruun Kal is the sole planet—lies on the nexus of several hyperspace lanes: the hub of a wheel called the Gevarno Loop, whose spokes join the Separatist systems of Killisu, Jutrand, Loposi, and the Gevarno Cluster with Opari, Ventran, and Ch'manss—all Loyalist. Due to local stellar configurations and the mass sensitivities of modern hyperdrives, any ship traveling from one of these systems to another can cut several standard days off its journey by coming through Al'Har, even counting the daylong realspace transit of the system itself.

None of these systems has any vast strategic value—but the Republic has lost too many systems to secession to risk losing any to conquest. Control of the Al 'Har nexus offers control of the whole region. It was decided that Haruun Kal is worth the Council's attention—and not solely for its military uses.

In the Temple archives are reports of the Jedi anthropologists who studied the Korun tribes. They have a theory that a Jedi spacecraft may have made a forced landing there, perhaps thousands of years ago during the turmoil of the Sith War, when so many Jedi were lost to history. There are several varieties of fungi native to the jungles of Haruun Kal that eat metals and silicates; a ship that could not lift off again immediately would be grounded forever, and comm equipment would be equally vulnerable. The ancestors of the Korunnai, the anthropologists believe, were these shipwrecked Jedi.

This is their best explanation for a curious genetic fact: all Korunnai can touch the Force.

The true explanation may be simpler: we *have* to. Those who cannot use the Force do not long survive. Humans can't live in those jungles; the Korunnai survive by following their grasser herds. Grassers, great six-limbed behemoths, tear down the jungle with their forehands and massive jaws. Their name comes from the grassy meadows that are left in their wake. It is in those meadows that the Korunnai make their precarious lives. The grassers protect the Korunnai from the jungle; the Korunnai, in turn—with their Force-bonded companions, the fierce akk dogs—protect the grassers.

When the Jedi anthropologists were ready to depart, they had asked the elders of ghôsh Windu if they might take with them a child to train in the Jedi arts, thus recovering the Force talents of the Korunnai to serve the peace of the galaxy.

That would be me.

I was an infant, an orphan, called by the name of my ghôsh, for my parents had been taken by the jungle before my naming day. I was six months old. The choice was made for me.

I've never minded.

It is the Korunnai that Depa came here to train and use as anti-government partisans. The civil government of Haruun Kal is entirely Balawai: off-worlders and their descendants, beneficiaries of the financial interests behind the thyssel bark trade. Government of the Balawai, by the Balawai, and for the Balawai.

No Korun need apply.

The government—and the planetary militia, their military arm—joined the Confederacy of Independent Systems as a cynical dodge to squelch an ongoing Judicial Department investigation into their treatment of the Korun natives; in exchange for the use of the capital's spaceport as a base to conduct repair and refit for the Al'har fleet of droid starfighters, the Separatists provided arms for the militia and turned a blind eye toward illegal Balawai activities in the Korunnal Highland.

But since Depa arrived, the Separatists have discovered that even the smallest bands of determined guerrillas can have a devastating effect on military operations.

Especially when all these guerrillas can touch the Force.

This was a large part of Depa's argument for coming here in the first place, and why she insisted on handling it personally. Untrained Force users can be exceedingly dangerous; wild talents crop up unpredictably in such populations. Depa's mastery of Vaapad makes her virtually unbeatable in personal combat, and her own cultural training—in the elegant philosophico-mystical disciplines of the Chalactan Adepts—makes her uniquely resistant to all forms of mental manipulation, from Force-powered suggestion to brainwashing by torture.

I believe she may have also nursed a private hope that some of the Korunnai might be persuaded to enlist in the Grand Army of the Republic; a cadre of Force-capable commandos could take a great deal of the pressure off the Jedi and accomplish missions that no clone troopers could hope to survive.

I suspect, too, that part of the reason she insisted on taking this mission was sentimental: I think she came here because Haruun Kal is where I was born.

Though this world has never been my true home, I bear its stamp to this day.

The Korun culture is based on a simple premise, what they call the Four Pillars: Honor, Duty, Family, Herd.

The First Pillar is Honor, your obligation to yourself. Act with integrity. Speak the truth. Fight without fear. Love without reservation.

Greater than this is the Second Pillar, Duty, your obligation to others. Do your job. Work hard. Obey the elders. Stand by your ghôsh.

Greater still is the Third Pillar, Family. Care for your parents. Love your spouse. Teach your children. Defend your blood.

Greatest of all is the Fourth Pillar, Herd, for it is on the grasser herds that the life of the ghôsh depends. Your family is more important than your duty; your duty outweighs your honor. But *nothing* is more important than your herd. If the well-being of the herd requires the sacrifice of your honor, you do it. If it requires that you shirk your duty, you do it.

Whatever it takes.

Even your family.

Yoda once observed that—though I left Haruun Kal as an infant, and returned only once, as a youth, to train in the Korun Force-bond with the great akks—he thinks I have the Four Pillars in my veins along with my Korun blood. He said that Honor and Duty are as natural to me as breathing, and that the only real difference my Jedi training has made is that the Jedi have become my Family, and the Republic itself is my Herd.

This is flattering. I hope it might be true, but I don't have an opinion on the subject. I'm not interested in opinions. I'm interested in facts.

This is a fact: I found the shatterpoint of the Gevarno Loop.

Another fact: Depa volunteered to strike it.

And another fact—

That she said: *I have become the darkness in the jungle.*

The spaceport at Pelek Baw smelled clean. It wasn't. Typical backworld port: filthy, disorganized, half choked with rusted remnants of disabled ships.

Mace stepped off the shuttle ramp and slung his kitbag by its strap. Smothering wet heat pricked sweat across his bare scalp. He raised his eyes from the ocher-scaled junk and discarded crumples of empty nutripacks scattered around the landing bay, up into the misty turquoise sky.

The white crown of Grandfather's Shoulder soared above the city: the tallest mountain on the Korunnal Highland, an active volcano with dozens of open calderae. Mace remembered the taste of the snow at the tree line, the thin cold air and the aromatic resins of the evergreen scrub below the summit.

He had spent far too much of his life on Coruscant.

If only he could have come here for some other reason.

Any other reason.

A straw-colored shimmer in the air around him explained the clean smell: a surgical sterilization field. He'd expected it. The spaceport had always had a powered-up surgical field umbrella, to protect ships and equipment from the various native fungi that fed on metals and silicates; the field also wiped out the bacteria and molds that would otherwise have made the spaceport smell like an overloaded refresher.

The spaceport's pro-biotic showers were still in their long, low blockhouse of mold-stained duracrete, but their entrance had been expanded into a large temporary-looking office of injection-molded plastifoam, with a foam-slab door that hung askew on half-sprung hinges. The door was streaked with rusty stains that had dripped from the fungus-chewed durasteel sign above. The sign said CUS-TOMS. Mace went in.

Sunlight leaked green through mold-tracked windows. Climate control wheezed a body-temperature breeze from ceiling vents, and the smell loudly advertised that this place was well beyond the reach of the surgical field.

Inside the customs office, enough flybuzz hummed to get the two Kubaz chuckling and eagerly nudging each other. Mace didn't quite manage to ignore the Pho Ph'eahian broadly explaining to a bored-looking human that he'd just jumped in from Kashyyyk and boy, were his legs tired. The agent seemed to find this about as tolerable as Mace did; he hurriedly passed the comedians along after the pair of Kubaz, and they all disappeared into the shower blockhouse.

Mace found a different customs agent: a Neimoidian female with pink-slitted eyes, cold-bloodedly sleepy in the heat. She looked over his identikit incuriously. "Corellian, hnh? Purpose of your visit?"

"Business."

She sighed tiredly. "You'll need a better answer than that. Corellia's no friend of the Confederacy."

"Which would be why I'm doing business *here.*"

"Hnh. I scan you. Open your bag for inspection."

Mace thought about the "old-fashioned glow rod" stashed in his bag. He wasn't sure how convincing its shell would be to Neimoidian eyes, which could see deep into the infrared.

"I'd rather not."

"Do I care? Open it." She squinted a dark pink eye up at him. "Hey, nice skin job. You could almost pass for a Korun."

"Almost?"

"You're too tall. And they mostly have hair. And anyway, Korunnai are all Force freaks, yes? They have powers and stuff."

"I have powers."

"Yeah?"

"Sure." Mace hooked his thumbs behind his belt. "I have the power to make ten credits appear in your hand."

The Neimoidian looked thoughtful. "That's a pretty good power. Let's see it."

He passed his hand over the customs agent's desk, and let fall a coin he'd palmed from his belt's slit pocket. The Neimoidian had powers of her own: she made the coin disappear. "Not bad." She turned up her empty hand. "Let's see it again."

"Let's see my identikit validated and my bag passed."

The Neimoidian shrugged and complied, and Mace did his trick again. "Power like yours, you'll get along fine in Pelek Baw," she said. "Pleasure doing business with you. Be sure to take your PB tabs. And see me on your way offworld. Ask for Pule."

"I'll do that."

Toward the back of the customs office, a large advertiscreen advised everyone entering Pelek Baw to use the probiotic showers before leaving the spaceport. The showers replaced beneficial skin flora that had been killed by the surgical field. This advice was supported with gruesomely graphic holos of the wide variety of fungal infections awaiting unshowered travelers. A dispenser beneath the screen offered half-credit doses of tablets guaranteed to restore intestinal flora as well. Mace bought a few, took one, then stepped into the shower blockhouse.

The blockhouse had a smell all its own: a dark musky funk, rich and organic. The showers themselves were simple autonozzles spraying bacterium-rich nutrient mist; they lined the walls of a thirty-meter walk-through. Mace stripped off his clothes and stuffed them into his kitbag. There was a conveyor strip for possessions beside the walk-through entrance, but he held on to the bag. A few germs wouldn't do it any harm.

At the far end of the showers, he walked into a situation.

The dressing station was loud with turbine-driven airjet dryers. The two Kubaz and the comedy team, still naked, milled uncertainly in one corner. A large surly-looking human in sunbleached khakis and a military cap stood facing them, impressive arms folded across his equally impressive chest. He stared at the naked travelers with cold unspecific threat.

A smaller human in identical clothing rummaged through their bags, which were piled behind the large man's legs. The smaller man had a bag of his own, into which he dropped anything small and valuable. Both men had stun batons dangling from belt loops, and blasters secured in snap-flap holsters.

Mace nodded thoughtfully. The situation was clear enough. Based on who he was supposed to be, he should just ignore this. But cover or not, he was still a Jedi.

The big one looked Mace over. Head to toe and back again. His stare had the open insolence that came of being clothed and armed and facing someone who was naked and dripping wet. "Here's another. Smart guy carried his own bag."

The other rose and unlooped his stun baton. "Sure, smart guy. Let's have the bag. Inspection. Come on."

Mace went still. Pro-bi mist condensed to rivulets and trickled down his bare skin. "I can read your mind," he said darkly. "You only have three ideas, and all of them are wrong."

"Huh?"

Mace flipped up a thumb. "You think being armed and ruthless means you can do whatever you want." He folded his thumb and flipped up his forefinger. "You think nobody will stand up to you when they're naked." He folded that one again and flipped up the next. "And you think you're going to look inside my bag."

"Oh, he's a funny one." The smaller man spun his stun baton and stepped toward him. "He's not just smart, he's funny."

The big man moved to his flank. "Yeah, regular comedian."

"The comedians are over there." Mace inclined his head toward the Pho Ph'eahian and his Kitonak partner, naked and shivering in the corner. "See the difference?"

"Yeah?" The big man flexed big hands. "What are you supposed to be, then?"

"I'm a prophet." Mace lowered his voice as though sharing a secret. "I can see the future . . ."

"Sure you can." He set his stubble-smeared jaw and showed jagged yellow teeth. "What do you see?"

"You," Mace said. "Bleeding."

His expression might have been a smile if there had been the faintest hint of warmth in his eyes.

The big man suddenly looked less confident.

In this he could perhaps be excused; like all successful predators, he was interested only in victims. Certainly not in *opponents*. Which was the purpose of his particular racket, after all: members of any sapient species who were culturally accustomed to wearing clothes would feel hesitant, uncertain, and vulnerable when caught naked. Especially humans. Any normal person would stop to put on pants before throwing a punch.

Mace Windu, in contrast, looked like he might know of uncertainty and vulnerability by reputation, but had never met either of them face-to-face.

One hundred eighty-eight centimeters of muscle and bone. Absolutely still. Absolutely relaxed. From his attitude, the pro-bi mist that trickled down his naked skin might have been carbon-fiber-reinforced ceramic body armor.

"Do you have a move to make?" Mace said. "I'm in a hurry."

The big man's gaze twitched sideways, and he said, "Uh—?" Mace felt a pressure in the Force over his left kidney and heard the sizzle of a triggered stun baton. He spun and caught the wrist of the smaller man with both hands, shoving the baton's sparking corona well clear with a twist that levered his face into the path of Mace's rising foot. The impact made a smack as wet and meaty as the snap of bone. The big man bellowed and lunged and Mace stepped to one side and whipcracked the smaller man's arm to spin his slackening body. Mace caught the small man's head in the palm of one hand and shoved it crisply into the big man's nose.

The two men skidded in a tangle on the slippery, damp floor and went down. The baton spat lightning as it skittered into a corner. The smaller man lay limp. The big man's eyes spurted tears and he sat on the floor, trying with both hands to massage his smashed nose into shape. Blood leaked through his fingers.

Mace stood over him. "Told you."

The big man didn't seem impressed. Mace shrugged. A prophet, it was said, received no honor on his own world.

Mace dressed silently while the other travelers reclaimed their belongings. The big man made no attempt to stop them, or even to rise. Presently the smaller man stirred, moaned, and opened his eyes. As soon as they focused well enough to see Mace still in the dressing station, he cursed and clawed at his holster flap, struggling to free his blaster.

Mace looked at him.

The man decided his blaster was better off where it was.

"You don't know how much trouble you're in," he muttered sullenly as he settled back down on the floor, words blurred by his smashed mouth. He drew his knees up and wrapped his arms around them. "People who butch up with capital militia don't live long around—"

The big man interrupted him with a cuff on the back of his head. "Shut it."

"Capital militia?" Mace understood now. His face settled into a grim mask, and he finished buckling down his holster. "You're the police."

The Pho Ph'eahian mimed a pratfall. "You'd think they'd hire cops who weren't so *clumsy*, eh?"

"Oh, I dunno, Phootie," the Kitonak said in a characteristically slow, terminally relaxed voice. "They bounced *real* nice."

Both Kubaz whirred something about slippery floors, inappropriate footwear, and unfortunate accidents.

The cops scowled.

Mace squatted in front of them. His right hand rested on the Power 5's butt. "It'd be a shame if somebody had a blaster malfunction," he said. "A slip, a fall—sure, it's embarrassing. It hurts. But you'll get over it in a day or two. If somebody's blaster accidentally went off when you fell—?" He shrugged. "How long will it take you to get over being dead?"

The smaller cop started to spit back something venomous. The larger one interrupted him with another cuff. "We scan you," he growled. "Just go."

Mace stood. "I remember when this was a nice town."

He shouldered his kitbag and walked out into the blazing tropical afternoon. He passed under a dented, rusty sign without looking up.

The sign said: WELCOME TO PELEK BAW.

Faces—

Hard faces. Cold faces. Hungry, or drunk. Hopeful. Calculating. Desperate.

Street faces.

Mace walked a pace behind and to the right of the Republic Intelligence station boss, keeping his right hand near the Merr-Sonn's butt. Late at night, the streets were still crowded. Haruun Kal had no moon; the streets were lit with spill from taverns and outdoor cafés. Lightpoles—tall hexagonal pillars of duracrete with glowstrips running up each face—stood every twenty meters along both sides of the street. Their pools of yellow glow bordered black shadow; to pass into one of the alley mouths was to be wiped from existence.

The Intel station boss was a bulky, red-cheeked woman about

Mace's age. She ran the Highland Green Washeteria, a thriving laundry and public refresher station on the capital's north side. She never stopped talking. Mace hadn't started listening.

The Force nudged him with threat in all directions: from the rumble of wheeled groundcars that careened at random through crowded streets to the fan of death sticks in a teenager's fist. Uniformed militia swaggered or strutted or sometimes just posed, puffed up with the fake-dangerous attitude of armed amateurs. Holster flaps open. Blaster rifles propped against hipbones. He saw plenty of weapons waved, saw people shoved, saw lots of intimidation and threatening looks and crude street-gang horseplay; he didn't see much actual keeping of the peace. When a burst of blasterfire sang out a few blocks away, no one even looked around.

But nearly everyone looked at Mace.

Militia faces: human, or too close to call. Looking at Mace, seeing only a Korun in offworld clothes, their eyes went dead cold. Blank. Measuring. After a while, hostile eyes all look alike.

Mace kept alert, and concentrated on projecting a powerful aura of *Don't Mess With Me.*

He would have felt safer in the jungle.

Street faces: drink-bloated moons of bust-outs mooching spare change. A Wookiee gone gray from nose to chest, exhaustedly straining against his harness as he pulled a two-wheeled taxicart, fending off street kids with one hand while the other held on to his money belt. Jungle prospector faces: fungus scars on their cheeks, weapons at their sides. Young faces: children, younger than Depa had been on the day she became his Padawan, offering trinkets to Mace at "special discounts" because they "liked his face."

Many of them were Korunnai.

FROM THE PRIVATE JOURNALS OF MACE WINDU

Sure. Come to the city. Life's easy in the city. No vine cats. No drillmites. No brassvines or death hollows. No shoveling grasser manure, no hauling water, no tending akk pups. Plenty of money in the city. All you have to do is sell *this,* or endure *that.* What you're really selling: your youth. Your hope. Your future.

Anyone with sympathy for the Separatist cause should spend a few days in Pelek Baw. Find out what the Confederacy is really fighting for.

It's good that Jedi do not indulge in hate.

The station boss's chatter somehow wandered onto the subject of the Intel front she managed. Her name was Phloremirlla Tenk, "but call me Flor, sweetie. Everybody does." Mace picked up the thread of her ramble.

"Hey, everybody needs a shower once in a while. Why not get your clothes spiffed at the same time? So everybody comes here. I get jups, kornos, you name it. I get militia and seppie brass—well, used to, till the pullback. I get everybody. I got a pool. I got six different saunas. I got private showers—you can get water, alcohol, probi, sonics, you name it—maybe a recorder or two to really get the dirt we need. Some of these militia officers, you'd be amazed what they fall to talking about, alone in a steam room. Know what I mean?"

She was the chattiest spy he'd ever met. When she eventually stopped for breath, Mace told her so.

"Yeah, funny, huh? How do you think I've survived this game for twenty-three years? Talk as much as I do, it takes people longer to notice you never really *say* anything."

Maybe she was nervous. Maybe she could smell the threat that smoked in those streets. Some people thought they could hold danger at bay by pretending to be safe.

"I got thirty-seven employees. Only five are Intel. Everybody else just works there. Hah: I make twice the money off the Washeteria as I draw after twenty-three years in the service. Not that it's all that hard to do, if you know what I mean. You know what an RS-Seventeen makes? Pathetic. Pathetic. What's a Jedi make these days? Do they even pay you? Not enough, I'll bet. They love that *Service is its own reward* junk, don't they? Especially when it's *other* people's service. I'll just bet."

She'd already assembled a team to take him upcountry. Six men with heavy weapons and an almost new steamcrawler. "They look a little rough, but they're good boys, all of them. Freelancers, but solid. Years in the bush. Two are full-blooded kornos. Good with the natives, you know?"

For security reasons, she explained, she was taking him to meet them herself. "Sooner you're on your way, happier we'll both be. Right? Am I right? Taxis are hopeless this time of day. Mind the gutter cookie—that stuff'll chew right through your boots. Hey, *watch* it, creepo! Ever hear that peds have the right-of-way? Yeah? Well, *your* mother eats *Hutt* slime!" She stumped along the street, arms swinging. "Um, you know this Jedi of yours is wanted, right? You got a way to get her offworld?"

What Mace had was the *Halleck* onstation in the Ventran system with twenty armed landers and a regiment of clone troopers. What he said was, "Yes."

A new round of blasterfire sang perhaps a block or two away, salted with staccato pops crisper than blaster hits. Flor instantly turned left and dodged away up the street.

"Whoops! *This* way—you want to keep clear of those little rumbles, you know? Might just be a food riot, but you never know. Those handclaps? Slugthrowers, or I'm a Dug. Could be action by some of these guerrillas your Jedi runs—lots of the kornos carry slugthrowers, and slugs *bounce*. Slugthrowers. I hate 'em. But they're easy to maintain. Day or two in the jungle and your blaster'll never fire again. A good slug rifle, keep 'em wiped and oiled, they last forever. The guerrillas have pretty good luck with them, even though they take a *lot* of practice—slugs are ballistic, y'know. You have to plot the trajectory in your head. Shee, gimme a blaster *anytime*."

A new note joined the blasterfire: a deeper, throatier *thrumm-thrummmthrummthrumm*. Mace scowled over his shoulder. That was some kind of light repeater: a T-21, or maybe a Merr-Sonn Thunderbolt.

Military hardware.

"It would be good," he said, "if we could get off the street."

While she assured him, "No, no, no, don't worry, these scuffles never add up to much," he tried to calculate how fast he could dig his lightsaber out of his kitbag.

The firing intensified. Voices joined in: shouts and screams. Anger and pain. It started to sound less like a riot, and more like a firefight.

Just beyond the corner ahead, white-hot bolts flared past along the right-of-way. More blasterfire zinged behind them. The firefight was overflowing, becoming a flood that might surround them at any second. Mace looked back: along this street he still could see only crowds and groundcars, but the militia members were starting to take an interest: checking weapons, trotting toward alleys and cross-streets. Flor said behind him, "See? Look at that. They're not even really *aiming* at anything. Now, we just nip across—"

She was interrupted by a splattering *thwop*. Mace had heard that sound too often: steam, superheated by a high-energy bolt, exploding through living flesh. A deep-tissue blaster hit. He turned back to Flor and found her staggering in a drunken circle, painting the pavement with her blood. Where her left arm should have been was only a fist-sized mass of ragged tissue. Where the rest of her arm was, he couldn't see.

She said: "What? What?"

He dived into the street. He rolled, coming up to slam her hip joint with his shoulder. The impact folded her over him; he lifted her, turned, and sprang back for the corner. Bright flares of blaster bolts bracketed invisible sizzles and finger snaps of hypersonic slugs. He reached the meager cover of the corner and laid her flat on the sidewalk, tucked close against the wall.

"This isn't supposed to happen." Her life was flooding out of the shattered stump of her shoulder. Even dying, she kept talking. A blurry murmur: "This isn't *happening*. It *can't* be happening. My—my *arm*—"

In the Force, Mace could feel her shredded brachial artery; with the Force, he reached inside her shoulder to pinch it shut. The flood trickled to sluggish welling.

"Take it easy." He propped her legs on his kitbag to help maintain blood pressure to her brain. "Try to stay calm. You can live through this."

Boots clattered on permacrete behind him: a militia squad sprinting toward them. "Help is on the way." He leaned closer. "I need the meet point and the recognition code for the team."

"What? What are you talking about?"

"Listen to me. Try to focus. Before you go into shock. Tell me where I can find the upcountry team, and the recognition code so we'll know each other."

"You don't—you don't understand—this isn't *happening*—"

"Yes. It is. *Focus.* Lives depend on you. I need the meet point and the code."

"But—but—you don't *understand*—"

The militia behind him clattered to a stop. *"You! Korno! Stand away from that woman!"*

He glanced back. Six of them. Firing stance. The lightpole at their backs haloed black shadow across their faces. Plasma-charred muzzles stared at him. "This woman is wounded. Badly. Without medical attention, she will die."

"You're no doctor," one said, and shot him.

2

CAPITAL CRIMES

He had plenty of time to get familiar with the interrogation room.

Four meters by three. Duracrete blocks flecked with gravel whose shearplanes glinted like mica. The walls from waist-high to ceiling had once been painted the color of aged ivory. The floor and lower walls used to be the green of wander-kelp. What was left of both paint jobs flaked in patches rimmed with mildew.

The binder chair that held him was in better condition. The clamps at his wrists were cold and hard and had no weakness he could touch; those at his ankles sliced pale gouges into the leather of his boots. The chest plate barely let him breathe.

No windows. One glowstrip cast soft yellow from the joining of wall and ceiling. The other one was dead.

The door was behind him. Twisting to watch it hurt too much. The durasteel table in the center of the room was dented and speck-led with rust—he thought it was rust. Hoped it was. On the far side of it was a wooden chair, its bow back stripped from wear.

His vest and shirt were tattered at the shoulder where the first bolt had struck. The skin beneath was scorched and swollen with a black bruise. Set on stun, the bolt had barely penetrated his skin, but the concussive force of the steam-burst still hit like a club. It had picked him up and spun him. The pounding in his skull implied that at least one shot had caught the side of his head. He didn't remember.

He didn't remember anything between that first shot and waking up in this binder chair.

He waited.

He waited a long time.

He was thirsty. Uneasy pressure in his bladder somehow made his head hurt worse.

Studying the room and assessing his injuries could occupy only so much of his time. Much of the rest of it, he spent replaying Flor's death.

He knew she was dead. She had to be. She couldn't have lived more than a minute or two after the militia stunned him; without his Force-hold to pinch off that brachial artery, she would have bled out in seconds. She would have lain on that filthy sidewalk staring up at city-dimmed stars while the last of her consciousness darkened, faded, and finally winked out.

Again and again he heard that wet splattering *thwop*. Again and again he carried her back under cover. And stopped her bleeding. And tried to speak with her. And was shot by men he'd thought were coming to help.

Her death had gotten inside him, down below his ribs. It ate at him: a tiny pool of infection that grew through the hours in that room until it became a throbbing abscess. Pain and nausea and sweats. Chills.

A fever of the mind.

Not because he was responsible for her death. It ate at him because he *wasn't*.

He'd had no idea she was about to walk into a blaster bolt. The Force never offered the faintest hint of a clue. No trace of a bad feeling—or rather: no hint that all the bad feelings he'd had were about to add up to something much, much worse.

Nothing. Nothing at all. That's what sickened him.

What happens to a Jedi when he can no longer trust the Force?

Was this what broke Depa?

He shook that thought out of his skull. He drove his attention into his visual field, focusing on cataloging the smallest detail of his prison. Until he could see for himself, he told himself solidly, he owed her the presumption of innocence. Such doubts were unworthy of her. And of him. But they kept creeping back, no matter how hard he stared at the mildew-eaten paint on the wall.

. . . I know you think I've gone mad. I haven't. What's happened to me is worse.

. . . I've gone sane . . .

He knew her. He *knew* her. To the marrow of her bones. Her most secret heart. Her cherished dreams and faintest, foggiest hopes. She could not be involved in massacres of civilians. Of *children.*

. . . nothing is more dangerous than a Jedi who's finally sane . . .

She couldn't.

But as seconds swelled to hours, the certainty in his head went hollow, then desperate. Like he was trying to talk himself into something he knew was wrong.

He felt the door behind him open. A damp breeze licked the back of his neck. Footsteps entered and clicked to one side, and he twisted to look: they belonged to a smallish human male, comfortably plump, wearing militia khakis that were improbably well starched, considering the heat and the damp. The man carried a snap-rim case covered in tanned animal hide. He brushed a wave of end-dampened hair the color of aluminum away from dark eyes, and offered Mace a pleasant smile. "No, please." He waved a hand toward the door. "Feel free to have a look."

Twisting farther, Mace could see down the corridor behind his binder chair. At the far end stood a pair of steady-looking militiamen with blaster rifles aimed at his face.

Mace frowned. An unusual position for guards.

"Is this clear enough?" The man moved around Mace to the table, never crossing their line of fire, and opened his animal-hide bag. "I'm told you have a bit of a concussion. Let's not make it fatal, shall we?"

The Force showed him a dozen places on that soft body where a single blow would maim or kill. This man was no warrior. But energy spidered outward from him in all directions: an important man. Mace found no direct threat in him, only a cheery pragmatism.

"Not talkative? Don't blame you. Well. My name's Geptun. I'm chief of security for the capital district. My friends call me Lorz. You can call me Colonel Geptun." He waited, still wearing that indifferently pleasant smile. After a few seconds, he sighed. "Well. We know who I am. And we know who you're not."

He flipped open the lid of Mace's identikit. "You're not Kinsal Trappano. I'm guessing not Corellian, either. Interesting history you don't have. Smuggler. Small-time pirate. Gunrunner. Et cetera and so forth." He settled into the wooden chair, laced his fingers together, and propped his hands on his belly. He watched Mace with that pleasant smile. Silently. Waiting for him to say something.

Mace could have kept him waiting for days. Without Jedi training, no human truly understands what patience is. But Depa was out there. Somewhere. Doing something. The longer it took him to reach her, the more of it she might do. He decided to talk.

A small victory for him, Mace thought. No loss for me.

"What am I charged with?"

"That depends. What have you done?"

"Officially."

Geptun shrugged. "Nothing's been filed. Yet."

"Then why am I being held?"

"We're interrogating you."

Mace raised an eyebrow.

"Oh, yes. We are." Geptun winked. "We are indeed. I'm a terrific interrogator."

"You haven't even asked me a question."

Geptun smiled like a sleepy vine cat. "Questions are inefficient. In your case, futile."

"You must be good indeed," Mace said, "to have figured that out without even asking one."

By way of reply, Geptun reached into the animal-skin case and pulled out Mace's lightsaber.

The glow rod shell had been stripped away. Traces of adhesive showed black against the metal. He hefted it in his hand, smiling. "And torture would probably be a waste of time, too, yes?"

He set the lightsaber on the table and spun it like a bottle. Mace could feel its whirl in the Force: feel exactly how to touch it with his mind, to lift it and trigger it and set it flashing upon Colonel Geptun, to slay or hold hostage, or to slash through the restraints that held him in the binder chair—

He let it spin.

The two shooters standing ready at the far end of the corridor made sense to him now.

His lightsaber's spin took on a wobble, slowed, and trickled to a stop, its emitter centered on his breastbone. "I believe that means you're It," Geptun said.

A neat trick. Mace measured him again. The colonel endured his scrutiny blandly. *"Geptun,"* Mace said, "could be a Korun name."

"And in fact it is," the colonel admitted cheerily. "My paternal grandfather came out of the jungle some seventy-odd years ago. This, ah, is not discussed. You understand. Not in polite society."

"Is that something you still have here? Polite society?"

Geptun shrugged. "My name's only a mild handicap. Maybe that trace of Korun blood is what makes me too proud to change it."

Mace nodded, more to himself than to the other. If the man had enough Force-touch to control the lightsaber's spin, he might easily have enough to conceal his intentions. Mace revised his threat assessment from Low to Unknown. "What do you want from me?"

"Well. That's the real question, isn't it? There are a variety of things you could do for me. You could, say, be a substantial boost to my career. A Jedi? Even your basic Jedi grunt might be valuable, to the right people. I mean, I've captured an enemy officer here, haven't I? The Confederacy might reward me handsomely for you. In fact, I know they would. And maybe even give me a medal." He tilted his head: a humorous sidelong look. "You don't seem concerned by the possibility."

If he were planning to turn Mace over to the Separatists, Geptun wouldn't be here. Mace waited. Silently.

"Ah, it's true," the colonel sighed after a moment. "I'm not political. And there's something else you might be able to do for me."

Mace kept waiting.

"Well. I see it like this. Here I have a Jedi. Probably an important Jedi, since we caught him next to the corpse of the planetary chief of Republic Intelligence." He winked at Mace again. "Oh, yes: Phloremirlla and I were old friends. Friends too long to let political differences come between us, eh?"

"I'm sure she'd be gratified by your obvious grief."

Geptun took this without a blink. It didn't even dent his smile. "Tragic. After so many years in so many dangerous places, to be cut down by a stray blaster bolt. Collateral damage. Merely a bystander. Hardly *innocent*, though, was she?"

It was possible, Mace reflected, that he might come to profoundly dislike this man. "If your men hadn't shot me, she'd still be alive."

He chuckled. "If my men hadn't shot you, I wouldn't have the pleasure of your company tonight."

"And has this pleasure been worth your friend's life?"

"That remains to be seen." Their gazes locked for a full second. Mace had seen lizards with more expressive eyes. Predatory lizards.

He revised his threat assessment again. Upward.

Geptun shifted his weight like a man getting comfortable after a large meal. "So. Back to this Jedi in question. I'm thinking this Jedi is also someone a little on the capable side. Even, perhaps, actively dangerous. Since he answers the description of a fellow who broke several bones belonging to a pair of my best men."

"Those were your best? I'm sorry."

"So am I, Master Jedi. So am I. Well. I fell to wondering what business might possibly bring an important, dangerous Jedi like yourself to our little backworld of Haruun Kal. You would hardly have come so far just to commit petty assault upon peace officers. I fell to wondering if your business might possibly have something to do with *another* Jedi. One who seems to be running around upcountry, doing all sorts of un-Jedi-ish kinds of things. Like murdering civilians. Might your business have something to do with her?"

"If it does?"

Geptun tilted his chair back and looked at Mace over the curves of his plump cheeks. "We've been hunting this Jedi for some time now. I've even posted a bounty. A *big* bounty. It's possible that if someone were to, mm—deal with—my *existing* Jedi problem, I might feel fully compensated. I might not even miss that reward we were talking about earlier."

"I see."

"Maybe you do. And maybe you don't. Here's the thing: I can't quite make up my mind."

Mace waited.

Geptun sighed irritably and settled his chair back on the floor. "You're not the easiest man to have a conversation with."

This didn't call for a reply, so Mace didn't make one.

"See? That's exactly what I'm talking about. Well. I suppose I just need a way to ease my mind, you understand? I'm right on the bubble, here: I can go either way. I'd like that reward. Yes, indeed I would. But given the choice, I'd prefer my, er, *upcountry* Jedi problem taken care of—but I'm not sure that's the best decision I could make right now. For my *future.* I'm wavering. You see? Teetering. I need a little reassurance. If you know what I mean?"

Now Mace finally understood what they were talking about. "How much reassurance do you need?"

Geptun's eyes glinted the same flat sheen as the shearplanes of the gravel in the walls. "Ten thousand."

"I'll give you four."

Geptun scowled at him. Mace stared back; his face might have been carved from stone.

"I can keep you here a *very* long time—"

Mace said, "Thirty-five hundred."

"You insult me. What, am I not worth even haggling with?"

"We *are* haggling. Thirty-two fifty."

"I'm wounded, Master Jedi—"

"You mean: Jedi Master," Mace said. "Three thousand."

Geptun's face blackened, but after a moment wasted trying to match uncompromising stares with Mace Windu—a losing proposition—he shook his head and shrugged again. "Three thousand. I suppose one must make allowances." He sighed. "There *is* a war on, after all."

They cut him loose at dawn.

Mace descended the worn stone sweep of the Ministry of Justice's front steps. The high cirrus over Grandfather's Shoulder bled morning. The lightpoles had gone pale. The street below was as restlessly crowded as ever.

He had his kitbag over his shoulder and his blaster strapped to his thigh. His lightsaber was in an inside pocket of his vest, concealed below his left arm.

He slid into the crowd and let its current carry him along.

Endless faces passed him, meeting his eyes incuriously or not at all. Carts clattered. Music trickled from open doorways and leaked from personal players. Once in a while the massive rumble of steamcrawler treads forced the crowds to one side or another; at such times the touch of unfamiliar flesh made his skin crawl. The smell of human sweat mingled with Yuzzem urine and the musky funk of Togorians. He smelled the unmistakable tang of t'landa Til elbow glands, and the smoke of portaak leaf roasting over lammas fires, and he could only marvel dully at how *alien* it all was. Of course, the alien here was Mace.

He could not guess what he should do next.

FROM THE PRIVATE JOURNALS OF MACE WINDU

I should have been working my way toward Depa already. I could have headed for the Highland Green Washeteria, to make new contact with the remaining Republic Intelligence agents onworld. I could have hired my own team: though the bribe to Geptun wiped out the credit account of "Kinsal Trappano"—it never contains more than a few thousand—that account is monitored by the Jedi Council. New funds would be added as required. A steamcrawler wouldn't be hard to come by, and the streets were filled with dangerous-looking people who might be willing to hire on. I could have done any number of things.

Instead, I drifted with the current of the crowds.

I discovered that I was afraid. Afraid of making another mistake.

It's an unfamiliar feeling. Not until Geonosis did I truly understand that such a thing was even possible.

At the Temple, we teach that the only true mistake a Jedi ever makes is to fail to trust the Force. Jedi do not "figure things out" or "come up with a plan." Such actions are the opposite of what being a Jedi means. We let the Force flow through us, and ride its currents to peace and justice. Most of Jedi training involves learning to trust our instincts, our feelings, as opposed to our intellects. A Jedi must learn to "unthink" a situation, to "unact": to become an empty vessel for the Force to fill with wisdom and action. We feel the truth when we stop analyzing it. The Force acts through us when we surrender all effort. A Jedi does not decide. A Jedi *trusts*.

To put it another way: we are not trained to think. We are trained to *know*.

But at Geonosis, our knowing failed us all.

Haruun Kal has already taught me that the tragedy of misjudgment that was Geonosis was not an isolated event. It can happen again.

Will happen again.

I don't know how to stop it.

To have come here alone made sense . . . but it was intellectual sense, and the intellect is a deceiver. To go after Depa myself feels right . . . but my feelings can no longer be trusted. The shadow on the Force turns our instincts against us.

I didn't know what to do, and I didn't know how to decide what to do.

There were instincts, though, that had little to do with Jedi training. It was one of these Mace followed when he felt a *Hey, buddy* nudge on his shoulder, and looked around to find no one there.

The nudge had come through the Force.

He scanned a sea of faces and heads and steamcrawler smoke. Limp café banners dripping in the moist air. A cart with a ragged mange-patched grasser in the traces. The driver flourished an electroprod. "Two creds, anywheres in town. Two creds!" Nearby, a Yuzzem with alcohol-bleared eyes snarled. He was harnessed to one of the two-wheeled taxicarts. He turned in the traces and snatched a human out of the seat, holding him overhead in one enormous hand while the other displayed wickedly hooked claws. His snarl translated: *No money? No problem. I'm hungry.*

Another nudge—

Mace got a glimpse of him this time. The crowd made one of those smoke-random rifts that let him see a hundred meters along the street: a slender Korun half Mace's age or less, darker skin, wearing the brown close-woven tunic and pants of a jungle ghôshin. Mace caught a quick flash of white teeth and a hint of startling blue eyes and then the young Korun turned and moved away up the street.

Those startling eyes—had Mace seen him before? On the street the night before, maybe: around the time of the riot . . .

Mace went after him.

He needed a direction. This one looked promising.

The young Korun clearly wanted him to follow; each time the crowds would close between them and Mace would lose him, another Force-nudge would draw his eyes.

The crowds had their own pace. The faster Mace tried to move, the more resistance he met: elbows and shoulders and hips and even one or two old-fashioned straight-arms to the chest, accompanied by unfriendly assessments of his walking manners and offers to fill that particular gap in his education. To these, he responded with a simple "You don't want to fight me." He never bothered to emphasize this with the Force; the look in his eyes was enough.

One excitable young man didn't say a word, deciding instead to communicate with a wild overhand aimed at Mace's nose. Mace gravely inclined his head as though offering a polite bow, and the young man's fist shattered against the frontal bone of Mace's shaven skull. He briefly considered passing along some friendly advice to the excitable youth about the virtues of patience, nonviolence, and civilized behavior—or at least a mild critique of the fellow's sloppy punch—but the agony on his face as he knelt, cradling his broken knuckles, put Mace in mind of one of Yoda's maxims, that *The most powerful lessons, without words are taught,* so he only shrugged apologetically and walked on.

The pressure of the crowds brought his pursuit up against the law of diminishing returns: Mace couldn't gain on the young Korun without attracting even more attention and possibly injuring any number of insufficiently polite people. Sometimes when the Korun flicked a glance back, Mace thought he might detect a hint of a smile, but he was too far away to read it: was that smile enouraging? Friendly? Merely polite? Malicious?

Predatory?

The Korun turned down a narrower, darker street, still shadowed with the lees of night. Here the crowds had given way to a pair of Yarkora sleeping off their evening's debauchery arm in arm, perilously close to a pool of vomit, and three or four aging Balawai women who had ventured out to sweep the walkstones in front of their respective tenement doorways. Their morning rite of mutual griping broke down as Mace approached. They clutched their brooms possessively, adjusted the kerchiefs that bound whatever thin hair they may have had left, and watched him in silence.

One of them spat near his feet as he passed.

Instead of responding, he stopped. Now off the main streets and away from the constant rumble of voice, foot, and wheel, he could hear a new sound in the morning, faint but crisp: a thin, sharp hum that pulsed irregularly, bobbing like a cup on a lazy sea.

Repulsorlift engine. Maybe more than one.

Echoes along the building-lined street made the sound come from everywhere. But it wasn't getting louder. And when he got another Force-nudge from Smiley up the street and moved on, it didn't get fainter, either.

On the opposite sides of the buildings around, he thought. *Pacing me.*

Maybe swoops. Maybe speeder bikes. Not a landspeeder: a landspeeder's repulsorlifts hummed a single note. They didn't pulse as the vehicle bobbed.

This was starting to come into focus.

He followed Smiley through a maze of streets that twisted and forked. Some were loud and thronged; most were quiet, giving out no more than muttered conversation and the thutter of polymer cycle tires. Rooftops leaned overhead, upper floors reaching for each other, eclipsing the morning into one thin jag of blue above permanent twilight.

The twisting streets became tangled alleys. One more corner, and Smiley was gone.

Mace found himself in a tiny, enclosed courtyard maybe five meters square. Nothing within but massive trash bins overflowing with garbage. Trash chutes veined the blank faces of buildings around; the lowest windows were ten meters up and webbed with wire. High above on the rim of a rooftop, Mace's keen eyes picked out a scar of cleaner brick: Smiley must have gone fast up a rope, and pulled it up behind him, leaving no way for Mace to follow.

In some languages, a place like this was called a dead end.

A perfect place for a trap.

Mace thought, *Finally* . . .

He'd begun to wonder if they'd changed their minds.

He stood in the courtyard, his back to the straight length of alley, and opened his mind.

In the Force, they felt like energy fields.

Four spheres of cautious malice layered with anticipated thrill: expecting a successful hunt, but taking no chances. Two hung back at the far mouth of the alley, to provide cover and reserves. The other two advanced silently with weapons leveled, going for the point-blank shot. Mace could feel the aim points of their weapons skittering hotly across his skin like Aridusian lava beetles under his clothes.

The repulsorlift hum sharpened and took on a direction: above to either side. Speeder bikes, he guessed. His Force perception expanded to take them in as well: he felt the heightened threat of powerful weapons overhead, and swoops were rarely armed. One rider each. Out of sight over the rims of the buildings, they circled into position to provide crossing fire.

This was about to get interesting.

Mace felt only a warm anticipation. After a day of uncertainty and pretense, of holding on to his cover and offering bribes and letting thugs walk free, he was looking forward to doing a little straightforward, uncomplicated buttwhipping.

But then he caught the tone of his own thoughts, and he sighed.

No Jedi was perfect. All had flaws against which they struggled every day. Mace's few personal flaws were well known to every Jedi of his close acquaintance; he made no secret of them. On the contrary: it was part of Mace's particular greatness that he could freely acknowledge his weaknesses, and was not afraid to ask for help in dealing with them.

His applicable flaw, here: he *liked* to fight. This, in a Jedi, was especially dangerous.

And Mace was an especially dangerous Jedi.

With rigorous mental discipline, he squashed his anticipation and decided to parley. Talking them out of attacking might save their lives. And they seemed to be professionals; perhaps he could simply *pay* for the information he wanted.

Instead of beating it out of them.

As he reached his decision, the men behind him reached their range. Professionals indeed: without a word, they leveled their weapons, and twin packets of galvenned plasma streaked at his spine.

In even the best-trained human shooter there is at least a quarter-second delay between the decision to fire and the squeeze on the trigger. Deep in the Force, Mace could feel their decision even before it was made: an echo from his future.

Before their fingers could so much as twitch, he was moving.

By the time the blaster bolts were a quarter of the way there, Mace had whirled, the speed of his spin opening his vest. By the time the bolts were halfway there, the Force had snapped his lightsaber into his palm. At three-quarters, his blade extended, and when the blaster bolts reached him they met not flesh and bone but a meter-long continuous cascade of vivid purple energy.

Mace reflexively slapped the bolts back at the shooters—but instead of rebounding from his blade, the bolts splattered through it and grazed his ribs and burst against a trash bin behind him so that it boomed and bucked and shivered like a cracked bell.

Mace thought: *I might be in trouble after all.*

Before the thought could fully form in his mind, the two shooters (a distant, calculating part of Mace's brain filed that they were both human) had flipped their weapons to autoburst. A blinding spray of bolts filled the alleyway.

Mace threw himself sideways, flipping in the air; a bolt clipped his shin, hammering his leg backward, turning his flip into a tumble, but he still managed to land in a crouch behind the cover of the alleyway's inner corner. He glanced at his leg: the bolt hadn't penetrated his boot leather.

Stun setting, he thought. *Professionals who want me* alive.

While he was trying to feel his way toward what they might try next, he noticed that his blade cast a peculiarly pale light. Much too pale.

Even as he crouched there, staring drop-jawed into the paling shaft, it faded, flickered, and winked out.

He thought: *And this trouble I'm in just might be serious.*

His lightsaber was out of charge.

"That's not *possible,*" he snarled. "It's not—"

With a lurch in his gut, he got it.

Geptun.

Mace had underestimated him. Corrupt and greedy, yes. Stupid? Obviously not.

"Jedi!"

A man's voice, from the alley: one of the shooters.

"Let's do this the easy way, huh? Nobody has to get hurt."

If only that were true, Mace thought.

"We got all kinds of stuff out here, Jedi. Not just blasters. We got glop. We got Nytinite. We got stun nets."

But they hadn't used any yet. Mercenaries, Mace decided. Maybe bounty hunters. Not militia. Glop grenades and sleep gas were expensive; a blaster bolt cost almost nothing. So they were saving a few credits.

They were also giving him time to think. And he was about to make them regret it.

"You want to know what else we got?" Mace could hear his smirk. "Look *up,* Jedi . . ."

Over the roof rims above, the pair of speeder bikes bobbed upward, visored pilots skylining themselves against the blue. Their forward steering vanes scattered mirror flashes of the sunrise across the courtyard floor. Their underslung blaster cannons bracketed Mace with plasma-scorched muzzles. He was completely exposed to their crossfire—but they weren't firing.

Mace nodded to himself. They wanted him alive. A hit from one of those cannons and they'd have to pick up his body with shovels and a mop.

But that didn't mean cannons were useless: a blast from the lead bike shattered a chest-sized hunk of the baked-clay wall two meters above him. Chunks and slivers pounded him and slashed him and battered him to the ground.

Heat trickled down his skin, and he smelled blood: he was cut. The rest was too fresh to know how bad it might be. He scrambled through the rubble and dived behind a trash bin. No help there: the speeder pilot blasted the bin's far side and it slammed Mace hard enough to knock his wind out.

Shot. Concussed. Cut. Battered. Bladeless.

Haruun Kal was pounding him to pieces, and he hadn't been onworld even a standard day.

"All right!" He reached up and splayed his hands above the trash bin so that the speeder pilots could see. He let his decharged lightsaber dangle, thumb through its belt ring. "All right: I'm coming out. Don't shoot."

The lead speeder drifted in a little as he worked his way out from behind the bin, hands high. The other speeder hung back for high cover. Mace picked his way to the alley mouth, took a deep breath, and stepped out from the corner. The two shooters slowly uncovered: one from behind a trash bin and the other stepping out from a recessed doorway. The two backups stayed at the corners of the alley's far mouth.

"You're pretty good," Mace said. "Among the best I've ever seen."

"Hey, thanks," one answered. From his voice, this was the one who'd spoken earlier. The leader, then, most likely.

His smile was less friendly than his tone. He and his partner both carried fold-stock blasters in the crooks of their arms. The men at the end of the alley had over–under blaster rifles combined with something large bore: grenade launchers or wide-galvenned riot blasters. "Coming from a Jedi like you, I imagine that's high praise."

"You certainly do come prepared."

"Yup. Let's have that blaster, eh? Nice and easy."

Slowly—*very* slowly—Mace switched his lightsaber to his left hand, inching his right down toward the Power 5's butt. "I wish I could tell you how many times teams like yours have come after me. Not just in alleys. On the street. Caves. Cliffs. Freighter holds. Dry washes. You name it."

"And now you're caught. Put the blaster on the ground and kick it toward my friend here."

"Pirates. Bounty hunters. Tribals. Howlpacks." Mace might have been reminiscing with old friends as he complied. "Armed with everything from thermal detonators to stone axes. And sometimes just claws and teeth."

The silent one bent down for the Power 5. His blaster's muzzle dropped out of line. Mace took a step to his left. Now the talker was in the line of fire from the two behind him.

Mace reached into the Force, and the alleyway crystallized around him: a web of shearplanes and stress lines and vectors of motion. It became a gemstone with flaws and fractures that linked the talker and his partner, the two shooters at the far end, the speeder bikes and their pilots, the twenty-meter-high buildings to either side—

And Mace.

No shatterpoint that he could see would get him out of this.

Doesn't mean I won't, he thought. *Just means it won't be easy. Or certain.*

Or even likely.

He took one deep breath to compose himself.

One breath was all it took. If the Force should bring death to him here, he was ready.

"Now the lightsaber," the talker said.

"You are better prepared than most." Mace balanced his lightsaber on his palm. "But like all those others, you've forgotten the only piece of equipment that would actually do you any good."

"Yeah? What's that?"

Mace's voice went cold, and his eyes went colder. "An ambulance."

The leader's smile tried to turn into a chuckle, but instead it faded away: Mace's level stare was a humor-free zone.

The leader hefted his blaster. "The lightsaber. Now."

"Sure." Mace tossed it toward him. "Take it."

His lightsaber tumbled through a long arc. In the Force he felt them all fractionally relax: the slightest easing of trigger pressure: the tiniest shift of adrenaline-charged concentration. They relaxed because he was now unarmed.

Because none of them understood what a lightsaber was.

Mace had begun the construction of his lightsaber when he was still a Padawan. On the day he first put hand to metal, he had dreamed that lightsaber for three years already: had imagined it so completely that it existed in his mind, perfect in every detail. Its construction was not creation, but actualization: he took mental reality and made it physical. The thing of metal and gemstone, of particle beam and power cell, was only an expression; his *real* lightsaber was the one that existed only in the part of the Force Mace called his mind.

A lightsaber was not a weapon. Weapons might be taken, or destroyed. Weapons were unitary entities. Many people even gave them names of their own. Mace would no more give a name to his lightsaber than he would to his hand. He was not the boy who first imagined its shape, forty-one years before; nor was his lightsaber identical to that first image in the dreams of a nine-year-old boy. With each new step in his ever-deepening understanding of the Force and his place in it, he had rebuilt his lightsaber. Remade it. It had grown along with him.

His lightsaber reflected all he knew. All he believed.

All he was.

Which was why it required no effort, no thought, to seize his lightsaber's tumbling handgrip through the Force and fire it like a bullet.

It screamed through the air and its butt took the talker between the eyes with a hollow stone-on-wood *whock*. The impact flipped him off his feet, unconscious or dead before he hit the ground. His hands spasmed on the blaster, and it gushed energy. Through the Force Mace nudged the blaster's muzzle to sweep the talker's partner and blow him spinning to the ground; Mace guided it farther upward, and hammering energy chewed an arc of chunks from the walls before it battered the steering vanes of the speeder bike above and behind him, smacking it into a spin that kept the pilot too busy hanging on to even think about firing a weapon.

The over–unders of the two at the alley mouth now coughed, but Mace was already in motion: he Force-sprang at a slant and met the far wall five meters up, then kicked higher and across to the opposite wall, up and back again, zigzagging toward the rooftops through a storm of blasterfire.

Belated grenades burst below: spit-white glop spewed across the alley, swirling the purple cloud of Nytinite anesthetic gas, but Mace was already well above their effect zone. He sailed up over the lip of the flat baked-tile roof and there were *people up there*—

The roof was cluttered with hods full of tiles and pots of liquid permacite and bundled tarpaulins that might have been keeping the winter rains out—but now had become camouflage for at least two men.

Lying concealed beneath the tarps, the men were invisible to the eye but Mace felt them in the Force: adrenaline shivers and the desperate self-control it took to remain motionless. Bystanders? Roofers caught in a sudden firefight, hiding for their lives? Reserves for the assault team?

Mace was not certain he'd live to find out.

Before he could touch down, the other speeder pilot cut off his path with a fountain of blasterfire that traversed back to intercept him. A shove with the Force dropped him short, but as he made contact with the roof, the pilot fired an impact-fused grenade at Mace's feet. Mace reached out and the Force slapped the grenade away from himself and the hidden men, but the cannon's blast stream hammered a line of shattered tiles and smoking holes in the rooftop straight at them.

So he sprang *toward* it.

An upward thrust with the Force lifted him over the blast stream, and he made his spring into a twisting dive-roll that brought him to his feet with his back to the massive communal chimney that rose from the center of the roof. The chimney shuddered with the impact of cannonfire on its far side. Through the Force he felt the other speeder bike circling toward an open shot.

Cannon holes in the roof, he thought. Those cannons left shattered gaps big enough to dive through. If he could drop through one into the building—

The chimney was only a meter taller than Mace was. He sprang to the top. Cannonfire blasted into its baked-clay wall, tracking up toward his legs. Before he could spot a roof hole big enough to dive through, the chimney bucked and began to crumble.

He clawed for his balance. A man shouted, *"Hey, Windu! Happy name-day!"* and Mace got a glimpse of tarpaulins flipping back, and blue eyes and white teeth, and something came tumbling toward him through the air—

It was shaped vaguely like a cryoban grenade but when Mace reached into the Force to slap it away, he *recognized* it: its feel was as familiar as the sound of Yoda's voice.

It was a lightsaber.

It was *Depa's* lightsaber.

Instead of slapping it away, Mace drew it toward him—and

through the Force he *felt* her, felt Depa as though she stood at his side and had taken his hand. Its grip smacked into his palm.

In the green flash of Depa's blade, the situation looked different.

The rest of the fight lasted less than five seconds.

The speeder bike above opened fire again and Mace slipped to one side, letting the Force move the blade. Blaster bolts ricocheted from the energy fountain and smashed the speeder's power cell, sending it flipping toward the ground within the alley's end. The blue-eyed Korun—Smiley, the one who had led him here—and the other man who had lain beneath the tarp held rapid-fire slugthrowers that they slipped over the roof rim to fill the alley below with a lethal swarm of bullets.

Two more Korunnai popped out of cover on the rooftop across the alley. One had a slugthrower: flame leapt from its barrel. The other—a big light-skinned Korun girl with reddish hair—stood upright, wide-legged, a massive Mer-Sonn Thunderbolt tucked into her armpit, showering the alley with howling packets of galvenned particle beam.

The other pilot didn't like the new odds: he power-slewed his speeder and shrieked away above the rooftops. Smiley yanked his barrel around and took aim at the pilot's back—but before he could fire, the speeder bike flipped in the air, tumbled out of control, and crashed through the wall of a distant building at roughly two hundred kilometers an hour.

Smiley waved a hand, and the Korunnai stopped firing.

The sudden silence rang in Mace's ears.

"Was that fun or *what?*" Smiley grinned at Mace, and winked. "Come on, Windu: tell me that didn't warm your shorts a little."

Mace dropped to the rooftop and angled Depa's blade to a neutral position. "Who are you?"

"I'm the guy who just slipped your jiffies off the roaster. Let's *go*, man. Militia'll be here any minute."

The two Korunnai across the alley were already sliding down slender ropes toward the ground. Smiley and his friend hooked grapnels that might have been made of polished brassvine over the lip of the roof and paid out rope below. His friend slung his slug rifle and slipped over the edge.

Mace scowled toward the column of smoke that now rose from the gaping hole the second speeder bike had left in the building blocks away. Smiley caught his look and chuckled. "Love that fungus: ate his fly-by-wire. Saved me a shot."

Mace muttered, "I'm just hoping nobody was home."

"Yeah, think of the mess." Smiley gave him that big white grin. "Forget about identifying bodies, huh? Better to just hose it out."

Mace looked at him. "I have a feeling," he said slowly, "that you and I aren't going to be friends."

"And that's got my heart pumping pondwater, let me tell you." Smiley took a rope in his hands and beckoned. "On the *double*, Windu. What do you want, an invitation? Flowers and a box of candy?"

The cascade of Depa's lightsaber highlighted both their faces the color of sunlight in the jungle. "What I want," Mace told him, "is for you to tell me what you were doing with this blade."

"The lightsaber?" The blue in his eyes sparked with manic fire. "That's my *credentials*," he said, and disappeared below the rim.

3

JUNGLE TO JUNGLE

Mace stood on the roof, staring into the emerald gleam of Depa's blade. Either she'd given it to Smiley, or he'd taken it off her corpse. Mace hoped it was the former.

At least, he thought he did.

The Depa he knew—would she lend out her lightsaber? Would she give away part of herself?

Something told him it hadn't exactly been a Concordance of Fealty.

After a few seconds, he released the activation plate. Her blade shrank and vanished, leaving behind only a tang of ions in the air. He slipped the handgrip into the inner pocket of his vest. It didn't go in easily: the grip was tacky with a thin layer of goo that had an herbaceous scent.

Some kind of plant resin. Sticky, but it didn't come off on his hand.

He shook his head, scowling at his palm. Then he sighed. And shrugged. Perhaps it was time he stopped expecting things on this planet to make sense.

He leaned out over the roof rim. Four bodies below in the alley, plus the pilot lying amid the wreckage of his speeder bike in the alley. Include the one who'd crashed into the building, and that was all of them.

Smiley and the Korunnai were swiftly and efficiently looting the dead.

Mace's jaw tightened. One of the dead—the talker, maybe—had a deep blood-lipped gash from ear to ear.

Someone had cut his throat.

A sick weight gathered in Mace's chest. Some things did make sense after all, and the sense this made turned his stomach.

The Force gave him no sign of guilt from any of them; perhaps the violence here was so recent that its echoes washed away any such subtleties. Or perhaps whichever of them had done this felt no guilt at all.

And these killers were his best hope—perhaps his only hope—of reaching Depa.

But he could not simply let this pass.

Another lesson of Yoda's came to mind: *When all choices seem wrong, choose restraint.*

Mace slid down the rope.

Smiley nodded him over. "You're a mess, you know that? Take that shirt off." He reached down to pull a medpac off a dead man's belt. "There'll be spray bandage in here—"

Mace took Smiley's upper arm with one hand. "You and I," he said, "need to reestablish our relationship."

"Hey—*ow,* huh?" Smiley tried to jerk free, and discovered that Mace's grip would not suffer by comparison with a freighter's docking claw: trying just hurt his arm. *"Hey!"*

"We got off on the wrong foot," Mace said. "We're going to make an adjustment. Do you think we can manage this peacefully?"

The other Korunnai looked up from their looting. They stood, faces darkening as they turned toward Mace and Smiley, shifting grips on their weapons. Fingers slipped through trigger guards.

"Bad idea," Mace said. "For everyone concerned."

"Hey, easy on the arm, huh? I might need it again someday—"

Mace's hand tightened. "Tell them what we're doing."

"You want to lay off the bone-crushing *grip?*" Smiley's voice was going thin. Beads of sweat swelled across his upper lip. "What, you like my arm so much you want to take it *home* with you?"

"This isn't my bone-crushing grip. This is my don't-do-something-stupid grip." Mace tightened it enough to draw a squeak of pain through Smiley's lips. "We'll graduate to bone-crushing in about ten seconds."

"Um . . . when you put it *that* way . . ."

"Tell them what we're *doing*."

Smiley twisted his neck to look over his shoulder at the other Korunnai. "Hey, you kids stand down, huh?" he said weakly. "We're just . . . uh, reestablishing our relationship."

"Peacefully."

"Yeah, *peacefully*."

The other three Korunnai let their weapons dangle from their shoulder slings and went back to looting the bodies.

Mace released him. Smiley massaged his arm, looking aggrieved. "What exactly is your malfunction, anyway?"

"You didn't lead me into a trap. You used me to lead *them* into a trap."

"Hey, Captain Obvious, news flash: this wasn't a trap."

Mace frowned. "Then what would you call it?"

"It was an *ambush*." Smiley smirked. "What, they don't teach Basic in Jedi school?"

"Do you know," Mace said, "that I disliked you the instant we met?"

"Is that Jedi-speak for *thank you so much for saving my lightsaber-waving butt*? Shee." He shook his head, mock-sad. "So what is it? What's your fuss?"

"I would have liked," Mace told him solidly, "to have taken them alive."

"What for?"

In Pelek Baw, Mace reflected, that was a fair question. Turn them over to the authorities? What authorities? Geptun? The cops who ran the strong-arm at the pro-bi showers? He took a deep breath. "For *questioning*."

"Everything needing to know, you?" This came from the big red-haired girl with the Thunderbolt. She looked up at Mace, still crouched beside a corpse. Her accent dripped high upland. "Are looking at it, you. Six Balawai scum. Over and done. Never another Korun's home burn. Never another herd slaughter, never another child murder, never another woman—"

She didn't finish, but Mace would read the final word in the smoke of hate that clouded her eyes. He could feel it in the anger and violation that pulsed from her into the Force. He could more than guess what she had been through; in the Force, he could feel how it had made her feel: sick with loathing, so wounded inside her heart that she could not allow herself to feel at all. His face softened for an instant, but he hardened it again. He knew instinctively that she wanted no pity. She was no one's victim.

If she saw how sorry he felt for her, she'd hate him for it.

So, instead, he lowered his voice, speaking gently and respectfully. "I see. My question, though: how are you certain that these men have done such things?"

"*Balawai,* them." She said it as if she were spitting out a hunk of rotten meat.

These were the people Depa had sent for him? The sick weight in his chest gathered mass.

He stepped away from Smiley and opened his fingers toward his lightsaber, where it lay beside the talker's throat-cut corpse. The decharged grip leapt from the ground to his hand.

"Listen to me. All of you."

The simple authority in his voice drew their eyes and held them. He said, "You will do no murder while I am in your company. Do you understand this? If you try, I will stop you. Failing that . . ."

Muscle bunched along his jaw, and his knuckles whitened on his lightsaber's handgrip. Smoldering threat burned the calm from his dark eyes.

"Failing that," he said through his teeth, "I will avenge your victims."

Smiley shook his head. "Um, *hello,* huh? Maybe you haven't noticed, but we're at *war* here. You get it?"

A thin whistling in the distance swelled to become a shriek. Other whistles joined in, rising in pitch and volume both. Sirens: militia units on their way. Smiley turned to his companions. "That's the bell, kids. Saddle up."

The Korunnai worked faster, stripping the corpses of medpacs, food squares, blaster gas cartridges. Credits. Boots.

"You call it war," Mace said. "But these were not soldiers."

"Maybe not. Sure got some nifty gear, though, don't they?" Smiley picked up one of the over–unders and sighted appreciatively along its barrel. "*Verrrry* nice. How else are we gonna get stuff like this? It's not like your bloody Republic sends us any."

"Is it worth their lives?"

"Shee. Little judgmental, aren't we? Didn't we just slip your jiffies off the roaster? A *thanks* wouldn't exactly be out of line—"

"It was you," Mace replied grimly, "who put my 'jiffies' *on* the roaster. And you took your time about slipping them off."

Though the mockery stayed in his tone, Smiley's eyes went remote. "I don't know you, Windu. But I know who you're supposed to be. She talks about you all the time. I know what you're supposed to be able to *do*. If they could have taken you—"

"Yes?"

His head flicked a centimeter to the right: a Korun shrug. "I would have let 'em. You coming, or what?"

Pelek Baw rolled past the groundcar's tinted windows. The vehicle bumped along on large toroidal balloons made of a native tree resin, and used laminated wooden bow slats as springs. The driver was local: a middle-aged Korun with a web of cataract across one eye and bad teeth stained red from chewing raw thyssel bark. Mace and the Korunnai sat behind him in the passenger cabin.

Mace kept his head down, pretending to be engrossed in cobbling together an improvised adapter to recharge his lightsaber from looted blasterpacks. It didn't require all that much of his attention; his lightsaber was designed to be easily rechargeable. In an emergency, he could even use the Force to flip a concealed lock on the inside of its hermetically sealed shell, opening a hatch that would allow him to manually switch out the power cell. Instead, he laboriously wired up leads from the blasterpacks and pretended to study their charge monitors.

Mostly, it was an excuse to keep his head down.

The first thing the Korunnai did once they were on their way was swiftly and efficiently field-strip the captured weapons, despite the cramped compartment and the jouncing ride. Mace guessed they must've had plenty of practice. All exposed parts, they rubbed with chunks of a translucent orange-brown resin that Smiley said was portaak amber: a natural fungicide that the ULF used to protect their weapons. This was the same resin that coated the handgrip of Depa's lightsaber.

Smiley passed Mace a chunk. "Better rub up yours, too. And you might consider getting yourself a knife. Maybe a slug pistol. Even with the amber, powered weapons are unreliable here." He told Mace to keep the chunk, and shrugged off his thanks.

Smiley's name was Nick Rostu. He'd introduced himself in the groundcar while he was spray-bandaging Mace's cuts and treating his bruises by a liberal use of the stolen—captured—medpac. Mace recalled a ghôsh Rostu that had been loosely affiliated with ghôsh Windu; that Nick had taken the Rostu name meant he must be nidôsh: a clan child, an orphan. Like Mace.

But not much like Mace.

Unlike his companions, Nick spoke Basic without an accent. And he knew his way around the city. Probably why he seemed to be in charge. Mace gathered from their conversation that Nick had spent much of his childhood here in Pelek Baw. After what he'd seen of the Korun children in this city, he refused to let himself imagine what Nick's childhood must have been like.

The big, emotionally ravaged girl they called Chalk. The other two looked enough alike to be brothers. The older, whose teeth showed scarlet thyssel stains, was called Lesh. The younger brother, Besh, never spoke. A knurl of scar joined the corner of his mouth to his right ear, and his left hand was missing its last three fingers.

In the groundcar, they spoke to each other in Koruun. Eyes on his lightsaber's handgrip, Mace gave no sign that he understood most of what they said; his Koruun was rusty—learned thirty-five standard years before—but serviceable enough, and the Force offered understanding where his memory might fail. Their chatter was mostly what he would expect from young people after a firefight: a mix of *Did you see when I—?* and *Wow, I really thought I was gonna*—while they sorted through the adrenaline-charged chaos of imagery that was inevitably the memory of battle.

Chalk glanced at Mace from time to time. *What's with Jedi Rockface?* she asked the others generally. *I don't like him. He looks the same when he's cleaning his weapons as he did while he was using them. Makes me nervous.*

Nick shrugged at her. *Would you be happier if he was like Depa? Count your blessings. And mind your mouth: she said he spent some time upcountry a few years ago. He might still speak some Koruun.*

Chalk's only response was a bleak silent scowl that twisted in Mace's stomach like a knife. *Like Depa . . .*

He burned to ask what Nick had meant by that—but he wouldn't. He couldn't. He couldn't ask them about Depa. He was half sick with dread already, which was no state in which to meet his former Padawan and examine her mental and moral health; he would need as clear and open a mind as all his Jedi training and discipline could produce. He couldn't risk contaminating his perceptions with expectations or hopes or fears.

They bounced and swayed through a part of town Mace didn't recognize: a tangle of shabby stone housing blocks that rose from a scree of wood-frame shanties. Though the streets were far less crowded here—the only foot traffic seemed to be surly, ragged-looking men, and furtive women peering from doorways or clustered in nervous groups—the groundcar still spent valuable minutes stopped at this corner and that bend and another angle, waiting in the blare of the steam horn for the way to clear. They'd have made better time in an airspeeder, but Mace didn't suggest it; flying, on this world, struck him as a chancy undertaking.

Though he couldn't say for certain that it would be any more chancy than spending more time with these young Korunnai. They worried him; they had enough Force-touch to be unpredictable, and enough savagery to be dangerously powerful.

And then there was Nick, who was at best marginally sane.

Back in the alley, standing among the corpses with the militia on the way, Mace had asked where their transport was, and why they weren't hurrying to meet it; he didn't want to get caught in another firefight.

"Relax. Neither do they." Nick had smirked at him. "What d'you think those sirens are about? They're letting us know they're coming."

"They don't try to catch you?"

"If they did, they'd have to fight us." He'd stroked his long-barreled slugthrower as though it were a pet. "Think they're gonna do that?"

"I would."

"Yeah, okay. But they're not Jedi."

"I've noticed."

Several of the weapons the Korunnai had left on the ground. Besh had picked up Mace's Power 5, frowned at it, then shrugged and tossed it back among the bodies. Mace had moved to retrieve it, and Nick had told him not to bother.

"It's mine—"

"It's junk," Nick countered. He picked it up. "Here, look."

He'd pointed it at Mace's forehead and pulled the trigger.

Mace managed not to flinch. Barely.

A wisp of greenish smoke had trailed downward from the grip.

Nick had shrugged and tossed the blaster back to the ground. "Fungus got it. Just like that second speeder bike. Some of those circuits are only nanometers thick; a few spores can eat right through 'em."

"That," Mace had told him, "was not funny."

"Not as funny as if I'd been *wrong*, huh?" Nick chuckled. "What's the matter, Windu? Depa says you got a great sense of humor."

Through clenched teeth Mace said, "She must have been joking."

In the car, he looked from one to another of the Korunnai. He could trust none of them. Though he felt no malice from them, he'd felt none from Geptun, either. But he did feel knotted around them a strangling web of anger and fear and pain.

Korunnai were Force-users. But they'd never had Jedi training. These radiated darkness: as though they came from some reversed universe, where light is only a shadow cast by the darkness of the stars. Their anger and pain beat against him in waves that triggered resonance harmonics in his own heart. Without knowing it, they called to emotions that Mace's lifetime of Jedi training was supposed to have buried.

And those buried emotions were already stirring to answer . . .

He recognized that he was in danger here. In ways deeper than the merely physical.

Now, sitting in the groundcar, waiting for his lightsaber to recharge, Mace decided that he should get some things straight with these four young Korunnai. And there'd never be a better time.

"I think we'll all speak Basic now," Mace said. "Any being will soon enough tire of listening to conversation in a foreign tongue." Which was not even a lie.

Chalk gave him a dark look. "Here, *Basic* is foreign tongue."

"Fair enough," Mace allowed. "Nonetheless: when I am in your company, that is what we will speak."

"Shee, pretty free with the orders, aren't we? No murder, no looting, speak Basic . . . ," Nick said. "Who said *you're* in charge? And if we don't feel like doing what we're told? What's it gonna be, Mister There-Is-No-Emotion? Harsh language?"

"I *am* in charge," Mace said quietly.

This was greeted with a round of half-pitying sneers and snorts and shaken heads.

Mace looked at Nick. "Do you doubt my ability to maintain a grip on the situation?"

"Oh, very funny," Nick said, massaging his arm.

"I won't bore you with the complexities of chain of command," Mace said. "I'll stick to facts. Simple facts. Straightforward. Easy to understand. Like this one: Master Billaba sent you here to bring me to her."

"Says who?"

"If she wanted me dead, you'd have left me in that alley. She wouldn't have sent you to divert or ditch me. She knows you're not good enough for that."

"Says *you* . . ."

"You're under orders to deliver me."

"Depa doesn't exactly give orders," Nick said. "It's more like, she just lets you know what she thinks you should do. And then you do it."

Mace shrugged. "Do you intend to disappoint her?"

The uncertain looks they now exchanged drove that sick knife deeper into Mace's gut. They feared her—or something to do with her—in a way that they did not fear him.

Nick said, "So?"

"So you need my cooperation." Mace checked the meter on the blasterpack: this one was depleted. He pulled the adapter out of his lightsaber's charge port.

Nick sat forward, a dangerous glint sparking in his blue eyes. "Who says we need your cooperation? Who says we can't just pack you up and send you Jedi Free Delivery?"

Instead of hooking in the next blasterpack, Mace balanced the lightsaber's handgrip on his palm. "I do."

Another glance made the rounds, and Mace felt swift currents ripple the Force back and forth among them. The brothers blanched. Chalk's knuckles whitened on the Thunderbolt. Nick's face went perfectly blank. Their hands shifted on their rifles.

Mace hefted the lightsaber. "Reconsider."

He watched each of them mentally calculate the odds of bringing a weapon to bear in the cramped cabin before he could trigger his blade. "Your chances come in two shapes," he said. "Slim, and fat."

"Okay." Nick carefully lifted empty hands. "Okay, everybody. Stand down. *Relax*, huh? Shee, how twitchy are *we*, huh? Listen, you need us, too, Windu—"

"*Master* Windu."

Nick blinked. "You're kidding, right?"

"I worked very hard to gain that title, and I've worked even harder to deserve it. I prefer that you use it."

"Um, yeah. I was saying *you* need *us,* too. I mean, you're not from around here."

"I was born on the north slope of Grandfather's Shoulder."

"Yeah, okay. Sure. I know: you're from here. But you're still not *from* here. You're from the galaxy." Nick's hands clutched as though he were trying to pull words from the air. "Depa says—you know what Depa says?"

"Master Billaba."

"Yeah, okay, sure. Whatever. *Master Billaba* tries to explain it like this. It's like, you live in the *galaxy,* y'know? The *other* galaxy."

The other galaxy? Mace frowned. "Go on."

"She says . . . she says that you—all of you, the Jedi, the government, *everybody*—you're, like, from the Galaxy of Peace. You're from the galaxy where rules are rules, and almost everybody plays along. Haruun Kal, though, we're a whole *different* place, y'know? It's like the laws of physics are different. Not opposite, not *up is down* or *black is white.* Nothing that simple. Just . . . different. So when you come here, you expect things to work a certain way. But they don't. Because things are *different,* here. You understand?"

"I understand," Mace said heavily, "that you're not my only option for local guides. Republic Intelligence set up a team to take me up-country—"

The looks exchanged among the Korunnai stopped Mace in midsentence. "You know something about that upcountry team." It wasn't a question.

"Upcountry team," Nick echoed derisively. "See, this is what I'm talking about. You just don't get it."

"Don't get what?"

Some of that manic glitter snuck back into his bright blue eyes. "Who do you think we left dead in that alley just now?"

Mace stared.

Nick showed him those gleaming teeth of his.

Mace looked at Lesh. Lesh spread his hands. His thyssel-stained smile was apologetic. "Does talk true, Nick: things are different, here."

Besh shrugged, nodding.

Mace looked at Chalk: at her eyes, incongruously dark in her fair-skinned face; at the way she cradled the massive Merr-Sonn Thunderbolt on her lap as though it were her child.

And many things suddenly fell into place.

"It was you," he said to her wonderingly. "You shot Phloremirrla Tenk."

The blistering afternoon sun dissolved the departing groundcar into heatshimmer and dust. Mace stood in the road and watched it go.

This far from the capital, the road was little more than a pair of ruts filled with crushed rock snaking through the hills. Green foliage striped its middle: the jungle reclaiming its own from the center out. For this short patch, the road paralleled the silver twist of Grandmother's Tears, a river of snowmelt from Grandfather's Shoulder that joined with the Great Downrush a few klicks from Pelek Baw. They were well above the capital now, on the far side of the great mountain.

Nick and the others were already hiking uphill through an ankle-high litter of bracken and scrub, weapons slung across their shoulders. The living wall of the jungle loomed twenty meters above. In the far distance, Mace could just make out a segmented line of gray blotches: probably tame grassers. The Balawai government used teams of the great beasts to clear the jungle back from the road.

"Master Windu—" Nick had stopped on the hillside above. He beckoned for Mace to follow, and pointed at the sky. "Air patrols. We need to make the tree line."

But still Mace stood in the road. Still he watched dust rise and twist in the groundcar's wake.

Nick had said: *You're from the Galaxy of Peace.*

And: *things are different, here.*

A deep uneasiness coiled behind his ribs. Were he not a Jedi and immune to such things, he might call it superstitious dread. An unreasoning fear: that he had left the galaxy behind in the groundcar; that civilization itself was bouncing away down the road to Pelek Baw. Leaving him out here.

Out here with the jungle.

He could *smell* it.

Perfume of heavy blooms, sap from broken branches, dust from the road, sulfur dioxide rolling down from active calderae upslope on Grandfather's Shoulder. Even the sunlight seemed to carry a scent out here: hot iron and rot. And Mace himself.

He could smell himself sweat.

Sweat trickled the length of his arms. Sweat beaded on his scalp and trailed down his neck, across his chest, along his spine. The tatters of his bloodstained shirt lay somewhere along the roadway, klicks behind. The leather of his vest clung to his skin, already showing salt rings.

He had begun to sweat before they'd even left the groundcar. He had begun to sweat while Nick explained why Republic-supported partisans under the command of a Jedi Master had murdered the station boss of Republic Intelligence.

"Tenk's been playing her own game for years now," Nick had said. "*Upcountry team,* my bloody saddle sores. You, *Master* Windu, were on your way to a seppie Intel camp in the Gevarno Cluster. It goes like this. One: she turns you over to the 'team.' Two: the 'team' reports an 'accident in the jungle.' Your body's never recovered—because you're getting what's left of your brains sucked out in a torture cell somewhere in Gevarno. Three: Tenk retires to a resort world in the Confederacy of Independent Systems."

Mace had been shaken. Too much of it made too much sense. But when he asked what evidence Nick had of this, the young Korun had only shrugged. "This isn't a court of law, *Master* Windu. It's a war."

"So you murdered her."

"*You* call it murder." Nick shrugged again. "I call it slipping your jiffies—"

"Off the roaster. I remember."

"We've been waiting for you for days. Depa—Master Billaba—described you to us and told us to watch for you at the spaceport, but we had a little militia trouble and missed you. We didn't pick you up again until you were coming out of the Washeteria with Tenk. And we almost lost you then, too—got a little hung up in a food riot. Then before we could get to you, you managed to get your Jedi butt stunned into next year. Fighting a pitched battle with the militia on an open street in Pelek Baw is not a high-percentage survival tactic, if you know what I mean."

"You couldn't have just *warned* me?"

"Sure we could. Which woulda decloaked us to Tenk and her Balawai pals. Gotten us killed for nothing. Because you wouldn't have believed us anyway."

"I'm not sure I believe you now." Mace had turned his lightsaber over in his palm, feeling the unpleasant way the portaak amber gripped his skin. "It's not lost on me that I only have your word on this. Everyone who might contradict your story is dead."

"Yeah."

"That doesn't seem to trouble you."

"I'm used to it."

Mace frowned. "I don't understand."

"That's what war *is*," Nick said. His voice had lost its mocking edge, and sounded almost kind. "It's like the jungle: by the time the Whatever-It-Is that's moving through the trees out there is close enough that you can see for sure what it is—or *who* it is—you're already dead. So you make your best guess. Sometimes you're right, and you take out an enemy, or spare an ally. Sometimes you're wrong. Then you die. Or you have to live with having killed a friend."

He showed his teeth, but his smile had no warmth left in it. "And sometimes you're right and you die anyway. Sometimes your friend isn't a friend. You never know. You *can't* know."

"I can. That's part of what being a Jedi is."

Nick's smile had turned knowing. "Okay. Take your pick. We're murderers who must be brought to justice. Or we're soldiers doing our duty. Either way, who else is gonna take you to De—uh, *Master* Billaba?"

Mace growled, "This is not lost on me, either."

"So what are you gonna do about it?"

He and the others watched Mace think it over.

And, in the end, the decision Mace reached surprised none of them. It disappointed only himself.

Nick had winked. "Welcome to Haruun Kal."

Now the groundcar's dust plume slipped into a fold of the hills, and was gone.

At the green wall above, Besh and Lesh had already vanished into the canopied shadow. Chalk and Nick waited for him just below the tree line, crouched in the scrub, watching the sky. Outlined against the green.

The wall of jungle was green only on the outside: between the leaves and trunks, among the fronds and flowers and vines, was shadow so thick that from out here under the brilliant sun, it looked entirely black.

Mace thought, *It's not too late to change my mind.*

He could leave Nick here. Could turn his back on Chalk and Besh and Lesh. Hike along the road, catch a ride into Pelek Baw, hop a shuttle for the next liner on the Gevarno Loop . . .

He knew, somehow, that this was his last chance to walk away. That once he crossed the green wall, the only way out would be *through*.

He couldn't guess what he might find on the way—

Except, possibly, Depa.

. . . you should never have sent me here. And I should never have come . . .

It was too late to change his mind after all.

He was in the jungle already.

He'd walked into it from the shuttle in the Pelek Baw spaceport. Maybe from the balcony on Geonosis. Or maybe he'd been just standing still, and the jungle had grown around him before he'd noticed . . .

Welcome to Haruun Kal.

His boots crunched through the husks of bracken as he toiled up the slope. Chalk nodded to him and vanished through the wall. Nick gave him a smile as if he knew what Mace had been thinking.

"Better keep up, Master Windu. Another minute, we woulda left you standing there. You want to be alone out here? I don't think so."

He was right about that. "If we should happen to get separated, is there a landmark I should make for?"

"Don't worry about it. Just keep up."

"But if we do, how will I find you?"

"You won't." Nick shook his head, smiling into the jungle. "If we get separated, you won't live long enough to worry about finding us. You get it? Keep up."

He walked into the trees and was swallowed by the green twilight.

Mace nodded to himself, and followed Nick into the shadows without looking back.

4

THE SUMMERTIME WAR

Single file through the jungle: Chalk picked their path, parting gleamfronds, tipping gripleaf trailers aside with the muzzle of the Thunderbolt. Mace followed perhaps ten meters back, with Nick close behind his shoulder. Besh and Lesh brought up the rear together, switching positions from time to time, covering each other.

Mace had to look sharp to keep track of Chalk. Once they were well into the jungle, he could no longer easily feel any of the Korunnai in the Force. His gaze had a tendency to slip aside from them, to pass over them without seeing unless he firmly directed his will: a useful talent in a place where humans were just another prey animal.

Occasionally a Force-pulse as unmistakable as an upraised hand came from one or another of the Korunnai, and they would all stop in their tracks. Then seconds or minutes of stillness: listening to wind-rustle and animal cries, eyes searching among green shadow and greener light, reaching into the Force through a riot of lives for—what? Vine cat? Militia patrol? Stobor? Then a wave of relaxation clear as a sigh: some threat Mace could not see or feel had passed, and they walked on.

It was even hotter under the trees than in full sunlight. Any relief due to shade was canceled by the damp smothering stillness of the air. Though Mace heard a constant ruffle of leaves and branches high above, the breeze never seemed to reach down through the canopy.

They broke out into a gap, and Nick called a halt. The jungle canopy layered a roof above them, but the folds of ground here were clear for dozens of meters around, smooth gray-gold trunks of jungle trees becoming cathedral buttresses supporting walls of leaf and vine. Upslope, a spring-fed pond brimmed over into a steamy sulfur-scented stream.

Chalk moved into the middle of the gap, lowered her head, and went entirely still. A Force wave passed out from her and broke across Mace and thirty-five years fell away: for a delicious instant he was once more a boy returned to the company of ghôsh Windu after a lifetime in the Jedi Temple, feeling for the first time the silken warmth of a Korun's Force-call to an akk . . .

Then it passed, and Mace was again a grown man, again a Jedi Master, tired and worried: frightened for his friend, his Order, and his Republic.

Within minutes a crashing outside the gap heralded the arrival of large beasts, and soon the jungle wall parted to admit a grasser. It lumbered into the gap on its hind legs, its four anterior limbs occupied with ripping down greenery and stuffing it into a mouth large enough to swallow Mace whole. It chewed placidly, bovine contentment in all three of its eyes. It turned these eyes toward the humans one at a time: first the right, then the left, then the crown, assuring itself that none of its three eyes spied a threat.

Three more grassers tore their way into the gap. All four were harnessed for riding, the wide saddles cinched above and below their foreshoulders, exactly as Mace remembered. One wore a dual-saddle setup, the secondary saddle slung reversed at the beast's mid-shoulder.

All four grassers were thin, smaller than Mace remembered—the largest of them might not have topped six meters at full stretch—and their gray coats were dull and coarse: a far cry from the sleek, glossy behemoths he'd ridden all those years ago. This was as troubling as anything he'd yet seen. Had these Korunnai abandoned the Fourth Pillar?

Nick reached up to take the knotted mounting rope of the dual-saddled grasser. "Come on, Master Windu. You're riding with me."

"Where are your akks?"

"Around. Can't you feel them?"

And now Mace could: a ring of predatory wariness outside the green walls: savagery and hunger and devotion tangled into a semi-sentient knot of *Let's-Find-Something-to-Kill*.

Nick rope-walked up the flank of the grasser and slid into the upper saddle. "You'll see them if you need to see them. Let's hope you don't."

"Is it no longer customary to introduce a guest to the akks of the ghôsh?"

"You're not a guest, you're a package." Nick slid a brassvine goad out of its holster beside the saddle. "Mount up. Let's get out of here."

Without even understanding why he did it, Mace moved away into the middle of the gap. One breath composed his mind. The next expressed his nature into the Force around him: Jedi serenity balancing buried temper, devotion to peace tipping the scales against a guilty pleasure in fighting. Nothing was hidden, here. Light and dark, pure and corrupt, hope, fear, pride, and humility: he offered up everything that made him who he was, with a friendly smile, lowered eyes, and hands open at his sides. Then he sent rippling through the Force the call he'd been taught thirty-five years before . . .

And he got an answer.

Slipping through the walls of the gap: measured tread blending seamlessly with wind-rustle and flybuzz: horned reptoid heads questing, lidless oval eyes of gleaming black—

"Windu!" A hiss from Nick. "Don't move!"

Triangular fangs scissored along each other as jaws that could crush durasteel worked and chewed. Steaming drool trailed down mouth folds of scaled hide thick enough to stop a lightsaber. Splay-toed feet with shovel-sized claws churned kilos of dirt with every step. Muscular armored tails as long as their landspeeder-sized bodies whipped sinuously back and forth.

The akk dogs of Haruun Kal.

Three of them.

Nick hissed again. "Back up. Just back up. Straight toward me. Very slowly. *Don't* show them your back. They're good dogs, but if you trigger their hunt–kill instincts . . ."

The beasts circled, switching tails that could break Mace in half. Their eyes, hard-shelled and lidless, glittered without expression. Their breaths all stank of old meat, and their hides gave off a leathery musk, and for an instant Mace was on the sand in the Circus Horrificus in the bowels of Nar Shaddaa, surrounded by thousands of screaming spectators, at the mercy of Gargonn the Hutt—

He understood now why he had done this. Why he'd had to.

Because in that instant's vision of a long-ago arena, Depa was at his side.

Was that their last mission together? Could it be?

It seemed so long ago . . .

FROM THE PRIVATE JOURNALS OF MACE WINDU

I had come to Nar Shaddaa to track down exotic-animal smugglers who had sold attack-trained akk dogs to the Red Iaro terrorists of Lannik—and Depa had followed me to the Smugglers' Moon because she had suspected I might need her help. How right she was: even together, we barely survived. It was a terrible fight, against mutated giant akks for the amusement of the Circus Horrificus patrons—

But remembering it in the jungle, I found that my eyes filled with tears.

On that day in Nar Shaddaa, she showed me blade work that surpassed my own; she had continued to grow and study and progress in Vaapad as well as the Force.

She made me so very proud . . .

It had been years since she had passed her Trials of Knighthood; she had long been a Jedi Master, and a member of the Council; but for that one day, we had again been Mace and Depa, Master and Padawan, pitting the lethal efficiency of Vaapad against the worst the galaxy could throw at us. We fought as we had so many times: a perfectly integrated unit, augmenting each other's strengths, countering each other's weaknesses, and on that day it seemed we should have never done anything else. As Jedi Knights, we were unbeatable. As Masters, members of the Council—

What have we won? Anything?

Or have we lost everything?

How is it that our generation came to be the first in a thousand years to see our Republic shattered by war?

"Windu!" Nick urgently hissed Mace back to the present.

Mace lifted his head. Nick stared down at him from three meters above the jungle floor. "Don't just *stand* there!"

"All right."

Mace lifted his hands, and all three akk dogs lay down. A touch of the Force and a turn of both palms, and the three dogs rolled onto their backs, black tongues lolling to the side between razor-sharp teeth. They panted happily, gazing at him with absolute trust.

Nick said something about dipping himself in tusker poop.

Mace moved to one dog's head, sliding the palm of his hand between the triangle that six vestigial horns formed on the akk's brow. His other hand he placed just beside the akk's lower lip, so that the creature's huge tongue could flick Mace's scent into the olfactory pits beside his nostrils. He moved from one to the next, and then to the last; they took his scent, and he took their Force-feel. With the severe formality such solemn occasions demanded they respectfully learned each other.

Magnificent creatures. So different from the mutant giants that Depa and he had fought in the Circus Horrificus. In the fetid depths of Nar Shaddaa, Gargonn had taken noble defenders of the herd and twisted them into vicious slaughterers—

And Mace could not help but wonder if something on Haruun Kal might have done the same to Depa.

"All right," he said, to everyone and no one. "I'm ready to go."

Every night, they made a cold camp: no fire, and no need for one. The akks would keep predators at bay, and the Korunnai did not mind the darkness. Though militia gunships did not fly at night, a campfire was sufficiently hotter than the surrounding jungle that it could be detected by satellite sensors; Nick explained dryly that you never knew when the Balawai might decide to drop a DOKAW on your head.

He said that the government still had an unknown number of DOKAW platforms in orbit; the De-Orbiting Kinetic Anti-emplacement Weapons were, basically, just missile-sized rods of solid durasteel with rudimentary guidance and control systems, set in orbit around the planet. Cheap to make and easy to use: a simple command to the DOKAW's thrusters would kick it into the atmosphere on a course to strike any fixed-position coordinates.

Not too accurate, but then it didn't have to be: a meteorite strike on demand.

For the Korunnai, campfires were a thing of the past.

Many of the nocturnal insects signaled each other with light, making the night sparkle like a crowded starfield, and the different kinds of glowvines were mildly phosphorescent in varying colors; they combined into a pale general illumination not unlike faint moonlight.

The grassers always slept standing, all six of their legs locked straight, eyes closed, still reflexively chewing.

The Korunnai had bedrolls lashed to their saddles. Mace used a wallet tent he kept in a side pocket of his kitbag; once he split the pressure seal with his thumbnail, its internally articulated ribs would automatically unfold a transparent skin to make a shelter large enough for two people.

They would sit or kneel on the ground, sharing their meals: once the food squares and candy they'd looted from the dead men ran out, their meals became strips of smoked grasser meat and a hard cave-aged cheese made from raw grasser milk. Their water came from funnel plants, when they could find them: waxy orange leaves that wrapped themselves in a watertight spiral two meters high, trapping rainwater to keep the plants' shallow root system moist. Otherwise, they filled their canteens from warm streams or bubbling springs that Chalk occasionally tasted and pronounced safe to drink; even the ionic autosterilyzer in Mace's canteen couldn't remove the faint rotten-egg taste of sulfur.

After they ate, Lesh would often pull a soft roll of raw thyssel bark from his pack and offer it around. Nick and Mace always refused. Chalk might take a little, Besh a little more. Lesh would use his belt knife to carve off a hunk the size of three doubled fingers and stuff it into his mouth. Roasted and refined for sale, thyssel was a mildly stimulating intoxicant, no more harmful than sweet wine; raw, it was potent enough to cause permanent changes in brain chemistry. A minute of chewing would pop sweat across Lesh's brow and give his eyes a glassy haze, if there was enough vinelight to see it by.

Mace learned a great deal about these young Korunnai—and, by implication, about the ULF—during these nights in camp. Nick was the leader of this little band, but not by any reason of rank. They didn't seem to have ranks. Nick led by force of personality, and by lightning use of his acid wit, like a jester in control of a royal court.

He didn't talk of himself as a soldier, much less a patriot; he claimed his highest ambition was to be a mercenary. He wasn't in this war to save the world for the Korunnai. He was in it, he insisted, for the *credits*. He constantly talked about how he was getting ready to "blow this bloody jungle. Out there in the galaxy, there's *real* cred-its to be made." It was clear to Mace, though, that this was just a pose: a way to keep his companions at arm's length, a way to pretend he didn't really care.

Mace could see that he cared all too much.

Lesh and Besh were in the war from stark hatred of the Balawai. A couple of years before, Besh had been kidnapped by jungle prospectors. His missing fingers had been cut off, one at a time, by the Balawai, to force him to answer questions about the location of a supposed treasure grove of lammas trees. When he could not answer these questions—in fact, the treasure grove was only a myth— they assumed he was just stubborn. "If you won't answer us," one had said, "we'll make sure you never answer anyone else, either."

Besh never spoke because he couldn't. The Balawai had cut out his tongue.

He communicated by a combination of simple signs and an extraordinarily expressive Force projection of his emotions and attitudes; in many ways, he was the most eloquent of the group.

Chalk proved a surprise to Mace; guessing what he had of what had happened to her, he'd expected that she would be fighting out of a personal vendetta not unlike Lesh and Besh. On the contrary: even before joining the ULF, she and some members of her ghôsh had hunted down the men who'd molested her—a five-man squad of regular militia, and their noncom—and given them the traditional Korun punishment for such crimes. This was called *tan pel'trokal*, which roughly translated as "jungle justice." The guilty men were kidnapped, spirited away a hundred kilometers from the nearest settlement, then stripped of equipment, clothing, food. Everything. And released.

Naked. In the jungle.

Very, very few men had ever survived *tan pel'trokal*. These didn't.

So Chalk did not fight for revenge; in her own words, "Tough girl, me. Big. Strong. Good fighter. Didn't want to be. *Had* to be. How I lived through what they did, me. Fought, me. Never *stopped* fighting. And lived through it. Now I fight so other girls don't *have* to fight. Get to be *girls*, them. You follow? Only two ways to stop me: kill me, or show me no girls have to fight."

Mace understood. No one should have to be that tough.

"I am impressed by how you move through the jungle," Mace said to her once, in one of these cold camps. "It's not easy to see you even when I know you're there. Even your grasser is hard to track."

She grunted, chewing bark. Her dismissive shrug was about as casual as Mace's question. That is: not very.

"That's an interesting way of using—" He dredged from the depths of thirty-five-year-old memory the Koruun word for the Force. *Pelekotan:* roughly, "world-power." "—*pelekotan.* Is this something you've always been able to do?"

What Mace was really asking—what he was afraid to ask outright: *Did Depa teach you that?*

If she was teaching Jedi skills to people who were too old to learn Jedi discipline . . . people with no defense against the dark side . . .

"You don't use *pelekotan,*" Chalk said. "*Pelekotan* uses you."

This was not a comforting answer.

Mace recalled that the strict, literal translation of the word was "jungle-mind."

He discovered that he didn't really want to think about it. In his head, he kept hearing: . . . *I have become the darkness in the jungle* . . .

The grasser's lumbering pace was smooth and soothing; to make better time, it walked on both hind and midlimbs. This put its back at such an angle that Mace's rear-facing saddle let him recline somewhat, his shoulders resting on the grasser's broad, smooth spine, while Nick rode the foreshoulder saddle, peering over the top of its head.

These long, rocking rides through the jungle struck Mace with a deep uneasiness. Facing only backward, he could never see what was ahead, only what they had already passed; and even that had meanings he could not penetrate. Much of what he looked at, he could not be wholly sure if it was plant or animal, poisonous, predatory, harmless, beneficial—perhaps even sentient enough to have a moral nature of its own, good or evil . . .

He had a queasy feeling that these rides were symbolic of the war itself, for him. He was backing into it. Even in the full light of day, he had no clue what was coming, and no real understanding of what had passed. Utterly lost. Darkness would only make it worse.

He hoped he was wrong. Symbols are slippery.

Uncertain . . .

During the day, he saw the akk dogs in glimpses through the jungle as they ranged the rugged terrain around. They went before and behind, patrolling to guard the others from jungle predators, of which these jungles hid many that were large enough to kill a grasser. The three akks were bonded to Besh, Lesh, and Chalk. Nick had no akk of his own. "Hey, growing up on the streets of Pelek Baw, what would I do with an akk? What would I feed it, people? Heh, well, actually, now that I think about it—"

"You could find one now," Mace said. "You have the power; I've felt it. You could have a Force-bonded companion like your friends do."

"Are you kidding? I'm too young for that kind of commitment."

"Really?"

"Shee. Worse than being *married.*"

Mace said distantly, "I wouldn't know."

Mace would often get drowsy from the heat and the grasser's smooth gait. What little sleep he got at night was plagued by fever-ish dreams, indistinctly menacing and violent. The first morning af-ter he'd triggered his wallet tent's autofold and tucked it back into its hand-sized pocket in his kitbag, Nick had heard his sigh and saw him rub his bleary eyes.

"Nobody sleeps well out here," he'd told Mace with a dry chuckle. "You'll get used to it."

Day travel was a dreamlike flow from jungle gloom to brilliant sun and back again as they crossed grasser roads: the winding strips of open meadow left behind by grasser herds as they ate their way through the jungle. These were often the only times he'd see Chalk and Besh and Lesh, their grassers, and their akks. Using the akk dogs to keep in contact, they could spread out for safety.

Open air was the only relief they got from the insects: it was the territory of dozens of species of lightning-fast insectivorous birds. The dogflies and pinch beetles and all the varieties of wasp and bee and hornet stuck mostly to the relative safety of shade. Mace's skin was a mass of bites and stings that required considerable exercise of Jedi discipline to avoid scratching.

The Korunnai occasionally used juices from a couple of different kinds of crushed leaves to treat particularly nasty or dangerous stings, but in general they seemed not to really notice them, in the way a person rarely notices the way boots unnaturally constrict toes. They'd had a lifetime to get used to it.

Though they could have moved faster by following the grasser roads, frequent overflights by militia gunships made that too risky: Nick informed him that people riding grassers were shot on sight. Every hour or two, the akks gave warning of approaching gunships; their keen ears could pick up the hum of repulsorlifts from more than a kilometer away, despite the jungle's constant buzz and rustle, whir and screech, and even the distant thunder of the occasional minor volcanic eruption.

Mace got enough glimpses of these gunships to have an idea of their capabilities. They looked to be customized versions of ancient Sienar Turbostorms: blastboats retrofitted for atmospheric close-assault work. Relatively slow but heavily armored, bristling with cannons and missile launchers, large enough to transport a platoon of heavy infantry. They seemed to travel in threes. The militia's ability to maintain air patrols despite the metal-eating fungi and molds was explained by the straw-colored shimmer that haloed them as they flew; each gunship was large enough to carry its own surgical field generator.

From the height of the brush and young trees on the grasser roads, the most recent ones they crossed seemed to be at least two or three standard years old. Mace mentioned this to Nick.

He grunted grimly. "Yeah. They don't only shoot *us,* y'know. When Balawai gunners get bored, they start blasting grasser herds. Just for fun. It's been a couple of years since we've been stupid enough to gather more than four or five grassers in any one place. And even then we have to use akks to keep them separated enough that they don't make easy targets."

Mace frowned. Without constant contact and interaction with others of their kind, grassers could become depressed, sick—sometimes even psychotic. "This is how you care for your herds?"

Though he couldn't see Nick's face, he could hear the look on it. "Got a better idea?"

Beyond winning the war, Mace had to admit he did not.

Something else bothered him: Nick had said *a couple of years*—but the war had begun only a few months before. When he mentioned this, Nick replied with a derisive snort.

"*Your* war began a few months ago. Ours has been going since before I was born."

So began Mace's lesson in the Summertime War.

Nick wasn't sure how it started; he seemed to think it was an inevitable collision of lifestyles. The Korunnai followed their herds. The herds destroyed the hostile jungle. The destruction of the jungle made Korun survival possible: keeping down the drillmites, and the buzzworms and the gripleaf and vine cats and the million other ways the jungle had to kill a being.

The Balawai, by contrast, *harvested* the jungle: they needed it intact, to promote the growth of all the spices and woods and exotic plant extractives that were the foundation of Haruun Kal's entire civilized economy—and grassers were especially partial to thyssel bark and portaak leaf.

Korun guerrillas had been fighting Balawai militia units in these jungles for almost thirty years.

Nick thought it probably started with some bust-outs—jungle prospectors down on their luck—deciding to blame their bad luck on Korunnai and their grassers. He guessed these jups got liquored up and decided to go on a grasser hunt. And he guessed that after they wiped out the herd of some unlucky ghôsh, the men of the ghôsh discovered that the Balawai authorities weren't interested in investigating the deaths of mere animals. So the ghôsh decided they might go on a hunt themselves: a Balawai hunt.

"Why shouldn't they? They had nothing left to lose," Nick said. "With their herds slaughtered, their ghôsh was finished anyway."

Sporadic raids had gone back and forth for decades. The Korunnal Highland was a big place. The bloodshed might die down for years at a time, but then a series of provocations from one side or the other would inevitably spark a new flare-up. Korun children were raised to hate the Balawai; Balawai children in the Uplands were raised to shoot Korunnai on sight.

It was a very old-fashioned war, on the Korun side. The metal-eating fungi restricted them mostly to simple weapons—usually based on chemical explosives of one kind or another—and living mounts instead of vehicles. They couldn't even use comm units, because the Balawai government had geosynchronous detector satellites in orbit that could pinpoint comm transmissions instantly. They coordinated their activities through a system of Force communication that was hardly more sophisticated than smoke signals.

By the time Nick was old enough to fight, the Summertime War had become a tradition, almost a sport: late in the spring, when the winter rains were long enough gone that the hills were passable, the more adventurous young men and women of the Korunnai would band together on their grassers for their yearly forays against the Balawai. The Balawai, in turn, would load up their steamcrawlers and grind out to meet them. Each summer would be a fever dream of ambush and counterambush, steamcrawler sabotage and grasser shooting. A month or so before autumn brought the rains again, everyone would go home.

To get ready for next year.

Some of Depa's dazzling success was now explained, Mace realized: she didn't have to *create* a guerrilla army. She'd found one ready-made.

Blooded and hungry.

"This Clone War of yours? Who cares? You think anybody on Haruun Kal gives a handful of snot who rules on Coruscant? We kill seppies because they give weapons and supplies to the Balawai. The Balawai support the seppies because they get stuff like those gunships. For free, too. They used to have to buy them and ship 'em in from Opari. You follow? This is *our* war, *Master* Windu." Nick shook his head with amused contempt. "You guys are just passing through."

"You make it sound almost like fun."

"Almost?" Nick grinned down at him. "It's the most fun you can have while you're sober. And you don't really have to be all that sober; look at Lesh."

"I admit I don't know a lot about war. But I know it's not a game."

"Sure it is. You keep score by body count."

"That's revolting."

Nick shrugged. "Hey, I've lost friends. People who were as much family to me as anyone can be. But if you let the anger chew you up inside, you're just gonna do something stupid and get yourself killed. Maybe along with other people you care about. And fear is just as bad: too cautious gets people just as dead as too bold."

"Your answer is to pretend it's *fun?*"

Nick's grin turned sly. "You don't pretend anything. You have to *let* it be fun. You have to find the part of yourself that *likes* it."

"The Jedi have a name for that."

"Yeah?"

Mace nodded. "It's called the dark side."

Night.

Mace sat cross-legged before his wallet tent, stitching a tear in his pants left by a brush with a brassvine. He had his fake datapad propped against his thigh; its screen provided enough light that he could do the needlework without drawing blood. Its durasteel casing showed black mildew and the beginning of fungal scarring, but it had been adapted for the Haruun Kal jungles, and it still worked well enough.

They'd finished their cheese and smoked meat. The Korunnai field-stripped their weapons by touch, reapplying portaak amber to vulnerable surfaces. They spoke together in low voices: mostly sharing opinions on the weather and the next day's ride, and whether they might reach Depa's ULF band before they were intercepted by an air patrol.

When Mace finished patching his pants, he put away the stitcher, and silently watched the Korunnai, listening to their conversation. After a time, he picked up the datapad's recording rod and flicked it on, fiddling with it for a moment to adjust its encryption protocol.

When he had it set to his satisfaction, he brought the recording rod near his mouth and spoke very softly.

FROM THE PRIVATE JOURNALS OF MACE WINDU

I've read war tales in the Temple archives, from the early years of the Republic and before. According to these tales, soldiers in bivouac are supposed to speak endlessly of their parents or their sweethearts, of the food they would like to eat or wine they wish they were drinking. And of their plans for after the war. The Korunnai mention none of these things.

For the Korunnai, there is no "after the war."

The war is all there is. Not one of them is old enough to remember anything else.

They don't allow themselves even a fantasy of peace.

Like that death hollow we passed today—

Deep in the jungle, Nick turned our grasser aside from our line of march to skirt a deep fold in the ground that was choked with a riot of impossibly lush foliage. I didn't have to ask why. A death hollow is a low point where the heavier-than-air toxic gases that roll downslope from the volcanoes can pool.

The corpse of a hundred-kilo tusker lay just within its rim, its snout only a meter below the clear air that could have saved it. Other corpses littered the ground around it: rot crows and jacunas and other small scavengers I didn't recognize, lured to their deaths by the jungle's false promise of an easy meal.

I said something along these lines to Nick. He laughed and called me a Balawai fool.

"There's no false promise," he'd said. "There's no promise at all. The jungle doesn't *promise*. It exists. That's all. What killed those little ruskakks wasn't a trap. It was just the way things are."

Nick says that to talk of the jungle as a person—to give it the metaphoric aspect of a creature, any creature—that's a Balawai thing. That's part of what gets them killed out here.

It's a metaphor that shades the way you think: talk of the jungle as a creature, and you start *treating* it like a creature. You start thinking you can outsmart the jungle, or trust it, overpower it or befriend it, deceive it or bargain with it.

And then you die.

"Not because the jungle kills you. You get it? Just because it *is what it is.*" These are Nick's words. "The jungle doesn't *do* anything. It's just a place. It's a place where many, many things live ... and *all of them die.* Fantasizing about it—pretending it's something it's not—is fatal. That's your free life lesson for the day," he told me. "Keep it in mind."

I will.

I have a feeling that his lesson applies equally well to this war. But how can I avoid pretending this war is something it's not? I don't yet know what real war really is.

So far, I have only impressions ...

Vast. Unknown, and unknowable. Living darkness. Deadly as this jungle.

And my guide cannot be trusted.

Day.

Mace stood in a universe of rain.

As though the jungle's trees and ferns and flowers had grown at the foot of a towering waterfall, rain pounded through leaf and branch with a roar that made conversation possible only in shouts. No waterproof gear could handle this; in less than a minute, Mace's clothes had soaked through. He dealt with it Korun-style: he ignored it. His clothes would dry, and so would he. He was more concerned with his eyes; he had to shelter them with both hands in order to look up against the rush. Visibility was only a handful of meters.

It was just barely good enough that he could see the corpses.

They hung upside down, elbows bent at a strange angle because their hands were still tied behind them. Living gripleaves twined around their ankles held them six meters above the jungle floor, low enough to bring their heads within an easy jump for a vine cat like the one an akk had chased off as Mace and Nick approached.

Mace counted seven bodies.

Birds and insects had been at them as well as the vine cats. They'd been hanging for a while. In damp gloom that alternated with thunderous downpours. And metals weren't the only thing that the local molds and fungi fed on. Through the colorless tatters that were all that remained of their clothing, it was impossible to tell even if they had been men or women. Mace was only moderately certain they had been human.

He stood beneath them, looking up into the empty eye sockets of the two that still had heads.

"Is this what you felt?" Nick shouted down from the saddle. His grasser reached for the gripleaves that held the bodies, and Nick jabbed its forelimb with his brassvine goad. The grasser decided to rip up some nearby glass-ferns instead. It never stopped chewing.

Mace nodded. Echoes of these murders howled in the Force around him. He'd been able to feel it from hundreds of meters away.

This place stank of the dark side.

"Well, now you've seen it. Nothing for us to do here. Come on, mount up!"

The corpses stared down at Mace without eyes.

Asking him: *What will you do about us?*

"Are they—" Mace's voice was thick; he had to cough it clear, and enough water ran into his mouth that he passed a few seconds coughing for real. "Are these Balawai?"

"How should I know?"

Mace stepped out from below the bodies and squinted up at Nick. A blaze of lightning above the canopy haloed the young Korun's black hair with gold. "You mean they could have been Korunnai?"

"Sure! What's your point?" He seemed puzzled that Mace would care one way or the other.

Mace wasn't sure why he cared, either. Or even *if* he cared. People are people. Dead is dead.

Even if these had happened to be the enemy, nothing could make this right.

"We should bury them."

"We should get out of here!"

"What?"

"Mount up! We're leaving."

"If we can't bury them, at least we can cut them down. Burn them. Something." Mace caught at the mounting rope as though his merely human strength might hold back the two-ton grasser.

"Sure. Burn 'em." Nick sputtered a mouthful of the drenching rain down the grasser's flank. "There's that Jedi sense of humor again . . ."

"We can't just leave them for the scavengers!"

"Sure we can. And we will." Nick leaned down toward him, and on his face was something that might have even been pity. For Mace, that is. For the dead, he seemed to feel nothing at all.

"If those are Korunnai," Nick shouted, not unkindly, "to give them any kind of decent burial will only light a giant *We-Were-Here* advertiscreen for the next band of irregulars or militia patrol. And give them a pretty good idea of when. If those are Balawai—"

He glanced up at them. Everything human left his face.

He lowered his voice, but Mace could read his lips. "If they're Balawai," he muttered, "this is already better than they deserve."

Night.

Mace woke from evil dreams without opening his eyes.

He wasn't alone.

He didn't need the Force to tell him this. He could smell him. Rank sweat. Drool and raw thyssel.

Lesh.

Barely a murmur: "Why here, Windu? You come here why?"

The wallet tent was pitch black. Lesh shouldn't even have known Mace was awake.

"What want here, you? Come to take her away from us, you? Said you would, she." His voice was blurry with the drug and with a childlike weepy puzzlement, as though he suspected Mace might break his favorite toy.

"Lesh." Mace pitched his voice deep. Calm. Assured as a father. "You have to leave my tent, Lesh. We can talk about this in the morning."

"Think you can? Huh? Think you *can?*" His voice thinned: a shout strangled to a whisper. Now Mace smelled machine oil and portaak amber.

He was armed.

"Don't *understand* yet, you. But find *out*, you will—"

Mace reached into the Force. He could feel him: crouched by Mace's ankle. Mace's bedroll was pinned beneath his boots.

A less-than-ideal combat position.

"Lesh." Mace added the Force to his voice. "You want to leave, now. We'll talk in the morning."

"*What* morning? Morning for you? Morning for me?"

Mace couldn't tell if he was saying *morning,* or *mourning.*

Something was still strong enough even in Lesh's thyssel-addled mind that he could resist Mace's Force-pushed order. "Don't know *anything,* you." His voice went thicker, hitching, as if he wasn't breathing well. "But teach you, will *Kar.* What you do, he knows. Teach you, will the akks. Wait, you. Wait and see."

Kar? There'd been a Kar Vastor mentioned in several of Depa's reports. His name had come up as a particularly capable leader of a commando squad, independent or semi-independent; Mace was unclear on the ULF's command structure. But Lesh breathed the name with a sort of superstitious awe . . .

And had he said *akks?* or *ax?*

"Lesh. You have to go. Now." Questions notwithstanding, Mace was not so foolish as to engage a bark-drunk man in conversation.

"Think you know her. Think she's yours. Teach you better. Maybe. Live long enough to learn, you? Maybe *not.*"

That was enough of a threat for a flick of the Force to bring his lightsaber to his hand. The sizzling flare of its blade cast purple-fringed shadows. But Lesh was not attacking.

He hadn't moved. His rifle was tucked crosswise into his lap.

Tears streamed down his face.

That was the blur in his voice. That was the thick hitch.

He was crying. Silently.

"Lesh," Mace began in astonishment, "what's the ma—" He stopped himself because Lesh was still bark-drunk, and Mace was still not a fool. Instead, he offered a hand towel from his kitbag. "Here. Wipe your face."

Lesh took it and smeared the streaks below his eyes. He stared down at the towel and knotted it between his fists. "Windu—"

"No." Mace held out his hand for the towel. "We'll talk in the morning. After you sober up."

Lesh nodded and sniffled against the back of his fist. With one last beseeching look at Mace, he was gone.

The night rolled on, slow and sleepless. Meditation offered less rest than sleep would, but no dreams.

Not a bad bargain.

In the morning, when he asked Lesh if he still wanted to talk, Lesh pretended he didn't know what Mace meant. Mace watched his back as he walked away, and a flash of Force intuition took him and shook him and he knew:

By nightfall, Lesh would be dead.

Day.

The akks' Force yammer was almost painful. They'd given this call often enough that Mace knew it now.

Gunships. More than one.

Mace could feel that Nick was worried. In the Force, dry-ice tension rolled off him. It was starting to affect Mace, too: breathing it in off Nick tied knots in Mace's stomach.

Air patrols had been dogging them all day long. Spiral routes and quarter-cutting: search pattern. It wasn't safe to assume they were looking for anything but the four Korunnai and Mace.

Tension twisted those knots in Mace's guts. How could people live their lives under this kind of pressure?

"Bad luck," Nick muttered under his breath. "Bad, bad luck."

They were exposed in a notch pass through a razorback ridge: some long-ago groundquake had knocked a gap here. A broad fan of scrub-clutched scree made the ramp they'd climbed up to the pass. They'd been picking their way through a jumble of boulders a few dozen meters wide, akks ranging before and behind; the sides of the gap were towering cliff faces hung with flowering vines and epiphytic trees that clung to the rock with root-fingered grips. The spine of the ridge was shrouded in low clouds. Only two or three hundred meters away, the slope on the far side led down into dark jungle beyond. They might be able to reach the trees before the air patrol overflew them—

But Nick reined in their grasser. "Lesh is in trouble."

Mace didn't have to ask how he knew: these young folk shared a bond almost as profound as the one they had with their akks.

Mace thought of his Force-flash from the morning. He said, "Go."

Nick wheeled the grasser and they galloped back through the notch. From Mace's rear-facing saddle, he watched Chalk overtaking them on her way back from her position on point. Her grasser was the fastest of the four, and it carried only half the load of Nick's.

As they cleared the crest of the pass, Mace used the Force to lift himself up so that he could stand on the saddle facing forward, his hands on Nick's back, leaning to see past his shoulder.

On the descending curve of the pass, someone was down. An akk dog nosed him nervously. Lesh. His grasser stood placidly a dozen meters away, ripping small trees from the cliff wall to fill its ever-chewing maw. Besh got there first; he swung down from his grasser and sprinted to his brother's side.

"Get up!" Nick shouted. "Mount up and *move!*"

Nick gestured, and in the Force Mace felt a tug as though an unseen hand had taken hold of his line of sight and dragged it out toward the jungle below: a pair of matte-dull specks of metal skimmed the canopy, trailing a shock wake of roiling leaves.

Gunships. Coming straight for the notch.

"Might not have seen us yet," Nick muttered to himself. "Might just be checking the pass—"

"They've seen us."

Nick looked down at Mace past his shoulder. "How do you know?"

"Because they travel in *threes.*"

His last word was swallowed by howls of repulsorlifts and snarling turbojets that brought a gunship slewing into the gap from the other side of the ridge. Mace expected it to swoop in for a strafing run, but instead it hovered, cycling its turbojets. "What are they doing?"

Nick scowled back at the gunship. "You've heard the expression, *We're cooked?*"

"Yes . . ."

Ventral bays swung open in the gunship's belly, and nozzles shaped like a chemical rocket's reaction chamber deployed in a wide-angled array. They belched jets of flame that hit the ground and splashed and ran like rivers of fire, coating rocks and filling crevices. In just over a second the whole end of the pass had become an inferno so intense Mace had to shield his face with his arm. The gunship swept toward them, burying the gap in fire.

"In this case," Nick said grimly, "it's not just an expression."

5

BLOOD FEVER

The gunship bore down on them, riding a towering fan of flame.

The grasser unleashed an earsplitting honk and threw itself into a shockingly fast sprint, bounding from rock to rock, bucking and twisting in the air. Nick unleashed an equally earsplitting stream of profanity as he wrapped his arms around its neck to hang on. Its forebody whipped back and forth, and all four of its arms windmilled in panic.

Mace gathered himself, feeling the flow of the Force, letting his mind link the path of the bucking grasser to the jets of the gunship's flame projectors. As the gunship sailed overhead, Mace stiffened his hand into a blade and jabbed the grasser in the nerve plexus below its midshoulder.

The grasser blared a yelp like the horn of an air taxi in heavy traffic and leapt five meters sideways—into the gap between the fringes of two flame streams, so that they roared around Nick and Mace, only a few splashes igniting patches of fur on the grasser's legs. Mace gestured, and the Force pushed air away from the burning fur, snuffing it within a bubble of vacuum.

The gunship thundered past, gouts of flame clawing toward Chalk. She slipped around to the chest of her grasser, and it cradled her in its forelimbs as it ran, shielding her with its body. Nick's curses strangled to coughs on the thick black petrochemical smoke.

The smoke burned Mace's eyes like acid, blinding him with tears. He used the Force to nail himself to the saddle, then by feel he flipped open the stolen medpac that hung from Nick's belt, and let the Force tell him which spray hypo to use. He jabbed it into Nick's back beside his spine, then triggered it against his own chest.

Nick twisted at the sting. "What the *frag*—?"

"Gas binder," Mace said. Intended for emergency use during fires on shipboard, the gas binder selectively scrubbed a user's bloodstream of a variety of toxins, from carbon monoxide to hydrogen cyanide. "Not as good as a breath mask, but it'll keep us conscious for a few minutes—"

"We get to be wide *awake* while we *burn to death?* Great! How can I ever *thank* you?"

The gunship heeled over as it slewed into a curve that would bring it around for another run. Flame raked the haunches of Chalk's grasser, and its whole flank caught fire. It screamed and threw up its hands as it pitched forward, thrashing on the burning rocks, sending Chalk tumbling hard into a boulder. Her Force-bonded akk, Galthra, bounded from crag to crag, howling fury, clawing at the air as though she wanted to reach up and drag the gunship down on top of her. Mace felt no fear from her: akks were bred on the slopes of active volcanoes, and their armored hide was tough enough to stop a lightsaber.

The gunship rounded its turn and streaked back toward Mace and Nick.

Mace reached deeper into the Force, opening himself, seeking a shatterpoint. The fluid situation in the notch pass gelled, then splintered into crystal: grassers and akks and people and gunships became nodes of stress, vectors of intersecting energy joined by flaws and fault lines. Mace's mouth set in a grim slit.

He saw one bare chance.

The gunship could pass above them and rain fire all day long; no lightsaber was going to deflect a wash of flame-fuel. But: if the militia in the gunship wanted to take out the akks as well . . .

The gunship's aft launchers coughed and concussion missiles streaked back down the pass toward Besh and Lesh. The shock of explosions made the inferno around Mace and Nick whip and jump and spit, and was answered by smaller detonations on all sides, as heat-stressed stone began to shatter. Red-hot shards of half-molten rock slashed through the flames. Wherever they landed they stuck, sizzling. Mace's vest smoldered, and Nick was kept too busy smacking flames off his tunic and pants to even remember to curse.

Mace used the Force to unclip the grenade pack Nick had taken off the mercenaries in Pelek Baw, then he snatched the captured over-under out of its scabbard on the grasser's harness.

Nick twisted again, eyes wild, barely hanging on. "What are you doing *now?*"

"Jump."

"*What—?*"

With a surge of the Force Mace yanked him out of the saddle an instant before a missile took their grasser full in the chest. The explosion blasted them tumbling through the air in a cloud of vaporized flesh and bone.

Through the Force Mace felt Nick's consciousness fuzz from the shock wave; he turned his tumble into a forward flip that landed him on his feet among the rocks. The Force whipped the over-under's sling up his arm to his shoulder to free his hands, then caught Nick's limp body and delivered him lightly to Mace's arms.

Nick looked up at him with eyes that didn't quite focus. "Wha—? Wha' happen—?"

"Stay here," Mace said. He tucked Nick into a gap between two house-sized boulders; their mass would take a long time to heat, even in the raging inferno. Meanwhile they'd offer shelter from the fire.

"Are you *crazy?*" Nick asked blurrily. "You know what kind of firepower those ruskakks pack?"

"Two Taim and Bak dual KX-Four ball turrets, port and starboard," Mace said absently as he crouched behind the rock, slapping a Nytinite grenade into the over-under while he waited for the gunship to finish its sweep. "Twin fixed-position Krupx MG-Three mini missile tubes fore and aft, a belly-mounted Merr-Sonn Sunfire One Thousand flame projector—"

"And their *armor!*" Nick said. His eyes were only now starting to clear. "What do we have that can punch through that *armor?*"

"Nothing."

"So what exactly do you think you're gonna *do?*"

Mace said, "Win."

The gunship hurtled past. In the bare second that Mace was in the gunners' blind zone he stood up and launched a Nytinite grenade in a high arc. In the Force he felt its path; as it overtook the gunship, only the subtlest of nudges was required to loop it directly in front of the gunship's starboard turbojet intake, which promptly sucked it in like a snapfish taking a bottle bug.

Metal screamed. Nytinite grenades didn't actually detonate; they were canisters that released jets of gas. That this one was a grenade was not pertinent. What *was* pertinent was that a half-kilo chunk of durasteel had been sucked into turbojet fans that were rotating at roughly one bazillion rpm.

In round numbers.

A wash of purple gusted out the exhaust, followed by white-hot chunks of the turbojet's internal fans. More superheated chunks ripped through the turbojet's housing, and the whole engine blasted itself to shards, sending the gunship slewing wildly sideways to bounce off the face of the cliff wall.

Mace looked down at Nick. "Any questions?"

Nick appeared to be in danger of choking on his own tongue.

Mace said, "Excuse me," and was gone.

The Force launched him over the rocks like a torpedo. He stayed low, blasting through flames too fast to get burned, skimming the slag beneath; kicking off from one boulder to another, he ricocheted across the pass toward Chalk and her aak, Galthra.

The two gunships approaching from below swooped up toward the gap. Besh's grasser was down, kicking, on fire, and screaming. Lesh's was already just a pile of ragged meat. A missile took one of their akks in the flank; though akk hide is nearly impenetrable, the hydraulic shock of the missile's detonation made a bloody hash of its internal organs. The akk staggered into the rocks before it fell. Besh dragged his brother through the flames into cover behind its massive armored body. The akk's body bucked and jounced as round after round of cannonfire slammed into it, making it twitch as though still alive.

Behind Mace, the pilot of the first gunship finally recovered control, shutting down the port turbojet and bringing the craft around on repulsorlifts alone. Mace could feel Chalk recovering consciousness among the burning rocks, but he didn't have time to do anything for her right now. Instead, he followed the drift of her awakening mind into the Force-bond she shared with Galthra. One second was enough for Mace to sound the depths of that bond: he took its full measure.

Then he just took it.

Galthra's bond with Chalk was deep and strong, but it was a function of the Force, and Mace was a Jedi Master. Until he released the akk, Galthra's bond would be with *him*.

Mace hurled himself flipping through the air as Galthra sprang down to meet him. She hit the ground already gathered for her next leap and Mace finished his flip to land standing on her back. She was not trained to carry a rider in battle, but the flow of the Force through their bond made them a single creature. Mace wedged his left foot behind her cowl spines and she sprang out into the pass, bounding a jagged path through the inferno of flame and bursting stone.

Crouching low to take some cover from Galthra's massive skull, Mace slipped a grenade from the pack into the over–under's launcher, then slung the weapon without firing. Behind him, he felt the forward missile ports of the damaged gunship cycle open.

Mace murmured, "Right on time."

He and Galthra reached the crest of the pass. The two gunships in front of him roared up the slope. The one behind launched a concussion missile at Galthra's back.

In the shaved semisecond after launch, that eyeblink when the missile seemed to hang in the air as though gathering itself for the full ignition of its main engine and the multiple dozens of standard gravities of acceleration it would pull in its lightning flight, the Force-bond between Mace and Galthra pulsed and the great akk made a sudden leap to the left.

The missile screamed past so close that its exhaust scorched Mace's scalp.

And one little nudge in the Force—hardly more than an affectionate chuck under the chin—tipped its diamond-shaped warhead up a centimeter or two, altering its angle of attack just enough that the missile skimmed the crest of the pass instead of impacting on the burning ground. It streaked on, punching black smoke into turbulence vortices that trailed its tail fins, until the lead gunship swooped up the far side of the pass and took the missile right up its nose.

A huge white fireball knocked it rearing back like a startled grasser, and black smoke poured from the twisted gap blown in its nose armor. Its turbojets roared, and smoke whipped from its screaming repulsorlifts as its pilot fought for control. The third gunship slewed, yawing wildly as it reversed thrust and dived to avoid ramming the other's rear end.

Mace and Galthra raced straight toward them.

As they passed the shuddering hulk of Chalk's grasser, Mace reached for the Thunderbolt. It flipped from the ground into his arms, its power pack nestling between his feet. He cradled the massive weapon at his hip, angled the barrel at the third gunship, and held down the trigger.

Mace surfed through the flames and black stinging smoke, over the slag of melting rock, through the thunder and shrapnel shrieks of bursting stone on the back of three-quarters of a metric ton of armored predator, firing from the hip, hammering out a fountain of packeted energy that ripped its way up the side of the gunship. The Thunderbolt didn't have the punch to penetrate the gunship's heavy armor plating, but that didn't matter; the roaring repeater was merely Mace's calling card.

Galthra shot down the slope beneath the gunships and Mace

turned to face them, riding backward, spraying the air with blaster-fire until the Thunderbolt overheated and coughed sparks and Mace cast it aside. The third gunship fired a pair of missiles, but Mace could feel their point of aim before they squeezed the triggers, and Galthra was so fast in response to his Force commands that neither of the missiles came close enough for its detonation to have so much as mussed his hair.

If he'd had any.

Now the gunship's side-mounted laser turrets rotated to track them, and through the Force Mace felt their targeting computers lock on. The two damaged ships reached firing position, and they also locked on. They were coordinating their fire: he could not hope to dodge. So he didn't bother. He brought Galthra to a halt beneath him.

He stood motionless, empty-handed, waiting for them to open fire.

Waiting to give them a brief tutorial on the art of Vaapad.

Their cannons belched energy and Mace threw himself into the Force, releasing all but his intention. It was no longer Mace Windu who acted: the Force acted *through* him. Depa's lightsaber snapped into his left hand while his own flipped into his right. The green cascade was a jungle-echo of the purple as they both met clawing chains of red.

On Sarapin, a Vaapad was a notoriously dangerous predator, powerful and rapacious. It attacked with its blindingly fast tentacles. Most had at least seven. It was not uncommon for them to have as many as twelve. The largest ever killed had twenty-one. The thing about a Vaapad was that you never knew how many tentacles it had until it was dead: they moved too fast to count. Almost too fast to see.

So did Mace's.

Energy sprayed around him, but only splatters of it grazed him here and there; the rest went back at the gunship. Though the Thunderbolt hadn't the power to penetrate their heavy armor, a Taim & Bak laser cannon is a whole different animal.

Ten bolts reached his blades. Two apiece went back at the damaged ships, bursting against their armor and knocking them reeling to break their target lock. The other six hammered the cockpit of the third gunship, blasting a gaping hole in its transparisteel viewport.

Mace dropped the lightsabers, swung the over–under forward on its sling, and fired from the hip. It belched a single grenade that the Force guided right through that hole into the cockpit. The grenade made a dull, wet-sounding *whump* inside the gunship. A fountain of white goo splashed out the hole.

Mace grunted to himself; he thought he'd loaded Nytinite.

Then he shrugged: *Eh. Same difference.*

One of the forward turbojets sucked strings of hardening glop through its intake, squealed, and chewed itself to shrapnel. The gunship lurched wildly; with the crew glued fast in the grenade's glop, there was nothing they could do except watch in horror as their ship careened into the face of the ridge and detonated in an impressive explosion that splashed flame three hundred meters down the slope.

Mace thought, *And now, for my next trick . . .*

He released the over–under and extended his hands and both lightsabers hurtled back to his grip—

But the two damaged gunships had peeled off and were already limping away into the smoke-stained sky.

He watched them go, frowning.

He felt oddly distressed.

Unhappy.

This had been . . . strange. Uncomfortable.

His rigorous self-honesty wouldn't allow him to deny the actual word that described the feeling.

It had been *unsatisfying.*

FROM THE PRIVATE JOURNALS OF MACE WINDU

I don't know how long I stood there, frowning into the sky. Eventually, I recovered enough of my equanimity to slide off Galthra's back and release my hold on her Force-bond. She bounded off, searching for Chalk upslope among the burning rocks.

Nick came stumbling down the slope, picking his way through the dying flames, avoiding the half-slagged rocks that still glowed a dull red. He seemed most impressed by the fight. Adrenaline drunk and childishly giggly, he seemed deliriously happy, bubbling over with jittery enthusiasm. I don't recall much of what he said beyond some nonsense about me being a "walking one-man war machine."

Something like that. I'm not sure the word he used was *walking*.

Most of what he said was lost in the roar that lived inside my head: a hurricane-whirl of the thunder of my heart, echoes of the battle's explosions, and the tidal surge of the Force itself.

When he reached me, I saw that he was wounded: blood washed down his face and neck from a deep gash along the side of his head— probably a graze from a rock splinter. But he just kept on about how he'd never seen anything like me until I stopped him with a hand on his arm.

"You're bleeding," I told him, but that dark gleam in his bright blue eyes never wavered. He kept going on about "Alone against three gunships. Three. *Alone.*"

I told him that I hadn't been alone. I quoted Yoda: " 'My ally is the Force.' " He didn't seem to understand, so I explained: "I had them outnumbered."

What happened next I remember vividly, no matter how much I wish I could wipe it from my mind. I couldn't tear my eyes from the two damaged gunships that by then were mere specks of durasteel soaring into the limitless sky.

Nick followed my gaze, and said, "Yeah, I know how you feel. Shame you couldn't roast all three, huh?"

"How I feel?" I rounded on him. "How *I* feel?"

I had a sudden urge to punch him: an urge so powerful the effort to restrain it left me gasping. I wanted—I *needed*—to punch him. To punch him in the *face*. To feel my fist shatter his jaw.

To make him shut up.

To make him *not look at me.*

The understanding in his voice—the knowledge in his cold blue eyes—

I wanted to hit him because he was right. He *did* know how I felt.

It was an ugly shock.

As he said: I'd wanted to destroy those other gunships, too. I wanted to rip them out of the sky and watch them burn. No thought of the lives I'd already taken in the first gunship. No thought of the lives I would take in the other two. In the Force, I reached out toward the burning wreckage on the ridge face above, searching among the flames; for what, I can't say.

I'd like to think I was feeling for survivors. Checking to see if there were any people, merely wounded, who might be saved from the wreckage. But I cannot honestly say that is true.

I might have just wanted to feel them burn.

I also cannot honestly say I'm sorry for the way the fight turned out.

Though I took their lives in self-defense, and the defense of others, neither I nor those I defended are innocents. I cannot honestly claim that my Korun companions are any more deserving of life than were the people in the gunship. What I did in the pass, I cannot call my duty as a Jedi.

What I did there had nothing to do with peace.

One might call it an accident of war: it happened that this small band of murderous guerrillas accompanied a Jedi Master, and so the spouses and children of a gunship crew have suffered a horrible loss. One *might* call it an accident of war . . . even I might call it that—

If it had been anything resembling an accident.

If I hadn't been *trying* to bring that ship down. If I hadn't felt the fever in my blood: blood fever.

The lust for victory. To win, at any cost.

Blood fever.

I feel it even now.

It's not overpowering; I haven't fallen that far. Yet. It's more a preference. An expectation. An anticipation that has been disappointed.

This is bad. Not the worst it can be, but bad enough.

I have long known that I am in danger here. But only now am I beginning to understand how dark and near that danger is; I never guessed how close Haruun Kal has already brought me to that fatal brink.

It is a side effect of the Force immersion of Vaapad. My style grants great power, but at a terrible risk. Blood fever is a disease that can kill anyone it touches. To use Vaapad, you must allow yourself to enjoy the fight. You give yourself to the thrill of battle. The rush of *winning*. This is why so few students even attempt the style.

Vaapad is a path that leads through the penumbra of the dark side.

Here in the jungle, that shadow fringe is unexpectedly shallow. Full night is only a step away. I must be very, very careful here.

Or I may come to understand what's happened to Depa all too well.

Mace lowered his head. The electric sizzle of combat drained from his limbs, leaving them heavy and hurting: he had a variety of superficial burns from plasma splatter and splinters of half-molten rock.

He made himself look back up the slope into the pass, through the dying flames and the black twists of fading smoke. In the pass above were dead akks, dead or wounded grassers, and Chalk and Besh and Lesh.

He recalled his Force-flash of this morning.

"Come on, settle down," he told Nick. It was astonishing how tired he'd suddenly become. "I think we have casualties."

They worked their way up the ramp of scree. Above, Chalk limped over to her wounded grasser and shook her head: it had been terribly burned. One whole flank was only a mass of char. She walked back up the six-meter length of its body, dropped to one knee, and stroked its head. It made a faint honk of pain and distress, and nuzzled her hand as Chalk drew her slug pistol and shot it just below its crown eye.

The pistol's single sharp pop echoed from the cliff walls that bound the notch. To Mace, it sounded like a punctuation mark: a period for the end of the battle. The echoes made it into sardonic applause.

Besh and Lesh still huddled in the shadow of the dead akk. With the akk on one side and a huge crag on the other to shelter them from the flames, Mace thought they might have made it through.

Chalk got there before Nick and Mace. All the way down from the corpse of her grasser, her eyes stayed locked on where the brothers must have been, and from her face Mace could tell that what she saw was bad. She glanced over at Nick as he and Mace came up, and she gave that same slow expressionless shake of the head.

Besh sat on the ground by the dead akk's head. Hugging his knees. Rocking back and forth. Scattered on the ground around him were contents of a standard medpac: hand scanner, spray hypos and bandages, bone stabilizers. He didn't seem to be injured, but he was pale as a dead man, and his eyes were round and blankly staring.

Lesh was in convulsions.

His face had twisted into a rigid mask, a blind gape at the empty afternoon sky. He bucked and writhed, hands clutching spastically, heels drumming the rocks. Mace's first thought was *head wound*—shrapnel or rock splinters in the skull could trigger such seizures—and he couldn't understand why Nick and Chalk and his own brother just stood as though they were helpless to do anything but watch him suffer. Dropping to a knee, Mace reached for the medpac scanner. Chalk said, "Leave it."

Mace looked up at her. She gave him the head shake. "Dead already."

Mace picked up the scanner anyway, and slid the medpac cover open to activate the display. The readout said Lesh wasn't wounded.

He was *infected.*

Unidentified bloodborne parasites had collected in his central nervous system. They had now entered a new stage in their life cycle.

They were eating his brain.

The previous night in the wallet tent made sense to Mace now: Lesh must have been sick with these parasites already. And Mace had thought it was nothing but stress and thyssel intoxication.

"Fever wasps," Nick said hoarsely. He was almost as pale as Besh. He could face violent death with a wink and a sarcastic one-liner, but this had his face shining with pale sweat. He stank of fear. "No telling when he might have been stung. Thyssel chewers go faster. The larvae like the bark. When they hatch—"

He swallowed and his eyes went thin. He had to look away.

"They'll hatch from his skull. *Through* his skull. Like an, an, an *eggshell*..."

The pure uncomplicated horror on his face told Mace this wouldn't be the first time he'd seen it happen.

Mace set the medpac on a cool spot by the dead akk. "It says here he can still be saved." It took only a second to charge a spray hypo with thanatizine. "We can put him in suspended animation. Slow down the ... wasp larvae ... until we can get him to Pelek Baw and a full hospital. Even if he's identified—"

Besh looked up at him, and shook his head in a mute *No*.

Mace brushed past him and knelt at Lesh's side. "We can save him, Besh. Maybe it'll mean giving him up to the militia, but at least he'll be *alive*."

Besh caught Mace's arm. His eyes were raw, spidered with blood. Again, he shook his head.

"Master Windu." Nick picked up the medpac case and glanced at the readout. "Lesh is way more advanced than this thing says."

"Medpac scanners are extremely reliable. I can't imagine it's wrong."

"It's not wrong," Nick said softly. He turned the case so that Mace could check the screen again. "These aren't Lesh's readings."

"What?"

Besh, looking at the ground, touched his own chest with the tips of his fingers, then sagged; he seemed to crumple in on himself, breath leaving him along with hope and fear. His Force aura shaded into black despair.

Mace looked from Besh to Nick and back again, and then at Lesh spasming on the rocks, and then at the spray hypo still clutched nervelessly in his hand. *Not because the jungle kills you,* Nick had said. *Just because it is what it is.*

Nick retrieved the medpac's scanner and waved it near Mace's head. "You're okay," he said thinly, licking pale sweat from his upper lip. "No sign of infestation." He turned to Chalk, frowning down at the medpac's readout.

His shoulders slumped and his hand started to shake.

He had no words, but he didn't need any. She read her fate on his face.

She stiffened and her mouth went thin and hard. Then she turned away and marched downslope.

"Chalk—" Nick called after her helplessly. "Chalk, wait—"

"Getting the Thunderbolt, me." Her voice was squeezed flat, as unemotional as a navcomp's vocabulator. "Good weapon. Will need it, you."

Nick turned his stricken look on Mace. "Master Windu—" He held out the medpac scanner imploringly. "Don't make me do my own reading, huh?"

Mace quickly scanned Nick's spine and skull. The readings indicated a clear negative, but Nick didn't seem much relieved.

"Yeah, well," he said with understated bitterness, "if I was gonna die in the next day or two, I wouldn't have to worry about taking care of *them*."

"Taking care of them?" Mace said. "Is there a treatment?"

"Yeah." Nick drew his pistol. "I got their treatment right here."

"That's your answer?" Mace stepped in front of him. "Kill your friends?"

"Just Lesh," he said, his voice grim and hard, even though it trembled a little, like his hand. He didn't have Chalk's mental toughness. His eyes watered, and his face twisted, and he could barely make himself look at his friends. "Time enough to take care of Besh and Chalk when they start the twitches."

Mace still couldn't believe Nick was serious. "You want to just *shoot* them? Like Chalk's grasser?"

"Not like her grasser," Nick said. His face had gone gray. "Not in the head. Scatters the larvae. Some of them will be developed enough to be dangerous." He coughed. "To us."

"So it's not enough that he dies." Mace breathed Jedi discipline into a wall around his heart: to lock down his empathic horror at the gray rictus of Lesh's face. Pink-tinged foam bubbled from Lesh's lips. "The . . . infested areas . . . have to be destroyed. Brain and spinal cord."

Nick nodded, looking even sicker. "With wasp fever, we usually burn the body, but . . ."

Mace understood. The escaped gunships would have transmitted their position. No telling what might already be on its way.

He could not believe what he was about to do. He could not even believe what he was about to *say*. But he was a Jedi. The purpose of his life was to do what must be done. To do what others would not, or could not.

No matter what it was.

He unclipped the lightsabers from his belt. His own and Depa's both.

Green blade and purple sizzled together in the smoke-hazed air.

Besh looked up from the ground. Chalk went still on the slope, the Thunderbolt cradled in her arms. Nick opened his mouth as though he wanted to say something, but didn't know what it might be.

They all stared at Mace as though they'd never seen him before.

"He's your friend. Your brother." Mace took a deep breath, steadying his own fear and revulsion and his dark, dark loathing for what he must do. "You might want to say good-bye."

Besh shook his head mutely. With an inarticulate sob compounded of grief and terror, he threw himself to his feet and stumbled away upslope.

Chalk only held Mace's eye for a second, and gave him one slow nod. Then she followed Besh. She put one strong arm around Besh's shoulders. Besh collapsed against her, sobbing.

Nick was the last. His eyes showed nothing but pain. Finally, he shook his head, and tears spilled onto his cheeks. "He's already gone." He touched Mace on the shoulder. "Master Windu—you don't have to do this—"

"Yes, I do," Mace said. "Or *you'll* have to."

Nick nodded reluctant understanding.

"Thanks. Windu, uh, Master, I—just—thanks." He turned and walked after the others. "I won't forget it."

Neither would Mace.

He stared down at Lesh between the two shining blades. He

reached into the Force, seeking to touch anything of the young man that might remain, to offer what little comfort might be his to give, but it was as Nick said: Lesh was already gone. A long moment passed while Mace composed himself, found an attitude of calm reverence, and consigned whatever might have been left of Lesh's consciousness or spirit to the Force.

Then he took a deep breath, lifted his blades, and began.

The razorback ridge eclipsed the southern sky behind them. The jungle canopy overhead glowed with early sunset; on the ground it was already twilight. The companions walked along a broad track crushed bare by repeated passages of steamcrawler treads. The canopy had arched over the track, joining above so that their path lay along a jungle-lined tunnel that wound and switchbacked up and down the folds that radiated from the ridge's north face.

Mace wore bacta patches trimmed to fit the worst of his burns. Nick's temple was shiny with spray bandage. Chalk wore a sling restraining the shoulder she'd separated when she tumbled into the rocks, and a compression wrap supported her twisted knee. Besh walked in expressionless silence. He might have been in shock.

What was left of Lesh was buried at the tree line.

Their backpacks were heavy with supplies scavenged from the dead grassers. Little of Mace's gear survived; his wallet tent, his changes of clothing, his own medpac and identikit, all had been destroyed with Nick's grasser. The war on Haruun Kal was erasing Mace's connections to life outside the jungle: of all the physical evidence that he had ever been anything other than a Korun, only the two lightsabers remained.

Even the fake datapad that he had carried all this way—its miniature subspace coil must have been damaged in the blast. He'd considered summoning the *Halleck* to evacuate Besh and Chalk for medical treatment, despite the fact that it would have severely compromised his mission here; the sudden appearance of a Republic cruiser in the Al'Har system would certainly have drawn entirely too much Separatist attention. But the datapad's holocomm had been unable to even pick up a carrier wave. His last link to what Depa called the Galaxy of Peace was as dead as the Balawai militia Mace had sent crashing into the razorback ridge.

A stroke of irony—the fake datapad's recording function still worked. Disguise had become reality: the datapad was a fake no longer. Mace had a superstitious hunch that this was somehow symbolic.

Galthra walked among them at Chalk's side instead of ranging around; she was the last of their akks. With a little luck, her presence alone might keep major predators at a respectful distance.

No gunships had yet come to the pass behind them. Mace found this inexplicable, and disturbing. Once in a while, Galthra gave a Force-twitch that may have meant she heard engines in the distance, but it was hard to tell. Mostly, she mourned her dead packmates: her Force presence was a long moan of grief and loss.

They pushed on. Nick set a killing pace. He had not spoken since they'd buried Lesh's remains.

Mace guessed that Nick was thinking about Besh and Chalk; he himself certainly was. Thinking about the fever wasp larvae that teemed within their brain and spinal cord tissue. They might have a day or two before dementia would begin. A day or two after that: convulsions and an ugly death. Besh walked with his head down, shivering, as though he could think of nothing else; Chalk marched like a war droid, as though suffering and death were too alien for her to even comprehend, let alone fear.

Mace matched Nick's pace, close by his side. "Talk to me."

Nick's eyes stayed on the jungle ahead. "Why should I?"

"Because I want to know what you have in mind."

"What makes you think I have *anything* in mind? What makes you think anything I might have in mind can make a *difference?*" His voice was angrily bitter. "We have two people about to go into second-stage wasp fever. No grassers. One akk. A handful of weapons, militia on our tail. And you and me."

His gaze slid sideways to meet Mace's. His eyes were red and raw.

"We're dead. You get it? Like that tusker in the death hollow: a few meters short of where we needed to be. We didn't make it. We're dead."

"For dead men," Mace observed, "we're making good time."

For an instant he thought Nick might crack a smile. Instead, Nick shook his head. "There's a *lor pelek* who travels with Depa's band. He's . . . very powerful. More than powerful. If we can get Besh and Chalk to him before they start the twitches, he might be able to save them."

Lor pelek: "jungle master." Shaman. Witch doctor. Wizard. In Korun legend, the *lor pelek* was a person of great power, and great peril. As unpredictable as the jungle. He brought life or death: a gift or a wound. In some stories, a *lor pelek* was not a being at all, but was rather *pelekotan* incarnate: the avatar of the jungle-mind.

Mace made a connection. "Kar Vastor."

Nick goggled at him. "How'd you know that? How'd you know his name?"

"How long before we reach them?"

Nick trudged on a few paces before he answered. "If we still had grassers, and akks for warding? Maybe two days. Maybe less. On foot? With only one akk?" His shrug was expressive.

"Then why march us so hard?"

"Because I *do* have something in mind." He flicked a sidelong glance at Mace. "But you're not gonna like it."

"Will I like it less than having to do to Besh and Chalk what I had to do to Lesh?"

"That's not for me to say." Nick's gaze went remote, staring off into the gloom-filled tunnel ahead. "There's a little outpost settlement about an hour west of here. Ones like it are strung out every hundred klicks or so along these steamcrawler tracks. They'll have a secure bunker, and a comm unit. Even though we—the ULF—don't use comms, we still monitor the frequencies. We get in there, we can send a coded signal to them with our position. Then we put Chalk and Besh in thanatizine suspension, sit tight, and hope for the best."

"A Balawai settlement?"

He nodded. "We don't *have* settlements. DOKAWs saw to that."

"These Balawai—they'll take us in?"

"Sure." Nick's teeth gleamed in the jungle twilight, and that manic spark kindled in his eyes. "You just have to know how to ask."

Mace's face darkened. "I won't let you harm civilians. Not even to save your friends."

"No need to scorch your scalp over that one," Nick said, trudging onward. "Out here, civilians are a *myth.*"

Mace didn't want to ask what Nick meant by that. He came to a stop on the rugged track. He saw again the holoprojected carnage spread across the Supreme Chancellor's desk; he saw again images of huts broken and burned, and nineteen corpses in the jungle. "You were right," he said. "I don't like it. I don't like it at all."

Nick kept walking. He didn't even look over his shoulder as he left Mace behind. "Yeah, well, as soon as you come up with a better idea," he said into the darkness ahead, "you be sure to let me know, huh?"

6

CIVILIANS

In this bunker, the air is closer to cool than any I've felt since the interrogation room in the Ministry of Justice. The bunker is set into the igneous stone of the hillside—mostly just a durasteel door across the mouth of a bubble some pocket of gas or softer stone once left in the granite here. Though it overlooks the remnants of the outpost compound below, it was clearly never meant to be a combat position: no gun ports. From the way it's constructed—excavated—I believe it was more along the lines of a panic room: a safe place to hole up in the event of an attack. A safe place to wait for help from the militia.

If so, it didn't work.

The night air gently curls around the twisted shards that are all that's left of the door; its whispering passage darkly echoes the violence that still hums in the Force around me.

I dare not meditate. The dark is too deep here. It has a tidal pull: a black hole that I've taken up too tight an orbit around, and it's tearing me in half. Gravity draws the near half of me in toward an event horizon that I'm afraid to even glimpse.

Behind me, lost in the night shadows against the stone, Besh and Chalk lie motionless, nearly as cool as the rock they lie on, in full thanatizine suspension. Only with the Force can I tell that they still live: their hearts beat less than once per minute, and an hour spans no more than ten or twelve shallow breaths. The fever wasp larvae in their bodies are similarly suspended; Besh and Chalk might survive a week or more like this.

Provided nothing eats them in the meantime.

Making sure they're safe is my job. Right now, it's my only job. And so I sit among the wreckage of this doorway and stare out into the infinite night.

The Thunderbolt rests on its bipod in the doorway, muzzle canted toward the sky. Chalk maintains her beloved weapon well; she insisted on field-stripping it one last time before she would let me inject her. I have test-fired it at intervals, and it's still working fine. Though I am trying to learn to feel the action of the metal-eating fungi in the Force, the way the Korunnai do, I prefer to depend on practical experiment.

There is little for me to do right now. I pass the time by recording this—and by thinking about my argument with Nick.

Back on the trail, Nick said that civilians are a myth. He meant, I found, that there are no civilians out here: that to be in the jungle is to be in the war. The Balawai government promulgates a myth of innocent jungle prospectors being massacred by savage Korun partisans. This, Nick says, is only propaganda.

Now, here in the ruins of this Balawai outpost, I find the thought oddly comforting—but earlier this evening I rejected the idea instinctively. It seemed to me nothing more than rationalization. An excuse. A sop to consciences haunted by atrocities. On the hike along the steam-crawler track that led us here, Nick and I went back and forth about it quite a bit.

According to Nick, civilians stay in the cities; the only real civilians on Haruun Kal are the waiters and the janitors, the storekeepers and the taxicart pullers. He said there's a reason why jungle prospectors carry such heavy weapons, and that reason has more to do with akk dogs than with vine cats. Balawai do not go into the jungle unless they're ready, willing, and able to kill Korunnai. Nobody on either side waits for the other to attack. In the jungle, if you don't strike first you're nothing but prey.

Then I asked him about the dead children.

It's the only time I've yet seen Nick angry. He wheeled on me like he wanted to throw a punch. "*What* children?" he said. "How old do you have to be to pull a trigger? Kids make *great* soldiers. They barely know what fear is."

It is wrong to make war on children—or *with* them—and I told him so. No matter what. They're not old enough to understand the consequences of their actions. He replied in staggeringly obscene terms that I should tell that to the Balawai.

"What about *our* children?" He shook with barely restrained fury. "The jups can leave their kids at home in the city. Where do we leave *ours?* You've seen Pelek Baw. You *know* what happens to a Korun kid on those streets—*I* know what happens. I was *one of them*. Better blown to pieces out here than having to—survive—like I did. So then, out here, how do you tell the gunners in those ships that the Korunnai they're happily blowing arms and legs off of, are only *kids?*"

"Does that justify what happens to the Balawai children? The ones who *don't* stay in the cities?" I asked him. "The Korunnai aren't firing down at random from a gunship. What's *your* excuse?"

"We don't *need* an excuse," he said. "We don't murder kids. We're the *good* guys."

"Good guys," I echoed. I could not keep a bitter edge from my voice: the holographic images shown to Yoda and me in Palpatine's office are never far beneath the surface of my mind. "I have seen what's left behind when your *good guys* are done with a jungle prospector outpost," I told him. "That's why I'm *here.*"

"Sure it is. Hah. Let me share something with you, huh?" Changeable as a summer storm, Nick's anger had blown away between one eyeblink and the next. He gave me a look of amused pity. "I've been waiting for *days* for you to bring that up."

"What?"

"You Jedi and your secrets and all that tusker poop. You think nobody else can keep their chip-cards close to the chest?" He rolled his eyes and waggled his fingers near his face. "Ooo, look out, I'm a Jedi! I know things Too Dangerous for Ordinary Mortals! Careful! If you don't stand back, I might tell you something Beings Were Not Meant to Know!"

It has occurred to me, on reflection, that Nick Rostu can be regarded as a test of my moral conviction. A Jedi might conceivably fall to the dark from the simple desire to smack the snot out of him.

At the time, I managed to restrain myself, and even to maintain a civil tone, while Nick revealed that he knew all about the jungle massacre and the data wafer.

It wasn't easy.

He told me that not only had he *been* there—at the very scene Yoda and I had viewed in Palpatine's office—he had been in the company of Depa and Kar Vastor when they'd thought the whole scheme *up*. He had helped them dress the scene, and later it was Nick himself who had tipped off Republic Intelligence.

Even now, hours later, it's hard for me to put into words how that made me feel. Disoriented, certainly: almost dizzy. Disbelieving.

Betrayed.

I have been carrying those images like a wound. They've festered in my mind, so inflamed and painful I've had to cushion them in layers of denial. Pain like that makes a wound precious; when the slightest touch is agony, one must keep the wound so protected, so sequestered, that it becomes an object of reverence. Sacred.

But Nick told the story like it had been just some kind of *practical joke.*

Hmm. I find now another word for how I felt. For how I *feel.*

Angry.

This, too, makes meditation difficult. And risky.

It is as well that Nick left on Galthra some hours ago. Perhaps before he returns—*if* he returns—I will have found a place in my mind to put these things he shared with me, where they will no longer whisper violence behind my heart.

The whole massacre was staged.

Not fake. The bodies were real. The death was real. But it was a setup. It *was* a practical joke. On *me.*

Depa wanted me here.

That's what this has been about. From the beginning.

That data wafer wasn't a frame, and it wasn't a confession. It was a *lure*. She wanted to draw me from Coruscant, bring me to Haruun Kal, and drop me into this nightmare jungle.

Many of the corpses were indeed jungle prospectors, Nick told me. Jups, when they're not harvesting the jungle, act as irregulars for the Balawai militia. They are vastly more dangerous than the gunships and the detector satellites and all the DOKAWs and droid starfighters and armies of the Separatists put together. They know the jungle. They live in it. They use it.

They are more ruthless than the ULF.

The rest of the corpses in that staged little scene—they were Korun prisoners. Captured by the jups. Captured and tortured and maltreated beyond my ability to describe; when the ULF caught up, the first thing the Balawai did was execute the few prisoners who were still alive. Nick tells me that none of them escaped. None of the prisoners. And none of the jups.

The children—

The children were Korunnai.

This Kar Vastor—what kind of man must he be? Nick told me it was Kar Vastor who nailed that data wafer into the dead woman's mouth with brassvine thorns. Nick told me it was Kar Vastor who persuaded the ULF to leave the corpses in the jungle. To make the scene so gruesome that I'd be sure to come here to investigate. To leave dead children—*their own dead children*—to the jacunas and the screw maggots and the black stinking carrion flies so full of blood they can only waddle across rotting flesh—

Stop. I have to stop. Stop talking about this. Stop thinking about it.

I can't—this isn't—

Nothing in this world can be trusted. What you see is not related to what you get. I don't seem to be able to comprehend any of it.

But I'm learning. In learning, I'm changing. The more I change, the more I understand. That's what frightens me. I shudder to think what will happen when I really begin to understand this place.

By the time I finally *get it,* who will I be?

I'm afraid that the man I was would despise the man I am becoming. I have a terrible dread that this transformation is exactly what Depa had in mind when she decided to draw me here. She said there was nothing more dangerous than a Jedi who'd finally gone sane.

I think she *is* dangerous.

I'm afraid she wants me to become dangerous, too.

I should—I need to change the—think about something other than—

Because I asked Nick about her.

I couldn't help myself. Hope blossomed along with my anger—if the holo was a setup, maybe what she'd said was no more than . . . atmosphere. Local color. Something.

Despite my determination to hold myself unbiased until I could see her, speak with her, feel her essence in the Force—despite my resolve to ask nothing, and hear nothing—despite all my years of self-discipline and self-control—

The heart has power that no discipline can answer.

So I asked him. I told him of Depa's words on the data wafer: how she called herself *the darkness in the jungle,* and how she said that she had finally gone sane.

How I fear that in fact she has fallen to the dark, and is irretrievably mad.

And Nick—

And Nick—

"Crazy?" he said with a laugh. "*You're* the one who's crazy. If she was crazy, nobody'd follow her, would they?"

But when I asked if he meant she was all right, he responded, "That depends on what you mean by *all right.*"

"I need to know if you've seen her act from anger, or fear. I need to know if she uses the Force for her personal gratification: for gain, or for revenge. I need to know how much hold the dark side has on her."

"You don't have to worry about that," he told me. "I've never met someone kinder or more caring than Master Billaba. She's not *evil.* I don't think she could be."

"This isn't about good and evil," I told him. "This is about the fundamental nature of the Force itself. Jedi are not moralists. That's a common misperception. We are fundamentally pragmatic. The Jedi is altruistic less because to be so is *good,* than because to be so is *safe:* to use the Force for personal ends is dangerous. This is the trap that can snare even the most good, kind, caring Jedi: it leads to what we call the dark side. Power to do good eventually becomes just power. Naked force. An end in itself. It is a form of madness to which Jedi are peculiarly susceptible."

Nick answered this with a shrug. "Who knows the real reasons why anybody does anything?"

This was not a comforting response, and the rest of what he told me was worse.

He says the words on that crystal are just how Depa talks, now. He says she has nightmares—that screams from her tent tear through the camp. He says no one ever sees her eat—that she's wasting away as though something inside is instead eating her . . . He says she has headaches that painkillers cannot touch, and sometimes cannot leave her tent for days at a time. That when she walks outside in daylight, she binds her eyes, for she cannot bear the light of the sun . . .

I am sorry I asked. I am sorry that Nick told me.

I'm sorry that he did not lie.

It is very un-Jedi to fear the truth.

I'll continue the story. Putting experience into words is a gain in perspective. Which I need. And it's a way to pass the hours of the night, which I also need. Even for a Jedi Master, accustomed to meditation and reflection—trained for it—there is such a thing as spending too much time alone with one's thoughts.

Especially out here.

This outpost settlement was built at the crest of a shoulder sloping down from the ridge. The ridge here isn't a razorback anymore, but rather a sine-wave wall of volcanic mounds. The settlement stands on a green-splashed outcrop; to either side of this jungle-clutched fist of stone are blackened washes where lava occasionally flows down from a major caldera, which is about six hundred meters above where I sit and record this. If you listen closely, you might hear the rumble. This microphone may not be sensitive enough. There—hear that? It's ramping up for another eruption.

These eruptions come regularly enough that the jungle doesn't have time to reclaim the lava's path; heat-scorched trees line the washes, with leaves cooked off on the lava side. Eruptions must not be too serious in these parts. Otherwise, why build an outpost here?

Well—

I suppose it could have been for the view.

The bunker itself is slightly elevated above the rest of the compound. From where I sit in the wreckage of the doorway, I can look down over a charred mess of tumbled and broken prefab huts and the shattered perimeter wall. Pale glowvine light shows gray on the steamcrawler track that switchbacks up the side of the shoulder.

Out across the jungle—

I can see for kilometers up here: ghost-ripples of canopy spread below, silver and black and veined with glowvines, pocked with winking eyes of scarlet and crimson and some just dull red: open calderae, active and bubbling in this volatile region. It's breathtaking.

Or maybe that's just the smell.

Another of the ironies that have come crowding into my life: all my worry about civilians, and battles, and massacres, and having to fight and maybe kill men and women who may be only civilians, innocent bystanders, and all my arguing with Nick and everything he told me—

All for nothing. Needn't have worried. When we got here, there was no one left to fight.

The ULF had been here already.

There were no survivors.

I will not describe the condition of the bodies. Seeing what had been done here was bad enough; I feel no urge to share it, even with the Archives.

I will grant Nick this: the Balawai at this outpost had clearly been no innocent civilians. The Korunnai had left the bodies draped with what must have been the most prized pieces of the jups' jewelery: necklaces of human ears.

Korunnai ears.

Based on the limited scavenger damage and the low decomposition, Nick guessed that the ULF band who'd done this might have passed through here no more than two or three days before. And there were certain, mmmm, signs—things done to the bodies—and echoes in the Force that don't seem to fade away, a standing wave of power, that suggests this had been the work of Kar Vastor himself.

The ULF guerrillas had also thoroughly looted this place; there is not a scrap of food to be found, and only useless bits and pieces of technology and equipment. The wreckage of two steamcrawlers lies tumbled downslope. The comm gear is gone as well, of course, which is why I alone am here to watch over Besh and Chalk.

When we found the comm gear gone, Nick's spirits collapsed. He seems to alternate despair with that manic cheerfulness of his, and it's not always easy to guess what will trigger either state. He let himself flop to the bloodstained ground, and gave us up for dead. He returned to his mantra from the pass: "Bad luck," he muttered under his breath. "Just bad luck."

Despair is the herald of the dark side. I touched his shoulder. "Luck," I told him softly, "does not exist. *Luck* is only a word we use to describe our blindness to the subtle currents of the Force."

His response was bitter. "Yeah? What *subtle current* killed Lesh? Is this what your Force had planned for *you?* For Besh and Chalk?"

"The Jedi say," I replied, "that there are questions to which we can never have answers; we can only *be* answers."

He asked me angrily what that was supposed to mean. I told him: "I am neither a scientist nor a philosopher. I'm a Jedi. I don't have to explain reality. I just have to deal with it."

"That's what I'm doing."

"That's what you're *avoiding.*"

"You have a Jedi power that can get all of us to Depa and Kar in a day? Or *three?* They're marching *away* from us. We can't catch up. *That's* reality. The only one there is."

"Is it?" I let a thoughtful gaze rest on Galthra's broad back. "She moves well through this jungle. I know that akks are not beasts of burden—but one man, alone, she might be able to carry at great speed."

"Well, yeah. If I didn't have to worry about you guys—" He stopped. His eyes narrowed. "Not a chance. Not a *chance,* Windu! Drop it."

"I'll watch over them until you get back."

"I said *drop it!* I'm *not* leaving you here."

"It's not up to you." I stepped close to him. Nick had to bend his neck to look up into my eyes. "I'm not arguing with you, Nick. And I'm not asking you. This is not a discussion. It's a briefing."

Nick is a stubborn young man, but he's not stupid. It didn't take him long to understand that until he met me, he didn't know what stubborn looked like.

We managed to rig an improvised bareback pad for Galthra; Nick and Chalk and I persuaded Galthra, through the Force, to bear Nick on her back as she had me, and carry him swiftly through the jungle on the trail of the departed Korunnai. The three of us watched them vanish into the living night, then Besh and Chalk arranged themselves as comfortably as possible on the bunker floor, and I injected them with thanatizine.

We all wait together, in the hope that Nick will win through the jungle, in the hope that he might find and bring back this Kar Vastor—this dangerous *lor pelek,* this terror of the living and mutilator of the dead—and that this man of no conscience or human feeling might use his power to save two lives.

I wonder what Kar Vastor will think, when he arrives, and finds what I have done to the scene of his victory.

I have spent some hours—between the time Nick left and the time I sat down here to record this entry—giving the dead a decent burial. Nick will no doubt laugh, and make some snide remark about how little I understand, how naive and unready I am for a part in this war. He'll probably ask me if burying these people makes them any less dead. I can only reply to this imagined scorn with a shrug.

I didn't do it for them. I did it for me. I did it because this is the only way I have to express my reverence for the life that was torn from them, enemy or no.

I did it because I don't want to be the kind of man who would leave someone—like *that* . . .

Anyone.

I sit here now, knowing that Depa has passed within a few klicks of here; that she stood, perhaps, on this very spot. Within the past forty-eight standard hours. No matter how deeply I reach into the Force—how deeply I reach into the stone beneath and the jungle around—I can feel nothing of her. I have felt nothing of her on this planet.

All I feel is the jungle, and the dark.

I think of Lesh a lot. I keep seeing how he writhed on the ground, twitching in convulsions, teeth clenched and eyes rolling, his whole body twisting with furious life—but the life that twisted him was not Lesh's. It was something that was eating him from the inside out. When I reached into the Force for him, all I felt was the jungle. And the dark.

And then I think of Depa again.

Perhaps I should listen more, and think less.

The eruption seems to be strengthening. The rumbling is loud as a Pelek Baw throughway, and tremors have begun to shake the stone floor. Mmm. And rain has begun, as it often will: triggered by particulates in the smoke plume.

Speaking of smoke—

Among the equipment looted by the ULF would have been, no doubt, breath masks; I may miss them more than anything else. I must have a care for my lungs. On this outcrop, I'm in little danger from lava, but the gases that roll downslope from such eruptions can be caustic as well as smothering. Besh and Chalk will be safer than I. Perhaps I should risk a hibernation trance; no predator will reach us through the eruption. Predators need to breathe, too.

And they—

That—

Wait, that sounded like—

Queer. Some Haruun Kal jungle predators mimic their prey's mating calls or cries of distress, to lure or to drive them. I wonder what kind of predator that one was: something that preys on humans, it must be. That cry almost got me. Sounded exactly like a child's scream of terror.

I mean, *exactly*.

And now this one—

Oh.

Oh, no.

That's *Basic*. Those *are* screams.
There are children out there.

Mace pelted downslope, running half blind through rain and smoke
and steam, navigating by ear: heading for the screams.

Smoke from the caldera above had smothered the glowvines; his
only light was the scarlet hellglow that leaked through cracks in the
black crusts floating on lava flows. Rain flashed to steam a meter
above the washes. A swirling red-lit cloud turned the night to blood.

Mace threw himself into the Force, letting it carry him bounding
from rock to branch to rock, flipping high over crevices, slipping past
black-shadowed tree trunks and under low branches with millime-
ters to spare. The voices came intermittently; in between, through
the downpour and the eruption and the hammering of his own
heart, Mace heard a grinding of steel on stone, and the mechanical
thunder of an engine pushed to the outer limits of its power.

It was a steamcrawler.

It lay canted at a dangerous angle over a precipice, only a lip of
rock preventing a fall into bottomless darkness. One track clanked
on air; the other was buried in hardening lava. Lava doesn't behave
as a liquid so much as a soft plastic: as it rolls downslope it cools, and
its piecemeal transition into solid rock can produce unpredictable
changes in direction: it forms dams and blockages and self-building
channels that can twist flows kilometers to either side, or even make
them "retreat" and overflow an upstream channel. The immense vehicle must have been trying to climb the track to the outpost when
one of the lava washes plugged, dammed itself, then diverted and
swept the steamcrawler off the track, down this rainwash gully until
it jammed against the lip of rock. The curl and roll of lava broke
through black patches of crust around it, scarlet slowly climbing the
crawler's undercarriage.

Though steamcrawlers were low-tech—to reduce their vulnerability to the metal-eating fungi—they were far from primitive. A kilometer below the caldera, the lava flow didn't come close to the

melting point of the advanced alloys that made up the steamcrawler's armor and treads. But lava was filling in the gap below its flat undercarriage until the only real question was whether the rising lava would topple the steamcrawler over the lip before enough heat conducted through its armor to roast whoever was inside.

But not everyone was inside.

Mace skidded to a stop just a meter upslope of where the flow had cut the track. The lava had slashed through the dirt to bedrock, making the edge of the gully where Mace stood into an unstable cliff, eight meters high, above a sluggish river of molten stone; the steamcrawler was a further ten meters down to his right. Its immense headlamps threw a white glare into the steam and the rain. Mace could just barely make out two small forms huddled together on the highest point: the rear corner of the cabin's heavily canted roof. Another crawled through the yellow-lit oblong of an open side hatch and joined them.

Three terrified children sobbed on the cabin roof; in the Force, Mace could feel two more inside—one injured, in pain that was transforming into shock, the other unconscious. Mace could feel the desperate determination of the injured one to get the other out the open hatch before the 'crawler toppled—because the injured one inside couldn't know that getting out the hatch wouldn't help any of them at all. They still faced a simple choice of dooms: over the precipice or into the lava.

Dead either way.

If, as some philosophers argued, there was a deeper purpose in the universe that the Jedi served, beyond their surface social function of preserving the peace of the Republic—if there was, in fact, a cosmic reason why Jedi existed, a reason why they were granted powers so far beyond the reach of other mortals—it must have had something to do with situations like this.

Mace opened himself to the Force. He could hear Yoda's voice: *Size matters not*—which, Mace had always privately considered, was more true for Yoda than it was for any of his students. Yoda would probably just reach out, lift the steamcrawler from the gully, and casually float it up the mountain to the outpost while croaking some enigmatic maxim about how *Even a volcano is as nothing, compared to the power of the Force . . .* Mace was much less confident in his own raw power.

But he had other talents.

A new tremor from the eruption shook the dirt cliff under his feet. He felt it sag: undercut by the river of lava, the shaking was rapidly destroying the cliff's structural integrity. Any second now it would collapse, sending Mace down into the river, unless he did something first.

The something he did was to reach deep through the Force until he could feel a structure of broken rock ten meters below him and five meters in from the face. He thought, *Why wait?* and shoved.

The dirt cliff shook, buckled, and collapsed.

With a subterranean roar that buried even the thunder of the eruption and the clamor of the steamcrawler's laboring engine, hundreds of tons of dirt and rock poured into the river of lava, organics bursting into flames that the growing landslide instantly smothered as it built itself into a huge wedge-shaped berm of raw dirt across the gully; as lava slowly bulged and climbed the upstream face, the downstream side of the cliff continued to collapse, piling over cooler lava that hardened beneath it, pushing the hotter, more liquid lava into a wave that washed around the steamcrawler's side, welled to the lip of the precipice, then plunged in a rain of fire upon the black jungle far below.

The landslide built into a wave of its own that filled in the gully as it rolled down toward the steamcrawler and the screaming, sobbing children—and on the very crest of that wave of dirt and rock, backpedaling furiously to keep from being sucked under by the landslide's roll, came Mace Windu.

Mace rode that crest while the wave sank and flattened and finally lurched to a halt, its last remnants trickling into a ridge that joined Mace's position with the corner of the steamcrawler's cabin. Nearly all his concentration stayed submerged in the Force, spread throughout the slide, using a wide-focus Force grip to stabilize the rubble while he scrambled down to the steamcrawler's roof.

On the roof were two young boys, both about six, and a girl of perhaps eight standard years. They clung to each other, sobbing, terror-filled eyes staring through their tears.

Mace squatted beside them and touched the girl's arm. "My name is Mace Windu. I need your help."

The girl sniffled in astonishment. "You—you—*my* help?"

Mace nodded gravely. "I need you to help me get these boys to safety. Can you do that? Can you take the boys up the same way I came down? Climb right up the crest. It's not steep."

"I—I—I don't—I'm *afraid*—"

Mace leaned close and spoke in her ear only a little louder than the hush of the rain. "Me, too. But you have to *act* brave. Pretend. So you don't scare the little boys. Okay?"

The girl scrubbed her runny nose with the back of her hand, blinking back tears. "I—I—*you're* scared, *too?*"

"Shh. That's a *secret.* Just between us. Come on, up you go."

"Okay . . . ," she said dubiously, but she wiped her eyes and took a deep breath and when she turned to the other two children her voice had the bossy edge that seems to be the exclusive weapon of eight-year-old girls. "Urno, Nykl, come on! Quit crying, you big *babies!* I'm going to *save* us."

As the girl bullied the two boys up onto the face of the slide, Mace moved on to the hatchway. Though it was a side hatch, the angle of the steamcrawler aimed it at the sky. Inside, the 'crawler's floor was sharply tilted, and the rain pounding through the open hatchway slicked the floor until it was impossible to climb.

Down at the lowermost corner of the rectangular cabin, a boy who seemed to be barely into his teens struggled one-handed to drag a girl not much younger up the steep floor. He had a foamy wad of blood-soaked spray bandage around one upper arm, and he was trying to shove the unconscious girl ahead of him, using the riveted durasteel leg posts of the 'crawler's seats like a ladder. But his injured arm could take no weight; tears streamed down his face as he begged the girl to wake up, *wake up,* give him a little help because he couldn't get her out and he wouldn't leave her, but if she'd just *wake up*—

Her head lolled, limp. Mace saw she wouldn't be waking up anytime soon: she had an ugly scalp wound above her hairline, and her fine golden hair was black and sticky with blood.

Mace leaned in through the hatchway and extended his hand. "All right, son. Just take my hand. Once we get you out of here, then I can—"

When the boy looked up, the tearful appeal on his face twisted into instant wild rage, and his plea became a fierce shriek. Mace hadn't noticed the swing-stock blaster rifle slung around his good arm; the first hint of its existence Mace got was a burst of hot plasma past his face. He threw himself backward out the hatch and flattened against the cabin wall while the hatchway vomited blasterfire.

The steamcrawler lurched, the hatch going even higher; his sudden movement had been enough to tip its precarious balance, toppling it toward the precipice.

Mace bared his teeth to the night. With the Force, he seized the steamcrawler and yanked it back into place—but a squeal from above grabbed his attention. In seizing the 'crawler he'd lost his Force-hold on the landslide, and the unstable mound of dirt and rock had begun to shift under the little girl and the two boys, sending them sliding down toward the lava.

Mace calmed his hammering heart and extended one hand; he had to close his eyes for a moment to reassert his control on the slide and stabilize it—but its shift had left it less solid than before. He could hold it for the minute or two it would take the girl and boys to reach the relative safety of the outcrop above, not much more. And now he could feel the 'crawler slowly tilting beneath him, leaning higher and higher toward the point of no return.

From inside the cabin he could hear the boy's terrified curses, and his shrieks about *kill all you fragging kornos.* Mace's eyes drifted closed.

This filthy war—

The boy and the girl in the steamcrawler were about to become casualties of the Summertime War . . . because when the boy had looked up, he could not see that a Jedi Master had come to his rescue.

He could see only a Korun.

To use the Force to disarm the boy, or persuade him, would break the hold he kept upon the landslide, which might cost the lives of the three children scrambling up its face. To reason with the boy seemed impossible—the boy would know too much about what Balawai can expect at the hands of Korunnai—and it would certainly take longer than they had. To abandon them was not an option.

Once he got the boy moving up the face of the landslide toward the others, he'd be able to bring the girl himself. But how to get the boy out?

Mace spun the situation in his mind: he framed it as a fight for the lives of these five children. All of them. A fundamental principle of combat: *Use what you're given.* How you fight depends on *whom* you fight. His first opponent had been the volcano itself. He'd used the power of the volcano's weapon—the lava, where it had undercut the cliff—to hold that power at bay.

His current opponent was not the boy, but rather the boy's experience of the Summertime War.

Use what you're given.

"Kid?" Mace called, roughening his voice. Making himself sound the way the boy would expect a Korun to sound, adopting a thick upland accent like Chalk's. "Kid: five seconds to toss that blaster out the hatch and come after it, you got."

"Never!" the boy screamed from inside. *"Never!"*

"Don't come out, you, and the next thing you see—the *last* thing you see, *ever*—is a grenade coming *in*. Hear me, you?"

"Go ahead! I know what happens if we get taken alive!"

"Kid—already got the others, don't I? The girl. Urno and Nykl. Gonna leave them all alone, you? With *me?*"

There came a pause.

Mace said into the silence, "Sure, go ahead and die. Any coward can do that. Guts enough to live for a while, you got?"

He was moderately sure that a thirteen-year-old boy who'd load up four other children and set out in a steamcrawler across the Korunnal Highland at night—a boy who'd rather die than leave an unconscious girl behind—had guts enough for just about anything.

A second later, he was proven right.

FROM THE PRIVATE JOURNALS OF MACE WINDU

From this doorway, I can see a spray of brilliant white flares—head-lamps of three, no, wait, *four* steamcrawlers—climbing the spine of the fold, heading for the broken track.

Heading for us.

Dawn will come in an hour. I hope we'll all live that long.

The eruptions have subsided, and the rain has trailed off to an inter-mittent patter. We've shifted some things around in the bunker. The three younger children are curled up on scavenged blankets in the back, asleep. Besh and Chalk now lie near the Thunderbolt, where I can keep an eye on them; I'm not at all sure that one of these children might not try to do them some harm. Terrel, a boy of thirteen who seems to be their natural leader, is remarkably fierce, and he still does not entirely believe that I'm not planning to torture all five of them to death. Yet even on Haruun Kal, boys are still boys: every time he stops worrying about being tortured to death, he starts pestering me to let him fire the Thunderbolt.

I wonder what Nick would say about *these* civilians. Are they a myth, too? Now all my work in cleaning up this compound does not seem pointless; the children have been through enough tonight without hav-ing to see what had been done to the people who'd lived here. Without having to see the kind of thing that has probably been done to people they know, at their outpost.

Possibly even to their parents.

I can't consider such questions right now. Right now, all I seem to be able to do is stare past the twisted jags of durasteel that once had been this bunker's door, watching the steamcrawlers' upward creep.

I don't need any hints from the Force to have a bad feeling about this.

In dejarik, there is a classic manuver called the fork, where a player moves a single holomonster into position to attack two or more of his opponent's, so that no matter which 'monster the opponent moves to safety, the other will be eaten. Caught in the fork, one's only choice is which piece to lose. The word has come to symbolize situations where the only choice to be made is a choice of disasters.

We are well and truly forked.

I know who these steamcrawlers are bringing: jungle prospectors from the same outpost as the children, fleeing the same ULF guerrillas whose attack had forced the children away—probably the same band that destroyed this outpost. I got the story from Terrel, while I was tending to his broken arm and the girl's scalp wound.

Their outpost had been the next one on this track, some seventy klicks to the north and east. They had come under attack by the ULF at dusk; Terrel's father had given him the task of gathering the other children and driving them to safety.

They'd had no way to know that the ULF had been to this outpost first.

Terrel's arm had been broken by either a bullet or a grenade fragment; he wasn't sure which. He told me proudly how he managed the dual-stick controls of the steamcrawler with only one hand, and how he had crashed into grassers as he broke through the Korun skirmish line, and how he was pretty sure he'd managed to run down "at least five or six fragging kornos."

He says such things defiantly, as if daring me to hurt him for it.

As if I ever would.

The older girl, Keela, has the most serious injury. In the steamcrawler's tumble down the gully, she was thrown from her seat. She has a skull fracture and a severe concussion. I was able to salvage a spare medpac from the 'crawler before it went over the precipice. She's in no grave danger, now, so long as she remains quiet and gets a few days' rest. The medpac had a new bone stabilizer, so Terrel's arm should heal nicely. The younger children—Urno and Nykl and the brave little girl Pell—have nothing worse than a few bruises, and scraped hands and knees from scrambling up the landslide.

So far.

I have not bothered to maintain my pretense of belonging to the guerrillas, though I have also avoided explaining who I really am. The children seem to have decided that I'm a bounty hunter, since I don't "act like a korno"—which is to say, I haven't tortured and killed them, as they were all half expecting, based on the tales they've heard from their parents. As they were all half expecting despite being alive right now only because I saved them. They have decided, based on their vast experience of bounty hunters—courtesy of countless half-cred holo-dramas—that Besh and Chalk are my prisoners, and that I'm going to deliver them to Pelek Baw for a big reward.

I have not disabused them of this notion. It's easier to believe than the truth.

But what should be merely a childish fancy has become unexpect-edly complicated and painful; even the kindest illusion will often cut deeper than any truth. One of the younger boys—rather arbitrarily—decided that I must be "just about the greatest bounty hunter there is." A six-year-old's instinctive reaction, I suppose. Soon, he got into a heated discussion with his brother, who insisted that "everybody knows" Jango Fett is the greatest living bounty hunter. Which led the first boy to ask me if *I* am Jango Fett.

I cannot help but wonder: if I had told them I'm a Jedi, who might this boy assume I am?

I was saved from answering by a scornful declaration from Terrel. "He ain't Jango Fett, stupid. Jango Fett's *dead. Everybody* knows that!"

"Jango Fett is *not* dead! He is not!" Tears began to well in the little boy's eyes, and he appealed to me. "Jango Fett ain't dead, is he? Tell him. Tell him he ain't dead."

At first, all I could think to say was "I'm sorry." And I was. I am. But the truth is the truth. "I'm sorry, but yes," I told them. "Jango Fett is dead."

"See?" Terrel said with terrible thirteen-year-old scorn. " 'Course he is, stupid. Some stinkin' Jedi snuck up behind him and stabbed him in the back with one of them laser swords."

Somehow this hurt even more. "It didn't happen that way. Fett was . . . killed in a fight."

"Tusker poop," Terrel declared. "No stinkin' Jedi could've took Jango Fett face to face! He was the *best.*"

With this I could not argue; I could only contend that Fett had not been stabbed in the back.

"What d'you know about it? Was *you* there?"

I could not—still cannot—bring myself to tell them just how *there* I had been.

And I cannot properly describe the wound Terrel's tone has opened within me: the way he says *stinking Jedi* tells me more than I want to know about what Depa has done to our Order's name on this planet. It was not so long ago that every adventurous boy and girl would have dreamed of being a Jedi.

Now their heroes are bounty hunters.

The line of steamcrawlers has halted half a kilometer below us— where the lava wash took out the track. This won't stop them for long; when the cliff collapsed, it made a natural dam across the break. In the hours since the eruption, I would guess that the lava has penetrated the rocks and dirt, and cooled enough to stabilize the slide. Intelligently cautious, they're testing its integrity before attempting to cross.

But I know they'll make it.

Then what will I do?

It seems I have no choices left. Surrender is not an option. To save Besh and Chalk—not to mention myself—I'll have to hold the children hostage.

This is how far I have fallen, even I, a Jedi Master. This is what a few days in this war has brought me to: threatening the lives of children I would give my own to save.

And if these Balawai call my bluff?

The best outcome I can then foresee: these children will have to watch as their parents, or their parents' friends, are killed by a Jedi.

Best outcome—the phrase is itself a mockery. On Haruun Kal, there seems to be no such thing.

Forked.

And yet, in dejarik, one doesn't get forked by accident. It's the result of a mistake in play. But where was my mistake that left us here?

Glow rods below. They've left the steamcrawlers and are advancing on foot. No one has called out. They will have tried to raise this outpost on comm; getting no answer, they'll approach with caution. I wouldn't be surprised if those glow rods are lashed to long sticks, to see if they draw sniper fire.

There are a *lot* of them.

Now, in desperation, I can only do as I always have, when I have faced impossible situations: I turn to Yoda's teachings for advice and inspiration. I can summon in my mind his wise green eyes, and imagine the tilt of his wrinkled head. I can hear his voice:

If no mistake have you made, yet losing you are . . . a different game you should play.

Yes. A different game. I need a different game. New rules. New objectives. And I need it in about thirty seconds.

Terrel? Terrel, come up here. All of you. Pell, wake up the boys. We're going to play a game.

[the voice of a boy, faintly]: "What kind of game?"

A new game. I just made it up. It's called *Nobody Else Dies Today.*

[another boy's voice, faintly]: "I was *'sleep.* 'S this gonna be a *fun* game?"

Only if we win.

7

GAMES IN THE DARK

These Balawai may have been irregulars, but they were both experienced and disciplined. Their recon squad entered the ruined compound in three teams of two, spread over 120 degrees of arc to give them overlapping fields of fire. While glow rods still waved halfway along the slope below, these six entered in total silence and deep shadow. They must have had some kind of night-vision equipment; if the Force hadn't let Mace feel the stark threat of their weapons' points of aim, he wouldn't have known they were there.

He stood in impenetrable shadow, looking out between the twisted jags of durasteel that were the remnants of the bunker's door. He could feel a darkness deeper than the night gathering upon the compound like fog rising from damp ground. The darkness soaked in through his pores and pounded inside his head like a black migraine.

There had never been light bright enough to drive back darkness like this; Mace could only hope to make of himself a light bright enough to cut through it.

I am the blade, he told himself silently. *I will have to be; there is no other.*

"Terrel," he said softly. "They're here. Go ahead, son."

"You're sure? I can't see anything," Terrel said from beside him. He wiped his nose, then made fists as though he were holding on to his courage with both hands. "I can't see anything at all."

"They will be able to see you," Mace said. "Call out."

"Okay." Staying in the shadows, he repeated, "Okay," but this time in a loud call. "Okay, hey, don't shoot, okay? Don't shoot! It's me!"

The night went silent. Mace felt six weapons trained on the bunker door. He murmured, "Tell them who you are."

"Yeah, uh, hey listen, it's Terrel, huh? Terrel Nakay. Is my dad out there?"

A woman's voice came out of the darkness to Mace's left, shrill with hope. "Terrel? Oh, *Terrel!* Is Keela with you—?"

The girl with the head wound held Pell and the two boys well back from the doorway, but when she heard the woman's voice she started unsteadily to her feet. "Don't go out there," Mace said. "And keep the smaller children still. We don't want anyone shot by accident."

She nodded and sank back to her knees, calling out, "Mom, I'm here! I'm okay!"

"Keela! Keela—Keela—is Pell with you?"

A man shouted from the center, *"Quiet!"*

"Rankin, it's Terrel and Keela! Didn't you hear them? Keela, what about Pell—"

"Hold your position, you stupid nerf! And shut up!" the man snarled. His voice was ragged: angry, exhausted, and desperate. "We don't know who *else* is here! This place is completely fragged."

"Rankin—"

"They could be *bait.* Shut your mouth before I shoot you myself."

Mace nodded to himself. He would have suspected the same thing.

"Terrel?" The man called out in a much softer tone: warily calm. "Terrel, it's Pek Rankin. Come on out where we can see you."

Terrel looked at Mace. Mace said, "You know him?"

The boy nodded. "He's—sort of a friend of my dad's. Sort of."

"Go on, then," Mace said gently. "Move slowly. Keep your hands in plain sight, away from your body."

Terrel did. Out from the bunker door, feeling his way down the grade toward the shattered huts. "Can somebody put on a light? I can't see."

"In a minute," Rankin's voice replied from the darkness. "Keep on coming this way, Terrel. You'll be all right. What happened to your 'crawler? How come you don't answer comm? Where are the other kids?"

"We had an accident. But we're okay. We're all okay. Okay?" Terrel caught his foot on a rock and stumbled. "Ow! Hey, the *light*, huh? I got one broken arm already."

"Just keep walking toward my voice. Are you alone? Where are the other kids?"

"In the bunker. But they can't come out," Terrel said. "And you can't go in."

"Why's that?"

Mace said, "Because *I'm* in here."

In the Force he felt their tension ratchet up, sharp as an indrawn breath. After a moment, Rankin's voice came out of the darkness. "And who might *you* be?"

"You don't need to know."

"Is that so? Why don't you step out where we can get a look at you?"

"Because the temptation to take a shot at me might prove over-whelming," Mace said. "Any bolts that miss will be bouncing around the inside of this bunker. Where there are four more innocent children."

A new man's voice rang out from the right, thin with fear and anger. "Two of those kids are my *sons*—if you hurt them—"

"All I have done," Mace said, "is tend their injuries and keep them sheltered. What happens to them now depends on you."

"He's telling the truth!" Terrel called. "He didn't hurt us—he *saved* us. He's *okay*. Really. He's just afraid you'll shoot him 'cause he's a korno!"

A burst of low, half-strangled profanity came from the right.

Terrel called hastily, "But he's not a *real* korno. He just looks like one. He talks almost like a regular person—and he's like, like a, a bounty hunter, or something . . ."

His voice trickled off, leaving a silence empty and ominous. Mace felt currents of intention shifting and winding through the Force; the Balawai must have been consulting in whispers on comm.

Finally, Rankin called out once more. "So? What do you want?"

"I want you to take these children and go away from here."

"Huh? What else?"

"That's all. Just take the children and go."

"Well. Aren't you generous," Rankin said, dry. Bitter. "Listen, I'm gonna make a light. Nobody get twitchy. I don't want to get fragged, okay?"

Mace said, "Light will be welcome."

Yellow-white glow flared behind a slab of tumbled wall, and a cell-powered glow rod came flipping through the air to land not far from Terrel's feet. It bounced, and rolled to a stop. Its half globe of up-angled light stretched the surrounding shadows toward the sky, painting them even darker.

Terrel held a hand at his chin to shade his eyes. "Hey, don't make me stand around alone out here, huh?"

"Come on over here, boy." A man stepped into view, moving slowly into the light. He held a blaster rifle in one hand, its barrel slanting down, carefully directed at the ground beside him. His other hand was up and forward, palm out. His clothing was scorched and stained, and one whole side of his head bore a clotted mass of spray bandage, the foam covering one eye. From his voice, this was Rankin. "Get yourself under cover."

Terrel looked back up at the bunker. Mace said, "Go ahead, son."

The voice of the man who'd claimed to be the boys' father snarled from the darkness. "Don't call him *son*, korno! You're not his father! Your stinkin' kind *killed* his father—"

"*Stow* that garbage!" Rankin barked, but too late: Terrel's face crumpled in tragic disbelief.

"Dad?" he said, sounding stunned and lost. "My dad?"

If eyes could shoot blaster bolts, Rankin's would have killed the man. "Get him out of here," he said. Another man, also wounded, stepped far enough into the light to fold Terrel in his arms and draw him away into the ring of darkness.

"Listen," Rankin said, looking up at the dark jagged mouth of the bunker. "I guess you don't want the children hurt. Neither do we. But we've got a serious problem here, okay? We got our *butts* shot off tonight. Our homes are destroyed. Half the people I know on this whole planet are *dead*. Those 'crawlers are stuffed with wounded, and we've got a load of kornos on our tails. We can't just *go*, get it? We *can't*. We need a place to hole up till dawn, that's all."

"You can't stay here," Mace said. "There are ULF guerrillas on their way here right now. Look at where you are. This place couldn't stand against them when it was *intact*."

"It doesn't have to. Gunships fly at dawn. We can hold out till then."

"You don't understand—"

"Maybe I don't. So? Not your problem, is it?"

"I have *made* it my problem," Mace said grimly. "You have no idea what this place is. What it has become."

"You know what happened here?" Rankin waved his rifle at the shattered huts. "Where is everybody?"

"Dead," Mace said. "Killed by the ULF. All of them."

"I don't think so. Where are the bodies? Think I've never seen a ULF action? I *know* the kind of things they do to our dead."

"Forget the bodies." Mace tried to massage the pain from his temple with the heel of one hand. How could the simple decency of burying the dead turn against him? "If you're here when the guerrillas arrive, they'll kill all of you, too. You care about your children's lives? Get them out of here."

"Hey, he didn't say *us*," said the father's voice from the darkness. "You catch that, Pek? 'Kill all of *you*,' he says. You catch *that*?"

"Shut up." Rankin didn't even glance in the father's direction. "Then why haven't you sent out the other kids already?"

"Because I don't know when the ULF will *get* here," Mace said impatiently. "This is the only place I can defend them. And if I had sent them out already, you'd have no reason to listen to me, would you? I'd be just another korno. One of you would have opened fire, and by now people would be dead. That's what I'm trying to *avoid*. Don't you understand? *We don't have time to argue.* On grassers, they can move as fast as a steamcrawler. Faster. They could be here *right now,* watching you from the jungle—"

Rankin shook his head. "That's why we need that bunker, you follow? We gotta get our wounded where we can protect them—"

"You *can't* protect them!" Mace's fists clenched until his fingernails drew blood from his palms. Why wouldn't they *understand?* He could feel the dark closing in upon them all like a strangler's noose. "*Listen* to me. This bunker couldn't help the people who lived here, and it can't help you. Your only hope is to take your kids and your wounded and *run.* All of you: *run.*"

"Some kinda stinkin' funny korno," the father's voice said from the shadows. "What's he so worried about *us* for?"

"That's not your business," Mace said. "Your business is to get yourself, your people, and these five children *out* of this place without anyone *dying.*"

"Maybe he's just tryin' to keep us out *here* where the stinkin' kornos can *get* us—"

"Didn't I tell you to *shut up?*" Rankin angled his good eye up toward the bunker. "You're askin' us to take a lot on faith, from some guy we can't even *see.*"

"You don't need to see me. All you need to see is this." With a twitch of the Force, Mace squeezed the Thunderbolt's trigger. A single packet of energy screamed into the sky and burst in a spherical flash of scarlet as it entered a low cloud. "That could as easily have been your head. I know exactly where you are. All *six* of you."

He paused for a second to let that sink in. "If I wanted you hurt, we wouldn't be talking. You'd already be dead."

The truth of this wiped Rankin's face clean of expression. Mace watched it hit home, and had just enough time to think that this might actually work—

Then streaks of blasterfire lit up the slope below.

The jungle thundered with scarlet explosions, multiple bolts flashing from the cover of steamcrawlers to shatter branches and blow rocks to splinters. The bursts were instantly echoed by smaller, whiter flares under the trees, crackling like a bonfire built of green logs: muzzle flashes.

Slugthrowers.

Shouts and screams from human throats underscored the whine of blasters and the shrieks of slugs hurtling in ricochets off steam-crawler armor.

"What did I tell you?" the father shrieked from the darkness. "What did I *tell* you? He kept us *yapping* and now we're *getting killed down there—!*"

"Don't do nothing stupid!" Rankin shouted. He hunched over in the glow rod's spill, his face desperate and frightened: a jacklighted ur-stag. "Look, nobody do *nothing—*"

"Rankin!" The Force gave Mace's voice the thunder of a signal cannon. "Pull your people back. A fighting retreat. Have them pull back here to the compound."

Below, a steamcrawler's turret gun spewed a stream of flame across an arc of jungle. Blood-colored light licked the bunker's ceiling.

"You said coming up here can't *help* us—"

"It can't. *I* can. Do it. It's your only chance."

Behind Mace, one of the boys had started to cry, and now the other one joined him. Pell said, "Mister? That's my *mom* out there." Her underlip twitched and her eyes welled. "Don't let them hurt her, okay? Don't let nobody hurt her."

Keela gathered Pell into her arms. "She'll be okay. Don't worry. She'll be okay." Her eyes begged Mace to make this true.

Mace stared down at them, thinking that if it were up to him, no one would hurt anyone. Anywhere. Ever. He said only, "Hang on. Be brave."

Pell sniffled and nodded solemnly.

Outside, Rankin was shouting into his comlink. "—*no,* blast it! Up *here.* Flares and flame projectors. Light 'em up and slow 'em down— and *get those 'crawlers in gear!*"

"Rankin, *don't!*" the father shouted. "Don't you *get* it? Once we're up here, he can *crossfire* our butts from the *bunker!*"

"Don't be stupid—"

"*Space* your *don't-be-stupid* talk! You know what's stupid? Talking to that korno like he's a *human being!* Believing one fraggin' word he says, *that's* stupid! Want to talk to the kornos? Talk with your *gun.*"

A star burst to life below and shot high into the air: a flare. It hung below the clouds, lighting the steamcrawlers, the jungle, and the outpost stark actinic white. Mace had to shield his eyes against the sudden glare, and he heard the father's harsh cry of triumph, and the Force snapped his lightsaber to his hand and brought the blade to life as a blaster rifle sang a rhythm fast as a hand could squeeze.

The father was no marksman; no bolt would have come within arm's length of Mace—but they would have bounced into the bunker. Amethyst light flashed to meet the red, and instead every bolt screamed away into the sky.

Mace stood in the doorway, looking down at Rankin's awestruck face past the guard angle of his lightsaber's blade. Rankin's mouth moved in breathless silence: *Jedi* . . .

Mace thought: *Looks like we lose.*

"Keela," Mace said without turning, his voice tight but dead level. "Get the children to the back. Lie down behind the bodies of the Korunnai: they are your best cover."

"What?" Keela stared at him blankly. "What? Who *are* you?"

From outside, the father's voice roared, "That's a *Jedi!*" An instant later, it was joined by another voice: higher, half broken, hoarse with grief, betrayal, and wild rage.

"A stinkin' Jedi! He's a *stinkin' Jedi!* Kill him! *Kill him!*"

The voice was Terrel's.

The Force moved Mace's hands faster than thought. Depa's lightsaber went to his left hand, to mirror his own in his right, and together they wove a wall across the mouth of the bunker, catching and scattering a flood of blasterfire.

Bolts splintered off in all directions; the erratic staccato of badly aimed shots took all his concentration and skill to intercept. Mace sank deeper and deeper into the Force, surrendering more and more of his conscious thought to the instinctive whirl of Vaapad, and even so some bolts slipped past him and whanged randomly around the inside of the bunker.

He was too deep in Vaapad to make a plan, too deep even to think, but he was a Jedi Master: he didn't have to think.

He *knew.*

If he stayed in this doorway, the children would die.

One step at a time, to give the shooters time to adjust their aim, Mace leaned into the gale of blasterfire and started down the exposed slope below the door. His blades flashing in blinding whirls of jungle green and sundown purple, spraying a spiked fan of deflected bolts toward the smoke-shrouded stars, he drew their fire down, away from the bunker's door. Away from their own children.

One step, then another.

He was aware, in an abstract, disconnected way, of an ache in his arms and the salt sting of sweat trickling into his eyes. He was aware of hot slashes of blaster grazes along his flanks, and of a chunk that had been torn from one thigh by a glancing hit. All these meant less to him than the new vectors of fire as he continued his relentless march and the jups broke from cover. He was also aware that not all the jups were shooting; he heard Rankin's desperate orders to cease fire, and felt in the Force an irrational blood hunger that kept the others squeezing triggers until their weapons began to smoke.

A blood hunger fed by the dark.

No. Not blood hunger.

Blood *fever.*

He felt people moving on all sides of him, *new* people, shooting and shouting and stumbling among the shattered huts. He felt their panic and fierce rage and the breathless desperation of their retreat. Massive shadows loomed in the Force, lumbering behemoths that roared with voices of fire: steamcrawlers backing into the ruined compound, treads crushing tumbled slabs of prefab walls, grinding the dirt over graves that Mace had dug only hours before.

The compound flooded with smoke and flame, with flashes of blaster bolts and snarls of hypersonic slugs. Mace paced through it all with relentless calm, his only expression a slight frown of concentration, his blades weaving an impenetrable web of lightning. He gave more and more of himself over to the Force, letting it move his hands, his feet, letting it guide him through the battle.

The dark power he had felt gather in the Force now rose around him to swallow the stars; it broke over him in a wave that pushed him down and caught him up and when he felt a hostile presence lunge toward his back he whirled with effortless speed and amethyst light splashed fire through the long durasteel blade of a knife held in a small hand. A sliced-off piece skittered across the ground and green energy dropped like an ax for the kill—

And stopped, trembling—

One centimeter above a brown-haired head.

Brown hairs curled, crisped, and blackened in green fire. A stub of knife, its new-cut edge still glowing hot, dropped from a nerveless hand. Stunned brown eyes, streaming tears that sparkled with brilliant green highlights, stared up at him from either side of Depa's blade.

"Stinkin' *Jedi,*" Terrel sobbed. "Go on an' kill me. Go on an' kill *everybody*—"

"You're not safe out here," Mace said. He threw himself backward and with a shove of the Force sent Terrel skidding toward the door of the bunker. A jet of flame howled through the space where they had stood.

Mace rolled to his feet, blades angled defensively before him, looking up at the looming turret gun of a steamcrawler as it traversed to track him. Someone inside had decided it would be worth Terrel's life to take out Mace. Mace didn't much care for that kind of math. He had a different equation in mind.

Four steamcrawlers divided by one Jedi equals one huge smoking pile of scrap.

The shatterpoints of the 'crawlers were obvious: neither the linked treads nor the traverse gears that rotated the turrets would stand against a single swipe of a lightsaber. In less than a second apiece, he could turn these armored behemoths into nothing more than hollow metal rocks—but he didn't.

Because that wouldn't *hurt* enough.

He wanted to hurt them worse than this black migraine was hurting him.

These people had attacked him when all he wanted was to help them. When he had been trying to *save* them. They had attacked him without regard for their own lives, or the lives of their children. They'd almost made him kill one of their children *himself.*

They were stupid. They were evil. They deserved to be punished. They deserved to die.

He saw it all in a single burst of image: a memory of something that hadn't happened yet. He saw himself dive headfirst under the steamcrawler and flip to his back, his twin blades carving through the 'crawler's lightly armored undercarriage. He'd come up in the passenger compartment, where one or two armed men might be guarding the wounded; he'd use their own blasterfire to take them out. Then cut his way into the cabin, take out the driver—then he'd wash the compound in flame projected from the steamcrawler's turret gun; the jups on foot would run and shriek as they burned. Then he would use the Force to flip his lightsabers through the air to carve gaps in the armor of the other steamcrawler, gaps through which his turret gun would pour flame, roasting drivers and passengers and wounded—thick meat-scented smoke would billow out the hatches . . .

They'd all die. Every single one of them.

It wouldn't take him a full minute.

And he'd *enjoy* it.

He was already running toward the steamcrawler, gathering himself for the headlong dive, when he finally thought, *What am I doing?*

He barely managed to turn his dive into a spring instead. He flipped upward through the air to land poised on the steamcrawler's outer deck beside the flame-gun turret. He let himself fall prone to the deck, using its bulk to cover him against blasterfire from the Balawai on the ground, and his whole body sagged as he tried to pull his mind back out from the Force.

It was too dark here. Too dark everywhere: thick and blinding, choking like the black smoke plume from the volcano's mouth above. He could find no light at all except the red flame that burned in his heart. His head pounded as though he were the one with fever wasps hatching inside his brain. As though his skull were cracking open.

Fatigue and pain rushed him, barreling him toward unconsciousness; drawing upon the Force to sustain himself drew in rage as well. He clung to the 'crawler's deck, pressing his face into the hot bullet-scarred armor. Every second he could hold himself still was another second for some of these men and women to live.

A howl welled up inside him: a roar of dark fury raised to the level of exaltation. He locked his teeth against it, but it rang in his ears anyway, echoing across the mountainside like akks calling with the voice of the blood fever itself—

Mace's breath caught in his throat. A voice inside him—how could it *echo?*

He raised his head.

That howling was akk voices after all.

They came up from the jungle, climbing the steep lava-cut sides of the outcrop, massive claws gouging furrows in the stone. Five, eight, a dozen: gigantic, armored, cowl spines bristling in full threat display, white foamy ropes of slaver looping from the corners of their dagger-toothed mouths.

Heavily armed Balawai fell back before them. The akks moved with the deliberate speed of creatures who had nothing to fear. Steamcrawler turret guns hosed them down with flame; they ignored it. They shrugged aside the minor stings of blaster hits. When they reached the crown of the outcrop, they began to pace around the outpost's perimeter, circling the shattered huts; their pace became a trot, then a gallop: a ring of armored predator, gradually tightening.

Mace recognized akk herding behavior: as though the Balawai were unruly grassers, the akks were forcing them into a single crowd in the central common area of the compound like a corral, working by pure intimidation. Any Balawai who tried to escape the ring was slammed back into it by the twitch of a massive shoulder or the sweep of an armored tail. No akk put its teeth on human flesh; even one jup who fired his rifle point blank into an akk's throat—use-lessly—received only a buffet from jaws that could as easily have bitten him in half.

Mace felt the dark thunder rising in the Force and he knew: the compound hadn't become a corral. It had become a slaughter pen.

A killing ground.

And then he felt the shadow of the butcher.

Mace looked upslope: there he was, standing on the rock above the bunker's door.

A Korun.

In the Force, he burned with power.

Huge: his sweat-glistening bare chest could have been fused together from granite boulders. His shaven skull gleamed more than two meters above his bare feet. His pants were crudely sewn from a vine cat's pelt. He raised arms like a spacescraper's buttresses over his head.

To each forearm was strapped some kind of shield: elongated teardrops of a mirror-polished metal. Their wide-curved ends extended around his massive fists, and they tapered to needle points a handspan behind his elbows.

Veins writhed in his forearms as his fists tightened. The edges of the shields blurred, and a high evil whine resonated in Mace's teeth.

The akk dogs turned to the man as though this were some kind of signal. As one, dogs and man together lifted their heads to the smothered stars and unleashed another dark blood-fever howl. It hummed in Mace's chest, and he felt the echoing answer it drew from his own rage, and he finally understood.

The rage wasn't all his.

His blood fever was an answer his heart gave to the call of the jungle. To the howl of the akks.

To the power of this man.

The Balawai had not run here of their own will; they had been *driven* here, herded to ground that had been soaked in violence and malice and savage blood fever only days before. What had been done in this place had been deliberate, the dark mirror image of a religious sanctification. The massacre here had been only a preparation, to prime the jungle for this dark rite.

Mace knew him now: this must be the *lor pelek*.

This was Kar Vastor.

His arms swept downward, and from beyond the ring of circling akks leapt six Korunnai, springing as high as Jedi but without Jedi grace. The Force thrust that propelled them felt like a grunt of pain. They flailed as though they clawed their way through the air, but they landed coiled, balanced, crouched to attack. All six were dressed identically to Vastor, and each bore those twin teardrop shields that snarled like overdriven comm speakers.

The Balawai met them with a storm of blasterfire. Bolts flashed and splattered and splintered upward into the clouds as the twin shields each man bore moved faster than thought.

The Balawai stopped firing.

Not a single Korun had fallen. Their flashing shields had intercepted every bolt.

They could only have learned this from a Jedi.

From one particular Jedi.

Oh, no, Mace thought.

Oh, Depa, no . . .

On the rock above, the *lor pelek* spread his corded arms, leaning out over the drop, toppling as though he thought he could fly—then at the last instant he sprang forward into a dive that carried him toward the center of the crowd of Balawai, where they massed around the steamcrawlers.

The killing began.

The Korunnai waded in without waiting for Vastor to land. They sprang among the mass of Balawai and swung those teardrop shields in short, vicious arcs, angled flat as though to cut with their edges—

And cut they did.

Their sizzling edges bit through blasters with tooth-grinding squeals; they slashed through flesh with a meaty squelch, and the blood on them shivered to mist. Scarlet clouds trailed them like smoke. Mace saw a man cut in half, and the shield came out his other side still shining like an ultrachrome mirror.

Shining like a vibro-ax.

Vastor touched down in the middle of the compound and rolled out of his fall without slowing. He flashed into an inhumanly fast sprint toward the very steamcrawler atop which Mace lay. Vastor's sprint became a headlong dive that carried him sliding between the treads.

The steamcrawler's armor hummed under Mace's hands, and a harsher squeal joined the chorus of snarling shields; he had to bite back an obscenity he'd learned from Nick.

Vastor was cutting through the 'crawler's undercarriage.

Had he stolen that dark dream right out of Mace's head?

Mace popped to his feet and both his lightsabers hummed to life. He felt Vastor in the Force: a torch that flared with darkness. He was almost through the undercarriage; once inside, he'd be loose among the wounded. The Force showed him how the wounded men and women inside the crawler had already pressed themselves away from the shining blades that sliced upward from below.

Mace decided it was time he introduced himself to this *lor pelek*.

He sprang into the air, flipping high over the steamcrawler's turret to land on its flat mid-deck armor directly above Vastor. A twitch of the Force reversed his grips so that the lightsabers' blades projected downward from his fists. Then he dropped to his knees, twisting to swing the blades in a circle around him.

A vibroshield is not the only thing that can cut steamcrawler armor.

A disk of that armor—edges still glowing from the lightsabers' cuts, Mace still kneeling in its center—dropped straight down like a free-falling turbolift.

Mace heard one explosive obscenity from below before he and the disk of armor flattened Kar Vastor like a fusion-powered pile driver.

The interior of the steamcrawler was crowded with wounded men and women. One of them brandished a heavy blaster; Mace slashed it in two with a flip of his lightsaber. "No shooting," he said, and the Force made his words into a command that sent several other blasters clattering to the floor.

Vastor lay pinned facedown to the deck, half stunned.

Mace leaned close to his ear. "Kar Vastor, I am Mace Windu. Stand down. That's an order."

A twitch of the Force was his only warning, but for Mace it was more than he needed. He threw himself into a back flip a quarter of a second before the disk of armor slammed upward to smash against the ceiling with a deafening clank. Before it could fall again, Vastor was on his feet. Then as the disk dropped, an ultrachrome flame licked through it, slicing it in half.

The pieces rattled back down through the hole Vastor had cut in the undercarriage.

Vastor faced Mace across the hole. Darkness pulsed at Mace through the Force, but on the *lor pelek*'s face was not anger, but instead inhuman focus: a primal ferocity like a krayt dragon surprised over the corpse of a bantha.

The way he had shrugged Mace off, the slicing of the armor disk: a predator's dominance display.

He raised his shield-clad hands in salute and rumbled something in a language that Mace didn't recognize—it didn't even sound like language at all: more like the growls and snarls of jungle beasts.

But as Vastor spoke, some power of the *lor pelek*'s unfurled his meaning inside Mace's mind.

Mace Windu, the *lor pelek* had said. *An honor. Why do you interfere in my kill?*

"There is no kill," Mace said. "Do you understand me? *No kill.* No more killing."

Vastor's smile was disbelieving. *No? Then what do you propose? Shall we lay down our arms?* He beckoned invitingly with one sizzling shield. *You first.*

The zings of blaster ricochets and the roar of steamcrawler turret guns came clearly through the gaps in the 'crawler's armor. "No *unnecessary* killing," Mace amended. "No more *massacres."*

Vastor's response had a quality of animal directness, straightforward and uncomplicated. *Massacres are necessary, dôshalo.*

"You and I are not dôshallai." Mace angled his lightsabers in a defensive X. "You are no clan brother of mine."

Vastor shrugged. *Where are Besh and Chalk?*

"In the bunker," Mace answered without thinking, his mind still whirling around the concept of a *necessary massacre.*

Vastor swept the wounded men and women in the steamcrawler's cabin with a contemptuous glare. *These will keep, dôshalo. They cannot escape. Follow me.* With a rush of the Force, he sprang straight upward through the hole Mace had cut.

That same rush of the Force tugged at Mace's will, inclining him to follow without thinking—but he understood now the power of this place, and of Vastor himself.

"You'll have to do better than that," Mace muttered.

He turned his attention to the terrified Balawai around him. He gestured, and all the discarded blasters flipped from the deck to hang in midair; with a single swift flourish he sliced every one of them in half, then cast their pieces out the hole. "Listen to me, all of you. You must surrender. It is your only hope."

"Hope of what?" a man said bitterly. His face was gray; he wore a bacta patch over a chest wound and clutched the stump of his wrist just above a wad of spray bandage that served him for a tourniquet. "We know what happens if we're captured."

"Not this time," Mace said: "If you fight, they will kill you. If you surrender I can keep you alive. And I will."

"We're supposed to just take your *word* for it?"

"I am a Jedi Master."

The man spat blood on the deck. "We know what that's worth."

"Obviously you don't." In the Force, Mace felt the dark flame that was the *lor pelek* fighting his way upslope toward the bunker. For an instant he was almost grateful—he'd be happy to leave the defense of Chalk and Besh in Vastor's hands—but then he remembered the children. The children were still inside.

Where Vastor was going.

Massacres are necessary.

"I won't argue." Mace moved to the rim of the hole Vastor had cut, and looked up through the one he'd cut himself, judging his clearance. "Fight to a sure death, or surrender to a hope of life. The choice is yours," he said, and threw himself upward into the burning night.

The whole compound was on fire: choking black smoke swirled above blazing lakes of flame-projector fuel. Blaster bolts flashed through every angle, their bursts an arrhythmic drumbeat under the howling chorus of the Korun shield-weapons. Vastor bounded up the slope toward the bunker in erratic zigzagging leaps, his shields flashing: catching stray bolts, carving metal, slashing flesh.

Mace dived from the top of the steamcrawler, flipped in the air, and hit the ground running. His blades wove a green and purple corona of power that splintered blasterfire into the sky.

A knot of Balawai huddled on their knees a few meters to the left of Mace's path, their hands finger-laced on the backs of their heads. Eyes closed against the horror around them, they screamed for mercy to a gore-smeared Korun whose face held nothing human. The Korun raised twin shields shrilling over his head, and with a roar of dark exultation he plunged them toward defenseless necks—

But before he could land the blow, the sole of a boot slammed his spine so hard that he flipped completely over and landed on his head.

The Korun sprang to his feet, unhurt and raging. "Kick *me?* Gonna *die,* you! Gonna *die*—"

He stopped, because to move another centimeter would have brought his nose in contact with the rock-steady purple lightsaber blade poised in front of his face. At the other end of that blade stood Mace Windu.

"Yes, I will," he said. "But not today."

The Korun's expression curdled like sour grasser milk. "Must be the Windu Jedi, you," he said in Koruun. "Depa's sire."

The word gave Mace a twinge; in Koruun, *sire* could mean either "master" or "father." Or both. He spoke in his rusty Koruun. "Don't kill not-fighters, you. Kill not-fighters and *you* die."

The Korun snorted. "Talk like a Balawai, you," he spat in Basic. "Don't take your orders, I."

Mace twitched his lightsaber. The Korun's eyes flickered. Mace returned to Basic as well. "If you want to live, believe what I say: what happens to them will happen to *you.*"

"Tell it to Kar Vastor," the Korun sneered.

"I intend to." Before the Korun could reply, Mace whirled and sprang for the bunker's door.

Mace didn't trouble with the distractions that had made Vastor's path jag like a bolt of lightning; he went straight for the door's shattered gape as though launched from a cannon. He reached it only steps behind the larger man.

And froze.

Froze despite the chilling whine of those teardrop shields, despite Vastor's rumbling snarl like the hunting-cough of a hungry vine cat. Despite a sound Mace could no more ignore than he could reverse the rotation of the planet: the shrieks of children screaming in terror.

The burning compound below lit the bunker's ceiling with shifting light the color of blood, casting Mace's shadow huge and wavering, indistinct but utterly black: a shadow that shrouded all within. The only light that fell upon the core of his shadow was the unnatural wash of mingled green and purple glare from his lightsabers.

Vastor stood within, hunched like a gundark, his right arm drawn back to strike. Dangling from hair tangled in Vastor's left fist, feet kicking above the floor, sobbing uncontrollably about how *all you stinkin' kornos have to die,* was Terrel.

"Vastor, *stop!*" Mace opened himself to the full flood of the Force, and used it to hammer at the *lor pelek's* will. "Don't do it, Kar. Put the boy down."

He might as well have not bothered; Vastor's answering snarl translated in Mace's mind as *When I am done with him.* The shield strapped to Vastor's left arm made a mirrored halo over Terrel's head, but now the other angled toward where Besh and Chalk lay. *Look there, and see what sort of creature I hold.*

"He's not some *creature,*" Mace responded with reflexive certainty. "He's a *boy.* His name . . . his name is . . ." His voice trailed away as his eyes finally made sense of what Vastor was pointing at. "Terrel . . ."

Besh and Chalk lay on the stone floor midway between where Vastor stood holding Terrel and where Keela, Pell, and the two younger boys cowered. The clothing of the thanatizine-bound Korunnai appeared inexplicably rumpled, even tattered, and over their torsos it glistened a wet oily black. A full second passed before Mace realized that it was the light from his blades that robbed color from the wet gleam on their clothes; he figured it out by the smell, strong even through the reek of the burning compound outside.

It was the smell of blood.

Someone had been hacking, inexpertly but with considerable enthusiasm, at the two helpless Korunnai.

Hacking at two human beings Mace had sworn to protect.

Hacking at sad Besh, who could not speak. Who'd lost his brother only yesterday.

Hacking at fierce Chalk, the girl who had made herself strong enough to survive anything. Anything but this.

They had lain down in this cold bunker floor and taken into their veins the drug that had swallowed them in a false death, trusting that a Jedi Master would watch over them to prevent a real one.

On the floor below Terrel's dangling feet was a short stub of knife, smeared with the same dark blood. The blade was only half a decimeter long, its tip now a sharp straight slant—

Terrel's knife. The one Mace had sliced in half on the slope outside.

Strength drained from Mace's knees. "Oh, Terrel," he said, letting his lightsabers swallow their blades. "Terrel, what have you *done?*"

Don't worry, was the meaning of Vastor's rumbling growl. *He won't do it again.*

Mace threw himself into a Force-spring, both his blades blazing to life again as he streaked through the darkness toward Vastor's back—and in that instant he saw himself arguing again with Nick on the trail, heard again his orders within this shattered bunker, saw the steamcrawler carrying children teeter at the lip of the precipice, saw Rankin step into the circle of light, faced Vastor inside a steamcrawler crowded with wounded. He couldn't see what he should have done differently—what he *could* have done differently and remained the Jedi he was—to lead to any moment other than this one: this moment where he knew already he would be too late, too slow, too old and tired, too beaten down by the inexplicable cruelties of jungle war—

Too useless to save the life of one single child.

Mace could only roar a futile denial as Vastor struck. The vibroshield sank deep into Terrel's body. And as the *lor pelek* ripped the life out of the boy, the blood fever told Mace what he should have done differently.

He should have killed Kar Vastor.

He'd been too late to save Terrel, but in the bunker there were four other Balawai children whom Vastor could reach with a single stride.

Still in the air, Mace drew back both lightsabers and whipped them forward and down with the full grim intention to carve Vastor into pieces so small it'd take a bioscan to tell they'd ever been human.

The *lor pelek* cast aside the boy's corpse with one flick of his massive wrist and whirled, shields flashing in the lightsaber glare as they flicked upward and met Mace's downward strokes. Mace used the Force to drive the blades; he would cut through the shields, through both of Vastor's arms, slash deep into his chest to quench the blades' fire in Vastor's smoking heart—

But the shields did not cut, and they did not give way.

Their singing whine hummed into Mace's hands, up his arms, to shiver in his chest and buzz in his teeth.

Then he was past, flipping over Vastor's head. Keela and Pell and the two boys shrieked and clung to each other on their knees, cowering back from his path. He landed and whirled to face the *lor pelek*, his blades crossed in the defensive X.

Vastor stared at Mace from a motionless fighting crouch. His eyes smoldered; his growl said, *We have gone to considerable trouble to bring you here, dôshalo. Must I kill you?*

"I told you before." Mace's growl matched Vastor's. "I am not your *dôshalo.*"

It will hurt Depa to find you dead. Stand down.

Mace's whole body thrummed with his need to strike: his need to dive into Vaapad and allow its dark storm to drive his blades. His veins sang with blood fever, and the black migraine hammered his skull. He needed to hit Vastor, to *hurt* him. To *punish* him.

But a lifetime of Jedi discipline held him in place. Jedi do not revenge. Jedi do not punish.

Jedi *defend.*

Mace ground his teeth together, panting harshly. "Leave this place, Kar Vastor. I won't let you harm these children."

Vastor lifted shields that still shone mirror bright; Mace's lightsabers had not even scarred their surface. Blood fever surged in Mace's heart. Vastor moved toward him with the ponderous menace of a hungry rancor. *I see flames in your eyes, Jedi Mace Windu: jungle green and stormcloud purple. I hear echoes of blood's thunder in your ears.*

He brought the curved backs of his vibrating shields together to make an earsplitting squeal that shot chills across Mace's back, and his fighting grin showed teeth filed sharp as a vine cat's. *You have decided to take my life.*

"I won't let you harm these children," Mace repeated.

Vastor shook his head in slow, grinning denial. *I have no interest in them. I do not make war on children.*

Mace's response was a grimly silent stare at Terrel's corpse.

He was man enough to kill, was the meaning of the shrug in Vastor's growl. *He was man enough to die. What he did was not war, but murder. What should I have done? Look around you, dôshalo: in this jungle, have you seen a jail?*

"If I had," Mace said through his teeth, "I would put you in it."

But instead you stand there, panting with hope and fear.

"Jedi do not fear," Mace told him. "Hope, I left behind on Coruscant."

You hope I will threaten the children. You fear I might not. You hope I will give you an excuse to kill me. You fear to simply act.

Mace stared.

In his reflection on Vastor's humming shields, he saw himself as though he looked upon a shatterpoint in his own nature.

What Vastor had said: it was true.

It was all true.

He burned with blood fever: ached to kill the *lor pelek* the same way that Vastor had killed Terrel. And for the *same reason.* In putting himself between Vastor and the children, he hadn't been seeking to defend innocent lives.

He'd been seeking justifiable homicide.

A perfectly Jedi murder.

Like a faceful of icy water, it shocked him from a dream: now for the first time, the flame-lit bunker looked *real.* Vastor was now human, only a man; a man of power, to be sure, but no longer the embodiment of the jungle's darkness. Terrel had been a boy, merely a child, yes, but a boy whose dead arms were still wet to the elbow with the blood of Chalk and Besh.

Until now, Mace had looked at them—at this whole *world*, and all that he had seen within it—with Jedi eyes: seeing abstract patterns of power in the swirling chiaroscuro of the Force, a punctuated rhythm of good and evil. His Jedi eyes had found him only what he'd already been looking for.

Without knowing it, he'd been seeking an enemy. Someone he could fight. Someone who would stand in for this war.

Someone he could blame for it.

Someone he could kill.

Now, though—

He looked at Vastor with his own eyes, truly open for the first time.

Vastor looked back intently. After a moment, the *lor pelek* relaxed with a sigh, lowering his weapons. *You have decided to let me live,* was the meaning of his wordless grumble. *For now.*

Mace said, "I am sorry."

For what? Vastor looked frankly puzzled. When Mace did not answer, he shrugged. *Now that I may safely show you my back, I will go. The fight is over. I must deal with our captives.*

He turned toward the bunker's door. Mace spoke to his back. "I won't allow you to kill prisoners."

Vastor stopped, glancing back over his shoulder. *Who said anything about killing prisoners? One of my men?* His eyes took a feral gleam from the light of Mace's blades. *Never mind. I know who it was. Leave him to me.*

Without another word, Vastor stalked out into the firelit night.

Mace stood in the flickering dark, his only light the shine from his blades. After a time, his hands went numb on the handgrips' activation plates, and his blades shrank to nothingness.

Now the only light was the bloody glow on the bunker's ceiling cast by the fires outside.

He noted absently that Besh and Chalk hadn't bled much from their wounds. The thanatizine, he guessed.

A low whimper from behind reminded him of the children. He turned and looked down at them. They quivered in a group hug so tight he couldn't see where one child ended and the next began. None of them returned his stare. He could feel their terror through the Force: they were afraid to meet his eyes.

He wanted to tell them that they had nothing to fear, but that would be a lie. He wanted to tell them that he wouldn't let anyone hurt them. That was another lie: he already had. None of them would ever forget seeing their friend killed by a Korun.

None of them would ever forget seeing a Jedi let that Korun walk away.

There were so many things he should say that he could only keep silent. There were so many things he should do that he could only stand holding his powered-down lightsabers.

When all choices seem wrong, choose restraint.

And so he stood motionless.

"Master Windu?" The voice was familiar, but it seemed to come from very far away; or perhaps it was only an echo of memory. "Master Windu!"

He stood staring into an invisible distance until a strong hand took his arm. "Hey, *Mace!*"

He sighed. "Nick. What do you want?"

"It's almost dawn. Gunships fly with the light. It won't take them long to get here. Time to saddle—" Nick's voice stopped as though he were choking on something. "Frag *me.* What did you—I mean, what did they—who would—how—?"

His voice ran down. Mace finally turned to face the young Korun. Nick stared speechlessly down at the bloody messes that were Besh and Chalk.

"The thanatizine has slowed their hemorrhaging," Mace said softly. "Someone who's good with a medpac's tissue binder might still be able to save their lives."

"And—and—and—are those *children*—?"

"Apparently some Balawai don't leave them in the cities after all."

"What are those *kids* doing here? What happened to them?"

Mace looked away. "I saved their lives." His shoulders lifted with his sigh, then fell. "Temporarily."

Nick grunted. "Huh. Always is."

Mace looked at him.

"When you save someone's life." Nick cocked his head in a Korun shrug. "It's always temporary, y'know?"

Mace drifted toward the bunker's shattered doorway. "I suppose it is. I'd never thought about it that way."

"Hey, hold on. Where do you think you're going?"

"Parents of these children were out there. They may still be alive."

"But Besh and *Chalk*," Nick insisted. "What about Besh and Chalk? You can't just walk out of here and *leave* them—"

"They are in your care now. I could not protect them." Mace lowered his head as he walked away, and lowered his voice as well. "I could not even protect myself."

"But Mace—Master Windu—" Nick called after him. *"Mace!"*

Mace stopped and looked back. Nick stood framed in the bunker's dark mouth, its twisted jags of durasteel surrounding him like teeth. "What about the kids? What am I supposed to do with them?"

"Pretend they are your own," Mace said, and turned away.

The compound was full of armed Korunnai, who were looting the scattered corpses with the same swift efficiency Mace had seen from Nick and Chalk and Besh and Lesh, back in that Pelek Baw alleyway. These Korunnai wore clothing that seemed to be all patches; most of the guerrillas bore wounds of one kind or another, and many of them showed signs of malnutrition. Only their weapons were well tended.

They clearly took better care of their blasters than they did of themselves.

As Mace moved through the compound, the new realness of the world he saw intensified, and fragmented: a scatter of hyper-real details that he could not fit into a complete picture.

Vivid as a nightmare.

A severed hand and forearm lay on the ground at the edge of a pool of burning flame-projector fuel, fingers slowly curling into a fist as it cooked.

A black splash of puddle that did not burn might have been water. Or blood.

A half-melted blaster gas cartridge ruptured, sending it skittering wildly across the ground, spraying a jet of bright green flame.

A pair of Korun teenagers danced like demented Kowakian monkey-lizards, dodging flame puddles as they tried to catch ration packs being flung out through the hatch of a smoking steamcrawler.

The sky burned with dawn as though the clouds had caught fire.

The twelve akks now stood in a ring around a couple of dozen shivering Balawai. The captives huddled together, holding each other, watching the guerrillas, eyes empty of hope and blank with terror.

The Korun whom Mace had kicked sat on the angled armor skirt of a steamcrawler beside the ring of akks, glaring at Mace as the Jedi Master diffidently approached. The Korun's shields were pushed up onto his forearms, freeing his hands, which were engaged in massaging a massive lump of black bruise over his right eye. The skin there had split, and half his face was painted with blood that had sprung from that bruise to join another trickle from a similar swelling on the same side of his mouth.

A flash of intuition connected the Korun's glare, the lumps on his face, and what the *lor pelek* had said to Mace as he had left the bunker.

Vastor must have a devastating left hook.

"Want what, you?" the Korun growled. He rose and pushed his shields back down to his fists, and they whined to life. "Want *what?*"

"Back off," Mace said expressionlessly. He walked past the bigger man. "I seem to have been looking for someone to kill. Don't let it be you."

He didn't need to introduce himself to the akk dogs who guarded the captives; the pack parted at his approach as though they recognized him instinctively. A simple question to the nearest captive led him to the father of the two young boys. When Mace told him that Urno and Nykl were still alive and as safe as any Balawai here could be, the man burst into tears.

Relief or terror: Mace could not tell.

Tears are tears.

Mace could summon no sympathy for him. He could not forget that this was the man who had fired the first shot into the bunker. Nor could he pass any sort of judgment upon him; he could not say that if this man had held his fire, any of the dead here would instead be alive.

Rankin was not among the captives. Nor was the girls' mother.

Mace knew neither had escaped.

Rankin . . . Though he and Mace could not have trusted each other, they had been, however briefly, on the same side. They had both been trying to get everyone out of here without anyone dying.

Rankin had paid the price of that failure.

Perhaps Mace had started paying it as well.

One more question to one more captive, and then the akks moved aside for him again.

Vastor was nearby, growling and barking and snarling the Korunnai into groups organized for the withdrawal. In his disconnected state, Mace felt no surprise to discover that he could not now understand the *lor pelek*. Vastor's voice had become jungle noise, freighted with meaning but indecipherable. Inhuman. Impersonal.

Lethal.

. . . not because the jungle kills you, Nick had said. *Just because it is what it is.*

Mace put out a hand to stop Vastor as the *lor pelek* swept by him. "What will you do with the captives?"

Vastor rumbled wordlessly in his throat, and now again his meaning unfurled in Mace's mind. *They come with us.*

"You can take care of prisoners?"

We don't take care of them. We give them to the jungle.

"The *tan pel'trokal*," Mace murmured. "Jungle justice." Somehow, this made perfect sense. Though he could not approve, he could not help but understand.

Vastor nodded as he turned to move on. *It is our way.*

"Is that different from murder?" Though Mace was looking at Vastor, he sounded like he was asking himself. "Can any of them survive? Cast out alone, without supplies, without weapons—"

The *lor pelek* gave Mace a predator's grin over his shoulder, showing his needle-sharp teeth. *I did,* he growled, and walked away.

"And the children?"

But Mace was talking to the *lor pelek*'s departing back; Vastor was already snapping at three or four ragged young Korunnai. What he might be ordering them to do, Mace couldn't say; Vastor's meaning had departed with his attention.

Mace drifted in the direction the last captive he'd spoken to had indicated. He stopped at the edge of a smoldering puddle of flame-projector fuel. It had burned nearly out; black coils of smoke twisted upward from only a few patches of dawn-paled flame.

A step or two in from the edge of the puddle lay a body.

It lay on its side, curled in the characteristic fetal burn-victim ball. One of its arms seemed to have escaped its general contraction. The arm pointed at the near rim of the puddle's scorch mark, palm-down, as though this corpse had died trying to drag itself, one-handed, from the flames.

Mace couldn't even tell if it had been a man, or a woman.

He squatted on his heels at the edge of the scorch, staring. Then he wrapped his arms around his knees, and just sat. There didn't seem to be anything else to do.

He had asked that last captive where she'd last seen the girls' mother.

He could not possibly determine if this corpse had once been the woman who'd given birth to Pell and to Keela; if this smoking mass of charred dead flesh had held them in its arms and kissed away their childish tears.

Did it matter?

This had been someone's parent, or brother, or sister. Someone's child. Someone's friend.

Who had died anonymously in the jungle.

He couldn't even tell if this corpse had been killed by a Korun bullet, or a vibroshield, or a Balawai blaster. Or if it had simply been unlucky enough to get in the way of a stream of fire from a steam-crawler's turret gun.

Perhaps in the Force, he might have been able to sense some answers. But he couldn't decide if knowing would be better than not knowing. And to touch the Force again in this dark place was a risk he was not prepared to take.

So he just sat, and thought about the dark.

Sat while the guerrillas splintered into bands that melted away down the mountainside. Sat while the prisoners were marched off in a gang, surrounded by akk dogs. Sat while the sun slanted past a pair of northeast peaks, and a wave of light rolled down the slope above him.

Vastor came to him, rumbling something about leaving this place before the gunships arrived. Mace did not even look up.

He was thinking about the light of the sun, and how it did not touch the darkness in the jungle.

Nick stopped on his way out of camp. In one arm, he carried Urno; Nykl slept against his other shoulder, tiny arms clasped around his neck. Keela stumbled along behind, one hand pressing against the spray bandage that closed her head wound while she used the other to lead little Pell. Nick must have asked Mace a question, because he paused at the side of the Jedi Master as though waiting for an answer.

But Mace had no answers to give.

When he got no response, Nick shrugged and moved on.

Mace thought about the dark. The Jedi metaphor of the dark side of the Force had never seemed so appropriate before—less the dark of evil than the dark of a starless night: where what you think is a vine cat is only a bush, and what appears to be a tree may very well be a killer standing motionless, waiting for you to look away.

Mace had read Temple Archive accounts written by Jedi who had brushed the dark and recovered. These accounts often mentioned how the dark side seemed to make everything clear; Mace knew now that this was only a delusion. A lie.

The truth was exactly opposite.

There was so much dark here, he might as well be blind.

Morning sun struck the compound, and brought gunships with it: six of them, a double flight, roaring straight in from the stinging glare of Al'har as it cleared the mountains. Their formation blossomed into a rosette as they peeled off to angle for staggered, crisscrossing strafing runs.

Mace still didn't move.

Might as well be blind, he thought, and perhaps he also said it aloud—

For the voice that spoke from behind him seemed to be answering.

"The wisest man I know once told me: *It is in the darkest night that the light we are shines brightest.*"

A woman's voice, cracking with exhaustion and hoarse with old pain—and perhaps it was only this voice that could have kindled a torch in Mace's vast darkness, only this voice that could have brought Mace to his feet, turning, hope blooming inside his head, almost happy—

Almost even *smiling*—

He turned, his arms opening, his breath catching, and all he could say was, "Depa . . ."

But she did not come to his embrace, and the hope inside him sputtered and died. His arms fell to his sides. Even prepared by what Nick had told him, he was not remotely ready for this.

Jedi Master Depa Billaba stood before him in the tattered remnants of Jedi robes, stained with mud and blood and jungle sap. Her hair—that had once been a lush, glossy mane as black as space, that she had kept regimented in mathematically precise braids—was tangled, spiked with dirt and grease, raggedly short as though she had hacked it off with a knife. Her face was pale and lined with fatigue, and had gone so thin her cheekbones stood out like blades. Her mouth seemed lipless and hard, and bore a fresh burn scar from one corner to the tip of her chin—but these were not the worst of it.

None of these were what kept Mace motionless as though nailed to the ground, even as gunships swept overhead and rained blaster-fire on the compound around them.

In the inferno of explosions, amid the whine of rock splinters and the hammering webwork of plasma, Mace could only stare at Depa's forehead, where she had once worn the shining golden bead of the Greater Mark of Illumination: the symbol of a Chalactan adept. The Mark of Illumination is affixed to the frontal bone of an adept's skull by the elders of that ancient religion, as a symbol of the Uncloseable Eye that is the highest expression of the Chalactan Enlightenment. Depa had worn hers with pride for twenty years.

Now, where the Mark had been was only an ugly ripple of keloid scar, as though the same knife that had slashed away her hair had crudely hacked the symbol of her ancestral religion from the bone of her skull.

And across her eyes, she wore a strip of rag tied like a blindfold: a rag as weathered and stained and ragged as her robes themselves.

But she stood as though she could see him all too well.

"Depa . . ."

Mace had to raise his voice to even hear himself through the roar of the repulsorlifts and the laser cannons and the exploding dirt and rock around him. "Depa, what happened? What has *happened* to you?"

"Hello, Mace," she said sadly. "You shouldn't have come."

PART TWO

VICTORY
CONDITIONS

9

INSTINCT

I finally understand what I'm doing here. Why I came. I understand the hypocrisy of that list of reasons I offered to Yoda and to Palpatine, in the Chancellor's office those weeks ago.

I was lying to them.

And to myself.

I must have seen the real reason I came here in the first instant I turned to her in the compound: in the pain-etched creases below her cheekbones. In the scar where the Mark of Enlightenment had been.

Yes: it wasn't really her. It was a Force-vision. A hallucination. A lie. But even a lie of the Force is more true than any reality our limited minds can comprehend.

In the rag that bound her eyes but did not blind her to the truth of me—

I found my conditions of victory.

I didn't come here to learn what has happened to Depa, nor to protect the reputation of our Order. I don't care what's happened to her, and the reputation of our Order is meaningless.

I did not come to fight this war. I don't care who wins. Because no one wins. Not in real war. It is only a question of how much each side is willing to lose.

I did not come here to apprehend or kill a rogue Jedi, or even to judge one. I cannot judge her. I have been on the periphery of this war for barely a double handful of days, and look what I am on the verge of becoming; she has been in the thick of it for *months*.

Drowning in darkness.

Buried in the jungle.

I didn't come here to stop Depa. I came here to *save* her.

I *will* save her.

And may the Force have mercy on any who would try to stop me, for I will have none.

FROM THE PRIVATE JOURNALS OF MACE WINDU

I don't remember leaving the compound. I suppose I must have been in some kind of shock. Not physical; my injuries are minor—though now the bacta patches from our captured medpacs are needed for more serious wounds, and the blaster burn on my thigh is angry and swelling with infection. But *shock* is the word. Mental shock, perhaps.

Moral shock.

A veil has fallen: between the moment when Depa came to me in the compound, and the moment I came back to myself on the slope below, there is in my mind mostly a blurred haze. In that blurred haze, I find two conflicting memories of our meeting there—

And both of them, it seems, are false.

Dreams. Imaginative reinterpretation of events.

Hallucination.

In one memory, she extends a hand toward me, and I reach to take it—but instead I feel a tug at my vest and her lightsaber leaps from its inner pocket and flips through the air to smack her palm. Blaster bolts from the gunships' laser cannons smash craters in the compound; each bolt makes rock and dirt explode like grenades; the air around us fills with red plasma and orange flame—and that old familiar half smile tugs up one corner of her lips and she says, "Up or down?" and I tell her *Up* and she leaps into an aerial roll over my head and I take a single step forward so that she lands with her back against mine—

And the feel of her back against my own, that strong and warm and living touch that I have felt so many times, in so many places, pulls the dread from my heart and the darkness from my eyes and our blades in perfect synchrony meet the fires from above and cast them back into the dawn-scorched sky—

As I said: a dream.

The other memory is a silent image of walking calmly at Depa's side through the rain of blasterfire, conversing with calm unconcern, as oblivious to the gunships as we are to the jungle, and to the sunlight of the dawn. In this dream or memory, Depa turns her blindfolded face toward me, her head cocked as though she can see into my heart. *Why have you come here, Mace? Do you even know?*

I don't hear these words: again like a dream, it seems we merely intend our meaning, and somehow make ourselves understood.

Why did you send for me? is my answer.

That's not the same thing, she reminds me gently. *You have to define your conditions of victory. If you don't know what you're trying to do, how can you tell when you've done it? Why have you come? To stop me? You can do that with one slash of a lightsaber.*

I suppose, I somehow reply, *I am trying to find out what has happened here. What is happening. To these people, and to you. Once I understand what's going on, I'll know what to do about it.*

The only thing you don't understand, says this blind dream-image of my beloved Padawan, *is that you already understand all there is to understand. You just don't want to believe it.*

Then the veil thickens, and deepens toward night, and I remember no more until sometime later—not too much later—when I was running helter-skelter down through the jungle, quite alone.

Bounding down a long, long slope half barren with old lava where it wasn't burned with new, I could feel the guerrillas somewhere ahead by the dark pall like smoke they trailed in the Force—and I could track them by the blood spoor their many wounded left on ground and rock and leaf.

And I remember skidding down the rim of a dry wash, and finding Kar Vastor waiting for me at the bottom.

Kar Vastor—

I have much to say of this *lor pelek*. Of the powers I have seen him wield, from the drawing of the fever wasps out of Besh and Chalk to the way the jungle itself seems to part for his passage and tangle itself behind. Of his followers: those six Korunnai he calls the Akk Guards, men he's made into lesser echoes of himself. How he has trained them in their signature weapons—those terrifying "vibroshields"—that he had designed and built. Even the smallest details: the primal ferocity of his gaze, the jungle-noise growl of his wordless voice, and how you hear his meaning as though it were your own voice whispering inside your head—all deserve more depth of comment than I can give them here.

I'm not sure why it took me so long to understand that he and I are natural enemies.

The *lor pelek* stood on the slope below Mace, holding the reins of a saddled grasser. The grasser kept one of its three eyes fixed warily on Vastor, and when he spoke, the grasser trembled as though it would shy away were it not held in place by an invisible force that overpowered its instincts.

Jedi Windu. You are sent for, dôshalo.

Mace did not need to ask by whom. "Where is she?"

An hour's ride ahead. Resting in her howdah. She no longer walks.

Mace felt dizzy; the world shifted focus as though he looked at its reflection in a rippling pool. "An hour . . . no longer *walks*—?" It made no sense, but in the Force it felt like the truth. "She was here— she was *just here*—"

No.

"But she *was*—she greeted me, and—" Mace passed a hand over his skull, checking for blood or swelling: searching for a head wound. "I returned her lightsaber—we fought—we fought the gunships—"

You fought alone.

"She was *with me . . .*"

I sent two of my men to check on you, when you did not join the march. They watched from below, hiding from the Balawai ships. They saw you: alone in the compound, your blades flashing against the blasterfire. My men say you drove them off single-handed, though they did not seem to be damaged. Perhaps you have taught Balawai to fear the Jedi blade. He showed Mace his sharp-filed teeth. *Nick Rostu spoke much of your victory at the pass. Even I might not be equal to such a feat.*

"She was with me." Mace stared at the traces of portaak amber that stained his palms. "We fought—or we spoke—I can't seem to remember—"

It is pelekotan *you recall.*

"The Force—? You're saying it was some kind of Force-vision?"

Pelekotan *brings us waking dreams of our desires and our fears.* Vastor's tone was grave, but not unkind. *When we desire what we fear and fear what we desire,* pelekotan *always answers. Have the Jedi forgotten this?*

"It seemed so *real*—it seemed more real than *you* do."

Vastor shrugged. *It was. Only* pelekotan *is real. Everything else is forms and shadows: less even than a cloud, or a memory. We are* pelekotan's *dream. Have the Jedi forgotten this as well?*

Mace didn't answer. He had only then become aware of the balanced weight of his vest: he put a hand to his right-side ribs, and felt through the stained panther leather the outline of a lightsaber, matching his own, which he wore on his left.

Depa's lightsaber.

And if what he'd seen in the compound had been a vision in the Force, what then? Did it change the truth he'd seen? Did it change the truth she'd seen in him?

From the Force, those truths become more real, not less.

"A dream," he heard himself murmur. "A dream . . ."

Vastor gestured for him to mount up. *Dream she may be, but refuse her summons and you will learn how swiftly dream turns to nightmare.*

Mace climbed into the saddle without telling the *lor pelek* that he already knew.

Some obscure impulse prompted him to ask: "And you, Kar Vastor: what visions does *pelekotan* bring to you?"

His response was a limitless stare, inhuman, as full of unguessable danger as the jungle itself. *Why should* pelekotan *show me anything? I have no fears.*

"And no desires?"

But he had already turned to lead the grasser away, and he gave no sign that he had heard.

FROM THE PRIVATE JOURNALS OF MACE WINDU

Kar Vastor led my grasser on foot; he was able to find a path through the densest, most tangled undergrowth so effortlessly that we could move at a steady trot. After a time, I began to believe—as I now do—that his ability to move through the jungle was only half perception; the other half was raw power. Not only could he sense a path where none could be seen, I believe he could at need make a path where none had existed.

Or perhaps *make* is the wrong word.

I never saw this power in action; I never saw trees move, nor knots of vines unbind themselves. Instead I felt a continuous current in the Force: a rolling cycle like the breath of some vast creature alone in the dark. Power flowed into him and out again, but I did not feel him use it any more than I feel my muscles use the sugars that feed them.

And that is exactly how it seemed: that we were carried through the jungle effortlessly, like corpuscles in its veins. Or thoughts in its infinite mind.

As though we were *pelekotan's* dream.

In that ride from the rear to the front of the guerrillas' line of march, I got my first view of the fabled Upland Liberation Front.

The ULF: terror of the jungle. Mortal enemy of the militia. Ruthless, unstoppable warriors who had driven the Confederacy of Independent Systems off this planet.

They were barely alive.

Their march was a ragged column of walking wounded, tracking each other through the jungle by splashes of blood and rich stink of infection. I would learn, later, during the days of hellish march, that this latest operation had been a series of raids on jungle prospector outposts; they were out here not to kill Balawai, but to capture medpacs, food, clothing, weapons, ammunition—supplies that our Republic cannot or will not provide for them.

They were heading for their base in the mountains, where they had gathered nearly all that was left of the Korun people: all their elders and their invalids, their children, and what was left of their herds. Living in confined, crowded space was unnatural for Korunnai. They had no experience with such conditions, and it swiftly took its toll. Diseases unknown in the civilized galaxy ravaged their numbers: in the months since Depa's arrival, dysentery and pneumonia had killed more Korunnai than had the militia's gunships.

These gunships circled like vultures over the jungle. The trees constantly hummed with the sounds of heavy repulsorlifts and turbofans. The hums rose to roars and fell to insectile buzzing, mingled to swarms and split to individuals that curved through the invisible sky. Now and again flame poured into the jungle from above, bringing harsh orange light to the gloom under the canopy, casting black shadows among the green.

I don't think they were actually expecting to hit anyone.

They harrassed us constantly, often firing down at random through the jungle canopy, or sweeping overhead to set vast swathes afire with their Sunfire flame projectors. To return fire would only fix our position for their gunners, and so all we could do was scurry along below the canopy and hope that we would not be seen.

The guerrillas barely seemed to notice. They slogged along—those who could walk—with heads down, as though they had already accepted that sooner or later one of those carpets of flame would fall upon them all. Korun to the bone, they never uttered a word of complaint, and nearly all could draw strength from the Force—from *pelekotan*—to keep them on their feet.

Those who could not walk were bundled like baggage upon the backs of their grassers. Most of the animals now bore nothing but wounded; the supplies and equipment looted from the Balawai rode crude but sturdy travois that the grassers dragged behind them.

On this march, too, the ULF would endure a new tactic from the militia: they had begun night raids. They didn't appear to have any hope of actually catching us—that wasn't the point. Instead, the gunships flew high overhead and fired laser cannons down at random. Just harassment. To spoil our rest. Keeping us awake and jumpy.

Wounded men and women need sleep to heal; none of them would get it. Every dawn, a few more would lie still and cold on their bedrolls when the rest of us arose. Every day a few more would stumble, blind with exhaustion, and stagger away from the line of march to lose themselves among the trees.

Usually permanently.

There are many large predators on Haruun Kal: half a dozen distinct species of vine cats, two smaller variants of akk dogs as well as the giant savage akk wolves, and many opportunistic scavengers such as the jacuna, a flightless avian creature that travels in bands of up to several dozen monkey-lizard-sized birds—which are equally adept at climbing, springing from branch to branch, or running on flat ground, and are not at all picky about whether what they eat is actually dead. And most of the large predators of Haruun Kal are intelligent enough to remember the good feeding to be had in the wake of a column of wounded Korunnai. Which is why stragglers rarely caught up with us again.

We were, as Nick would say, a walking all-you-can-eat buffet line.

This is also why the ULF didn't have to post much of a guard on the prisoners.

There were twenty-eight, all told: two dozen jungle prospectors and the four surviving children. The jups were left to stagger along supporting each other as best they could, dragging those who could not walk on smaller versions of the travois hauled by the grassers.

They were watched by only a pair of Vastor's Akk Guards and six of their fierce akk dogs; as Vastor led Mace past, he explained that the guards and dogs were there only to make sure the Balawai did not steal weapons or supplies from wounded Korunnai, or otherwise attack their captors. The guards didn't need blasters; any prisoner who wished to escape into the jungle was welcome to.

That is, after all, what was going to happen to them anyway: stripped of everything but their clothing and boots, they would be turned loose in the jungle, left to make their way to whatever safety they might be able to find.

Tan pel'trokal. Jungle justice.

Mace leaned alongside the grasser's neck, to speak softly for Vastor's ears alone. "How do you know they won't double back along the line of march? Some of your wounded are barely walking. These Balawai might think it worth the risk to steal weapons or supplies."

Vastor gave a grin like a mouthful of needles. *Can you not feel them? They are* in *the jungle, not of the jungle. They cannot surprise us.*

"Then why are they still here?"

It's light, Vastor rumbled, with a wave of the wrist at the green-lit leaves above. *The day belongs to the gunships. We give prisoners* tan pel'trokal *after sunset.*

"In the dark," Mace murmured.

Yes. The night belongs to us.

Mace remembered the recording of Depa's whisper: . . . *I use the night, and the night uses me* . . . It gave his chest a heavy ache. His breath came hard and slow.

Nick was down with the prisoners, leading by the reins a mangy, underfed grasser. This grasser had another dual-saddle setup like the one that had been blown to bits on Nick's grasser back in the notch pass; each saddle was big enough to hold two children. Urno and Nykl rode in the upper, forward-facing saddle, gripping the heavy pelt of the grasser's ruff, peering out from below its ears. Keela and Pell rode in the lower saddle, facing the rear and clinging to each other in mute despair.

Seeing those four children reminded the Jedi Master of the child who was not there, and he had to look away from Kar Vastor. In his head he saw the *lor pelek* holding the corpse of a boy. He saw the gleam of the shield through the wet streaked sheen of Terrel's blood.

He could not meet Vastor's eyes without hating him.

"And the children, too?" The words seemed to swell up Mace's throat and push themselves out at the other man. "You give them to the jungle?"

It is our way. Vastor's growl softened with understanding. *You are thinking of the boy. The one in the bunker.*

Mace still could not meet his eyes. "He was captured. Disarmed."

He was a murderer, not a soldier. He attacked the helpless.

"So did you."

Yes. And if I am taken by the enemy, I will get worse than I gave. Do you think the Balawai will offer me a clean, quick death?

"We're not talking about them," Mace said. "We're talking about you."

Vastor only shrugged.

Nick caught sight of them and gave a sardonic wave. "I'm not really a baby-sitter," he called. "I just play one on the HoloNet."

His tone was cheerful, but on his face the Jedi Master could read the clear knowledge of what would happen to these children at sunset. Mace's own face hurt; he touched his forehead and discovered there a scowl. "What's he doing here?"

Vastor stared past Nick, as though to look upon him would be a compliment the young Korun did not deserve. *He cannot be trusted with real work.*

"Because he left me behind to save his friends? Chalk and Besh are veteran fighters. Aren't they worth the effort?"

They are expendable. As is he.

"Not to me," Mace told him. "No one is."

The *lor pelek* seemed to consider this for a long time as he walked on, leading Mace's grasser. *I do not know why Depa wanted you here,* he said at length. *But I do not have to know. She desires your presence; that is enough. Because you are important to her, you are important to our war. Much more important than a bad soldier like Nick Rostu.*

"He's hardly a bad soldier—"

He is weak. Cowardly. Afraid of sacrifice.

"Risking his mission—his life—for his friends might make Nick a bad soldier," Mace said, "but it makes him a good man." And because he somehow could not resist, he added: "Better than *you.*"

Vastor looked up at the Jedi Master with jungle-filled eyes. *Better at what?*

FROM THE PRIVATE JOURNALS OF MACE WINDU

I don't see Vastor as evil. Not as a truly bad man. Yes, he radiates darkness—but so do all the Korunnai. And the Balawai. His is the darkness of the jungle, not the darkness of the Sith. He does not live for power, to cause pain and dominate all he surveys. He simply *lives*. Fiercely. Naturally. Stripped of the restraints of civilization.

He is less a man than he is an avatar of the jungle itself. Dark power flows into him and out again but it does not seem to touch him. He has a savage purity that I might envy, were I not a Jedi and sworn to the light.

Black is the presence of every color.

He doesn't make the darkness, he only uses it. His inner darkness is a reflection of the darkness of his world; and it darkens the world around him in turn. Internal and external darkness create each other, just as do internal and external light: that is the underlying unity of the Force.

As Depa might say, he didn't start this war. He's just trying to win it.

And that was it, right there: my Jedi instincts had made a connection below the threshold of my consciousness. Vastor. The jungle. The akk dogs, and the humans who had been made into Vastor's pack. Depa. Darkness so deep it was like being blind. Nick's words: *The jungle doesn't promise. It exists. Not because the jungle kills you. Because it is what it is.*

The war itself.

Only later, when I would spend a full day riding alongside Depa's howdah on the dorsal shell of her immense ankkox, when I would have to lean close to the gauzy curtains to catch her half-whispered words, would I understand where my instincts were leading me.

There are times when her voice is strong and clear, and her arguments lucid, and if I close my eyes and ignore the rocking of the ankkox's gait, the insect stings and rich floral rot of the jungle, I can imagine us chatting over a couple of cups of rek tea in my meditation chamber at the Jedi Temple.

In those times, she makes a terrifying sense.

"You still think like a judicial," she told me once. "That's your fundamental error. You still think in terms of *enforcing the law*. Upholding the *rules*. You were a great peace officer, Mace, but you're a terrible general. That's what cost so many lives at Geonosis: we went in like judicials. Trying to rescue hostages without loss of life. Trying to *keep the peace*. The Geonosians already *knew* we were at war—so only a few of us survived . . ."

"And if I thought like a general, what should I have done?" I asked her. "Let Obi-Wan and Anakin die?"

"A general," murmured the shadow through the curtains, "would have dropped a baradium bomb on that arena."

"Depa, you can't be serious," I began, but she had stopped listening to me.

"Win the war," she went on. "Win at the cost of two Jedi, one Senator, and a few thousand of the enemy."

"At the cost of everything that makes Jedi what we are."

"Instead, a hundred and more Jedi died, and you have a galaxy at war. Millions will die, and millions more will end up like that boy Kar killed: twisted, angry, and evil. Gather a million corpses, and tell them your ethics outweighed their lives . . ."

To this I have no easy answer, even now.

But as Yoda says: *There are questions for which we can never have answers. We can only be answers.*

That is what I must try to be, for I know, now, what it means to be a keeper of the peace in the Galaxy of War.

That is: it means nothing at all.

There is no peace. What we thought was the Great Peace of the Republic was only a dream from which our galaxy has now awakened. I doubt we'll ever fall back into any dream like that again.

In the Galaxy of War, no one sleeps that well.

This understanding came later; at the time, as I sat in the grasser's saddle and looked down at Kar Vastor, the prisoners behind us and Depa's ankkox still unseen ahead, I had only a notion—a hunch—a mass of unprocessed feelings and unsorted ideas.

An instinct.

But somehow my instincts seemed to be working again . . . which is why I chose to send Vastor on without me. As I asked Depa a thousand times, when she was my Padawan—

Is the true lesson what the teacher teaches, or what the student learns?

A few paces beyond where the Balawai prisoners stumbled along the jungle floor, Mace Windu reached past the grasser's nose and took its reins in one hand. "This is far enough. Leave me here."

Vastor stopped, looking back over his massive shoulder. *Depa awaits.*

"She's waited for weeks. She'll wait a few hours more." For the first time since the battle at the notch pass, Mace felt calm. Sure. On solid ground. "Go on without me. I will attend her when I choose."

You are sent for. She is not to be defied. Vastor turned and tugged on the reins, but Mace had them in his fist, and they might as well have been bolted to a cliff.

Vastor's eyes flickered with distant danger: lightning from a storm below the horizon. *You will regret this.*

"I am a Jedi Master, and a Senior Member of the Jedi Council," Mace said patiently. "I am a general of the Grand Army of the Republic. I am not to be *sent for.* If she wants to see me, she will find me at the steamcrawler track before dusk."

The lightning in the *lor pelek*'s eyes came closer. *I have said I will deliver you.*

Mace matched his stare exactly. "Funny: that's almost what Nick said. He didn't have much luck with it either."

My orders—

"Are your problem." Mace let the reins fall and spread his open hands. He went perfectly still, perfectly relaxed, perfectly calm, except for the sizzle of the Force that arced like static electricity from the two lightsaber handgrips to his empty palms. "Unless you choose to make them *our* problem. You can do that right now, if you like."

Vastor let the reins drop as well. He stepped away from the grasser and turned to face the Jedi Master squarely. His immense shoulders bulged, and muscles across his chest went rigid in acid-etched definition. The air shimmered like a mirage around him: anger beat against Mace like a hot wind in the Force. *You will come with me.*

"No."

Dark power clutched at Mace's will. *You will come with me.*

Slowly, reluctantly, Mace slid himself out of the saddle and slipped to the ground. He took two steps toward Vastor.

And stopped.

"I no longer enjoy your company," the Jedi Master said. "Go now. Do not return to me without Depa."

Vastor's eyes widened. His mouth worked soundlessly.

"You and I should not be alone together. There may be a fight."

Tendons stood out in Vastor's neck, winching his head downward and pulling his lips away from his sharp-filed teeth. *I do not wish to fight you, dôshalo.* Despite the rage smoking off him in the Force, his voice was soft. *Depa will be angry to find you dead.*

"Then you'd best be on your way," Mace replied reasonably. "Don't want to make Depa angry, do you?"

Apparently he didn't: Vastor's growl thinned to a snarl of frustration. *And what should I tell her you are doing here?*

"Nothing that I can be bothered to explain to you." Mace turned back to his grasser and took its reins once more. "Any questions Depa might have, she should ask me herself."

Though pretending to busy himself with adjusting the grasser's tack, Mace paid absolute attention to Vastor's white-hot stare burning its way into his shoulder blades. He stayed loose and balanced, ready to spring in any direction should the *lor pelek* lunge for his back.

Instead, he only heard a snarl and a growl and several short, deep yips: Vastor had said something to one of the Akk Guards who watched the prisoners. With one last glare that Mace could feel as though a lens focused sunlight on his skin, Vastor whirled away and plunged into the jungle, loping up the line of march.

Mace watched him go, bleak satisfaction on his face. He thought: *So much for being the welcome guest.*

The Akk Guard whom Vastor had spoken to gave Mace a dire look, echoed by the three akk dogs nearby. Mace ignored them all, and a few seconds later the Akk Guard stomped off to find his partner and the other akks. Mace caught Nick Rostu's eye and beckoned. Nick turned the children's grasser over to one of the Balawai and trotted over to the Jedi Master, keeping one eye turned toward the departing Akk Guard. "Shee. Those guys give me the creeps. Looked a little tense there, Master Windu. What did the big guy say to you?"

"Here, hold him." Mace handed the grasser's reins to Nick. "How much did you hear?"

"Some of what *you* said. Got some guts, you do." Nick stretched up to scratch the grasser on the side of its neck. "But Vastor—maybe you've noticed? You can only understand him when he's talking directly to you. When he's talking to somebody else, he always sounds like he's growling or whistling or making some other kind of animal noises and stuff."

"Yes, I had noticed something like that," Mace said slowly, nodding. "But I'd thought it was just me. Back at the outpost . . . things were confusing."

"That's why it's kind of like you're talking to yourself, you get it? In *my* head, he talks like a Pelek Baw curb-monkey. So what did he say to you?"

"He was," Mace said dryly, "trying to impress me with his sense of duty."

"So: what now? You didn't dust off the most dangerous man in the Korunnal Highland just to come and have a chat with the president of Rostu Jungle Nannies Inc. You have a move to make."

Mace nodded. "*We* have a move to make. Mount up. You're going to lead these prisoners to the steamcrawler track so that the militia can find them and pick them up."

Nick's mouth dropped open. "We . . . *me?* Why would I want to do something like *that?*"

"Because I gave them the word of a Jedi Master that if they surrendered I would keep them from harm. I will not be made a liar."

"What's your word got to do with *me?*"

"Nothing at all," Mace said. "I'm sure you *enjoy* thinking about Keela being disemboweled by a vine cat. When you think of Pell, do you see her starving to death in a gripvine nest or having her eyes pecked out by jacunas?"

Nick looked sick. "Hey, easy with that tusker poop, huh?"

"You think the boys will be gored by tuskers, or shredded by brassvines? Maybe they'll get lucky and fall into a death hollow. At least that is relatively swift, as their lungs are eaten by caustic fumes, and their own tears scald their faces like acid . . ."

The young Korun turned away. "You have any idea what Kar and Depa will *do* to me?"

"You've been over the ground in this region. If I lead them myself, I'll end up losing us all in the jungle. Mount up. Right now."

Nick snorted. "Shee, still pretty free with the orders, aren't we? What if I just don't wanna? What if I *do* like thinking about all that stuff? What if I *want* those people dead? What then?"

Mace went still. He stared off into the jungle, his eyes filled with its darkness. "Then I will beat you into unconsciousness," he said quietly, "and ask someone else."

He looked at Nick.

Nick swallowed.

Mace said, "I won't tell you again."

Nick mounted up.

"Kar Vastor," the Jedi Master said, looking again into the jungle, this time up the line of march where the *lor pelek* had vanished, "is not the most dangerous man on the Korunnal Highland."

Nick shook his head. "You only say that because you don't really know him."

"I say that," Mace Windu replied, "because he doesn't know *me.*"

10

A JEDI'S WORD

The prisoners limped along in ragged knots, holding each other up and nervously eyeing the pacing akk dogs. Mace forced his way through the tangled undergrowth toward them, Nick close behind on the grasser.

"Am I missing something here?" Nick leaned over to speak softly, one arm bent across the back of the grasser's thick neck. "Last night these ruskakks were trying to carve off a hunk of roast Windu."

"This *tan pel 'trokal.*" Mace's voice was equally low and far more grim. "You approve of it?"

"Sure." Nick glanced at the grasser that the children rode, and swiftly looked away. "Well, in principle, anyway . . ." His vivid eyes went narrow and cynical. "Wasn't too long ago Kar used to just kill them all. Can't afford to feed 'em. What else should we do? Givin' them the justice was Depa's call."

"Oh?"

"Makes sense, don't it? If the Balawai think we'll kill 'em anyway, why should they surrender? Every one of them'd fight to the death. That gets expensive, y'know? So we give 'em to the jungle. At least they got a chance."

"How many survive?"

"Some."

"Half? A quarter? One in a hundred?"

"How should I know?" Nick shrugged. "Does it make a differ-ence?"

Mace Windu said, "Not to me."

Nick closed his eyes and leaned his head against the grasser's ear as though exhausted, or in pain. "You've gone bats, haven't you," he said. "You're completely insane."

Mace stopped. A twitch of frown drew a vertical crease between his eyebrows. "No. Just the opposite, in fact."

"What's *that* supposed to mean?"

But Mace was already walking away.

Nick muttered a curse on all fraggin' Jedi who used nikkle nuts for brains, then goaded the grasser along after him.

When the prisoners saw them coming, a man's voice said, "It's the Jedi . . . No, the other one. The *real* Jedi." Mace thought this voice might belong to the man he'd spoken to in the steamcrawler this morning: the gray-faced one with a chest wound and a missing hand, who would not believe in a Jedi's word.

Mace chose not to ask what he meant by *the real Jedi*.

Some few of the prisoners clustered toward him, straightening their clothing and forcing their faces into expressions of hope; most just stopped where they were, swaying with exhaustion or stumbling against the great gray trees. Some grabbed handfuls of vines to lower themselves slowly to the ground.

A few tens of meters downslope, the two Akk Guards stared up at Mace with undisguised hostility. Two of the six akk dogs on prisoner duty slouched sullenly nearby.

The children's grasser was led by a man whom Mace recognized as Urno and Nykl's father. The only clean spots on his dirt- and blood-smeared face were the twin tracks from his eyes to his chin, rinsed white by tears. He dropped the reins and threw himself on the ground at Mace's feet. "Please—please, Your Honor—Your Highness—" he sobbed, facedown into the jungle floor, "please don't let them kill my boys. Do what you want with me—I deserve it, I know, I'm sorry for what I done, but my boys . . . it's not their fault, they didn't do nothing—please, I don't—I never met a Jedi before—I don't even know what I should call you—"

"Stand up," Mace said sternly. "Jedi are not to be knelt to. We are not your masters, but your servants. Stand up."

Slowly, the astonished man pulled himself to his feet. The back of his hand smeared a streak of mud below his nose. "Okay," he said. "All right. What's coming to me—I can take it like a man . . . but my boys—"

"What's coming to you is your life, and possibly your freedom as well."

The man blinked, uncomprehending. "Your Honor—?"

"Call me Master Windu." Mace swept past him and opened his arms, beckoning to all the prisoners. "Gather 'round. I'll need you all to stick closer together. There will not be enough of us to look after stragglers."

"Sir?" Keela said as the children's grasser caught up. She had twisted sideways in the lower saddle to stare at Mace with damp, bloodshot eyes. "Sir, what are they going to do with us? Where's Mom? Are you gonna let them put us out in the jungle?"

Mace met her tear-blurred gaze squarely. "No. I'm going to send you back to the city. You're going home. All of you."

Nick muttered, "Don't make promises you can't keep."

"I never do."

"You don't think Kar and those Akk Guards down there are gonna have something to say about it?"

"I'm aware of their opinion already. I have my own."

"The *tan pel'trokal*—"

"Means nothing to me," Mace said. "I don't care about jungle justice. I care about Jedi justice. And I will see it done."

"Jedi justice, my weeping saddle sores. You still don't get it, do you? Jedi *anything* doesn't mean *squat* out here—"

"I understand the rules now. You read them to me yourself; then Kar Vastor taught me what they mean. Now I can start to play."

"That's just *it*," Nick insisted. "You're in the *jungle*, now. There *are* no rules."

"Of course there are. Don't be an idiot."

Nick blinked. "You're kidding, right? You're making a joke."

"Stay here and watch," Mace told him, working his way down toward the guards. "Then tell me what you think of my sense of humor."

The same Akk Guard whom Mace had kicked now moved to block the Jedi Master's path. The swellings Vastor's fist had left on the man's face had gone as purple-black as the thickening clouds overhead. Muscle bunched like blocks of duracrete under the skin of his bare chest. "Where going, Windu?"

Mace had to tilt his head back to meet the Korun's stare. "I don't know your name."

"You can call me—"

"I didn't ask your name," Mace cut him off. "I just don't know it. I don't need to. You should get out of my way."

The guard's eyes looked scalded, and more than slightly crazed. "Out of *your* way, little Jedi?"

"I am taking the prisoners to the steamcrawler track." Mace nodded in that general direction. "I can go past you, or I can go over you. You pick."

"*Over* me? Can fly, you?" The vibroshields strapped to his forearms snarled to life. He raised them to either side of Mace's face. "Draw your toy weapon, little Jedi. Go ahead. Draw."

"My lightsaber? Why should I?" Mace raised a finger to tap his own forehead. "This is the only weapon I need."

"Yeah?" A sneer: "What, *think* me to death, you gonna?"

"You misunderstand." By way of explanation, he splattered the Korun's nose with a sharp head-butt.

The Korun staggered backward. Mace moved with him in perfect synchronization as though they were dancing, hands gripping the man's massive biceps. When the Korun started to recover his balance, his head naturally coming forward once more, Mace yanked on his arms, pulling him into another head-butt that brought Mace's forehead and the point of the Korun's chin together with a crack as sharp as a breaking rock.

Mace stepped back to let the semiconscious man collapse. The other guard snarled and lunged at Mace's back, only to find himself facing the business end of a sizzling purple lightsaber.

"He's alive," Mace said calmly. "So are you. For now. The next one of you pathetic nerfs who raises a hand to me will die for it. Do you understand?"

The Korun only stared at him with murder on his face.

"*Answer* me!" Mace roared. With a convulsive snarl, he threw his lightsaber on the ground at the Korun's feet. Faster than the eye could follow, his hand flashed out, his thumb hooking the Korun's cheek while his fingers dug in behind the hinge of the man's jaw. He yanked the Korun's face to within a centimeter of his own, and there was open raging madness in his eyes. *"DO YOU UNDERSTAND ME?"*

The Korun's mouth worked in speechless shock. Mace howled into his face, *"YOU WANT TO DIE? YOU WANT TO DIE RIGHT NOW? MAKE A MOVE! DO IT! DO IT AND DIE!"*

The astonished Korun could only blink and mumble and try to shake his head. Mace released the man's face with a contemptuous shove that sent the guard stumbling backward. Mace opened his empty hand, and his lightsaber flipped up from the ground and smacked into his palm. He tucked it back into the holster inside his vest.

"Never get in my way." His voice was again icily calm. "Ever."

He turned his eye to the pair of akk dogs, who were up and growling like looming thunderheads, spines bristling across their armored shoulders.

Mace stared at them.

First one, then the other, lowered its head and flattened those spines. Tails tucked low, the akk dogs backed away.

Mace looked upslope, where Nick stood gaping in blank wonder. The captives huddled even closer together, none daring to make eye contact. Mace beckoned.

By the time Nick and the grasser that carried the children arrived, the downed Akk Guard was stirring. But when he opened his eyes to find Mace still standing over him, he decided to stay on the ground.

"Okay, I admit it," Nick said as they passed by the guards and the dogs. "That *was* pretty funny. And a little scary: I've never seen you angry before."

"You still haven't," Mace said softly. "Remember those rules of the jungle I was talking about? You just saw one in action."

"What rule was that?"

"When the big dog's walking," said Jedi Master Mace Windu, "little dogs step aside."

Icy rain splashed down through the canopy, and thunder rolled like turbojets of gunships passing overhead. Though the day had reached only midafternoon, the storm wrapped the jungle in late-twilight gloom. Mace walked a few paces behind Nick's bedraggled grasser. Raindrops tapped his skull, and a chilly rivulet twisted along his spine. In places where the leaf mold gave way to bare ground, mud sucked at his boots with every step. Sometimes he sank in deeply enough that the mud leaked over his boot tops. Only by drawing strength from the Force could he keep moving.

He could not imagine what the march must be like for the wounded prisoners.

Every once in a while, a hunk or two of the hail that the thunderhead above spat down would bounce all the way through the layers of leaf and branch and vine and give someone a knock. By the time they reached ground level, most of these hailstones had melted down to about half the size of Mace's fist: too small to be dangerous, though still large enough to raise stinging welts on his head. The Balawai prisoners gathered ones that fell nearby, sucking on them to melt them in their mouths. With a bit of wiping, these hailstones made the cleanest source of water they were likely to find—they carried only the faintest sulfurous traces of volcanic smoke and gases.

In the Force, Mace felt the hot fierce sting of an approaching akk dog; a moment later he felt a Force-nudge on his right shoulder blade. He reached up to tug on Nick's ankle. "Keep them going," he said, raising his voice over the hiss of the rain. "I'll be right back."

A few steps off their line of march, a man's shadow began to take shape through the rain-blurred gloom. Mace walked toward it, weaving between trees and moving vines aside with a gesture, to find the bruised Akk Guard heading for him carrying one of the Balawai. Behind the guard, the great akk Mace had felt made a gray silhouette.

"Fell out, this one. Think he's fevered, me." The guard set the Balawai on his feet. It was the wounded man with the missing hand. "Better keep someone with him, you."

Mace nodded as he looped the man's good arm over his shoulders. "Thank you. I'll look after him." The Balawai gazed at him without recognition.

The guard frowned down at them. "Gonna kill you for this, Kar is. Know that, you?"

"I appreciate your concern."

"No concern. Just tellin'. That's all."

"Thank you."

The guard frowned a moment longer, then gave an elaborate shrug before he turned away and faded once more into the gloom.

Mace thoughtfully watched him go. The two Akk Guards hadn't been hard to co-opt; while Nick wrangled the Balawai into something resembling marching order, Mace had worked his way back upslope to where one stood watching him, while the one he'd knocked down still sat on the ground massaging his broken nose.

Mace squatted beside him. "How's your face?" he'd asked gravely.

The guard's voice was half muffled by his hands. "Why care, you?"

"It's no dishonor to lose to a Jedi," Mace had said. "Here, let me see."

When the astonished Akk Guard took his hands away from his face, Mace put his hands to either side of the man's nose and popped the bones straight with one brisk twisting squeeze. The sudden sharp pain made the Korun gasp, but it was over so quickly he didn't even have time to yelp.

After that he could only blink in wonder. "Hey—hey, feels *better*, that. How'd you—"

"Sorry I lost my temper," Mace said, standing to include the other Akk Guard. "But I can't back down from a challenge. You understand."

The two Korunnai exchanged a glance, and they both nodded reluctantly, as Mace had known they would: Vastor had trained them like dogs, and like dogs their only answer to the pat on the head that followed the kick was to wag their tails and hope they weren't in trouble anymore. "I think you're both solid," Mace went on. "Strong fighters. That's why I went at you so hard: respect. You're too dangerous for me to play games with."

The Korun with the broken nose had said in a tone of generous concession, "Got a stone-sweet head-butt, you." He chuckled, crossing his eyes to look at the bloodied swelling between them. "Best I ever ate."

Now the other Akk Guard could not resist chiming in. "And that grab on my face—was a Jedi thing, that? Never seen it before, me. Maybe teach me, you?"

Mace had no more time for pleasantries. "Listen: I know taking the prisoners will cause trouble with Kar. And I know you'll be in trouble for letting them go with me. Why don't you stay with us? Bring your dogs. Keep the Balawai in line, and don't let any of them get lost. It's not like Kar won't know where we're going. I told him myself. And if you're along, he won't have any trouble finding us: you can feel each other in *pelekotan*. Right?"

Again they had exchanged glances, and again they had nodded.

"If Kar wants these prisoners, he can take them from me himself. How can he blame you for losing if *he's* afraid to step up?"

To a dark-soaked Korun, this was undeniable logic.

"Right," the bruised guard said happily. "Right. Thinks you're a tumblepup in vine cat skin, him? Let *him* yank your tail. Will find out quick enough, I think."

And so Mace Windu had acquired a pair of Korun shepherds for his flock of Balawai.

Mace had cemented Nick's assistance with a similar technique. As they were about to turn aside from the ULF column, Mace had stood thoughtfully alongside Nick's grasser. "Nick," he'd begun, "I'm going to need an aide."

The young Korun had squinted suspiciously down from the saddle. "An aide? What for?"

"Like you said when you picked me up in Pelek Baw: I'm not from around here. I need someone who can look after me, give me advice, that kind of thing—"

"You want advice? Flush the fraggin' Balawai and shag your Jedi butt back up the column. Make some kissy-face with Kar and Depa before they chop you into sausage. Any other advice you want, feel free to ask."

"That's what I'm doing."

"Huh?"

"I need someone who knows his way around out here. Someone I can trust."

Nick snorted. "Good fraggin' luck. I wouldn't trust *anyone* out here—"

"I don't," Mace told him. "Except you."

"Me?" Nick shook his head. "You really *have* gone bats. Haven't you heard? I'm the least trustworthy guy in the ULF. I'm the weak coward, right? I'm the useless butter-brain who couldn't even get you out here from Pelek Baw without screwing it up—and now I'm screwing up *again* by playing along with this whole nikkle-nut *Free-the-Balawai* parade—"

"You're the *only* trustworthy man I've met on Haruun Kal," Mace had said solidly. "You're the only man I can trust to do the right thing."

"Hoo-fraggin'-ray. Look where it's gotten me."

"It's gotten you," Mace said, "a chance to join the personal staff of a general of the Grand Army of the Republic."

"Yeah?" Nick began to look interested. "What's it pay?"

"Nothing," Mace admitted, and Nick's face fell, but the Jedi Master went on, "Though when I leave this planet, I'll be taking my staff with me."

Nick's eyes recovered a little spark.

"With a brevet rank of, let's say, major? And once we get to Coruscant, I'll be needing staff instructors to train officers in guerrilla tactics. A few months as an urban- and jungle-warfare consultant affiliated with the Jedi Temple should make you pretty attractive to all those mercenary captains out there. You might even get your own company. Isn't that what you want? Or am I confusing you with some *other* Korun whose fondest dream is to travel the galaxy as a mercenary?"

"You bet your sweet—I mean, No, *sir*. General. Major Rostu at the general's service. Sir. Uh—is there any kind of swearing-in, or anything?"

"I hadn't really thought about it," Mace admitted. "I've never inducted anyone into the Grand Army of the Republic before."

"I feel like I should raise my right hand or something."

Mace nodded thoughtfully. "Put your left hand over your heart, raise your right and stand at attention."

Nick did so. "This is—uh, y'know, I feel kind of funny about this—"

"It is not to be undertaken lightly. The Force stands witness to such oaths."

"Sure enough." Nick swallowed. "Okay, I'm ready."

"Do you solemnly swear to serve the Republic in thought, in word, and in deed; to defend its citizens, resist its enemies, and champion its justice with the whole of your heart, your strength, and your mind; to forswear all other allegiances; to obey all lawful orders of your superior officers; to uphold the highest ideals of the Republic, and at all times to conduct yourself to the credit of the Republic as its commissioned officer, by witness of, aid from, and faith in the Force?"

Didn't sound bad at all, Mace thought. *I should probably write that down.*

Nick blinked silently. His eyes looked glassy, and he licked his lips.

Mace leaned toward him. "Say *I do*, Nick."

"I—I guess I do," he said in a tone of wondering discovery, as though he had just learned something astonishing about himself. "I mean: yes. I do."

"Come to attention, and salute."

Nick had snapped to in very creditable fashion, though he still looked a bit dazed. "Hey—hey, I *feel* something. In the *Force*—" His daze was replaced by open astonishment. "It's *you.*"

"A soldier at attention does not speak, except to answer direct questions. Is this understood?"

"Yes, sir."

"What you feel is our new relationship: it has a resonance in the Force not unlike the bond of an akk to its human."

"So I'm your *dog*, now?"

"Nick."

"Right, right, shut up. I know. Uh—sir."

"At ease, Major," Mace had said as he finally returned the young Korun's salute. "Move them out."

Now as the departing Akk Guard disappeared into the rain, Mace carried the wounded Balawai back to the group of exhausted prisoners. He couldn't find anyone among them who even *looked* strong enough to support this man's weight over the jumbled tree roots and through the calf-deep mud, so he just shrugged and joined the march, holding the Balawai's arm around his neck.

Heads down, shoulders hunched against the icy downpour, they slogged on.

They broke out of the trees on a small promontory that ended in a sheer cliff. Jungle swarmed its base a hundred meters below. They had been sidestepping down a long switchback, heading for the canyon floor. Half a klick behind, a ribbon of waterfall steamed down a thousand-meter drop; the far canyon wall was a riot of greens and purples and bright shining red that eclipsed half the sky. The thunderstorm swept to their rear as Mace and Nick broke out from the trees, and in the near distance through the canyon's mouth ahead, only a klick away—glowing now with afternoon sun blazing red-slanted from a crystal sky—lay the broad bare-dirt curve of the steamcrawler track.

Mace and Nick were both on foot. The feverish Balawai was tied into the grasser's saddle.

"There it is," Nick said. His voice was low and grim. "Pretty, ain't it?"

"Yes. Pretty." Mace stepped around the grasser. "Pity we didn't make it."

Any Force-sensitive could have felt the menace that lay across their path; to Mace, it felt like an arc of forest fire ripping through the trees. He couldn't feel exactly what was down there, but he knew it was Vastor: whatever forces he had brought after them now sealed the mouth of the canyon.

Nick nodded. He unslung his rifle, checked the clip, and cocked it. "Just couldn't move fast enough." He glanced back to where the Balawai were now struggling out to the fringe of the undergrowth. He shook his head. "Only needed an hour. That's all. One more hour, we woulda been clear."

"What's going on?" The boys' father joined them near the rim of the cliff. "Is that the track? Why have we *stopped?*"

The Akk Guard with the bruised face came out of the trees; the six dogs and the other guard were fanned out behind the prisoners. He nodded toward the thick arc of danger that all but the grassers and the Balawai could feel ahead. "Hard luck, huh? Told you Kar would come, me."

"Yes." Mace folded his arms. "It was too much to hope that he might let us go." He turned to the Akk Guard. "You can go to him, if you like."

"Maybe will, us." The Korun had recovered some of his former swagger. His chest swelled out, and he looked down at Mace with an air of contempt that might have been convincing, if he hadn't been so careful to keep himself just out of arm's reach. "Not going nowhere, you, huh?"

Mace glanced at Nick; Nick shrugged dolefully. Mace said, "It seems not."

Knots of exhausted Balawai untied themselves and frayed to pieces to let the departing Akk Guard through. He joined the other, and along with the dogs they faded into the trees beyond the reach of the afternoon sun.

Nick fingered his rifle. "Think they'll really go down there to Kar?"

"Not at all," Mace said crisply. "They'll move up the switchback to cut off our retreat."

"Don't much like the sound of that. What's *our* move?"

"You tell me, Major."

Nick blinked. "You're kidding."

"Not at all. Given our victory conditions—saving as many of these people's lives as possible—what should we do?"

"I can't believe you're asking *me.*"

"What I'm asking you," Mace said, "is not what we're going to do, but what we *should* do. Let me put it another way: what does *Kar* think we'll do?"

"Well . . ." Nick looked back up the trail, then forward down toward the mouth of the canyon and the steamcrawler track. "We should split up. If we all stay together, we all get caught either by whatever Kar's got below, or the guards and the ULF behind us. If the prisoners scatter, some might slip through while Kar's rounding up the rest."

"Exactly." Mace pointed at the boys' father. "You. Get the others out of the trees. I want all of you on this rock. On your knees, with your hands behind your heads."

The Balawai gaped. "Are you *crazy?*"

"Y'know," Nick said, sighing, "I ask him that all the time. Somehow I never get a straight answer."

Mace folded his arms across his chest. "All those who don't want to do what I say are welcome to take their chances with the jungle and the ULF."

The man turned away, shaking his head.

"What *are* we gonna do?" Nick asked.

"Something else."

"Y'know, if you hadn't told Kar about going to the steamcrawler track, he wouldn't be down there right now."

"Yes: he would have overtaken us in the jungle, and we wouldn't have had a chance."

"Wait—wait, I *get* it—" Understanding dawned on Nick's face.

Mace nodded. "Back under the trees, the prisoners would have scattered. Some might have escaped as you say. He's *expecting* us to scatter, just as you did. From his point of view, it's the obvious move: let some die to save the rest. That's why I expected Kar to try this, instead: find a place where he could trap everyone. Because Kar and I have this in common: with these people, it's all or nothing. He wants to give them all to the jungle. I want to send them all home." Muscle bunched along Mace's jaw. "I am not willing to purchase life with death, unless that death is my own."

Nick looked impressed. "Kar's not an easy man to lie to. He's so hooked into *pelekotan* that lying's a tricky business; I once saw him yank out a guy's *tongue*—"

Mace gave him a sidelong look. "Who lied? I told him that he and Depa would be able to find me at the steamcrawler track this afternoon. The lie is in what he assumed I meant, not in what I said."

"And you had me lead, because you figured he'd be able to guess what route I'd take—and you brought the Akk Guards along so that he'd be able to *track* us . . ."

Mace nodded.

"But *why?*"

"To get us all in a place just like this. Here, I'm sure he thinks he has everyone boxed."

"And he *does.*"

"So he's in no hurry to come and collect us. Now: what's the steamcrawler track good for, in view of our purpose? It's a broad open area, where any passing gunship will spot these people, and it's clear enough to use as a landing zone."

"Yeah . . ."

"So how much good does it do him to cut us off from an open area—" Mace reached inside his vest and pulled out the lightsabers. He tossed Depa's to Nick, who caught it reflexively. "—when all we need is a little time, and we can make one of our own?"

Nick stared down at the lightsaber in his hand. "It could work," he admitted. "And you want *me* to teach people warfare?"

Mace shrugged. "This isn't warfare, it's dejarik."

"Yeah, sure. When Kar shows up, you can be the one to clear the board. Go right ahead." He ducked his head gloomily. "He's gonna kill us both, y'know."

Mace's lightsaber found his palm, and a meter-long fountain of energy grew from its emitter. "That remains to be seen."

FROM THE PRIVATE JOURNALS OF MACE WINDU

It took only minutes to clear a landing zone. I had used the Force to pile some of the smaller trees, intending to kindle their damp wood with my blade to make a huge smoking bonfire, but I didn't have to; before we had even cleared the zone, three flights of gunships swarmed overhead. They didn't seem to have much difficulty understanding the situation: twenty-eight kneeling Balawai with fingers laced together behind their necks must have made matters clear enough.

"Looks like we pulled it off," Nick said, though he seemed to take little satisfaction from success. "We saved 'em. Wish they could return the favor."

We had barely begun cutting when we had both felt Vastor's forces drawing tight around us: a living noose. Nick had commented that my little deception hadn't fooled him for long.

I didn't answer. I had a feeling that in this particular game of dejarik, Kar was not my true opponent.

One of the gunships circled close overhead: offering itself as bait, to see if hidden guns would open fire when it came within range. And in the Force, I could feel the gunners inside it targeting Nick and me with laser cannons; only our proximity to the Balawai held them back.

As Nick would say: it was time to saddle up.

But before we left, I crouched beside the father of Urno and Nykl. "I want you to take a message to Colonel Geptun."

He looked dazed, and his words slurred with exhaustion. "Geptun? The security chief in Pelek Baw? How am I supposed to get in to see *him?*"

"He'll debrief you personally."

"He will?"

"Tell him the Jedi Master has handled his Jedi problem. Tell him that if he disarms his irregulars and withdraws the militia from the highland, this war is over. He has my word on it."

The man goggled at me as though antlers had suddenly sprouted from my forehead—and his astonishment was no greater than Nick's.

"One more thing: remind him that in less than a week I've solved a problem he couldn't manage in four months."

I rose, and stood over him so that my shadow fell across his face.

"Tell him that if he does not do as I suggest, *he'll* be the problem. And I will solve *him*."

I led Nick off into the jungle without waiting for a reply.

I did stop for a moment, though, and looked back through the trees, to where the boys' father held them in his arms as they waited for the descending gunship.

To where Keela held Pell, both of their heads lowered against the leaf-whirl thrown up by the ship's turbojets.

I don't expect to be forgiven. I don't even hope for it. I only hope that someday, these children may be able to look at a Jedi without hatred in their hearts.

That's the only reward I want.

Night was falling, and the sun slanted low through the canyon mouth. Navigating was easy: they loped through the thickening twilight, heading directly toward where the Force showed Mace maximum threat.

"So, you've handled the militia's Jedi problem, have you?" Nick muttered as they jogged under the trees. "That'll come as a surprise to Kar and Depa, I'm guessing."

"I'm not interested in Kar," Mace said. "I'm only interested in Depa. Where's the nearest subspace comm?"

Nick shrugged. "The Lorshan Pass caverns. That's our base—it's only a couple of days away, if we can ever lose the fraggin' gunships. That's where we're heading anyway. Why?"

"Less than a day after you get me subspace comm, Depa and I will be leaving this planet. I am willing to waste no more time. I need subspace to call for extraction."

"And me, right? You wouldn't leave your whole staff behind, would you?"

"You have seen what my word is worth."

"You think maybe you could, like, send me out *first?* Because, y'know, I don't want to be anywhere in this whole *sector* when Kar finds out she's leaving."

"Leave Vastor to me."

"And, uh, Master General, sir? Have you considered what you're gonna do if she doesn't want to go?"

"It's not up to her."

"She could have gotten out of here weeks ago, if she wanted. How are you gonna make her go?"

Mace said, "I have a hostage."

"A *what?* Are you allowed to do that? I mean, do Jedi *take* hostages?"

"There is one hostage a Jedi may lawfully take. I hope it won't come to that."

"Have you considered that she might not give a bucket of tusker poop about this hostage?"

"I have," Mace said. His voice was cold, but the thought made a hot knife twist in his belly.

Nick stopped in his tracks. He said weakly, "Have you considered that neither of us might *live* that long?"

He said this because of the twelve snarling akk dogs who had materialized around them as though the jungle had birthed them from the twilight.

Fury chuffed into the Force like the steam from their nostrils.

Moving out of the gloom-haunted trees came all six of the Akk

Guards. They wore their vibroshields pushed up over their biceps, freeing their hands for the assault rifles and grenade launchers they carried.

Weapons for hunters stalking human prey.

All six wore the human equivalent of the akks' snarls.

None of them spoke.

It was possible, at that moment, that none of them remembered how.

The Force hummed with anger, as though every one of them resonated on a single harmonic. Mace felt, then, the power of the Force-bonds that linked them—but not to each other. Not one of the Akk Guards had a link with a dog like the one Chalk had had with Galthra.

All eighteen of them, dogs and men alike, were Force-bonded not with each other, but each with one single other, as though they were spokes on a wheel of which he was the hub.

The anger Mace felt was Kar's.

He recognized its distinctive flavor.

He said, "I think Kar might be a little upset about those prisoners after all."

Nick stood with his back against Mace's: where once Depa would have been.

Where Depa *should* have been.

Where, in any sane universe, she would be right now.

Mace heard the familiar snap of an igniting blade and turned to Nick. "Give me that."

The young Korun's eyes flared green with the blade's glow. "What am I supposed to fight with, then? My rapierlike *wit?*"

Which would do him as much good as a lightsaber against twelve akk dogs, but Mace didn't tell him that. "You won't be fighting."

"Says you."

Instead of arguing, Mace reached over the blade and finger-snapped the end of his nose as though flicking away a fly.

Nick blinked, flinching, blurting a reflexive obscenity, and by the time he remembered that he'd had a lightsaber in his hand, the lightsaber was in Mace's.

"Vastor is a predator, not a HoloNet villain: they're not holding us here so that he can gloat. If he planned to kill us, we'd already be dead."

"So why are they holding us here?"

A massive shadow approached through the trees: low and huge, with side-bent legs and immense splay-clawed feet.

Nick breathed, "Oh, I get it. He's bringing Depa."

11

HOSTAGE

The immense shadow crashed closer, its walk a symphony of splintering trees.

It was an ankkox.

A massive armored saurian, the ankkox was the largest land animal of Haruun Kal. Ankkoxes were twice the size of grassers—more than half again the mass of a full-grown bantha—but built low and wide, with a broad dorsal shell like an oval soup plate turned upside down. The dorsal shell of this one was nearly three meters wide, and well over four meters long. A drover's chair was bolted to the top of the ankkox's crown shell, a convex disc of armor that capped the beast's head; when an ankkox retracted its head and legs, its crown shell and all six knee shells fit into gaps in its armor as snugly as air locks, enabling the ankkox to survive washes of volcanic gas that it couldn't outrun.

This drover did not sit, but stood wide-legged on the crown armor behind the chair, brandishing a long pole that ended in a sharp-looking hook, to use as a goad in directing the ankkox's path. Two teardrop-shaped shields of ultrachrome were pushed up onto his biceps.

Kar Vastor.

He moved only to direct the ankkox. His face held no expression. He did not even look at Mace and Nick.

The air around him shimmered with his rage.

Smaller trees the ankkox shouldered aside; underbrush it simply crushed beneath its speeder-sized feet. To get the ankkox through tree gaps too small to pass its huge shell where the trees were too large to overbear, Vastor would reach out with his goad, indicating specific points on their trunks—which would be struck by some whirring object, invisibly fast, that impacted with enough power to shatter the trunks and let it pass: the creature's tail mace.

The only part of the ankkox's body that was not armored was its extensile, muscular, surprisingly flexible tail. The tail was tipped with a thick round ball of armor, and an adult ankkox could snap its tail faster than the human eye could see, using that mace to accurately strike targets up to eight meters away with enough power to stun an akk dog or shatter a small tree.

There was a time, before the reopening of Haruun Kal to the civilized galaxy, when a mace taken from a juvenile ankkox was the traditional weapon of Korun herders: dangerous to acquire. Difficult to use. Deadly in effect.

On the central bulge of this ankkox's dorsal shell had been built a howdah: a small curtained cabin framed with lammas wood, two meters by three, barely larger than the long padded chaise within. The draped canopy stood slightly higher than Mace was tall, bounded by a polished rail perhaps a meter above the shell. The curtains, not to mention the fine-worked wood itself, were probably spoils looted from some Balawai's home. Multiple layers of gauzy lace, the curtains were translucent as smoke.

With the sunset behind, Mace could see her silhouette.

The ankkox crunched to a ponderous stop, settling onto its ventral shell with a long hiss through its teeth like gas venting from pneumatic landing jacks. Vastor tucked the goad into its holster bolted to the ankkox's crown shell, then stepped forward over the drover chair and folded his thick-muscled arms.

He stared down into the eyes of the Jedi Master.

The akk dogs started to growl low in their throats, a sound more felt than heard, like the subterranean precursor of a coming groundquake.

The wind died; even the rustle of leaves went silent.

In the hush of fading day, the Force showed Mace a shatterpoint.

The darkness of the jungle, not of the Sith.

Life without the restraints of civilization.

"We're done," Nick said. "You get that, don't you? We're as done as a week-old roast. What do they call it in the army? Aid and comfort to the enemy?"

"Be quiet. Don't draw attention to yourself."

"Great idea. Maybe they'll forget I'm here."

"This isn't about aid and comfort to the enemy," Mace said. "If this were going to be anything military, they'd put us under arrest. We'd be taken back to have some kind of show trial witnessed by the rest of the ULF. Instead, we're out here in the jungle, and the only witnesses are Kar, Depa, and these akks—human and saurian."

"So they're just gonna kill us."

"If we're lucky," Mace said, "it's going to be a dogfight."

"A *dog*fight? If we're *lucky*? Okay, sure. Let's not even try to make sense. Just tell me what I'm supposed to do."

"You're supposed to remember that you are an officer of the Grand Army of the Republic."

"I just took the fraggin' oath three *hours* ago—"

"Three hours or thirty years. It makes no difference. You have sworn to conduct yourself to the credit of the Republic as its commissioned officer."

"So that kind of rules out wetting my pants and sobbing like a baby, huh?"

"Stay calm. Show no weakness. Think of Vastor as a wild akk: do nothing to trigger his prey drive. And shut up."

"Oh, sure. Is that an order, General?"

"Will making it an order help you *do* it?"

Above on the ankkox's shell, Vastor had been staring silently while an aurora of rage built in the air around him. Only now did Mace meet the *lor pelek*'s gaze.

Mace allowed his lip to curl with a hint of contempt.

Nick whispered, "What are you *doing?*"

Mace's gaze never wavered. "Nothing you need concern yourself with."

"Um, maybe I should have told you," the young Korun muttered nervously. "Kar doesn't like to be stared at."

"I know."

"It gets him mad."

"He's already mad."

"Yeah. And you're makin' him madder."

"That's my intention."

"Y'know," Nick said, "I'm gonna give up asking if you're crazy. Let's consider it a standing question, huh? Every time you open your mouth, go ahead and assume I'm wondering if nikkle nuts have started falling out your earholes. 'Good morning, Nick.' Are you crazy? 'Nice day, isn't it?' Are you crazy?"

Mace hissed from the side of his mouth, "Will you be *quiet?*"

"Are you crazy?" Nick ducked his head. "Sorry. Just a reflex."

Vastor's jaw worked, and a wordless growl escaped from his tight-drawn lips.

You were sent for.

Mace sighed, looking bored.

Vastor's growl thickened.

Defiance carries a price.

Nick cocked his head, frowning. "This isn't about the prisoners?"

Mace looked at him sidelong: Nick had understood. So Vastor was talking to both of them—or rather, to Mace, but at least partially for the benefit of Nick. He glanced up at the howdah.

Likely for the benefit of Depa as well.

"Of course it's about the prisoners," Mace said softly. "He's just warming up. Play along."

Mace hooked his thumbs in his belt and walked casually forward. "I told you already: I am not to be sent for. Since you have brought her to me as ordered, I'll see her now."

The shimmer around Vastor deepened, but he held himself perfectly still. His growl sharpened into a vine cat's hunting cough. *I don't take orders. Depa is here at her own request.*

"Oh?"

She came to say good-bye.

"I'm not going anywhere."

Vastor's response was a silent grinning gape that showed all his inhumanly sharp teeth. He gestured, and the ring of akks and humans parted before him.

"I told you he's gonna kill us!" Nick hissed. "I *told* you! Shee, I *hate* it when I'm right!"

"Like I said before: think of Vastor as a wild akk. He won't kill us unless there's no other way to get what he wants."

"Yeah? What does he want?"

"Same as any akk dog: to assert his dominance. Defend his territory. And his pack."

"And you think he won't kill us for taking those prisoners?"

Mace shrugged. "Not you, anyway. You're subordinate: you don't really count."

"Oh, sure. Thanks a *lot*—" Nick stopped in mid-sarcasm and looked thoughtful. "Know what? I think I actually *mean* that."

"You're welcome."

Vastor spun the hooked goad, and the ankkox lumbered toward Mace and Nick, its tail mace whipping through threatening arcs around it.

"So, what?" Nick kept on under his breath. "You think he's just gonna throw you out of here? 'You got till sundown to get off my planet'?"

"Something like that."

"What about this hostage you were talkin' about?"

"We'll see if we need him."

"Um, it's not *me*, is it? Because, y'know, to tell you the truth, I don't think Depa likes me all that much—or even, y'know, any. At all."

"Hush."

The ankkox stopped. The beak-curve of the crown armor on its landspeeder-sized skull lowered to the ground at Mace's feet. The beast's eyes were orange and gold and as large as Mace's head, and they peered up from under the curve of armor with melancholy saurian patience.

Vastor vaulted to the ground. *Make your good-byes. Then you are leaving.*

"Nice doggy . . ." Nick said with a sickly forced smile. He gave a weak laugh. "Nice—"

Vastor's immense left arm flashed at Nick in a blinding palm slap that would have taken his head right off before he could even blink—but that massive arm was intercepted by the heel of Mace's open hand.

Mace's fingers locked momentarily around Vastor's wrist. "He's with me," he said, and before the *lor pelek* could react, he released Vastor and backhanded Nick off his feet.

Nick lay crumpled on the leaf mold, stunned, staring up at Mace in astonishment. Through their Force-link, Mace sent a pulse of private reassurance: an invisible deadpan wink.

Nick played along. "What was *that* for?"

The Jedi Master jabbed a finger at his face. "You are an officer in the Grand Army of the Republic. Act like one."

"How does one *act?*"

Mace turned back to Vastor. "I apologize for him."

Vastor grunted. *His mother should apologize.*

"Any problem you have with him, you bring to me." Mace had to bend his neck back to look up into the *lor pelek*'s eyes. "I struck one of your men, earlier. I apologize for that as well." He met Vastor's glare lazily. "I should have hit *you.*"

You are Depa's Master, and my dôshalo, and I do not wish you harm. Vastor's rumble went low and silken. *Don't touch me again.*

Mace sighed, still looking bored. He said to Nick, "Don't get up," and to Vastor, "Excuse me," and he sidestepped the *lor pelek* to vault onto the dorsal shell of the ankkox.

He had time to wonder if his pretense of confidence was fooling anyone.

*   *   *

Mace looked up at the howdah, now only a step or two away. His mouth had gone entirely dry.

He still couldn't feel her.

Even this close, finally, after all this time, whatever presence she cast in the Force blended invisibly into the jungle night around them.

The sick weight gathered in his chest again: the one that had been born weeks ago in Palpatine's office. The one that had grown heavier in Pelek Baw, and had nearly crushed him last night in the outpost bunker. That weight had lifted somehow through this long afternoon: maybe it was because he'd been so sure he was doing the right thing.

The only thing.

And now he was a meter away from being face to face with her: his Padawan: his protégée: the woman for whose sake he had left behind Coruscant and the Jedi Temple and the simple abstractions of strategic war. For whose sake he had plunged into this jungle. Had subjected himself to the harsh, complicated, intractable reality behind the strategies that had seemed so simple and so clean back in the sterile chambers of the Council.

He discovered that once again, he didn't know what he should do.

Just seeing her shadow on the curtains had loosened his grip on right and wrong.

Palpatine's words echoed inside his head:

Depa Billaba was your Padawan. And she is still perhaps your closest friend, is she not?

Is she? Mace thought. *I wish I knew.*

If she must be slain, are you so certain you can strike her down?

Right now, he wasn't entirely certain he could *look* at her.

He was that frightened of what he might see.

. . . I have become the darkness in the jungle . . .

A slim brown hand took one edge of the curtains. Long fingers, but strong: nails broken, and black with grime—the shape of the palm, the faint rolling texture of vein and tendon and bone, that he knew as vividly as he did his own—and the curtain was streaked with mold and stained, and hand-patched with dark thread that showed like scars against the lace, and it draped around her hand as she drew it slowly aside, and Mace's heart hammered and he nearly turned away, because he should have known he wouldn't meet her in the dawn, at the beginning of a day, even among a firestorm raining from gunship cannons; he should have known that was only wishful thinking, a solace from the Force; he should have known that they would only meet again in the twilight shadow—

But fear, too, leads into the dark.

He thought, *I have met the darkness in this jungle already. I've felt it in my own heart. I have fought it hand to hand and mind to mind. Why should I fear to see it on her face?*

The knot in his gut untied itself.

All his anxiety drained from him. All his darkness trickled away. He stood empty of everything save for fatigue and the pains of his battered flesh, and a calm Jedi expectation: ready to accept the turn of the Force, no matter what it may bring.

She drew the curtain aside.

She sat on the edge of a long, padded chaise. She wore the tatters of Jedi robes over the rough homespun of a jungle Korun. Her hair was as he had seen at the outpost: ragged, greasy, hacked short as though she'd used a knife to trim it without the benefit of a mirror. Her face was every bit as thin as he had seen it: her cheekbones sharp, and her jaw going prominent. The burn scar was there, from one corner of her hardship-thinned mouth to the point of her jaw—

But instead of a blindfold, she wore the strip of dirty rag tied around her forehead, concealing the Greater Mark of Illumination.

Or the scar it had left behind . . .

The Lesser Mark still glinted gold on the bridge of her nose, and though her eyes were bloodshot and pain-haunted, her gaze was clear, and level, and, after all, she was Depa Billaba.

Whatever had happened to her; whatever she had seen, or done.

She was still Depa.

With an effort that nearly broke Mace's heart, she curved her mouth into a smile, and she extended a hand that trembled, just a little, as Mace reached to take it. It felt fragile in his, as though her bones were as hollow as a bird's, but her grip was strong and warm.

"Mace," she said slowly. A single jewel of a tear welled in one eye. "Mace. Master Windu."

"Hello, Depa." He opened his vest and produced her lightsaber. "I have kept this safe for you."

As she reached for it her hand trembled even more. "Thank you, Master," she said slowly, with exhausted formality. "I am honored to receive it from your hand."

Her smile turned more genuine. She looked down at her lightsaber, turning it over and over in her hand as though she didn't quite remember what it was for. She lowered her head until he could no longer see her eyes. "Oh, Mace . . . How could you?"

"Depa?"

"How could you be so arrogant? So stupid? So *blind?*" Though her words were angry, her voice was only tired. "I wish . . . You should have *come* to me, Mace. Straight to me. Those people—they're not worth this. Not worth you not *knowing.* You should have *asked* me— I could have told you—"

"Why innocent children had to die?"

Her head hung even lower. "We all have to die, Mace."

"I'm not here to argue with you, Depa. I'm here to take you home."

"Home . . ." she echoed, and raised her head again. Her eyes were event horizons: infinitely deep, and infinitely dark. "You use that word as though it means something."

"It does to me."

"But it doesn't. Not anymore. Not even to you. You just haven't realized it yet." She sighed a bleak, bitter chuckle as dark as her eyes and swung her trembling hand at the jungle around them. "This *is* home. As much *home* as any place will ever be. For any of us. For all of us. That's what I brought you here to learn, Mace. But now you've messed everything up. It's falling apart and flying off in all directions. It's all wrong, and it's all too late, and I should have known it would happen like this, I should have known because you're just too blasted *arrogant* to *mind your own business!*" Her voice had risen to a screech, and a drop of blood seeped from a crack in her lower lip.

"*You* are my business here."

"Exactly. *Exactly!*" She snatched his wrist and yanked him down toward her with astonishing strength. "*I* was your business here. Those people had *nothing to do with you.* Nor you with *them.* But you can't stop being a Jedi," she said bitterly. "No matter what. With the existence of the *whole Jedi Order* at stake, *you* had to play HoloNet hero. Now your business here is *ruined.* Destroyed. Everything is *wasted.* It's too late. Too late for all of us. You have to leave here, Mace. You have to leave right now, or Kar will kill you."

"I'm planning on it," Mace agreed. "And you're coming with me."

"Oh," she said. The fire inside her dwindled, and her strength with it. Her hand went slack on Mace's arm. "Oh . . . you think—you think I can just *leave* . . ."

"You *must* leave, Depa. I don't know what you think is holding you here—"

"You don't understand. How could you? You haven't *seen*—I haven't *shown* you—You can't possibly understand . . ."

Mace thought of his hallucination at the outpost. "I understand," he said slowly, "all there is to understand. And now I believe it."

"Do you understand that *I am not in command* here?"

Mace shrugged. "Is anyone?"

"Exactly," she said. "Exactly. Master Yoda—Master Yoda would say, *You see, but you do not see.*"

"Depa—"

"You are alive *right now* because Kar doesn't want to *upset* me. That's the only reason. Not because I can *order* him. To do anything. Because I *asked* him. I asked to give you a chance to *run away.* Because Kar—because Kar *likes* me—"

Mace turned and looked down at the people and akks in the jungle. Twilight was deepening, and glowvines were beginning to pulse to life. The akks stirred uneasily, muttering deep half growls down in their enormous chests. Nick sat on the ground, knees drawn up and wrapped by his arms. He kept his head down, studiously avoiding looking at Vastor. The *lor pelek* paced back and forth in front of the ankkox's head, stalking like a hungry vine cat, flicking glances up at Mace and Depa and away again, as though he did not want to be caught looking.

"*Vastor* commands the ULF—?"

"*There is no ULF!*" Depa hissed. "The ULF is a *name,* that's all. I *made it up!* The Upland Liberation Front is a make-believe bogey on which to blame every raid and ambush and theft and petty sabotage and I don't know what all. The militia's going crazy looking for a pattern to our strikes. Trying to figure out our *strategy.* Because there is no pattern. No strategy. There is no ULF. There is just this clan, and that family, and one gang here and another there. That's all. Ragged Korun bandits and murderers."

"Your reports—"

"Reports." She looked like she wanted to grab him and shake him, but was just too tired. "What should I have told you? You've seen a little of Haruun Kal. What could I have said to make you understand?"

"You don't have to make me understand. All you have to do is come with me."

"Mace, *listen to me:* I *can't.*" She sagged, and lowered her face into her hands. "Kar is willing to let you go *only* because I am staying. To keep you *away* from me. If I leave with you . . . Going through the jungle, Mace: think of it. On foot, on grassers. Even in a steam-crawler. All the way back to Pelek Baw? Haven't you seen enough of him today to know that nowhere in the jungle could you ever be safe?"

The weight in Mace's chest lightened, just a bit. He swallowed, and found that his breath came more easily.

She was afraid for him. She had not fallen so far that she no longer cared.

That was his victory right there.

"We won't be going through the jungle," he said. "I have a ship on-station with a battalion of troopers. My comm's damaged, or we'd be on our way right now. Nick says you have subspace at the Lorshan Pass caverns. We can be out of the system less than a day after we get there."

She lifted her head again, and there was still no hope in her eyes. "It'll take two days to get there. If you're still here in two *hours*, Kar will kill you. Two *minutes*."

"Leave Vastor to me." Mace leaned forward, resting his forearms on the howdah's polished rail. "I am not leaving without you."

"You *have* to."

"Let me put it another way."

Mace took a deep breath. "Master Depa Billaba: by my authority as a Senior Member of the Jedi Council, and general of the Grand Army of the Republic, you are hereby relieved of command of Republic forces on Haruun Kal, uniformed and irregular. You are relieved of all duties and responsibilities in the action on this planet. You are suspended from the Jedi Council, pending investigation of your actions on Haruun Kal, and you are ordered to proceed with all due speed to Coruscant, where you will present yourself to the Council for judgment."

Depa shook her head. "You can't—you can't—"

"Depa," Mace said sadly, "you are under arrest."

"This is *ridiculous*—"

"Yes. And absolutely serious. You know me, Depa. How many arrests did we make, all those years? You know I will deliver my prisoner, or die in the attempt."

She nodded slowly, and she found a smile once more: a sad, quiet smile, edged with bitter knowledge. "Will you accept my parole? If I give my word not to . . . attempt escape?"

"I will always trust you, Depa."

Sudden tears sparkled again in her eyes, and she turned her face away. "How many times are you going to make me save your life?"

"Just this once more," he said. "You can come with me, or you can watch me die. Your choice."

Her shoulders twitched, and shook, and Mace for a moment thought she might be sobbing, but then her soft dry chuckle reached his ears.

"I have missed you, Mace." Her eyes sparkled with tears. "I can't tell you how I've missed you. Of course you knew exactly the spot where my defenses would crumble. But I'm not your real problem," she said tiredly. "What are you going to do about Kar?"

"You're my only problem," Mace told her. "I found your shatter-point; do you think I'd miss his?"

"I think he doesn't have one."

"That," said Mace Windu, "remains to be seen."

"You and your shatterpoints." Her sad smile was dazzling on her tear-stained face. "Who but Mace Windu would think to take *him-self* hostage?"

Mace's head twitched to the right in a Korun shrug. "I was the only one available."

Mace leapt lightly down from the ankkox. "Kar Vastor. We need to talk."

We do not. Vastor did not meet his eyes. *As you said: the next time we meet, there may be a fight.*

"What I said was," Mace replied lazily, "the next time we're *alone* together, there may be a fight. But I gave you too much credit. I mean, that *is* why you brought all your puppies along, isn't it? You certainly didn't seem interested in standing up to me without them."

Vastor's head turned like a steamcrawler's gun turret. *What?*

"You have a problem with me?" Mace spread his hands. "I'm right here."

Tendons in Vastor's neck cranked his head down a centimeter at a time. *She doesn't want you hurt.*

"Depa? Do you plan to hide behind her forever?" Mace folded his arms. "Always find a reason to back down, don't you? I admire your . . . *creativity.*"

The Akk Guards stared.

All twelve akk dogs hunched and coiled their haunches, tails whipping forward past their shoulder spines: ready to pounce. Vastor snarled and lunged convulsively past Mace. He snatched Nick's arm and hauled the young Korun to his feet, holding him out toward Mace.

"Hey, y'know, *ow*, huh?"

I have grassers saddled and supplied. Take them and the boy and go.

His filed-sharp teeth seemed to glow in the vine-lit gloom. *Take them and live.*

"You know," Mace said, "I don't much care for your tone."

Vastor's eyes widened. His mouth worked silently.

"And take your hand off my aide. Now."

Vastor found his voice: a roar of black rage. A violent shove sent Nick stumbling forward. Only a grab at Mace's shoulders kept him on his feet. He looked up into the Jedi Master's eyes and gave him a sickly grin. "Remember that question I wasn't gonna ask anymore?"

GO. Vastor's roar carried tectonic power. *Go before I forget my promise to spare you.*

Mace turned to one of the Akk Guards. "Does he always yammer like this? He'd quiet down if you got him fixed."

The guard went pale. He shook his head urgently. "Really, really don't want to talk to Kar like this, you. Really really really."

"Oh, right. Sure. He's not so good with Basic." Mace hooked his thumbs inside his vest.

Tendons stood out like cables in the *lor pelek*'s neck. His shimmering rage went scarlet, glowing in the twilit gloom, as though his skin were lava pouring from a volcano's mouth.

Slowly, deliberately, his left hand tucked behind the shield on his right arm. He pulled it down into fighting position, carefully avoiding its razor edges. Just as slowly and deliberately, he did the same with the other.

Muscle rippled in his arms as he squeezed the handgrips, and the shields whined to life. He brought them together back to back, generating an earsplitting squeal that made even the akk dogs flinch.

From behind Mace's shoulder, Nick whispered, "Are you *sure* I'm not allowed to wet myself?"

Mace walked calmly out of the center of the ring, straight toward Vastor, thumbs still hooked inside his vest. "You do that a lot. No doubt your puppies find it pretty scary."

Looking straight up into Vastor's eyes, Mace swung his vest open to display the handgrip of his lightsaber.

Then he shrugged out of the vest, folded it once, and tossed it over his shoulder with effortless accuracy, right into the hands of an astonished Nick Rostu. With his lightsaber still inside it.

"That's how much you scare *me.*"

Vastor's shields parted, and the jungle went silent.

"Everybody here knows this has nothing to do with Depa," Mace said. "This has to do with those Balawai you were too stupid and weak to hold."

Vastor's legs coiled like the akks' haunches. *They were mine! MINE! Mine to kill. Mine to spare. They were MINE to give to the justice of the jungle—*

"Until you met me. Then they were *mine,*" Mace said. "Mine to let go."

I'll show you stupid and weak—

"You already have."

Vastor shifted his weight to throw himself into a leap, but then froze as though an invisible leash had snapped tight around his neck. He glanced back at the shadow behind the curtains of the howdah for a moment. When he turned toward Mace once more, his lips were drawn back in a predator's grin, and his eyes burned like twin calderae.

Depa prefers that you live. But she doesn't mind if you get hurt.

Mace shrugged. "As long as she won't mind when *you* get hurt."

Vastor began to unbuckle his shields. Mace turned his back on the *lor pelek* contemptuously and strolled toward the center of the ring of akks and people.

There was nothing either slow or deliberate about the way Vastor shook the shields off his arms: a whipping snap of the wrist that flung them down to clatter against the rim of the ankkox's shell.

Nick held the bundle of Mace's vest and weapon uncertainly. "Um, guess I should have told you: that big-dog stuff doesn't work on Kar."

"On the contrary," the Jedi Master replied softly. "It's working perfectly."

Nick blinked.

Mace said, "As for you, though—"

"Don't worry about me. I know exactly what to do." He tucked

Mace's vest under one arm and trotted toward the nearest Akk Guard. "A hundred credits says the Jedi makes Kar cry like a baby! Who's in?"

The *lor pelek* crouched and lowered one hand to the ground, digging in the leaf mold, his sweat-glistening chest heaving, breath pumping darkness into him and out again. Gathering rage. Gathering power.

The shimmer around him had gone from red to black.

Mace shook his arms loose. "Rules?"

Vastor's reply was the snort of a hunting akk. *Jungle rules.* A burst of power launched the *lor pelek* as a human missile, clawing his way through the twilight toward the Jedi Master.

Jungle rules it is, then, Mace thought, and leapt to meet him in midair.

12

JUNGLE RULES

They collided with a crash that shook the jungle around them. The collision was not just of two human bodies, but of two node-channels of the Force: invisible energy crackled, and vivid blue gap-sparks arced from leaf to leaf in the canopy above. For a moment, they hung in the air, supported by power, grappling, tearing at each other's flesh. The akk dogs lunged and whirled and slashed the air with their tails. The guards clashed together their shields, roaring with ferocious animal exuberance.

Vastor seemed to be all teeth and claws and fierce snarling assault. Arms like girders of durasteel caught Mace in an unbreakable hug, pinning the Jedi's elbows to his creaking ribs. Mace answered swifter than thought with an instinctive head-butt that split the skin on one of Vastor's cheekbones. The *lor pelek* lowered his head to Mace's shoulder as though to snuggle in like a lover—then sank his needle teeth deep into Mace's neck, chewing for his carotid artery.

Mace jerked a knee up to slam the inside of Vastor's thigh; Vastor only grunted and bit down harder, twisting his head from side to side like an akk worrying off a tusker's leg. His jaw pressure on the artery was restricting its blood flow; billowing clouds of darkness gathered in Mace's brain—but when Mace fired the knee again, Vastor jerked his legs out of the way.

Mace's knee caught him a decimeter below the navel.

This brought a sharper grunt and a snarl that vibrated in Mace's neck, but instead of withdrawing his knee for another strike, Mace dug it in harder, forcing Vastor's body away from his own. This created just enough space that Mace could slip one arm up between their chests, and could stab his stiffened fingers into the notch of Vastor's collarbone.

And shove.

With a convulsive gasp of astonishment, the *lor pelek* released Mace's neck. Mace kept on shoving, jamming his fingers into Vastor's windpipe. Vastor gagged, and his massive arms loosened.

They fell together, tumbling, and as Mace finally pushed Vastor off him he managed to sneak in a quick snapping kick to the point of Vastor's chin that sent the *lor pelek* whirling like a topspun ball.

Mace recovered his Force-touch in time to flip upright and land in a balanced crouch; Vastor landed on all fours, absorbing the shock as effortlessly as a vine cat.

They looked at each other.

Blood ran from the bite wound on Mace's neck, painting his shoulder and part of his chest scarlet, but it was only a trail, not a jet: the artery must have remained intact. A similar trail rolled from Vastor's split cheek and dripped from his jaw.

Neither man appeared to notice.

Vastor's growl resonated in Mace's chest. *Not many men can break my grip. You won't do it twice.*

Mace didn't answer. Vastor was probably right.

He was suddenly, acutely aware that he hadn't slept since the night before the fight in the notch pass. The night when a bark-drunk Lesh had come to him in tears, to tell him what Kar and the Akk Guards would teach him, if he lived long enough.

It seemed like years ago.

He wondered briefly if the *lor pelek* would have gone ahead and torn out his throat despite what he claimed Depa had told him, or if he would have settled for the strangle.

He decided he could live without knowing the answer.

That is, if he lived at all.

Vastor stalked toward him on all fours. *Was that Jedi fighting? Poking and pinching? A little jab to stop the big dog? I am not impressed.*

Mace stood motionless except for the heaving of his chest. He knew already he could not match Vastor for raw power. With each breath, he stripped away another layer of restraint and inhibition. Another layer of serenity. He had to move his inner peace out of the way to let in the joy. The thrill. The sheer *okay-why-not-let's-FIGHT.* Because Vaapad was more than just a form of lightsaber combat.

It was a state of mind.

Night had deepened upon the jungle, and around them glowvines began to pulse faintly. To use Vaapad now, out here, was incredibly dangerous—almost as dangerous as *not* using Vaapad.

The ultimate answer for power is skill.

"Want to be impressed?" Mace said. "Let's see the impression my boot makes on your face."

Without warning, Vastor's stalk became a lightning lunge, fingers hooked like talons, his arms sweeping wide to close on Mace once more—but Mace wasn't there anymore. A slight sidestep and a weave of his head snuck him to the outside of Vastor's lunge, and his fist whipped backhand to snap Vastor in the base of the skull as he passed: a knockout blow.

But Vastor must have felt it coming; he pitched forward, rolling with the punch so that it flipped him end for end. He landed in perfect balance and sprang again, straight up; the kick Mace had aimed at his kidneys only grazed his calf muscle. He used the impact to whirl in the air so that he could fall upon the Jedi Master like a branch leopard taking a tusker.

But what he fell upon was Mace's fist, driven upward into his solar plexus by the combined power of the Force and nearly fifty years of Jedi combat training.

Mace's hand sank in to the wrist, and Vastor's fighting snarl became an agonized struggle for breath. Mace used the Force to hurl him off and send him tumbling through the air to slam into the flank of an agitated akk dog. Eyes glazing, half stunned, the *lor pelek* slid bonelessly down the akk's armored ribs, and staggered as his feet skidded over gnarled roots.

Before he could find his balance, Mace was on him. "Impressed yet?"

Standing toe to toe, the top of Mace's head barely came to the level of Vastor's chin, and you could have tucked Mace's whole thick-muscled upper body inside Vastor's chest with room to spare. And even hurt, lurching drunkenly, Vastor still could whip his arms in blindingly fast raking slaps at Mace's head and wounded neck.

But where Vastor's speed was blinding, Mace's was *invisible*.

Not one of those slaps connected.

Before Vastor could even focus his eyes, Mace had hit him six times: two thundering hooks to his short ribs, a knee slamming hard into the same thigh he'd hit before, an elbow snapping up to the point of his chin, and two devastating palm strikes to either hinge of his jaw.

An ordinary man would have been unconscious. Vastor seemed to be getting *stronger*.

Vastor fired another of those blinding slaps. This time, instead of ducking, Mace countered with a whirring hook that met the *lor pelek*'s swinging arm directly on the nerve that ran up the inside of the biceps. Vastor threw the other even harder—which only made the inside of that arm connect that much harder with Mace's counterhook.

Vastor's mighty arms spasmed and dropped limply to his sides.

"This is called Vaapad, Kar." A fierce light burned in Mace's eyes. "How many arms do you see?"

Then he hit Vastor twice in the nose before the *lor pelek* could even blink.

Vastor howled in pain and raging disbelief, falling back against the akk dog's flank once more, twisting and turning to try to find some way to avoid the Jedi's flashing hands.

Mace stayed with him, pinning him to the akk's flank, fists whirling through Vaapad flurries, striking not to disable or to kill, but instead to *hurt:* stinging flicks to soft tissue, smashing ears and nose, stabbing up under the chin.

The akk dog suddenly lurched away from them, giving Vastor half a meter of clearance. The *lor pelek* sprang sideways, diving away.

Mace let him go. "Go on and run, Kar. This is over. You lose. *I'm* the big dog here—"

Vastor turned his dive into a roll and spun to face the Jedi Master from one knee, and before Mace had even finished speaking the Force whirled around him and Mace found himself wrenched off the ground, hurtling backward through the air to slam against the smooth-barked gray trunk of a meter-thick lammas tree. The whole tree shivered with the impact, and a spiral galaxy birthed itself inside Mace's head.

He thought, *I was wondering when we'd get to this part.*

Vastor's face tightened. Strength must have been returning to his nerve-punched arms already, because he managed to raise one and gesture as though throwing a stone; Mace was whirled forward from the tree to crash against the skull of an astonished akk dog.

The impact folded him over the dog's head and blasted the breath from his lungs; the dog's crown spines gashed Mace's abdomen, and when it tossed Mace aside with a twitch of its head like a Nymalian water-ox, his blood ran down the black outer shells of its eyes.

Jedi Padawans learn to counter Force kinesis before they even begin lightsaber training. Still in the air, Mace sensed the flow of power that held Vastor's grip upon him; with a sigh, he allowed his center— Vastor's point of Force contact—to relax and ground Vastor's power back into the jungle around them . . .

And that jungle came to life.

A gripleaf trailer snaked down from above and seized one of Mace's ankles in its unbreakable clutch. His airborne tumble became a wide-swinging head-down arc.

Gripleaf trailers only grew tighter as their victim struggled, and their fibers were nearly as strong as durasteel cable; they could not be broken by mortal strength. This one squeezed his ankle, drawing blood with the edges of its sharp waxy leaves. Another trailer reached toward his other ankle, and from his upside-down vantage he could see a thick blade-thorned length of brassvine curving toward his neck.

He almost reached into the Force for his lightsaber—

But that would be admitting defeat.

Time to be clever.

He used the Force to shove the gripleaf trailer so that the arc of his swing sent him whirling out over the ring of dogs and men. One of the Akk Guards smirked at him as he swung overhead: "Big dog? More like little tusk-pig."

When his swing carried him back in, Mace reached down and grabbed the Akk Guard by the arm, yanking him into the air. Drawing upon the Force for a burst of strength, Mace whipped the astonished Guard up and over and used the edge of his razor-sharp shield to slice through the trailer before releasing him to flail helplessly through the air and crash into the jungle darkness.

Mace turned his own fall into a flip that landed him on an akk dog's shoulders. He bounded off into the air—

And Vastor's Force grip seized him again.

Vastor was on his feet now, and his arms didn't seem hurt at all. His blood-smeared mouth spread wide in a howl of triumph as he yanked Mace through the multicolored glowvine-shaded night, pulling him in while he opened his arms for that lethal embrace.

Mace thought: *Well, if you insist . . .*

Instead of resisting or grounding the power of Vastor's Force grip, Mace added his own strength to it. The speed of his flight suddenly doubled; Vastor had only time to widen his eyes in dismay as Mace flipped headfirst in the air. The top of his head speared into Vastor's gut and drove the *lor pelek* to the ground as though he'd been hit by a concussion missile.

On the other hand, Vastor's stomach wasn't much softer than that lammas he'd slammed Mace into; the impact didn't do Mace's head a lot of good, either.

Another spiral galaxy blossomed where the first had been as Mace rolled off him, lying on his back while he watched stellar clusters wheel inside his skull. Vastor lay beside him, making faint panting noises while he tried to pull air into his spasming chest.

Vastor's breath began to return in great whooping gasps, and Mace knew his time was running out. He shook the stars out of his head and reached down to his ankle to unwrap the severed gripleaf trailer. Limp now, dying, it was unresisting as an ordinary rope; Mace took one end in each fist, and as Vastor rolled over and gained his hands and knees, Mace slipped a loop of the trailer over the *lor pelek's* head from behind and tightened it around his throat.

Vastor straightened and his hands went to his throat, clawing at Mace's improvised garrote, but not even he was strong enough to break a gripleaf trailer with his bare hands. His face darkened, swelling with blood; the back of his neck bulged; veins writhed across his temples and forehead.

Ten seconds, Mace thought, hanging on, wedging his knees into Vastor's back. Ten seconds and out.

Vastor got one foot under him.

Mace swallowed, gasping for breath as he tried to tighten the trailer around the *lor pelek's* throat.

Pure will powered Vastor to his feet. He didn't even seem to notice the weight of a large Jedi Master hanging down his back.

Mace thought: *Here it comes.*

In an eyeblink, Vastor's grip shifted from the gripleaf trailer to Mace's wrists. He threw himself forward, bent at the waist, and with a surge of incredible strength yanked the Jedi Master over his head and slammed him bodily to the dirt.

The impact replaced the stars in Mace's head with billowing black nebulae; he'd never gotten his breath back properly after landing on the akk dog, and now he couldn't breathe at all. The jungle above faded into a black haze; through the darkness descending inside his skull, he barely caught a glimpse of Vastor leaping into the air to drop a body-slam that would finish him. With a gasp, he rolled aside, and Vastor landed hard on the ground beside him.

Mace dizzily tried to pull himself up to his hands and knees; Vastor was still down, his hands clawing weakly at Mace's flanks.

Mace pushed him off and made it to his knees. Vastor rolled onto his side, found a tree trunk, and pulled himself up it, leaning on it drunkenly.

Though Mace couldn't breathe—could barely see through the black-and-red haze inside his head—he could draw upon the Force to throw himself upright, and he lunged at Vastor, whirling, hands clasped together to deliver every erg of power at his command into one last thundering punch that lifted Vastor bodily off the ground, flipped him over backward, and dropped him on the back of his neck.

Mace swayed, almost out on his feet. The jungle hazed in and out of focus. All he could clearly see was the *lor pelek* climbing to his feet.

Vastor was *smiling*.

Is that the best you have?

"I'm just—" Mace gasped for breath. His arms came up slowly; each one felt like it was made out of collapsium. "Just getting *started*—"

One of those open-handed slaps flashed out of the darkness; the next thing of which Mace was aware was a bell-like ringing in his ears, and the grip of Vastor's huge hand around his neck, holding him up off the jungle floor.

Mace's eyelids fluttered open. Vastor's blood-smeared grin was the only thing in the world.

Vastor growled, *How many arms do you see?*

Mace didn't answer.

He certainly didn't see the one attached to the hand that snuffed the world like a blown-out candle.

In the darkness, a smell of ammonia and rotten meat: predator breath.

A dry rough tongue the size of his lost kitbag licked him back to consciousness, and Mace opened his eyes.

The Akk Guards were crowded around him, leaning over, their faces in deep shadow, haloed by the pulsing light of the glowvines in the canopy; one now pushed the nose of the akk dog who'd been licking Mace's unconscious body so that the great beast backed up.

Kar Vastor stepped into the gap. He squatted on his haunches at Mace's side. His face was lumped up, and blood still trickled from his split cheek, but his grin was fiercer than ever.

He barked something, and one of the Akk Guards stepped away for a brief moment. Mace heard Nick say, "Hey, cut it out. Hey, *ow,* huh? Come on, lay off the arm, you *know* I'm good for it—"

The Akk Guard returned, dragging Nick.

Vastor growled.

Nick said, "Hey, why are you telling *me*—?"

Vastor's growl sharpened, and Nick flinched away from him. He looked uncertainly up at the Akk Guard who held his arm, back at Vastor, then down at Mace.

"He, uh—" Nick swallowed hard. "—he wants me to say so everybody hears it: *You can get up, if you want . . ."*

Mace's eyes drifted closed. He didn't answer.

Vastor made a rumbling noise.

"He says, *Come on. You wanted to be the big dog. Get up and fight."* Nick lowered his voice. "I mean, you *can* get up, right? If you want to— I mean, I got *odds,* it's worth *five hundred creds,* I'll split it with you—"

Mace opened his eyes. "No."

Vastor's rumble broadened humorously, as though the *lor pelek* was a groundquake telling a joke.

"Um, he—he wants to know, *No, what?* That is—y'know, no to the *money?"*

"No," Mace said. He couldn't find a place on his body that did not hurt. "No more fighting. I've had enough. You win."

Vastor seized Mace's shoulder in one enormous hand and stood, pulling the Jedi Master upright without apparent effort. Now his growl once more became words in Mace's mind.

Tell them. Tell them who is the big dog here.

Mace hung his head, careful not to meet Vastor's eye. "You are." He coughed, and blood bubbled from his smashed mouth. "You're the big dog."

Nick looked stricken.

Tell them you were wrong to take my prisoners. Tell them you were wrong to let them go.

Mace kept his eyes on the ground at his feet. Blood from the shallow akk-spine gouges in his belly ran down his legs. "I was wrong to take your prisoners. I was wrong to let them go."

Tell them you are sorry that you challenged me, and you will never do it again.

Mace's only motion was to glance up at the howdah on the back of the ankkox. Now after dark, the curtains were opaque. He couldn't tell if Depa was even in there.

He lowered his head once more.

"I am sorry that I challenged you. I will never challenge you again."

A twitch of motion in his peripheral vision: Nick had let Mace's vest unroll from his hand. Now he held it alongside his leg. He gave it another suggestive twitch.

Mace could feel the lightsaber within it.

He met Nick's eye. Nick deliberately looked away, miming a nonchalant whistle, while he twitched the vest one more time.

A twist of the Force—no more effort than Nick expended to wiggle the vest—would bring that lightsaber to Mace's hands.

Mace said slowly, "Kar?"

Vastor hummed a *yes.*

"My weapon is in that vest. May I have it?" He kept his eyes fixed resolutely on the *lor pelek*'s chest. "Please?"

Vastor released his shoulder with a contemptuous shove, and extended a hand for the vest. Nick looked at Mace with open shock, as though he'd been unexpectedly betrayed.

Mace looked at the ground.

Vastor took the vest, and pulled Mace's lightsaber out of its pocket. *This is yours?*

"Yes, Kar," Mace said quietly. "May I have it, please?"

Vastor gave a sidelong glance at an Akk Guard, and purred something. The guard smirked, nodding.

"Please," Mace repeated humbly. "It's my only weapon. I won't be much good to anyone without it."

You're not much good to anyone with it, Vastor grunted. He held it out to Mace, but when the Jedi Master extended a hesitant hand to take it, Vastor flipped it carelessly away from him. The Akk Guard he'd purred at snatched it from the air.

The guard held it in one hand. The vibroshield on his other arm whined to life.

"Hey, Kar, c'mon, lay off, huh?" Nick's face was twisted in an ongoing wince; it was painful to pity someone previously respected. "You won, didn't you? Isn't that enough? Why do you have to be such a—"

Vastor interrupted the young Korun with a backhanded cuff that knocked him to the ground. He never even looked at him; his gaze was still on Mace Windu.

The Jedi Master seemed not even to notice Nick lying on the ground, cradling his bloodied mouth, cursing continuously into his hand. "Don't," Mace said brokenly. "Don't. You don't understand—a Jedi's lightsaber—"

Can be destroyed as easily as a Jedi Master. Vastor flicked his fingers as though brushing off a fly, but before the Akk Guard could bring the lightsaber's handgrip against the edge of his shield—

"Kar . . ."

Through the gauzy opacity of the curtained howdah above, Depa's voice had an eerie power, and it seemed to come from everywhere at once.

"To send him out into the jungle without his weapon would be murder, Kar. He is not the enemy."

Not your enemy. Perhaps.

"Please, Kar. Keep it safe for him, and return it to him when he departs."

He is departing now.

"He cannot travel," Depa said. "Can you not feel it? You hurt him, Kar. Hurt him badly. He needs rest, and medical treatment. Let us take him to the base. He can ride the ankkox with me. Keep his lightsaber yourself. You've shown him he cannot face you without it."

Vastor's inhuman stare searched the blank face of the howdah, but now night had fully fallen. Glowvine light shimmered off the curtains, and nothing could be seen within.

Finally he gave an irritable shrug and extended a hand. The Akk

Guard tossed the handgrip back to him, and Vastor tucked it into the waistband of his vine cat leather pants.

He cast Mace's vest to the ground at the Jedi Master's feet.

Did it hurt even more, knowing she was watching?

He no longer sounded mocking; this came in the tone of simple curiosity.

Slowly, painfully, like an old man protecting arthritic knees, Mace bent down to retrieve the vest. He said, "I'm not sure it *could* have hurt much more."

You might remember that this all began because you refused to come when I told you.

This began, Mace thought, *when I was summoned to the private office of Chancellor Palpatine.* But he said nothing.

Because you refused to do what you were told.

"Yes," Mace said. "Yes, I remember." He picked up the vest and slipped it on. The sting of dirt in open wounds announced that the lammas tree's bark had torn his back.

If there is a next time, dôshalo, it will be your last time.

"Yes, Kar. I know." He looked at Nick, who was now sitting on the ground staring balefully at Vastor. "Come on," Mace said softly. "I'll need you to help me up onto the ankkox."

FROM THE PRIVATE JOURNALS OF MACE WINDU

Vastor was willing to let Nick help me, and treat my more serious injuries with supplies from a captured medpac. He was willing to believe the battering he'd inflicted on me was nearly crippling.

It wasn't far from the truth.

Nick was still simmering as he helped me to my feet, muttering under his breath a continuous stream of invective, characterizing Vastor as a "lizard-faced frogswallower," and a "demented scab-chewing turtlesacker" and a variety of other names that I don't feel comfortable recording, even in a private journal.

"That's enough," I told him. "I have gone to considerable trouble to keep us both alive, Nick. I'd prefer we stay that way."

"Oh, sure. Nice job on that." His voice was bitter, and he didn't want to meet my eyes.

I told him I was sorry about his hundred credits, and pointed out to him gently that no one had told him to bet on me.

He turned on me then, instantly furious, hissing savagely to keep his voice down, as the Akk Guards and the dogs were still milling about. "This isn't about *credits!* I don't *care* about the credits—" He stopped himself, blinking, and his familiar smile flickered briefly across his lips. "Shee. Did I really just *say* that? Wow. So okay, sure, that was a lie: I care about the creds. I care a *lot.* But that's not why I'm angry."

I nodded, and told him I understood: he was angry at me. He felt like I'd let him down.

"Not *me,*" he said. "I mean, come *on:* Jedi are supposed to *stand* for something, aren't you? You're supposed stand up for what's *right.* No matter what." Angry at me as he may have been, he still swung his head under one of my arms and held it across his shoulders, so he could help me walk.

It was appreciated. Only as the adrenaline and concussion shock were wearing off did I begin understand what a beating I had taken; later, with access to the medpac's scanner, I would discover two cracked ribs, a severe ankle sprain from the gripleaf trailer, a moderate concussion, and some internal bleeding, not to mention the bite wound on my neck and an astonishing variety of scrapes and bruises.

As Nick helped me up onto the ankkox, I discovered what had made him so angry with me: more than anything else, it was that I'd declared we had been wrong to free the prisoners.

"I don't care what you say," he muttered darkly. "I don't care what *Kar* says. There were kids there. And wounded. I mean: those Balawai, they weren't evil. They were just people. Like us."

"Nearly everyone is."

"We did the right thing, and you know it."

It dawned on me then that Nick was proud of himself. Proud of what we had done. It may have been an unfamiliar feeling for him: that peculiarly delicious pride that comes from having taken a terrible risk to do something truly admirable. Of overcoming the instinct of self-preservation: of fighting our fears and winning.

It is the pride of discovering that one is not merely a bundle of re-flexes and conditioned responses; that instead one is a thinking being, who can choose the right over the easy, and justice over safety. The pride Nick took in this made me proud of him, too—though of course I could not tell him so. It would only have embarrassed him, and made him regret speaking at all.

I hope I never forget the fierce conviction on his face as he helped me climb the extended leg of the ankkox and clambered up onto its dorsal shell. "Just because Kar beat you like a rented gong doesn't mean he was *right*. Just because he won doesn't mean you were wrong to challenge him. I can't believe you'd ever say those things."

His answer came from within the curtained darkness of the howdah at the top of the curved shell.

"If you spend much time around us, Nick, you will learn . . ." Depa's voice was strong and clear and as sane and gentle as it has always been in my heart. "You will learn that Jedi do not always tell the truth."

Nick stopped, suddenly scowling as though he found himself unex-pectedly deep in thought. "Don't always—hey . . ." he muttered suspi-ciously. "Hey, wait one *second* here—"

She pulled back the curtain once more, and pushed open the small swing gate in the rail. "Come on in. You look like you might want to lie down."

"I might," I admitted. "This hasn't been my best couple of days."

She took my hand to steady me as I stepped into the howdah, and she made room for me on the chaise. "I have to hand it to you, Mace," she said with a softly ironic smile. "You still take a beating as well as any man in the galaxy."

Nick's eyes bulged as though his head might explode. "I knew it!" He shook a fiercely triumphant fist in my face. "I *knew* it. I *knew* you could take him!"

I told him to keep it down, because Vastor and the Akk Guards were still moving through the trees nearby, and I had no idea how sharp Vastor's ears might be. I didn't tell him to shut up altogether because it wouldn't have done any good.

"I've got you figured. You hear me? I've got your Jedi butt scanned to the twelfth *decimal* point! I shoulda *known* you were gonna dive when you started in on Kar like that—you were spinning him up to make the confrontation more *personal,* like. The more you insulted him, the less he was gonna worry about taking anything out on *me.* And you kept on taunting him so that booting your Jedi can into next week felt so good that he basically *forgave* you for letting those Balawai go!"

I told him he was half wrong.

"Which half?"

Depa answered for me. "The part about letting Kar win."

She knows me so well.

"You mean he really beat you?" Nick couldn't seem to believe it. "He really, really beat you?"

"We share a bond in the Force now, Nick. Did it *feel* like I threw the fight?"

He shook his head. "It felt like you were a smazzo drummer's trap skin."

"As you said earlier: Vastor is a difficult man to lie to. He would have known if I was holding back. Then the beating would have been much worse, and he might very well have killed me. What I did was pick a fight I knew I couldn't win."

"Couldn't?"

"Vastor is . . . very powerful. Half my age and twice my size. Training and experience can compensate only up to a point. And he is naturally ferocious in a way that no Jedi can duplicate."

"You're telling me you twisted his nose like that, *knowing* he was gonna beat you so bad your whole *family* would bleed?"

I shrugged. "I didn't have to win. All I had to do was fight."

"Kar's shatterpoint," Depa murmured. "You saw it all along."

I nodded. Nick wasn't familiar with the term; when I described *shatterpoint* as a critical weakness, he shook his head. "I didn't see anything weak out there."

With a sidelong glance at Depa's thoughtful frown, I quoted Yoda: *"You see, but you do not see.*

"Kar's great strength is his instinctive connection to *pelekotan.* The jungle lives in him as much as he lives in it. And like I keep telling you: even in the jungle, there are rules."

I explained that a fight between Kar and myself was inevitable: two alpha males in the same pack. I could smell it on him even during the battle at the outpost when we first met. My only hope of a good outcome was to make it personal and immediate.

And unarmed.

If the fight hadn't happened, he and the Akk Guards might very well have killed Nick and me both for setting free the prisoners. If he and I had gone at it blade to shield, I would be dead now—even if I'd killed him, the guards and the dogs would have torn me to shreds—and Depa, too, if she'd tried to save me; we'd only barely survived being attacked by three akks in the Circus Horrificus.

Against a dozen—

Well. It didn't happen that way. Because I knew what Kar really wanted, in the grip, as he was, of his alpha-male jungle instincts.

He wanted me to *submit*.

And like many other pack hunters, once his rival submitted, his instincts led him to allow that rival to peacefully sniff around the fringes of his pack—so long as I did not renew my challenge.

"That's why you gave him your lightsaber? So he wouldn't feel threatened?"

I shook my head, and for a moment I was tempted to smile. "No, I would have let him cut it up."

"You would?"

"If it would make him more comfortable with letting me stay? Of course. A lightsaber can be repaired or rebuilt. But I admit, Depa's idea was a stroke of genius."

She smiled at me. "I am a bit proud of myself for that."

Nick again expressed his confusion, and I explained. "Even with the Force, I can't pick Kar out from the jungle around us. He is so much a part of it, and it of him, that he is practically invisible. My lightsaber, on the other hand—"

"I get it!" Nick breathed. "As long as he carries it—"

"Exactly." I could feel it even now: I knew without thinking its precise position relative to my own. "It is a bell collar that Depa managed to buckle onto a singularly ferocious vine cat."

"Wow. I mean, wow. Y'know, everybody *hears* about how scary Jedi are—but those stories aren't the half of it," he said. "Your *real* powers don't have anything to do with lightsabers or picking up things with your minds . . ." Nick shook his head uncomprehendingly. "It's not *natural*—not just taking the beating, but bowing *down* like that . . . and being able to come up with stuff like giving Kar the lightsaber—"

"It requires a certain detachment of mind. When your emotions are not involved, answers are often obvious."

"It's still not natural. Can I just say, here, how much you two creep me out?"

"When I was Mace's student," Depa mused, "he would often remind me that nothing about being a Jedi is natural."

"I thought you guys were all about going with the flow and using your instincts and stuff . . ."

"The difference," I said, "lies in the instincts themselves. It is possible for an untrained Force-user to wield as much power as the greatest of Jedi—look at Kar. But untrained, the instincts he falls back on are those granted him by nature. It is another of the central paradoxes of the Jedi: the 'instincts' we use are not instinctive at all. They are the product of training so intense that they replace our natural ones. That's why Jedi must begin at such an early age. To replace our natural instincts—territoriality, selfishness, anger, fear, and the like—with the Jedi 'instincts' of service, serenity, selflessness, and compassion. The oldest child ever accepted for training was nine—and there was much debate over that. A debate that has continued, I might add, for more than ten years.

"Being a Jedi is a discipline *imposed* upon nature, just as civilization is, at its root, a discipline imposed upon the natural impulses of sentient beings.

"Because *peace* is an unnatural state.

"Peace is a product of civilization. The myth of the peaceful savage is precisely that: a myth. Without civilization, all *existence* is only the jungle. Go to your peaceful savage and burn his crops, or slaughter his herds, or kick him off his hunting grounds. You'll find that he will not remain peaceful for long. Isn't that exactly what happened here on Haruun Kal?

"Jedi do not fight for peace. That's only a slogan, and is as misleading as slogans always are. Jedi fight for *civilization*, because only civilization *creates* peace. We fight for justice because justice is the fundamental bedrock of civilization: an unjust civilization is built upon sand. It does not long survive a storm.

"Kar's power comes from natural instinct—but he is also *ruled* by instinct, in a way no Jedi ever is. A single Jedi who succumbs to his natural drives for power, for respect, for success or revenge, could do damage that is literally unimaginable."

"Mace," Depa interrupted me softly, "are we still talking about Kar? Or is this about Dooku?"

Or, I wondered silently, was it about *her?* . . .

I sighed and lowered my head, suddenly aware of how exhausted I was. But still I finished the thought, less for Nick's benefit than for Depa's.

And my own.

"Our only hope, against beings whose instincts control them, is to absolutely and utterly control our own."

13

JEDI OF THE FUTURE

N ight in the jungle.

Korun bedrolls scattered in clumps. Low voices blending into the background mutter of the jungle. Smells of hotpack ration squares and smoke from homemade cigarras of green rashallo leaves.

Mace sat on a borrowed bedroll a few meters from where Depa's wallet tent had been pitched in an abandoned ruskakk nest under a tangled arch of thyssel bushes. While Nick treated his injuries, he had been watching her vague silhouette cast on the tent wall by the light of a captured glow rod.

When the light winked out, it was as though she'd never even been there.

The muddy pastel pulse of glowvine light had Nick squinting at the medpac's scanner. "Looks like we took care of your internal bleeding," he said. "One more shot of anti-inflammatory, to keep the concussion swelling in your brain under control . . ."

Mace leaned his head to one side as Nick pressed the spray hypo against his carotid artery. The Jedi Master stared sightlessly off through the night; he didn't even feel the brief sting of the injection.

He was tracking his lightsaber.

"He's not settling," Mace said.

"Who's not what?"

"Vastor. He's pacing. Circling. Like a rancor staked out in the desert."

"You surprised?"

"I shouldn't be. He probably senses that even though the fight was real, my submission was fake. He's just not sure what to do about it."

Nick clipped the spray hypo back into its receptacle. "Unless your idea of fun is quality time with me and a medpac, I'd suggest you stay out of his way." He tapped the bacta patch that covered the bite wound on Mace's trapezius. "You wouldn't *believe* how many different kinds of lethal bacteria I found in there. I do *not* want to know what he's been *eating.*"

"I am less concerned with what he's eating," Mace said, "than with what's eating *him.*"

"One easy guess." Nick nodded toward Depa's tent. "How is she?"

Mace shrugged. "As you saw."

"No—I mean, that whole dark side crap. Like what we were talking about before I left you at the outpost."

"I . . . can't say." Mace's habitual frown deepened. "I would like to say she's fine. But what I would *like* has little to do with what *is.* She seems . . . unstable."

"Well, y'know, a few months in the war could do that to anybody."

"That's what I'm afraid of."

FROM THE PRIVATE JOURNALS OF MACE WINDU

I am not sure what time it is. After midnight, I suspect, with some hours to go before dawn. I cannot be more accurate, as this datapad's chronometer function has suffered the same fate as its concealed transmitter. There is a time of night here when even the glowvines mute their light, and the prowling predators go quiet, and sleep seems the only activity that has meaning.

Yet here I am awake, though I have slept little in the past three days. It was Depa's scream that woke me.

A raw shriek of impossible anguish, it yanked me from nightmares of my own. It was not fear, that scream, but suffering so profound that it could have no other expression.

Her scream woke her as well, and her first thought was to open her tent and exhaustedly reassure us that it had been only a dream. That seems always to be her first thought: to reassure the Korunnai, and me. From this I take considerable comfort.

It's the third time this has happened so far tonight.

And yet—injured as I am, and unused to sleeping on a Korun bedroll on the open ground—I find I have slept as well as I have yet managed on this planet.

Depa's screams are a *mercy*.

Because my own nightmares don't wake me.

My nightmares suck me down, drowning me in a blind gluey chaos of anxiety and pain; they are more than simple anxiety dreams of wounds or suffering or the varieties of gruesome maiming, dismemberment, and death available in the jungle.

In my dreams here, I have seen the destruction of the Jedi. The death of the Republic. I have seen the Temple in ruins, the Senate smashed, and Coruscant itself shattered by orbital bombardment from immense ships of impossible design. I have seen Coruscant, the seat of galactic culture, become a jungle far more hostile and alien than any on Haruun Kal.

I have seen the end of civilization.

Depa's screams bring me back to the jungle and the night.

A week ago, I could not have imagined that to wake up in this jungle would be a relief.

FROM THE PRIVATE JOURNALS OF MACE WINDU

Tomorrow we leave this place.

This is what I've been telling myself all day long, riding cross-legged on the ankkox's shell, talking with Depa. I should say: listening to her, for she seems to hear me only when it suits her. All day, I left the shell only to stretch my legs or relieve myself . . . and sometimes as I would climb up the shell to my spot, she'd be talking already, in that same low blurry murmur she used to speak with me—as though our conversation had been going on in her head, and my arrival was only a detail.

When the gunships came and rained fire upon us, or blasted away randomly with their cannons, the guerrillas who were lucky enough to be near the ankkox often ducked beneath it for shelter, but Depa never did, so neither did I. She lay on her chaise within the howdah, and I sometimes leaned my back against its polished rail, so that her soft voice drifted in over my shoulder.

We covered many kilometers today. The ground is rising; as the jungle thins we can move much more swiftly. It is not for nothing that a Korun does not speak of distance in kilometers, but in travel time.

The same thinning of the jungle that increases our speed also leaves us more exposed to the gunships that seem now to be patrolling in an organized search pattern.

I have much to tell of this day that has passed, and yet it's difficult for me to begin. I can only think of tomorrow, of meeting Nick, and finally calling down the *Halleck* to carry us away.

I burn for it.

I have discovered that I *hate* this place.

Not very Jedi of me, but I cannot deny it. I hate the damp, and the smell, and the heat, and the sweat that trickles constantly around my eyebrows, trails down my cheeks, and drips from the point of my chin. I hate the stupid bovine complacency of the grassers, and the feral snarls of the half-wild akk dogs. I hate the gripleaves, and the brassvines, the portaak trees and thyssel bushes.

I hate the darkness under the trees.

I hate the war.

I hate what it's done to these people. To Depa.

I hate what it's doing to me.

The *Halleck* will be cool. It will be *clean*. The food will have no mold or rot or insect eggs.

I know already what I will do first, aboard ship. Before I even visit the bridge to salute the captain.

I will take a *shower*.

The last time I was clean was on the shuttle, in orbit. Now I wonder if I'll ever be clean again.

When I stepped off the shuttle at the Pelek Baw spaceport, I remember looking up at the white peak of Grandfather's Shoulder, and thinking that I had spent far too much time on Coruscant.

What a fool I was.

As Depa described me: Blind, ignorant, arrogant fool.

I was afraid to learn how bad things might be here, and the worst of my fears didn't even approach the truth.

I can't—

I feel my lightsaber coming this way. I will continue later.

FROM THE PRIVATE JOURNALS OF MACE WINDU

Kar was ostensibly stopping at Depa's tent to discuss tomorrow's march before she settles in for the night; I suspect that his true aim was to check on me.

I hope he is satisfied by what he found.

This morning, I asked Depa why she hadn't left when the Separatists pulled back to Gevarno and Opari. Why she clearly would stay even now, were I not extorting her cooperation.

"There is fighting to be done. Can a Jedi walk away?" Her voice was muffled, coming through the curtains. She did not invite me inside this morning, and I did not ask why.

I'm afraid that she was in a state that neither of us wanted me to see.

"To fight on after the battle is done—Depa, that is not Jedi," I told her. "That's the dark."

"War is not about light or dark. It is about winning. Or dying."

"But here you've already won." I thought back to the words of my strange waking dream. Her words, or the Force's, I did not know.

"Perhaps I have. But look around you: is what you see a victorious army? Or are they ragged fugitives, spending the last of their strength to stay a step ahead of the gallows?"

I have enormous sympathy for them: for their suffering and their desperate struggle. It is never far from my thoughts that only chance—a whim of Jedi anthropologists and the choice of some elders of ghôsh Windu—separates their fate from my own.

I could too easily have grown to become Kar Vastor myself.

But I said none of this to Depa; my purpose here was not to muse upon the twists in the endless river that is the Force.

"I understand their war," I told her. "It's very clear to me why they fight. My question is: Why are *you* still fighting?"

"Can't you *feel* it?"

And when she spoke, I could: in the Force, a relentless pulse of fear and hatred, like what I had felt from Nick and Chalk and Besh and Lesh in the groundcar, but here amplified as though the jungle had become a planetwide resonance chamber. It was hate that kept the Korunnai fighting on, as though this whole people shared a single dream: that all Balawai might have a single skull, bent for a Korun mace . . .

She said: "Yes: our battle is won. Theirs goes on. It will never be over, not while one of them still lives. The Balawai will never stop coming. We used these people for our own purposes—and we got what we wanted. Should I now throw them *away?* Abandon them to *genocide,* because they are no longer *useful?* Is that what the Council orders me to do?"

"You prefer to stay and fight a war that is not yours?"

Her voice gathered heat. "They *need* me, Mace. I am their only hope."

That heat quickly faded, though, and she went back to her exhausted mumble. "I've done . . . things. Questionable things. I know. But I have seen . . . Mace, you cannot *imagine* what I have seen. As bad as it is—as bad as I am . . . Search the Force. You can *feel* how much worse everything could be. How much worse it *will* be."

With this, I could not argue.

"Look around you." Her mumble took on a bitter edge. "Think about everything you've seen. This is a *little* war, Mace. A little sputtering on-again, off-again series of inconclusive skirmishes. Until the Republic and the Confederacy mixed into it, it was practically a sporting event. But look at what it's done to these people. Imagine what war will do to those who've never known it. Imagine infantry battles in the fields of

Alderaan. DOKAWs striking spacescrapers on Coruscant. Imagine what the galaxy will be if the Clone War turns serious."

I told her it was already serious, and she laughed at me. "You haven't *seen* serious yet."

I told her I was looking at it.

And I think, now, of the clone troopers on the *Halleck,* and how their clean crisp unquestioning bravery and discipline under fire is as far from these ragged murderers as it is possible to be for members of the same species . . . and I remember that the Grand Army of the Republic numbers 1.2 million clone troopers—just enough to station a single trooper—one lone man—on each planet of the Republic, and have a handful of thousands left over.

If this Clone War escalates the way Depa seems to think it will, it will be fought not by clones and Jedi and battle droids, but by ordinary people. Ordinary people who will face one stark choice: to die, or to become like these Korunnai. Ordinary people who will have to leave forever the Galaxy of Peace.

I can only hope that war is easier on those who cannot touch the Force.

Though I suspect the truth is exactly opposite.

There were hours, too, when we did not speak. I sat beside the howdah while she dozed in the afternoon heat, drowsy myself with the ankkox's rocking gait and the unchanging flow of the trees and vines and flowers, and I listened to her dream-mumbles, and was shocked, sometimes, by her sudden nightmare shrieks, or the agonized moans that her migraines might pull from her lips.

She seems to suffer from an intermittent fever. Sometimes her speech becomes a disjointed ramble through imaginary conversations that shift from subject to subject with hallucinatory randomness. Sometimes her pronouncements have an eerie sibylline quality, as though she prophesied a future that had no past. I've occasionally tried to record these on this datapad, but somehow her voice never comes through.

As though our talks are my own hallucination.

And if so—

Does it matter?

Even a lie of the Force is more true than any reality we can comprehend.

FROM THE PRIVATE JOURNALS OF MACE WINDU

Much of the day we spent talking about Kar Vastor. Depa has spared me many of the less savory details, but she has told me enough.

More than enough.

For example: when he calls me dôshalo, it's not just an expression. If what he has told Depa is the truth, Kar Vastor and I are the last of the Windu.

The ghôsh into which I was born—and with which I lived for those months in my teens, while I returned to learn some of the Korun Force skills—has apparently been destroyed piecemeal over the past thirty years. Not in any great massacre, or climactic last stand, but by the simple, brutal mathematics of attrition: my ghôsh is just another statistical casualty of a simmering guerrilla war against an enemy more numerous, better armed, and equally ruthless.

Depa told me this hesitantly, as though it were horrible news that must be broken gently. And perhaps it is. I cannot say. She seems to think it should matter a great deal to me. And perhaps it should.

But I am more thoroughly Jedi than I am Korun.

When I think of my dôshallai dead and scattered, Windu heritage and traditions perishing in blood and darkness, I feel only abstract sadness.

Any tale of pointless suffering and loss is sad, to me.

I would change them *all* if I could. Not just my own.

I would certainly change Kar's.

It seems that as a young man, Kar Vastor was fairly ordinary: more in touch with *pelekotan* than most, but not in any other way unsual. It was the Summertime War that changed him, as it has changed so much on this world.

When he was fourteen, he saw his whole family massacred by jungle prospectors: one of the casual atrocities that characterize this war.

I do not know how it is that he alone escaped; the stories Depa has heard from various Korunnai are contradictory. Kar himself, it seems, will not discuss it.

What we do know is that after witnessing the murders of his entire family, he was left alone in the jungle: without weapons, without grassers, without akks or people, food or supplies of any kind. And that he lived in the jungle—alone—for more than a standard year.

This is what he meant when he said he had survived *tan pel'trokal*.

The term has an irony that only now do I begin to appreciate.

The *tan pel'trokal* is a penalty devised by Korun culture, to punish crimes deserving death. Knowing that human judgment is fallible, the Korunnai leave the final disposition of the sentence to the jungle itself; they consider it a mercy.

I would say: it is a mercy they grant themselves. Thus can they take life without the shame of bloodied hands.

In Kar's case, he faced his *tan pel'trokal* for the crime of being Korun. He was as innocent—and as guilty—as the Balawai children to whom he was planning to do the same. Their crimes were identical: they were born into the wrong family.

He was, at the time, perhaps a year older than Keela.

But there was no Jedi nearby to save him, and so he had to save himself.

I believe that his ability to form human speech was part of the price he paid for his survival. All Jedi know that power must be paid for; the Force maintains a balance that cannot be defied. *Pelekotan* traded him power for his humanity.

I sometimes wonder if the Force does the same for Jedi.

He and his Akk Guards clearly have much in common with Jedi: they seem to be our reflections in a dark mirror. They rely on instinct; Jedi rely on training. They use anger and aggression as sources of power; our power is based upon serenity and defense. Even the weapon he and his Akk Guards carry is a twisted mirror image of ours.

I use my sword as a shield. They use their shields as swords.

Depa tells me that these "vibroshields" are Kar's own design. Vibro-axes are common equipment among jungle prospectors, used for harvesting lumber and clearing paths through stands too thick for their steamcrawlers to crush through; since the sonic generators that power vibro-axes are fully sealed, they are remarkably resistant to the metal-eating molds and fungi.

And the metal itself . . . well, that's an interesting story of its own. It seems to be an alloy that the fungi don't attack. It is extremely hard, and never loses its edge. Nor does it rust, or even tarnish.

It also seems to be a superconductor.

This is why my blade could not cut it: the entire shield is always the same temperature throughout. Even the energy of a lightsaber is instantly conducted away. Hold a blade against it long enough and the whole thing will melt, but it cannot be cut. Not by an energy blade.

File the data.

When Kar accepts a man into his Akk Guards, the man builds his own weapons, not unlike the tradition in the spirit of which Jedi construct our lightsabers.

It strikes me now that Kar may have hit upon this idea from stories of Jedi training I shared with my long-lost friends in ghôsh Windu, thirty-five years and more ago: Korunnai have a living oral tradition, and stories are passed through families as treasured possessions.

I have not shared this speculation with Depa.

And Depa swears that she did not teach Kar and his guards the Jedi skill of interception; she says Kar knew this already when she first met him. If what she says is true, he must have taught himself—and he probably got the idea from those same stories that I, in my thoughtless youth, innocently shared with my innocent friends.

And so: in some odd, circuitous way, Kar Vastor may be my fault.

The source of this metal is a mystery; though Kar never speaks of it to anyone, I believe I know what it is.

Starship armor.

Thousands of years ago—before the Sith War—when shield generators were so massive that only the largest capital ships could carry them, smaller starships were armored with a mirrorlike superconducting alloy, which was sufficient to resist the low-fire-rate laser cannons of the day.

I think Kar, somewhere out in the jungle of the Korunnal Highland, sometime during his yearlong *tan pel 'trokal,* had stumbled upon the ancient Jedi starship whose crash stranded on this planet his ancestors, and my own.

It was earlier this evening that I learned the real truth of Kar Vastor. Not only who he is, and *why* he is—

But what he *means.*

Somewhere along our line of march Kar had located a cave that he deemed adequate to shelter a fire from gunship or satellite detection, and that night he set about curing Besh's and Chalk's fever wasp infestation. Besh and Chalk had remained in thanatizine suspension, tied to a grasser's travois like a bundle of cargo. The crude hacking Terrel had done to them had been mostly repaired with tissue binders from a captured medpac, though of course the wounds could not heal; the body's healing processes are suspended by thanatizine as well.

Depa was in attendance, as was I, as well as a select few others. A pair of the Akk Guards had carried her, chaise and all, in from her howdah. She lay back with one slim arm across her eyes; she was having another of her headaches, and the light from the fire of tyruun, the local wood that burns white-hot, was causing her pain. I suspect she might have preferred to skip the whole business.

Even so, when Kar laid the still forms of Besh and Chalk facedown on the mossy floor of the cave and tore open the backs of their tunics, Depa stirred and sat forward. Though she continued to shade her eyes, firelight gave them glitters of silver and red. She watched raptly, her small white teeth fixed in her lower lip, worrying the corner of her mouth near the burn scar.

Kar simply squatted beside the two, humming tunelessly under his breath, while a Korun I did not recognize injected them with the antidote. Vastor's humming deepened, and found a pulsing rhythm like the slow beat of a human heart. He extended his hands, and closed his eyes, and hummed, and I could feel motion in the Force, a swirl of power very unlike any I've felt from a Jedi healer—or anyone else, for that matter.

A streak of red painted itself along their spines, and a moment later this red suddenly blossomed into the glistening wetness of fresh blood oozing through their skin—and details, I suppose, are unnecessary. Suffice it to say that Kar had somehow used the Force—used *pelekotan*—to *persuade* the fever wasp larvae that they were in the wrong place to hatch: using the same animal tropism that draws them from the site of the wasp sting to cluster along the victim's central nervous system, Kar induced them to *migrate*—

Out of Besh and Chalk entirely.

And such was his power that the entire wriggling mass of them—nearly a kilo all told—squirmed its way straight into the tyruun blaze, where the larvae popped while they roasted with a stench like burning hair.

In the midst of this extraordinary display, Depa leaned close to me and whispered, "Don't you ever wonder if we might be *wrong?*"

I didn't understand what she was talking about, and she waved her fine-boned hand vaguely toward Vastor. "Such power—and such control—and never a day of training. Because what he does is *natural*: as natural as the jungle itself. We Jedi train our entire lives: to control our natural emotions, to overcome our natural desires. We give up so much for our power. And what Jedi could have done this?"

I could not answer; Vastor has power on the scale of Master Yoda, or young Anakin Skywalker. And I had no desire to debate with Depa on Jedi tradition, and the necessary distinction between dark and light.

So I tried to change the subject.

I told her that Nick had shared with me the truth of the faked massacre and her message on the data wafer, and I reminded her that she had yesterday alluded to having some plan for me: something she wanted to teach me, or to show me. So I asked her.

I asked what she had hoped to accomplish by drawing me here.

I asked what are *her* victory conditions.

She said that she wanted to tell me something. That's all. It was a message she could have sent on a subspace squawk: a line or two, no more. But I had to be in the war—see the war, eat and drink, breathe and *smell* the war—or I wouldn't have believed it.

She told me: "The Jedi will lose."

There in the cave, as fever wasp larvae snapped and crackled in the tyruun flames, I countered with numbers: there are still ten times as many Loyalist systems as Separatist, the Republic has a titanic manu-facturing base, and huge advantages in resources . . . the beginnings of a whole list of reasons the Republic will inevitably win.

"Oh, I know," was her response. "The Republic may very well win. But the *Jedi* will lose."

I said I did not understand, but I now believe that is not true. The truth, I think, is what the Force said to me in the image of Depa back at the outpost: that I already understand all there is to understand.

I just don't want to believe it.

She said that I had foreshadowed the defeat of the Jedi myself. "The reason you freed the Balawai, Mace," she said, "is the same reason that the Jedi will be destroyed."

War is a horror, she said. Her words: "A *horror.* But what you don't understand is that it *must* be a horror. That's how wars are won: by in-flicting such terrible suffering upon the enemy that they can no longer bear to fight. You cannot treat war like *law enforcement,* Mace. You can't fight to protect the innocent—because *no one is innocent."*

She said something similar to what Nick had said about the jungle prospectors: that there are no civilians.

"The *innocent citizens* of the Confederacy are the ones who make it possible for their leaders to wage war on us: they build the ships, they grow the food, mine the metals, purify the water. And only they can stop the war: only their suffering will bring it to a close."

"But you can't expect Jedi to stand by while ordinary people are hurt and killed—" I began.

"Exactly. That is why we cannot win: to win this war, we must no longer *be* Jedi." She speaks of this in the future tense, though I suspect that in her heart—in her conscience—the Jedi are dead already. "Like dropping a bomb into the arena on Geonosis: we can *save* the Republic, Mace. We *can.* But the cost will be our principles. In the end, isn't that what Jedi are for? We sacrifice everything for the Republic: our families, our homeworlds, our wealth, even our lives. Now the Republic needs us to sacrifice our consciences as well. Can we refuse? Are Jedi traditions more important than the lives of billions?"

She told me how she and Kar Vastor had managed to drive the Separatists off this world.

The CIS had been using the Pelek Baw spaceport as a base for the repair, refit, and resupply of the droid starfighters they used to picket the
Al'Har system. These operations required large numbers of civilian employees. Her strategy was simple: she proved to these civilian employees that the Separatist military and the Balawai militia together were
powerless to protect them.

There was no pitched battle. Nothing heroic or colorful. Just an unending series of gruesome killings. One or two at a time. At first, the
Separatists had flooded Pelek Baw with their forces—but battle droids
are as vulnerable to the metal-eating fungi as are simple blasters, and
soldiers of flesh and blood die just as easily as civilians. The essence of
guerrilla warfare: the real target is not the enemy's emplacements, or
even their lives.

The target is the enemy's will to fight.

Wars are won not by killing enemies, but by terrorizing them until
they give up and go home.

"That's why I brought you to Haruun Kal," she said. "I wanted to
show you what *winning* soldiers will look like." She pointed past the
fire. "That is the Jedi of the future, Mace. Right there."

She was pointing at Kar Vastor.

Which is why at this black hour, long after midnight and long before
dawn, as the glowvines weaken and predators go quiet, when only
sleep has meaning, I lie upon my bedroll and stare at the black leaves
above, and think of tomorrow.

Tomorrow we leave this place.

Back to worlds where showers are just clean water, instead of pro-bi
mist. Back to worlds where we sleep indoors, on bedrolls, with clean
bleached-fiber sheets.

Back to worlds that still lie, however temporarily, within the Galaxy
of Peace.

14

FINAL ENTRY

The air above the Lorshan Pass was so clear that the sky-colored peak Mace could barely discern in the distant south might have been Grandfather's Shoulder itself. There was a pall of brown haze down in that direction that he suspected was the smog over Pelek Baw. In the nearer distance, tiny silver flecks of gunships patrolled the jungle canopy below the pass. A lot of gunships: Mace had counted at least six flights, possibly as many as ten, weaving among the hills.

The occasional silent flash of cannonfire, or curling black smoke from flame projectors, he actually found comforting: it meant the militia thought the guerrillas were still down among the trees.

He sat cross-legged on the shadowed dirt of the cave mouth's floor, his datapad slung on his shoulder. Only two meters away, brilliant late-afternoon sunlight slanted across the cliffside meadow: a grassy sward, relatively flat for a few tens of meters before it curled over the lip of the cliff and dropped half a klick to the pass below.

Easily large enough for a Republic Sienar Systems *Jadthu*-class lander.

Mace determinedly avoided staring up into the sky. It would get there when it got there.

Only minutes to go, now.

He found himself tallying the list of injuries Haruun Kal had inflicted upon him, from the stun-blast bruises through flame burns, cracked ribs, a concussion, and a human bite wound. Not to mention innumerable insect bites and stings, some kind of rash on his right thigh, and blistering around his toes that was probably a persistent fungal infection . . .

And those were only the physical injuries. They would heal.

The nonphysical injuries—to his confidence, his principles, his moral certainties . . . to his heart—

Those couldn't be treated with spray bandages and a bacta patch.

Behind him, Nick's pacing had scuffed a path through the thin layer of dirt to the stone of the cave floor. He picked up his rifle from where it leaned against the wall, checked the action for the dozenth time, and set it back down again. He did the same with the slug pistol holstered at his thigh, then looked around for something else to do. Not finding anything, he went back to pacing. "How much longer?"

"Not long."

"That's what you said the last three times I asked."

"I suppose it depends on what you mean by *long.*"

"You sure she's coming?"

"Yes," Mace lied.

"What if they get here before she does? I mean, we're not gonna have time to lag around *waiting* for her—not with gunships and who-knows-what-all tracking the lander through the atmosphere. If she's not here—"

"We'll worry about that if it happens."

"Yeah." Nick started pacing from the back to the front of the cave, instead of side to side. "Yeah."

"Nick."

"Yeah?"

"Settle down."

The young Korun stopped, winced an apology at Mace, adjusted his tunic, and ran his thumbs around the drawstring waistband of his pants as though they were chafing him. "I don't like waiting."

"I've noticed."

Nick squatted alongside the Jedi Master and nodded at the data-pad. "Got any games on that thing? Shee, I'd even play dejarik. And I *hate* dejarik."

Mace shook his head. "It's my journal."

"I've seen you talking into it. Like a diary?"

"Something like that. It's a personal log of my experiences on Haruun Kal. For the Temple Archives."

"Wow. Am *I* in there?"

"Yes. And Chalk, and Besh, and Lesh. Depa and Kar Vastor, and the children from the outpost—"

"Wow," Nick repeated. "I mean, *wow*. That's really cool. Do all Jedi do that?"

Mace stared out over the rugged terrain below the pass. "I don't think Depa has." He sighed, and once more stopped himself from checking the sky. "Why do you ask?"

"It's just—well, it's weird, y'know? Thinking about it. I'm gonna be in the *Jedi Archives* . . ."

"Yes."

"Twenty-five thousand years of records. It's like—like I'll be part of the history of the whole galaxy!"

"You would be, regardless."

"Oh, yeah, sure, I know: everybody is. But not everybody's in the Jedi Archives, are they? I mean, my name'll be there *forever.* It's like being immortal . . ."

Mace thought of Lesh, and of Phloremirlla Tenk. Of Terrel and Rankin. Of corpses burned to namelessness, left on the ground at the outpost.

"It is," he said slowly, "as close to immortality as any of us will ever come."

"Could I listen to some?" Nick tried an encouraging nod. "Not like I'm nosy or anything. But it'd pass the time—"

"Are you certain you want to know what I think of you?"

"Sure I'm—why? Is it bad?" he asked with an anticipatory wince. "It's really bad, isn't it."

"I am teasing you, Nick. I can't play it for you. It's encrypted, and only the archive masters at the Temple have the code key."

"What, you can't even listen to it yourself?"

Mace hefted the datapad in his hand; it seemed such a small, insubstantial thing, to carry so much doubt and pain.

"Not only does encryption keep its contents secure, it protects me from the temptation to go back and edit entries to make myself look better."

"You'd do that?"

"The opportunity has not presented itself. If I had the chance . . . I can't really say. I hope that I would resist. But Jedi or not, I am still human." He shrugged. "I should make a last entry, preparatory to my formal report to the Council on our return to Coruscant."

"Can I listen?"

"I suppose you can. I have nothing to say that you don't already know."

FROM THE PRIVATE JOURNALS OF MACE WINDU [FINAL HARUUN KAL ENTRY]

Major Rostu and I wait in a cave at the Korun base in the Lorshan Pass; Depa—

[Male voice identified as NICK ROSTU, *major (bvt), GAR]:* "Hey, is that on? So they can, like, *hear* me?"

Yes. It's—

[Rostu]: "Wow. So some weird alien Jedi a thousand years from now can pull this out and it'll be like I'm saying *Hi* to him from a thousand years ago, huh? Hi, you creepy Jedi monkeyhunker, whoever you—"

Major.

[Rostu]: "Yeah, I know: *Shut up, Nick.*"

[sound of a heavy sigh]

Depa is to meet us here.

She has some strategem to get Kar Vastor and his Akk Guards far enough away for us all to make a clean extraction; she did not offer details, and I did not ask.

I was afraid to hear what she might have told me.

The signal was sent early this morning, using the same technique her sporadic reports had. Instead of a straight subspace transmission—which would be intercepted by the militia's satellites and allow them to pinpoint our location—she broadcast the coded extraction call on a normal comm channel, using a tight beam that they bounced to the HoloNet satellite off one of the mountains within our line of sight; the comm signal also contains a Jedi priority override code that hijacks part of the local HoloNet capacity, and uses *that* to send the actual extraction code to the *Halleck*. It is very safe, though there is always data loss from beam scatter.

I heard the acknowledgment myself, in the base's comm station.

The *Halleck* is on its way.

We arrived at this base about a standard hour after sunrise. The *Halleck* is probably insystem by now. The base itself is . . . not what I was expecting.

It's less a military base than an underground refugee camp.

The complex is enormous, a randomly dug hive that honeycombs the whole north wall of the pass; a number of access tunnels extend well downslope, to concealed caves deep in the jungle. Some of the caverns are natural: volcanic bubbles and water channels eroded by drainage from the snowcapped peaks above. The inhabited caverns have been artificially enlarged and smoothed. Though there is no mining industry on Haruun Kal, and thus no excavation equipment to be had, a vibro-ax cuts stone almost as easily as wood; many of the smaller chambers have pallet beds, tables, and benches of stone cut and dressed by such blades.

Which would make it relatively comfortable, were it not so crowded.

Thousands of Korunnai cram these caverns and tunnels and caves, and more trickle in every day. These are the noncombatants: the spouses and the parents, the sick and the wounded. And the children.

The global lack of mining equipment means that ventilation is necessarily rudimentary, and sanitation virtually nonexistent. Pneumonia is rampant; antibiotics are the first thing to run out in the captured medpacs, and there is nowhere in the caverns one can go and not hear people wheezing as they struggle to pull their next breath into wet, clogged lungs. Dysentery claims lives among the elderly and the wounded, and with sanitation basically at the level of buckets, it will only get worse.

The largest caverns have been given over to the grassers. All the arriving Korunnai bring whatever grassers survive the trip; even in wartime, the Fourth Pillar holds them in its grip. These grassers spend their days crowded together with no food and little room to move; they are all sickly, and restive. There have been fights between members of different herds, and I am told several die each day: victims of wounds from fighting, or infectious disease from the close quarters. Some, it seems, simply surrender their will to live; they lie down and refuse to get up, and eventually starve.

The Korunnai tend them as best they can; improvised fences of piled cut rock separate the various herds, and they are driven out the access tunnels in turns to forage in the jungles below the pass, under the watchful eyes of herding akks. But even this half measure is becoming problematic: as more and more grassers arrive, the Korunnai must take the herds farther and farther afield, to avoid thinning the jungle so much that it might reveal the base's location.

I do understand, now, why Depa doesn't want to leave.

We rode her ankkox right up one of the concealed tunnels. When we left the gloom of the jungle for the deeper darkness underground, Depa pulled back the curtains of her howdah and moved forward to the chair mounted on the beast's crown armor, and she seemed to inhale serenity with the thick stinking air.

Everyone we passed—everyone we *saw*—

There was no cheering, or even shouts; the welcome she got was more profound than anything that can be expressed by voice.

A woman, huddled against a sweating stone wall, caught sight of Depa, and pushed herself forward, and her face might have been a flower opening toward the sun. Depa's mere presence brought light to her eyes, and strength to her legs. The woman struggled to rise, pulling herself up the tunnel wall then leaning upon it for support, and she stretched a hand toward us, and when Depa gave her a nod of acknowledgment, the woman's hand closed to catch Depa's gaze from the air; she pressed that closed hand to her breast as though that one simple glance was precious.

Sacred.

As though it was exactly the one thing she needed to keep on living.

And that's what our welcome here was: that woman, multiplied by thousands. The warriors and the wounded. The aged. The sick and the infirm, the children—

Depa is more than a Jedi to them. Not a goddess—Force-users themselves, they are not easily impressed by Jedi powers. She is, I think, a totem. She is to them what a Jedi should be to everyone, but writ so large upon their hearts that it has become a form of madness.

She is their hope.

[Rostu]: "It's true, y'know."

Nick?

[Rostu]: "You think things are bad here? Okay, sure: they're bad. Not just *here* here. The whole highland. Bad enough. But you got *no idea* what it was before Depa—y'know, we're *not* the bad guys here."

No one has suggested that you are. Nor are you the good guys. I haven't *seen* any good guys.

[Rostu]: "So far? I've seen *one*. No: two."

You have?

[Rostu]: "All that good guy, bad guy stuff goes out the air lock pretty fast, doesn't it? I mean, you know why Pelek Baw withdrew from the Republic? It's got nothing to do with 'corruption in the Senate' and all that political tusker poop, either. The Balawai joined the Confederacy because the seppies promised to *respect* their *sovereignty*. Get it? Planetary *rights*. And the only planetary right the Balawai *care* about is the right to *kill us all*. The seppies park their droid starfighters and support staff at the spaceport, and all of a sudden the militia has an unlimited supply of gunships, and the Balawai have made it *illegal* for a Korun to be outside the city limits of Pelek Baw, and pretty soon they start rounding up Korunnai from *inside* the city, too—not everybody, you understand, just the criminals. The beggars, and street kids. And troublemakers. For the record, a *troublemaker* is any Korun who says Word One about the way we're treated.

"They had a camp for us. I was there. That's where Depa found us. You think things are ugly here? You should see what she *saved* us from.

"So maybe we went from living there to dying here. So? You think there's a *difference?* You think that was *better?*

"You go live in a cage if you want. Me? I'll die a free man. *That's* what Depa is to us.

"That's who you're taking away."

She would be leaving you soon, regardless.

[Rostu]: "Says you."

She is dying, Nick. The war is killing her. This *planet* is killing her. The Korunnai are killing her.

[Rostu]: "Nobody here would *ever* hurt her—" Not on purpose.

But she is drowning in your anger, Nick.

[Rostu]: "Hey, I'm just mildly cranky."

Not you personally. *All* of you. This whole place.

The unending violence . . . without hope, or remedy . . .

A Jedi's connection to the Force amplifies everything about us: it invests our smallest actions with the greatest conceivable weight. It makes us *more* of whatever we already are. If we are calm, it gives us serenity. If we are angry, it fills us with the rage of a god. Anger is a trap. You might think of it as a narcotic, not unlike glitterstim. Even the slightest taste can leave you with an appetite that never fades.

This is why we Jedi must strive always to build peace within ourselves: what is within will be reflected by what is without. The Force is One. We are part of the Force; it will always be, at least partially, whatever we are.

Just as it is too late for Kar Vastor to become a Jedi, it is too late for Depa to become a *lor pelek.* She is willing to give her life to help your people. Are you willing to take it?

[Rostu]: "Hey, don't look at me like that. I'm on *your* side, remember?"

So.

The *Halleck* must be insystem by now; we should be seeing a lander's vapor trail any minute.

And Depa is headed up to meet us.

[Rostu]: "She is? What, you can feel her?"

Not directly. But—characteristically—part of her plan to keep Kar and his Akk Guards out of our way included retrieving my lightsaber. In details like this—these little considerations, her automatic kindness—I find my hope that she is not wholly lost.

Though I can rebuild my blade, she—

There was a sadness—

Melancholy resignation: that is the best I can describe her expression, when she promised my lightsaber's return. Though the weapon is itself no great thing, she seemed near tears.

"I could not bear for your journey here to cost you anything more than it already has," she told me this morning, as I left her to come up here to wait.

I can feel clearly the approach of my lightsaber; and now I feel hers, as well. Winding toward us through the natural fissures in the rock that make a passageway from this cave to the interior caverns. It is odd—in an apprehensive, *premonition-of-dreadful-tragedy* sort of way—that I can feel Depa, the Depa I know, only in her weapon.

[Rostu]: "Um, does that appre-pre-whatever of dreadful tragedy by any chance translate into Basic as *I have a bad feeling about this?* Because, y'know, now that you mention it—"

I feel it too—but I have had only bad feelings ever since I came to this planet.

[Rostu]: "I've been wondering—I mean, we've been up here a *long* time. Haven't you started to wonder if Depa *didn't* send us up here so she could get Kar out of the way? If she sent us up here to get *us* out of the way?"

This has occurred to me. I have refused to allow myself to consider it. Depa is not like that; she is not given to trickery, much less betrayal. She has said she will join us here. That means she *will* join us. Here.

She's only steps away—

[Rostu]: "Or maybe, y'know: not."

You . . .

[Rostu]: "That's far enough. Stop! I mean it."

[The final sound on Master Windu's Haruun Kal journal is a nonverbal vocalization similar to a large predator's warning growl.]

[END JOURNAL]

15

THE TRAP

Nick stood in a classic shooter's stance, slug pistol in his right hand, left shoulder forward, right arm straight across his body, left hand cupping his right and the pistol's butt.

His target was a needle-pointed grin just visible within the fissure at the back of the cave.

Mace came to his feet smoothly but deliberately, without any sudden motion. "Don't do it, Nick."

"I'd rather not," Nick admitted. "But I will if I have to."

"I've seen him block blaster bolts. He can do the same with bullets. You won't have a chance."

"Says you." Nick's voice was uncharacteristically calm and flat, and his hands were as steady as the mountain around them. "You haven't seen me shoot."

"This is the wrong time to show me." Mace put one hand on Nick's arm and let its tired weight pull the pistol down. "Come on out, Kar."

The darkness in the fissure gathered itself into the shape of the *lor pelek*. His vibroshields were pushed back onto his upper arms.

In his hands he held two lightsabers.

Mace sagged as all hope and faith drained out of him. Only exhaustion remained.

He had been trying so hard, for so long, to believe in her, and in himself, and in the Force. He had *made* himself believe: he had ruthlessly disciplined his mind against any dread of failure. After all, this was *Depa*, his Padawan, almost his *child*—he had known her all her *life*—

All but her first few months, and her last few months.

Vastor walked past Nick without a sideways glance, holding the lightsabers on his open palms.

A peace offering.

She asked me to—

"I know," Mace murmured.

She said she did not want you to lose anything more by coming here than you already have.

"I haven't."

And it was true: he had lost nothing real. Not on Haruun Kal. He had lost her before he'd ever set foot on the shuttle's landing ramp. He had lost her before the massacre and the message on the wafer. He had lost her before he even sent her here.

Depa Billaba was another casualty of his failure at Geonosis.

She was just taking longer to die.

All he had lost on Haruun Kal was an illusion. A dream. A hope so sacred that he had not dared to admit it, even to himself: a fantasy that someday the galaxy would be again at peace.

That everything would go back to normal.

Do you need to sit down, dôshalo? Vastor's purr was guardedly concerned. *You look unwell.*

"So this is the kiss-off, huh?" Nick had his gun back in its holster, but he looked like he was shooting at Vastor inside his head. "Pretty scummy trick, if you ask me."

Tell your boy to mind his tongue when he speaks of Depa.

Mace only shook his head silently. He was out of words.

"I mean, that's *low*. And I know something about low, if you know what I mean. The kiss-off's bad enough, but to send her lightsaber along so you'd think it was *her*—"

"That's not why she sent it," Mace said softly. "Kar's giving them both to me."

Vastor's growl was absolute as a vine cat's stare: pitiless but some-how not unsympathetic. *She said you would understand.*

Mace nodded distantly. "She has no use for it anymore."

Nick frowned at him. "She doesn't?"

"It is the weapon of a Jedi."

"Oh."

"Yes."

Mace lowered his head.

"She's trying to tell you—"

"Yes."

Mace closed his eyes.

He could no longer bear to look at this place.

"It's killing her," he said faintly. "Being here. Doing these things. If she stays, she will die."

Everyone dies, dôshalo. But Haruun Kal is her problem. This is her place. She knows it now. She belongs here. The jungle isn't killing her.

You are.

Mace opened his eyes to meet the *lor pelek*'s concentrated stare.

She never stops thinking of you, Vastor rumbled. *What is killing her is imagining what you must think of her. What she knows you think of what she has done, and will do. She measures herself by your standards; that your standards are fatally wrong doesn't make her failure to live up to them any less painful.*

You are her sire, Mace Windu. Do you not understand how much she loves you?

"Yes." He wished she could understand how much *he* loved *her* . . . But if she did, would she have done anything differently? Or would she only be in even greater pain? "Yes, I do."

This is why she sent me to deliver these weapons, and her good-byes. She could not face you.

Mace breathed a heavy sigh, then straightened his shoulders. "She," he said slowly, sadly, reluctantly, "will have to get over that."

Eh?

"I'm sorry this is painful for her. It's not fun for me either; the clos-est thing to fun I've had on this planet was being beaten into unconsciousness," he said. "I told her I would not leave this world without her. And I won't. Nothing has changed."

You think not? Step out here, dôshalo. The *lor pelek* walked out of the cave shadow into the brilliant red-smeared afternoon on the cliffside meadow. *This is not the only cave on this mountain.*

Mace followed him, and Kar waved a lightsaber at the vast mountainside, pocked with shadows. *In one of them waits one of my men. Over the past months, we have captured some heavy infantry weapons from the Balawai. One of those weapons is a shoulder-fired proton torpedo launcher.*

"Threats will not move me, Kar. I have told her that I will die here rather than leave her behind."

You misunderstand. The torpedo is not for you; if I want you dead, I can kill you myself.

"That," said Mace Windu, "remains to be seen."

Soon the lander will arrive to take you away from here. If you do not leave on it, my man will destroy it. Your pilots, and gunners, and soldiers, and whoever else who has come to bring you away: they will all die.

Now Mace did, finally, look into the sky. Limitless turquoise: the only clouds to be seen were vapor trails along the horizon.

You see? You are not the only one here who can take hostages.

"Do you know," Mace said wonderingly, "that I am almost grateful to you for this?"

I understand: it makes what you must do much easier.

"Yes. Exactly. You have made my choice for me."

"What's wrong?" Nick asked from the shadows. "What's he saying to you? We're still leaving, aren't we?"

"A great deal is wrong," Mace replied. "He has said nothing of consequence, and no, we are not leaving. Not without Depa."

Vastor's head drew down, and his eyes flickered danger. *I do not make idle threats.*

"That you are here means I did not know Depa as well as I thought I did. That the two of you would expect me to bow to this threat means that she knows me even less."

The lander will be destroyed. It will be as though you have killed them yourself.

"There is no *as though.*" Mace turned and lifted his head to look Kar Vastor in the eye. "What it will be is you, Kar Vastor, taking up arms against the Republic."

The Republic has nothing to do with this. This is personal. You cannot pretend—

"I placed Depa under formal arrest three days ago. She gave me her parole—that is to say, her word of honor as a Jedi that she would not attempt to escape, or otherwise avoid returning to answer for her actions before the Jedi Council. She has violated her word, and her honor. I must now take her into custody. And you, as well."

Me? You are mad.

"Kar Vastor," Mace said flatly, "you are charged with the murder of Terrel Nakay."

"Uh, Master, mm, General—? Sir? You sure you know what you're doing?"

Vastor stared in blank disbelief. *Your men will die.*

"They are soldiers, and this is a war. They understand the risks they face," Mace said. "Do you?"

What risks?

"When your man fires upon the lander, you will have committed treason. Implicated in your crime, Depa will face the same charge. You are placing her in capital jeopardy: that is, she will be executed along with you."

Vastor's growl did not now carry words. Only contempt and anger.

"Perhaps you should order your man to stand down. While you still can."

Depa is right: Jedi are insane.

"Ever since I came to this planet, people have been telling me how crazy I am. They've told me this so many times that I had started to wonder if it might be true. Now, though, I understand: you don't say this because it's true. Not even because you think it's true. You say it because you *hope* it's true. Because if I am insane, you aren't really the revolting slime-hearted vermin that, down deep, you know you are."

But Vastor no longer seemed to be listening. He had folded his massive arms so that the lightsabers in his hands disappeared behind his ultrachrome-shielded biceps. He paced meditatively away from Mace, strolling toward the meadow's cliff lip, and stared out over the vast roll of jungle below. The vista was alive with gunmetal specks and distant flashes of cannonfire.

Many gunships patrol today, he hummed. *More than I have ever seen.*

"Mace—" Nick hissed from the cave behind. "You know that bad feeling I was talking about? It's getting worse."

"Yes."

"Maybe you better get back in here where it's safe."

"Nowhere is safe," Mace said, and walked out to join Vastor at the edge of the cliff.

I have tried, Vastor purred when Mace reached his side. *I have done all that can be asked of me. Not even Depa can say I did not try to spare your life. But you will not be reasonable.*

"It is not in my nature."

It is as you said earlier: you have made my choice for me. There is only one way to protect her from you.

"That is true."

Mace reached down inside himself until he found the calm center within his exhaustion and his pain. He breathed himself into that center until he was fully within it, and all pain and fatigue and doubt were left behind outside.

"Do we fight, now?"

We must.

It is bitter, that we last men of ghôsh Windu must be enemies. I wish this could have turned out differently, but I did not expect it would. Depa has told me that you do not lose well.

"I haven't had much practice."

Vastor bent his head in a regretful nod of respect. *Good-bye, Mace, Jedi of the Windu.*

A tiny surge of the Force—

Just a twitch. A shrug. The slightest nudge, not even directed at Mace; sent off somewhere into the trees below the pass—

A signal.

The scene, frozen in time, locked in the amber of Mace's Force-sense: Vastor standing with arms folded, not the slightest hint of threat, his shields pushed high on his arms, those arms still crossed to bury the lightsabers that he held under his massive biceps—

Mace beside him, exposed on the lip of the cliff, unarmed—

Gunships rippling the jungle canopy far below in shock wakes, silent with distance—

Nick behind in the cave, rifle leaning against the rock, one hand yanking the butt of his holstered pistol in a draw that to ordinary eyes would be blinding—

And a man hidden in the shadows of the jungle a kilometer away, smoothly squeezing the trigger of a high-powered sniper's blaster rifle to send one single packet of murderous scarlet energy clawing up toward the meadow from the jungle below—

Centered on Mace Windu's heart.

All this Mace kenned in a single instant, effortlessly, and the shatterpoint he found and struck by instinct was Vastor's balance at the lip of the cliff.

Calmly, without any particular haste, Mace put his hand on Vastor's shoulder and gave the *lor pelek* a shove.

Over the edge.

Vastor's eyes bulged astonishment as he toppled forward and his arms uncrossed to windmill for his balance. His teetering swung his head just far enough in the right direction that the bullet from Nick's slug pistol scorched Vastor's temple instead of blowing his brains out through his eyes; as his arms whirled, his grip on the lightsabers loosened. Mace reached into the Force, snatching them both, triggering them to flaring life and bringing them to his hands with an easy six or seven milliseconds to spare before he needed them to splatter aside the bolt from the jungle below.

Vastor's vine cat reflexes whirled him in the air and latched his hands onto the rock face a meter below the lip of the cliff. His confederate in the jungle poured fire up at Mace to drive him back, while Nick ran out of the cave behind him, shouting *"Did I get him? Is he dead? Is he dead?"* until Vastor threw himself back up into the meadow, bringing his vibroshields into fighting position with a surge of the Force.

Nick fired as fast as his finger could jerk the pistol's trigger and bullets clanged off Vastor's flashing shields—

And Mace just stood there.

Staring into his blade.

In the Force, the world had turned to crystal.

The purple flame of his blade splintered flaws throughout the planet. Stress fractures spidered from his blade to Vastor, to Nick, into the mountain behind, into the pass below, and to space above, racing in outrippling waves that joined him with what *was,* but also with what *had been,* and what *would be.*

Triggering his blade here, now: it was a shatterpoint of the Summertime War.

His consciousness splintered along with the world, flashing instantly along the fault lines and vectors of effect: for a single instant, he was in direct and intimate contact with many different times and places.

He saw it all.

As though from some impossible distance, he saw the Balawai prisoners kneeling on the promontory, and how gunships had arrived almost before he'd even lit the wood he'd piled up to make a signal fire.

He saw the gunships arrive at the outpost, only minutes after he had ignited this weapon to defend the children in the bunker from the hasty fire of their own people's weapons.

He saw Vastor below the outpost's ruins, and heard again his growled meaning: *My men say you drove them off single-handed, though they did not seem to be damaged. Perhaps you have taught Balawai to fear the Jedi blade.*

But they did not fear it, he knew.

He saw the gunships at the notch pass: flying *away* only seconds after he first flashed his blades. They had been *ordered to withdraw.*

Because he'd been *alone.*

Because if he was killed *before* he reached Depa and her guerrillas, it wouldn't solve the militia's *Jedi problem.*

He saw himself in the Pelek Baw alley, staring in disbelief at his depowered lightsaber.

He saw the hours he'd spent in the binder chair in that dirty room in the Ministry of Justice, waiting; that long wait hadn't been an interrogation technique. Geptun had never intended to interrogate him in the first place.

Following that stress fault back in time, he saw a shielded room in the Ministry of Justice, where technicians made cut after cut with his lightsaber. Where they had shot the blade with blaster bolts and bullets, and used it to cut thyssel, and lammas, and portaak leaves, duracrete, transparisteel.

So that they could measure and record the emission signature of this blade.

So that their satellites would recognize it whenever it was used. No matter what it might be used for.

That's why his blade had been out of charge. Geptun had probably had no idea about that upcountry team; he'd *wanted* Mace to get out of Pelek Baw.

Wanted him to make contact with Depa and the "ULF."

Wanted to find where all the missing Korunnai had been hiding.

Now in the meadow, other stress faults connected his mind to dozens of gunships that converged on the Lorshan Pass. Gunships packed with eager troops, trailing billows of hate and fear and fierce anticipation like the ash plume from an erupting volcano.

One fracture terminated at an orbiting satellite that whizzed across the face of the planet at almost twenty-eight thousand kilometers per hour, and through the fracture he could feel a silicon brain make an electronic connection. He could feel the execution of a simple command program, and he could feel automated clamps releasing huge durasteel bars layered in ablative shielding, and he could feel primitive guidance jets driving them into the atmosphere at an angle too steep for any spacecraft to survive.

But these were not spacecraft, and they were not intended to survive.

Vastor was still in the air, and Nick was still twisting to track him with his blazing pistol, when Mace Windu whipped his arms straight and shouted, *"Stop!"*

The Force blasts that accompanied the Jedi Master's command clubbed Nick to the ground and sent Vastor spinning against the mountain's face above the cave.

"What are you *doing?*" Nick rolled to his feet and snapped the pistol back into line. "He just tried to *frag* you—*kill* him!"

Vastor crouched above, clinging to the rock like a krayt dragon. *No more talking. It is time to fight.*

"Yes," Mace Windu said. "But not each other. *Look around you!*"

He swung his arm toward the jungle below the pass.

All the patrolling gunships, the dozens that had leisurely crisscrossed the jungle all these past days, now traced converging streaks that would intersect at the Lorshan Pass.

Nick swore, and Vastor's growl lost meaning.

"And there," Mace said, pointing to what seemed to be a slowly developing dark cloud, high above the mountains, but was in fact the smoke from ablative shielding burning off in the atmosphere.

The center of the cloud grew red, then orange, then pale as a blue-white star: ion thrusters kicking in.

Nick frowned. "That can't be the lander—the angle's all wrong, and it's coming in *way* too fast."

"It isn't," Mace said. "I should say, *they aren't.*"

"I'm not gonna like this, am I?" Nick passed a hand over his eyes. "Oh, nuts. Ohhh, nuts nuts *nuts*. You're about to tell me those are DOKAWs."

"At least five. More to follow."

YOU! Vastor's explosive roar seemed to yank him off the rock face and carry him raging to the meadow. He shook a sizzling shield at Mace. *This is YOUR fault! YOU have brought them here!*

"There will be time later to argue blame." Mace let the lightsabers' blades shrink to nonexistence. "There's something we need to do right now."

"What's that?"

The Jedi Master looked from the *lor pelek* to the young Korun officer, then into a sky at the durasteel missiles streaking through the atmosphere.

At thirty thousand kilometers per hour, and accelerating.

Mace Windu said, "Run."

They ran.

PART THREE

SHATTERPOINT

16

SHOCKWAVES

A fully-assembled De-Orbiting Kinetic Anti-emplacement Weapon (DOKAW)—hardened durasteel spear, ablative shielding, miniature ion drive, and tiny attitude thrusters—massed slightly more than two hundred kilograms. By the time the spear impacted a target at ground level, the shielding, the drive, and the attitude thrusters, as well as a fair bit of the hardened durasteel itself, would have all burned away; the final warhead massed in the general neighborhood of one hundred kilograms, slightly more or less depending on angle of entry, atmospheric density, and other minor concerns.

These concerns were minor because the DOKAW was not, in itself, a particularly sensitive or sophisticated weapon; its virtues lay more in the the realm of being inexpensive to produce and simple to operate, which is why it was found mostly in more primitive backworld areas of the galaxy. It was vulnerable to counterfire from turbolaser batteries, for example. It was also largely useless against a target capable of even rudimentary evasive action, and once its attitude thrusters had burned away, mere atmospheric disturbances would be sufficient to push it off course, making it less than ideally accurate against stationary targets smaller than a medium-sized town. Because, after all, it was basically just a hundred-kilo hunk of durasteel.

Ideal accuracy, though, was also a minor concern, because at the point of impact, this hundred-kilo spear of hardened durasteel was traveling at well over ten kilometers *per second*.

In a word:

WHAM.

Mace, Nick, and Kar had reached the widening throat of the first of the major caverns when the floor dropped out from under them for one astonishing second, then jumped back up and smacked them tumbling through the air toward the jagged rock roof overhead.

The blast transcended sound.

Mace controlled his spin instinctively so that he could absorb the impact against the roof with bent legs. His Force-hold caught Nick a meter short of severe head trauma; then as they both fell back toward the floor, the pressure-wave of superheated air that shrieked in through the fissure from the meadow cave sent them skidding and bouncing and rolling over the rough-cut floor in a hailstorm of rock shards and burning dirt.

Mace kept his Force-hold on Nick; as they skidded to a stop in the nightmare of dust and smoke and screaming, he set Nick on his feet and crouched beside him. "Stay up!" he shouted. "Stay low but *off the floor!*"

He huddled there, hands jammed against his ears, bounced by another blast—lesser—and another lesser still, the natural inaccuracy of the DOKAWs causing some scatter. A final convulsion of the mountain cracked the roof of the cavern and rained boulders at random. Some screams were crushed to gurgles; others scaled up to shrieks of agony.

Two seconds passed—two more—and Mace sprang to his feet. Light from glowglobes made luminous spheres that could not overlap through the thick swirl of dust and smoke that stung tears into his eyes; one incautious breath sent him into a paroxysm of coughing. He yanked Nick to his side—the young Korun had an arm over his streaming eyes and he was hacking into his other hand—and Mace grabbed the hem of his homespun tunic with both hands.

"Hey—*hackhagh*—hey, what are you—"

"We need your shirt."

With one twist he ripped the tunic in half up the back; another twist continued the rip from collar to waist in front. He left half in Nick's hands while he tied his own half over his face in a sort of hood. The cloth was coarse enough to see through, and it cut the dust and smoke from intolerable down to merely hellish.

While Nick imitated him, Mace picked his way around the rubble and over dead and wounded Korunnai toward a gleam of ultra-chrome under a huge slab of stone. He dropped to his heels beside it and gestured, clearing smaller rocks away from the *lor pelek*.

"Kar? Can you hear me?"

Even hoarse with dust and pain, Vastor's growl had a sardonic edge. *Better stand back. When you're around, big hard things seem to fall on my head.*

Mace breathed himself into his center, and found the slab's shatterpoint. "Don't move."

His blade flared, bit in, and the slab cracked in two over Vastor's back. A shrug of Vastor's huge shoulders shifted the two pieces enough that he could push himself up to his knees between them. He was caked with dust, and blood trickled from an ugly gash over one ear.

You could have killed me. You should have.

"You're no good to me dead," Mace said. "Is there a hardpoint in this base? A hardened bunker, preferably airtight?"

The heavy weapon lockup. It can be sealed.

"All right. Get all the non-ambulatory sick and wounded in there and seal it up. When the militia comes, they'll start with gas."

Vastor and Nick exchanged grim looks.

Mace glanced over his shoulder. "Nick. You're with me. Let's go."

We'll never hold them. Not for a day. Not an hour.

"We don't have to hold them ourselves. I have a medium cruiser in-system that's carrying a regiment of the finest soldiers this galaxy has ever seen." Mace put one hand on Vastor's shoulder, and the other on Nick's, and there was a strange shine to his dark eyes. "We aren't going to hold them. We aren't even going to fight them. With the *Halleck* for air cover and the troopers holding the ground, those twenty landers can evacuate this entire place within hours."

"Grassers and all?"

Mace nodded. "We just have to get them here."

DOKAWs pounded the mountain. Korunnai ran and screamed and bled. Some tried to help the wounded. Some died. Some huddled shivering against the nearest wall.

Mace kept moving. Nick trotted at his heels. Sometimes shockwaves knocked them down. Sometimes the dust was so bad that Mace had to light their way with scatter from his and Depa's blades.

"Why do you need *me*? You were in the comm center this morning," Nick gasped through a mouthful of dust that his spit had turned to mud. "I'm good with a medpac. You go on. I can look after wounded—"

"*That's* why."

Bladelight picked up jagged gleams ahead: the corridor was blocked with a sloping wall of tumbled rock.

"This is the only way I know to the comm center," Mace said. "I'm hoping you know another."

Nick muttered a curse under his breath as he leaned on the slope of boulders. "How deep is the rubble? Can you cut—" His eyes widened. "Hey, there are *people* in there! Trapped! I can feel them— we've got to get them out!"

"I feel them too. The fall's not stable," Mace said. "Shifting and cutting will take more time than we have: the first mistake would bring tons of stone down on their heads. We need another way to the comm center."

"But—we can't just *leave* them in there—!"

"Nick. Try to focus. Will they be safer out *here?*"

"Well, I . . ." Nick frowned. "Well . . ."

"Listen to me. There will be cave-ins throughout these caverns. We can dig survivors out *later*. We have to make sure enough people live through this to do the digging. Yes?"

Nick nodded reluctantly.

"Then let's go."

The comm center was just a small natural cave with rude plank ta-bles, a few homemade chairs, and some equipment. "Probably not much left of the relay antennas," Nick muttered as they trotted toward it.

"It's a little late to worry about concealing our position," Mace re-minded him. "And subspace won't have any trouble going through rock."

Nick squinted at the doorway, cursed, and broke into a sprint. "The surgical field's down!" He darted inside.

Mace went after him, but stopped in the doorway.

The subspace comm unit lay on the floor, among the splinters of the plank table; its housing looked like someone had rolled it down a mountainside and dropped it off a cliff. The realspace-frequency units, less durable, were crushed. Nick was cursing continuously un-der his breath as he knelt over the two Korun commtechs, who lay motionless on the floor as though they were simply taking a nap in the ruins of their post.

Mace said, "Nick."

"They're dead," the young Korun said thickly. "They're both dead. Not a mark on them. And—"

"Nick, come out of there."

Nick prodded one's head with his finger . . . which gave, deform-ing spongily, as though the man's skull were soft foam. "And they're *squishy* . . ."

"We have to leave this place. Now."

"What could *do* that to a man?"

"Concussion," Mace said. "Shock transmission. This room must be part of a solid structure that reaches to the surface—"

"You're saying . . ." Nick looked at the walls around him with widening eyes. "You saying if another DOKAW hits the same spot, while I'm still in *here*—"

"I'm *saying*—" Mace urgently extended a hand, "—cover your ears and *jump*."

Mace took his own advice then drew on the Force to suspend them both, and the air in the comm cave pounded them like they were caught in the palm of a giant's handclap. He let the shock send them whirling back along the passage away from the comm center, them released his Force-hold and rolled to his feet.

Nick was saying something as Mace pulled him upright, but Mace heard only a distant mutter over the high singing whine in his ears. "You'll have to speak up."

Nick cupped one hand to his ear. "What?"

"Speak *up*!"

"What? You'll have to speak up!"

Mace sighed and shoved Nick stumbling along the corridor; he turned, reaching into the Force as he extended a hand, and the subspace unit floated out the doorway, down the passage and into his arms.

He jogged after Nick while their stunned eardrums recovered. Three minutes' scramble brought them to a a nexus of intersecting passageways, some cut, some natural. "This will have to do."

"Do for what? What's left?" Nick sagged against the wall, panting. "And what are you lugging that fraggin' thing around for?"

Mace set the comm unit on the passage floor. He pulled off his improvised dust-mask and frowned at the rear access panel; fasteners unscrewed themselves and floated to a neat little pile in a dimple in the rock, joined shortly by the access panel itself. Mace examined the leads and contacts inside the unit for a moment, then nodded.

He opened his hand and his lightsaber jumped to it from its pocket inside his vest. A flick of the Force tripped the handgrip's secret interior latch; a curved section of the grip popped open, and Mace pulled out the power cell. Another flick of the Force bent a pair of lead-panels inside the comm unit's guts. Mace wedged the powercell between them, and the unit's ready-lights came on.

"Hold this here," Mace said. Nick held the energy cell in place while Mace keyed the *Halleck*'s emergency channel.

"*Halleck*, this is General Windu. This is a priority clear-call, intiation code oh six one five. Acknowledge."

The comm unit crackled to life in a burst of ECM static. A stolid voice came faintly through the buzz: "Response . . . one nine."

"Verification seven seven."

"Go a . . . General."

"Captain Trent, I need your status."

"Regret to in . . . Cap . . . bridge crew . . . ously wounded. This is Commander Urhal . . . der heavy . . . Repeat: We are under heavy DSF attack."

Nick frowned. "DSF?"

"Droid starfighter." Mace keyed the transmitter. "Can you hold?"

". . . gative. Too many . . . sustained heavy . . . shields and armor, but . . ."

Through the bursts of static and washes of white hiss, the acting captain of the *Halleck* sketched their situation: An unknown number of Trade Federation droid starfighters had been lying in wait, deactivated and drifting outside the system's ecliptic plane amid cometary dust and debris of ancient asteroids. The commander guessed that it was something about the lander itself that had triggered them; they had attacked as soon as the extraction lander undocked and made for orbit. The lander had been lost with all hands, and the DSFs had quickly overwhelmed the *Halleck*'s escort complement of six starfighters; they were pounding the cruiser with everything they had. The ship Mace had been looking to for rescue was already fighting for its life.

And losing.

Mace balanced on his heels, staring into the rock wall beside him.

The granular surface gleamed with sweat condensed from his breath, and flecks of mineral sparkled within it, but Mace didn't see any of that. He wasn't looking at the stone. He was looking *into* the stone. Through the stone.

Into the Force.

"So that's it, then, huh?" Nick's words came distantly to Mace's ears, hollow and faint, as though he spoke from the bottom of a well. "There's no way we can evacuate."

"That's it, yes. No way." This was a reflexive echo; Mace was barely aware of what Nick had said, and not at all aware that he had answered. "No way . . ."

His consciousness was elsewhere.

"Have I mentioned how much I *hate* this place? Every time I come here it's like being buried alive . . ."

Into the Force—

Mace wasn't actually *looking*, not really; the sense he used was not sight. This sense invaded the Force, touching power and letting the power touch it, shading the power then drawing on the shade it created to deepen its own shade, feeding upon the Force and feeding the Force in a regenerative spiral, gathering strength, spidering outward from this specific nowhere-in-particular-right-now to the general all-where of every time: from a crossroads inside a mountain that stood in a jungle the size of a continent, on a world that whirled through a galaxy that was rapidly becoming a jungle of its own.

This sense brought to his perception the stress-vectors of reality. It was more than the searching of a shatterpoint, it was as though this single moment existed in a crystal shell, and if he could strike it in *exactly the right way*, the shell enclosing this one would shatter as well—and the shell enclosing that shell, and on, and on, a single stroke whose shockwaves would propagate outward to crash through the trap that held not only him and Nick, but Depa and Kar and the Korunnai, the world of Haruun Kal, the Republic, perhaps the galaxy itself: more than a chain of shatterpoints, it was a *fountain* of shatterpoints. A cascade.

An avalanche.

If he could only find the spot to strike. . . .

Faintly, distantly, resonating from the here-and-now to Mace's everywhere-at-once: "We're *trapped* in here . . . The whole fraggin' planetary *militia* is outside, and there's *nobody* who can get here to help us, and we're *all* gonna *die*. This is a *stupid* place to die. Stupid, stupid, stupid."

"Stupid," Mace echoed. "Stupid, yes . . . Stupid! *Exactly!*"

"Are you even *listening* to me?"

"You," Mace said, his gaze slowly returning from the stone depths he had been contemplating, "are *brilliant*. Not to mention lucky."

"Ex*cuse* me?"

"Some years ago, the Jedi Order contemplated using droid starfighters for antipirate work—convoying freighters, that sort of thing. Do you know why we decided against it?"

"Do I care?"

"Because droids are *stupid*."

"Wow, *that's* a relief! I'd *hate* to be killed by a *genius*—"

Mace turned back to the comm unit and keyed the transmit once again. "Commander, this is General Windu. All the troops—get them loaded onto the remaining landers, and get those landers on course for the original coordinates. *All* of them. The original coordinates. Do you copy?"

"Yes, sir. But . . . no match for DSF . . . casualties . . . lucky if half of them make atmosphere . . ."

"That's not your problem. Once the landers are away, you will withdraw. Do you copy? This is a direct order. When the landers are away, the *Halleck* will jump for Republic space."

". . . landers . . . only sublight. With no hyperdrive, how will you . . . ?"

"Commander, is there so little for you to do right now that you can afford the time to argue with me? You have your orders. Windu out."

He plucked the powercell out of the back of the comm unit and returned it to the handgrip of his lightsaber. "Who's the best shooter you know?"

Nick shrugged. "Me."

"Nick . . ."

"What, should I lie?"

"All right. Second best."

"Who's still alive?" Nick thought for a second or two. "Chalk, maybe. She's pretty good. Especially with the heavy stuff. Or she would be if she could, y'know, *walk* . . ."

"She won't have to. Let's go."

Nick stayed against the wall, shrugging hopelessly. "Why bother? It's not like we can *get* anywhere, right? With the ship gone, there's nowhere to go."

"There is. And we will go there."

"Where?"

"I'm not going to tell you."

"You're not?"

"I have had enough," Mace said, "of being told I'm insane."

Nick rose warily, eyeing Mace as though the Jedi Master might be a worrt in disguise. "What are you talking about? You just *said* there's no way we can evacuate."

"We're not going to evacuate. We're going to *attack*."

Nick gaped. "*Attack?*" he echoed numbly.

"Not just attack. We are going to *beat* them," said the Jedi Master, "like a rented gong."

17

SEEKER

T he air in the weapons bunker was thick with the ozone tang of a surgical field and the rank pheromonal stink of human fear. The few heavy weapons that the guerrillas had cached were piled haphazardly outside the door to make room for the endless flood of stretchers carried by grim-faced Korunnai, bearing the sick and the wounded. Mostly sick.

Mostly children.

Mostly silent and round-eyed.

The bearers would stumble whenever another DOKAW shook the mountain, and sometimes dump those they carried; many of the invalids bled from fresh scrapes. Nick threaded his way around them to look for Chalk; the Korun girl had not left Besh's side since they both awakened from thanatizine suspension.

Mace had stopped outside the doorway. His defocused stare gathered the inventory of the weapons there, and plugged them into his calculations: new data that made his image of the coming battle shift and flow and remold itself like a stream of hardening lava. A tripod-mounted EWHB-10 with an auxiliary fusion-generator pack. Two shoulder-fired torpedo launchers, with four preloaded launch tubes apiece. A rack of twenty-five proton grenades, still in its factory-sealed case.

That was all he'd need.

The rest of the weapons were not relevant.

Nick came out the doorway, moving hesitantly, as though in pain. "They're not in there."

"No?"

Nick shook his head toward one of the stretcher-bearers. "They told me—there's not enough room for all the . . . So Kar—" He swallowed, forcing distress off his face and out of his voice. "All we're putting in here is people who'll *live*."

Mace nodded. "Where are the others?"

"We call it the dead room. Follow me."

The dead room was a huge cavern hung with night. The only light was soft yellow spill from a scatter of handheld glow rods. Unlike the other inhabited chambers, the floor of this one had not been leveled with vibro-bladed adzes, but had instead been cut into tiered ledges that followed the natural contour of the rock.

The ledges were packed with the dying.

No surgical field here: the air was thick with fecal stench, and the sickly sweet odor of rotten meat, and the indescribable smell of spores released by fungi feeding on human flesh.

Nick halted a few paces in from the entrance and closed his eyes. A moment later, he sighed and pointed up toward a far corner. "Over there. See that light? Something's happening; I think Kar's with them."

"Good. We need him, and we're running out of time."

They had to tread carefully to climb the levels of ledges without stepping on people in the gloom.

Besh lay stretched out, motionless, barely breathing, on a ledge near the ragged curve of the cavern ceiling. Vastor knelt beside him, eyes closed, one hand above Besh's heart. The medpac tissue-binder that had closed the wounds left by Terrel's knife had lost its glossy transparency, blackening and curling like dead skin, and the wounds had erupted into cruciferous bulbs of fungus that floresced faintly, iridescent green and purple pulsing in the shadows cast by Chalk's glow rod.

Chalk sat cross-legged on Besh's other side, her own chest bulky with spraybandage; head low, she sponged at the growths on Besh's chest with a damp rag. Even from meters away, Mace caught a strong odor of alcohol and portaak amber.

Nick stopped a couple of meters short and gave Mace a significant look, nodding toward the others as if to say, *This was your idea. Leave me out of it.*

Mace approached slowly, staying on the next ledge down. He stopped when he reached them and spoke softly to Chalk. "How is he?"

She wouldn't look at him. "Dying. How are you?"

She dipped her rag into the bucket, brought it out again, sponged, and returned it to the bucket with numb mechanical persistence: doing it to be doing something, though she showed no sign of hope that it might help.

"Chalk, we need you to come with us."

"Not leaving him, me. Needs me, him."

"*We* need you. Chalk, you have to trust me—"

"*Did* trust you, me. So did *Besh.*"

Mace had no answer.

Nick came to Mace's shoulder. "The Archives are starting to look pretty good right now."

The Jedi Master squinted at him.

Nick shrugged. "Hey, it's the only immortality any of us can hope for, right?"

"And how do you achieve immortality," Mace murmured, "if my journal is buried under a mountain on Haruun Kal?"

"Uh. Yeah." Nick looked like his stomach hurt. "That could be a problem."

"Forget about immortality. Let's concentrate on not dying *today.*"

Vastor's eyes were closed, and the Force shimmered around him. Mace could feel some of what the *lor pelek* was doing: searching within Besh's chest for the essential aura of the fungus that was killing him, focusing power upon it to burn it out spore by spore.

Another shockwave rattled the cavern. Loose rock clattered from the ceiling.

"Kar," Mace said, "this is not the way. We don't have time."

Vastor's eyes stayed closed. His expression did not so much as flicker. *Is there something better for me to be doing right now?*

"As a matter of fact," Mace said, "yes. There is."

Does it involve killing Balawai?

Mace said apologetically, "Probably not more than a thousand. Maybe two."

Vastor opened eyes filled with *pelekotan's* darkness. Chalk lifted her head, rag hanging forgotten from her fist.

"So," said Mace Windu. "Are we on?"

Smoke and dust clouded the huge cavern; it reeked of grasser fear-musk, of dung and urine and blood, and with each new DOKAW-shock the smell got worse.

Torchlight flared and blazed and vanished again. The stinking fog swirled with gigantic shapes: grassers bucking and clawing at each other, some with jaws panic-locked on their own or others' limbs. They charged at random, slamming into each other, trampling the injured and their own young. Korunnai darted among them, appearing from the smoke and vanishing again, hands full of sharp goads and blazing torches as they fought to separate the knots of shrieking, honking, fear-crazed beasts.

A swirl opened a gap: a looming akk dog paused to stare into Mace's eyes, measuring him with saurian malice as a thick rope of bloody drool looped from its jaws, then it ponderously turned aside and slipped into the murk, tail tapering so smoothly it might have been dissolving.

Mace threaded through the chaos.

Behind him followed a pair Korunnai, carrying a stretcher that held the EWHB and its generator. Two more brought the shoulder-fired torpedo launchers and the preloaded tubes on another stretcher. Chalk half-walked, her arm looped over Nick's shoulders as he helped her along.

Five more pairs of Korunnai trotted around the circumference of the caverns, sidling past all the confusion and riot; one of each pair carried a homespun sack holding five proton grenades apiece, and the others carried torches. Each pair soon slipped down a different one of the five vast passages along which grassers were daily driven to graze.

Erratic booming shivered the air, sharper and much smaller than the DOKAW-shocks, but still powerful enough to vibrate the floor. Mace pointed toward the source of the booming: a side cave where the great ankkox paced in restless fury. The concussions were its angrily whipping tail mace striking the walls and floor of its pen.

The nearest Korun stretcher bearer saw his gesture, and they moved in that direction, followed by Nick and Chalk.

Mace paused, and looked back over his shoulder. At the mouth of an upper passageway stood Kar Vastor and his Akk Guards. Behind them crouched all twelve of Vastor's Force-bonded akks. The *lor pelek* met Mace's gaze and nodded.

Mace returned the nod, spreading his hands as though to say, *Whenever you're ready.*

Vastor and his akks marched grimly down into the grasser cavern. The akks spread out in huge leaping springs, knocking over panicked grassers on all sides, crouching over them to let drool fall from razor teeth and moisten the fur on their necks. The humans stayed together in a flying wedge with Vastor at the point, moving in to manually separate struggling grassers, intimidating the winners and slaughtering any who had been too badly injured to walk.

Mace watched, stonefaced. It was wasteful. It was brutal.

It was necessary.

He turned once again to his own task.

He gestured and the mass of struggling beasts and men parted before him, and the smoke and dust cleared, and he saw her.

She sat on a ledge like a natural gallery that coursed one long-curving wall of the cavern. Her feet hung over the lip, dangling free: a child in a chair too tall for her. Her face was buried in her hands, and even from across the cavern his chest ached with a silent echo of her sobs.

And when he reached her side, he still did not know what to say.

"Depa . . ."

She lifted her head and turned to meet his eyes, and knowing what to say would not have helped him because he could not speak.

The rag—the one she had worn across her brow these past days—was gone. On her forehead—

On her forehead, where the Chalactan Greater Mark of Illumination should have been—

As it had been in his hallucination, days ago at the jungle prospector outpost: on her brow was only an ugly keloid ripple of scar. As though the Greater Mark of Illumination had been carved from the bone of her skull with a blunt knife. As though the wound it left behind had festered, and had not been treated.

As though it festered still . . .

The Lesser Mark, called the Seeker, still gleamed at the bridge of her nose. The Lesser Mark is fixed between the eyes of one who aspires to become a Chalactan adept: it symbolizes the centered self, the shining vision, the elegant order that seeking illumination creates within the seeker. The Greater Mark is called the Universe; it is an exact replica of the Seeker, writ large. It is fixed to the frontal bone in a solemn ceremony by the Convocation of Adepts, to welcome another to their company. The two, together, represent the fundamental tenet of Chalactan philosophy: As Without, So Within. The Adepts of Chalacta teach that the celestial order, the natural laws that govern the motion of planets and the wheel of galaxies, regulate as well the life of the Enlightened.

But for Depa, the universe was gone. All that remained was the Seeker.

Alone in the void.

"Mace . . ." Her face twisted once more to tears. "Don't look at me. You can't look at me. You can't see me like this. Please . . ."

He lowered himself to one knee beside her. He reached a tentative hand for her shoulder; she clutched his fingers and pressed his hand in place, but turned her face away.

"I'm so sorry . . ." Her head twitched as though she shook tears out of her eyes. "I'm sorry for everything. I'm sorry things can't be different. Better. I'm sorry *I* can't be better . . ."

"But you can." He squeezed her shoulder. "You can, Depa. You have to."

"I'm so lost, Mace." Her whisper could not be heard in the riot of the cavern, but Mace could *feel* her meaning, as though the Force itself murmured in his ear. "I'm so *lost* . . ."

The Depa of his hallucination—what had she told him?

He remembered.

"It is in the darkest night," he said gently, "that the light we are shines brightest."

"Yes. Yes. You always say that. But what do you know about dark?" Her head sagged, chin to her chest, as though she could no longer think of a reason to hold it up. "How does a blind man know the stars have gone out?"

"But they haven't," Mace said. "They still burn as bright as ever. And as long as people live around them, they will need Jedi. Like I need you now."

"I am . . . I'm not a Jedi anymore. I quit. I resign. I withdraw. I thought you understood that."

"I do understand it. I don't accept it."

"It's not up to you."

He pulled his hand from her shoulder and rose, looming above her. "Get up."

She sighed, and once again a smile struggled onto her tearstained lips. "I'm not your Padawan now, Mace. You can't order me—"

"*Get up!*"

Reflexes burned into her by more than a decade of unquestioning obedience yanked her instinctively to her feet. She swayed dizzily, and her mouth hung slack.

"Minutes from now, nearly a thousand clone soldiers of the Republic will reach this position."

New light kindled in her glazed eyes. "The *Halleck*—they can *save* us—"

"No," Mace said. "Listen to me: *We* have to save *them*."

"I—I don't *understand*—"

"They are coming in under fire. This entire system is a *trap*. It's been a trap all along. The Separatist pullback was *bait*, do you understand that?"

"No . . . it's not true, it's *not true!*" But the flash faded from her eyes, and she sagged. "But of course it's true. How could I have thought otherwise? How could I have thought I would win?"

"They've caught a medium cruiser. Not to mention two members of the Jedi Council. The *Halleck* may already be destroyed. The clone soldiers are coming in aboard the surviving landers. They will be pursued by Trade Federation droid starfighters: faster, more maneuverable, and better-armed than the landers. If our men are pinned between the starfighters and the militia, they won't have a chance. Whatever chance those men will have, *we* have to give them. *You* have to give them."

"Me? What can *I* do?"

He opened his vest. Her lightsaber floated out of its inner pocket. It bobbed gently in the air between them.

"You can make a choice."

She looked from the lightsaber to his eyes and back again; she stared at the handgrip as though her reflection in its portaak amber–smeared surface might whisper the future. "But you don't understand," she said faintly. "No choice of mine can matter here . . ."

"It does to me."

"Have you learned *nothing* on this world? Even if we *do* save them—it *doesn't matter*. Not in the jungle. Look *around* you. This isn't something you can *fight*, Mace."

"Of course it is."

"It's not an enemy, Mace. It's just the jungle. You can't do anything about it. It's just the way things are."

"I think," Mace said gently, "that you're the one who has failed to learn the lessons of Haruun Kal."

She shook her head hopelessly.

"Don't tell me you can't fight the jungle, Depa," he said. "That's what Korunnai *do*. Don't you understand that? That's what their whole culture is *based on*. Fighting the jungle. They use grassers to attack it, and akks to defend themselves from its counterattacks. That's what the Summertime War is *about*. The Balawai want to *use* the jungle: to live *with* it, to *profit* from it. The Korunnai want to beat it into submission. To make it into something that is no longer trying to eat them alive. Now, think: *Why do Korunnai do that?* Why are they enemies of Balawai? Why are they enemies of the jungle?"

"A riddle for your Padawan?" she said bitterly.

"A lesson."

"I am done with lessons."

"We are never done with lessons, Depa. Not while we live. The answer is right before your eyes. Why do Korunnai fight the jungle?"

He opened his hand as though offering her the answer on his palm.

Her eyes fixed on the handgrip of her lightsaber, floating between them, and something entered them then: some faint whisper of breeze from a cool clean place, a breath of air to ease her suffocating pain.

"Because . . ." Her voice was hushed. Reverent.

Awed by the truth.

"Because they are descended from *Jedi* . . ."

"Yes."

"But . . . but . . . you can't fight the way things *are* . . ."

"But we do. Every day. That's what Jedi *are*."

Tears streamed from her reddened eyes. "You can never win—"

"*We,*" Mace corrected her gently, "don't have to win. We only have to fight."

"You can't . . . you can't just *forgive* me . . ."

"As a member of the Jedi Council—you're right. I can't. As your Master, I *won't*. As your friend—"

His eyes stung. The smoke, perhaps.

"As your friend, Depa, I can forgive everything. I already have."

She shook her head speechlessly, but she lifted a hand.

Her hand shook. She made a fist, and bit her lip.

He said, "Take your weapon, Depa. Let's go save those men."

She took it.

18

UNCONVENTIONAL WARFARE

The militia landed in waves.

Before the plume of dirt and smoke had subsided from the last impact of a DOKAW into the mountain, gunships swooped over the jungles below the pass, disgorging dozens, then hundreds of arpitroops: airborne soldiers equipped with disposable repulsor packs, which lowered them briskly through the canopy below. They fanned out into the jungle bearing electronic sniffers that could detect certain chemicals in grasser urine in concentrations of only a few parts per billion. They swiftly located the five main tunnels to the partisan base and marked each one with high-powered beacons.

The gunships' laser cannons blasted away the jungle canopy and surrounding trees to create a free-fire zone at the mouth of each tunnel. A kilometer away, a similar technique had been used to clear a landing zone for the troop shuttles, which were waiting onstation to drop five hundred soldiers each before circling back to the embarkation area on the outskirts of the city of Oran Mas, fifty klicks to the northwest.

By the time the grasser tunnels had been marked, at least five thousand militia regulars were on the ground, marching toward the zone of engagement.

Ten thousand more followed close behind.

The militia bore arms that the Grand Army of the Republic itself might envy; provided by the Separatists, which was backed by the financial might and industrial capacity of the Trade Federation and the manufacturing guilds, this armament had been financed by a generous slice of the thyssel bark trade.

Standard combat equipment for the regular militia on Haruun Kal included the Merr-Sonn BC7 medium blaster carbine with the optional rocket-grenade attachment, six antipersonnel fragmentation grenades, and the renowned close-combat trench-style vibroknife, the Merr-Sonn Devastator, as well as Opankro Graylite ceramic-fiber personal combat armor. In addition, every sixth soldier carried a backpack flame projector, and each platoon of twenty was equipped with the experiemental MM(X) dual-operated grenade mortar, also from Merr-Sonn.

Fifteen thousand regulars. Thirty-five GAVs (ground assault vehicles: converted steamcrawlers, retofitted with chemical cannons firing explosive shells in addition to their flame projectors, and high-velocity repeating slug rifles blister-mounted through their side armor). Seventy-three Sienar Turbostorm close-assault gunships.

All this converged on the cavern base at the Lorshan Pass.

To oppose them, the Korun partisans had roughly four hundred actives, of whom two-thirds were walking wounded, and over two thousand noncombatants, consisting mainly of the elderly and the very young. They were armed with a variety of light slug rifles, a very few light and medium energy weapons, a small stockpile of grenades, two Krupx MiniMag shoulder-fired proton torpedo launchers, and one Merr-Sonn EWHB-10 heavy repeating blaster.

The partisans on Haruun Kal excelled at guerrilla operations, but they were less successful in conventional actions. In fact, in conventional engagements between regular militia and the Korunnai, the militia had crushed the partisans in every encounter. At the Lorshan Pass, they quite understandably expected not only to triumph, but to permanently break the back of the Korun resistance.

*   *   *

Most of the militia regulars at the Lorshan Pass never saw combat. While they were still establishing positions at the mouths of the access tunnels—before they'd so much as fired one blaster or launched a single grenade—the ground shook and the mountain roared, and mighty gusts of dirt and smoke blew out from four of the tunnel mouths.

Scouting parties—a few of the bravest enlisted men, creeping tentatively into the dark—discovered that these tunnels had been entirely sealed with uncountable tons of rock. This left the bemused militia with little to do except break out ration packs and do their best to relax, while taking turns scanning the mountain above with simple nonpowered binoculars for any signs of partisan activity.

Only one tunnel remained open. The regulars at the mouth of this tunnel had a somewhat different experience of the battle.

The detonation of the proton grenades in the other tunnels was taken by the militia unit commander as an opportunity. The tunnel his men faced was intact; he assumed this meant whatever explosives had been used for the local mines had misfired or otherwise failed to activate. He ordered his grenade mortars forward, and launched into that tunnel a number of gas grenades loaded with the nerve agent Tisyn-C.

His men were first astonished, then dismayed, as these same grenades came rocketing back out the tunnel's mouth to land in their own emplacements. Tisyn-C was heavier than air, and though their Opanko Graylite combat armor was rated to protect them from gas exposure, none of the regulars wished to test this capability with a nerve agent known to produce convulsions and dementia, followed by paralytic respiratory failure and death. As the white cloud rolled in to their improvised emplacements, the militia rolled out.

And so they were in the open, more concerned with what was among them than with what might be coming next, when they were hit by the grasser stampede.

Grassers were not bred to fight. Just the opposite, in fact: for seven hundred generations, Korunnai had bred their grassers to be docile and easily led, obedient to commands from their human handlers and their akk dog guardians, and to grow large and fat to provide plenty of milk, meat, and hide.

On the other hand, an adult grasser bull could mass over one and one half metric tons. His gripping limbs—the middle and forward pairs—were powerful enough to uproot small trees. One of the grassers' favorite treats was brassvine thorns, which had a hardness approaching durasteel; bored grassers had been known to worry off chunks of armor from steamcrawlers.

And seven hundred generations was not all that long a span, on an evolutionary scale.

These grasser bulls had been forced into confined quarters for weeks, under incredible stress and in constant danger from each other. Today they had endured a shattering bombardment that was entirely beyond their comprehension; the most closely analogous event for which their evolutionary instincts had prepared them was a volcanic eruption. The instinctive grasser response to eruption was blind panic.

Honking, hooting grassers flooded from the tunnel mouth. The regulars discovered that a blaster rifle was only of marginal use against a 1,500-kilo monster crazed by an overload of stress hormones. They also discovered that limbs powerful enough to uproot small trees were easily capable of pulling a man's legs off, and that jaws that could dent armor plate could, with a single chomp, make such a bloody mush of a man's head that one couldn't tell fragments of his helmet from fragments of his skull.

The regulars had better luck with their rocket-propelled fragmentation grenades. Fired from point-blank range, one of these grenades could penetrate a grasser's torso, and its detonation inside would make a satisfyingly shredded hash of that particular grasser. And with five GAVs at hand—though their turret guns could not traverse swiftly enough to track the leaping, twisting, sprinting grassers, a steady burst from one of their high-velocity slug repeaters was usually enough to drop a grasser in its tracks—the militia would have survived the grasser stampede with only an acceptable number of losses.

Would have, that is, if the grassers had not been followed by dozens of akk dogs.

Where the grassers had been panicked, acting at random, trying only to survive and escape, the akk dogs pounced like the pack-hunting predators they were: organized, intelligent, and lethal. They bounded among the militia, shredding men with their clashing teeth and breaking them with swipes of their tails. Their keen senses could often tell in an instant if a downed man was incapacitated or only faking; those soldiers who tried to play dead were soon no longer playing.

The slug repeaters of the GAVs were useless against the akks' armored hide, and their turret guns were of even less use against the agile akks than they'd been against the blundering grassers. The infantry had nothing that could scratch them; they began to scatter, triggering the akks' herding instincts. The akks overleaped them and slaughtered the leaders, sending the rest retreating in disorder to the killing ground at the tunnel's mouth.

The militia unit commander, who from his post in the turret of a GAV had seen his dream of victory morph into a nightmarish massacre in less than two minutes, did the only thing he could do.

He called in an airstrike.

The gunships in action at the Lorshan Pass were still engaged in shuttling soldiers from the embarkation point at Oran Mas. When they received the unit commander's call, at least one third were already headed in the direction of the pass. The Sienar Turbostorm was not by any means a fast ship—it could barely reach point-five past sound speed in a steep dive—but only seconds later the sky over the pass cracked open with two dozen sonic booms. The gunships shed velocity by heeling over and using their repulsorlift engines like retrothrusters. Their troop bays swung open, disgorging twenty arpitroops at a belch, then the gunships righted themselves and swooped upon the battlefield, spraying missiles from their forward batteries.

The missiles ripped into the battlefield indiscriminately, crushing akks but also shredding the soldiers they fought. The akks' only defense against concussion missiles was evasive action, and they scattered into the trees. Seeing a chance for a daring stroke, the unit commander ordered a charge by his five GAVs: they would drive right up the tunnel ahead with his own in the lead, crushing grassers and knocking aside akk dogs. More heavily armored than the gunships above, he felt they had little to fear—a feeling which he had less than one second to regret as a pair of proton torpedoes streaked from the tunnel's mouth and blew his GAV to scrap.

At this point, finally, the partisans deployed their one and only piece of mobile artillery: Twelve metric tons of ankkox lumbered from the mouth of the tunnel.

The drover who stood on its armored head was a Korun as tall as a Wookiee, with shoulders like a rancor's and a pair of ultrachrome teardrops fastened to his forearms.

The Korun gestured, and the twisted pile of smoking scrap that had been the unit commander's GAV squealed as it flattened beneath the ankkox's massive feet. He swung one arm, and the ankkox's tail mace blurred through the air, knocking the turret gun of the next GAV spinning so that its point-blank shot instead detonated against the armor of the one behind.

Two pairs of Korunnai, nearly as large as the one on the ankkox, and similarly armed, crouched on either curving flank of the beast's dorsal shell; one of each pair wore the bulky, unwieldy shoulder unit of a proton torpedo launcher, while the other tended their supply of disposable loader tubes. They had four apiece, and they seemed to have no interest in conserving them. Torpedo after torpedo streaked from the launchers, first destroying the remaining GAVs, then curving upward to blast gunships from the sky.

A few heroic soldiers of the militia tried to scramble close enough to the ankkox to attack the Akk Guards with small arms, only to be sent spinning through the air, chests crushed with blinding efficiency by blurred blows of the ankkox's tail mace.

At the crest of the ankkox's dorsal shell, where once had stood a howdah of polished lammas, a heavy repeating blaster had been bolted directly to the beast's armor. Its power generator was tended by a young Korun male with vivid blue eyes and a manic grin, and it roared a continuous song of destruction, spraying high-energy particle beam packets across the field of battle.

The gunner on this weapon was a Korun girl with pale skin and startling red hair, whose feel for the weapon was such that she could be seen to fire with her eyes closed, unerringly hammering the cockpits and cannon turrets of even those gunships that screamed past on transsonic strafing runs. Streaking concussion missiles were met tens of meters away with bursts of blasterfire; not one got through.

Nor could the gunships stand off and pound her in a laserfire duel; not only did her every shot rock their ships, spoiling their target locks, but she was defended by a Korun man and a Chalactan woman who handled Jedi energy blades as though they'd been born with them in hand.

Two gunships that tried to attack went down in flames.

Others peeled away, swinging around to take cover behind shoulders of the mountain. An instant later, three gunships appeared in formation straight up the mountain's face, diving, but firing repulsors to slow their dive to not much faster than a man might run. Ventral doors retracted to expose their belly-mounted Sunfire flame projectors.

A wave of unstoppable fire swept down.

The *Jadthu*-class landing craft carried by the *Halleck* were modified Incom shuttles not unlike the ones that ferry passengers to and from the liners that ply the Gevarno Loop. With reclining chairs replaced by benches, and transparisteel by armor plate, each was capable of carrying up to sixty fully outfitted troopers. Roughly box shaped, they were rear loading, so that they could be packed in a solid block, four ships by five, and socketed against a cruiser's hull, facing outward.

A simple design, they were easy and inexpensive to build, and were convenient to transport. Heavily armored, they were also capable of absorbing incredible punishment.

This was a good thing, because they lacked hyperdrives, and they paid for their durability with a maneuverability quotient that had been compared unfavorably to a Hutt on an oil slick.

Their only armament was a pair of dual-laser turrets fore and aft, and an Arkayd Caltrop 5 chaff gun, which could spray a cloud of sensor-distorting durasteel slivers in any direction. Gunners on the landers had discovered in their very first engagement that at the speeds of starfighter combat, the chaff sprayed by the Caltrop 5 was itself a highly effective weapon: like a miniature asteroid field, it would disastrously perforate any craft unwise or unlucky enough to fly through it, especially droid starfighters which sacrificed armor for greater maneuverability, depending on energy shields for defense—which would not, of course, do them any good at all against chaff.

When the *Halleck*—fully engaged and heavily damaged by the clouds of droid starfighters that whirled around it—blew the docking clamps and streaked for hyperspace, there were nineteen landers, bearing a total of 977 clone troops, including pilots and gunners.

These landers had no fighter cover: the *Halleck*'s fighter escort had been destroyed in the first minutes of the engagement. Their sole defense beyond their own guns were five Rothana HR LAAT/I gunships. These had been detailed to the mission as antipersonnel cover for the landers, should they be forced to make a pickup in a hostile-fire zone. While these gunships had been retrofitted with sublight drives for orbital use, the LAAT/I had never been intended to dogfight against the electronic reflexes of droid starfighters.

They were, however, manned by clone troopers, whose reflexes were not much slower. Which is why sixteen of the landers and three of the gunships reached the atmosphere.

One full wing of droid starfighters—sixty-four units—followed them in.

Fourteen landers reached the Korunnal Highland. Pursued by fifty-eight starfighters.

None of the gunships survived.

By the time they were within sight of the Lorshan Pass there were twelve landers, of which five were heavily damaged. Forty starfighters trailed them with relentless electronic persistence.

And streaking across the curve of the horizon in front of them came three more wings of starfighters, on course to intercept.

The trio of gunships ignited the mountainside. A wall of flame rolled downslope toward the battlefield at the tunnel mouth.

Militia regulars fled in all directions, slipping on blood and skidding through shreds of trees and grasser flesh. Wounded grassers screamed and thrashed, akk dogs snarled and leaped and bit, and the ankkox opened its huge armored throat to unleash a roar that knocked loose rock down the mountain above. Several of the regulars tried to dive for cover under the ankkox's shell, only to be smashed to sprays of pulp by the ankkox's tail mace.

At the crest of the dorsal shell, Chalk growled a continuous stream of curses as she struggled to swing the heavy repeater's barrel in a direction it had never been designed to point: nearly straight up. From his position tending the EWHB's fusion generator, Nick looked at Mace and pointed an accusing finger up at the incinerating flood washing down upon them. "Was *this* part of your *plan?*"

"Of course." Mace tucked his lightsaber back into its holster and looked up, measuring the approach of the gunships. "Everyone down!" he shouted. "Take cover under the shell!"

Depa threw herself forward over the ankkox's crown shell, flipping in the air to land beside the creature's immense head, one hand on the nostril flap beside its mouth, on the opposite side from Kar Vastor. The Akk Guards abandoned their expended torpedo launchers and slid down the shell's curve to leap from its rim. Nick said, "This is the part you didn't want to tell me, huh?"

Mace said, "Help Chalk."

Chalk was still struggling with the heavy repeater, lying on her back with her legs beneath the tripod; Nick had to pry her hands off it and drag her free. "Can I just say I *hate* your plans? *All* of them. How did you figure this was a *good* idea?"

Mace nodded to Kar, and the ankkox's tail swung over its back; Mace grabbed it with both hands, just below the huge knot of armor at its end. "Because if I'd tried this during those transsonic strafing runs," he said calmly, "all that would have been left of me is a red smear on a windscreen."

At the Force command of Kar Vastor, the ankkox snapped its tail into a wide whirl, yanking Mace into the air and spinning him once around the outer rim of its shell to get the feel for his added weight. Then with a whipcrack that blurred the world, it fired him straight up the side of the mountain as though he'd been shot from a torpedo launcher.

Hurtling into the path of the descending gunships, Mace reached through the Force to seize the support strut that divided the windscreen of the gunship in the middle, and pulled. He twisted in the air, whirling through a whistling arc, and reeled himself in as though he were on a towline. His boots thumped solidly to either side of the strut and stuck there, cemented by the Force, facing forward and looking down between the toes of his boots at the twin dumbstruck gapes of the gunship's pilot and its navigator.

The navigator just stared, unable to comprehend this inexplicable apparition. The pilot had better reflexes: The gunship lurched as he released the control yoke and clawed at his sidearm, clearly prepared to sell his own life and the lives of his crew for one shot at the Jedi Master through the hole the pilot assumed Mace's lightsaber was about to slice in the windscreen.

But Mace only shook his head as though mildly disappointed. He waggled an admonitory finger, as though they were schoolboys caught playing a naughty game.

The puzzlement this inflicted upon them was cleared up when they heard a pair of crisp clicks, which were the sounds of the safety levers of their seat-ejectors flipping to "armed." They had barely enough time to register what was happening—not nearly enough time to react—as the activator plates on both seats pressed themselves, and explosive bolts blew the transparisteel windscreen up and out a millisecond before their helmets would have done it for them.

Mace caught the barest flashing glimpse of the identically outraged looks on their faces as the repulsorlift pods on their ejection chairs shot them spinning out over the jungle. One of them howled something obscene. The other just howled.

Mace kicked off from the rim of the roof and dropped into the empty cockpit. A gesture toward the nav console deactivated the belly-mounted Sunfire flame projector. A similar gesture toward the pilot's console engaged the soft-touchdown failsafe on the autopilot, then he opened the cockpit door and walked calmly into the troop bay.

The bay was littered with leaves and mud and food wrappers, as well as bits and pieces of miscellaneous equipment forgotten or discarded by departed militia regulars. The access hatches to the port and starboard ball turrets were directly across from each other in front of the turbine mounts, two thirds of the way aft.

Mace passed between them, then turned and folded his arms.

He could hear, faintly through the sealed hatches, the honking of the ejection-alert klaxon, and he didn't need to touch the Force to mentally see the gunners in either turret frantically unbuckling the safety straps that secured them to the turrets' fighting chairs. The manual dogs on the hatches clacked sharply, but the desperate gunners found both hatches unaccountably jammed until they started putting their whole weight behind slamming their shoulders into them.

Which is when Mace's Force-hold went from keeping them shut to yanking them open, so that the two gunners practically flew into the troop bay, collided helmet-to-helmet with a gunshot *crack!* and collapsed. One of them, tougher than his counterpart, held on to consciousness, struggling dazedly to find his feet until Mace's foot found him.

To be precise: Until the toe of Mace's boot found, crisply, the point of the gunner's chin.

The unconscious man fell on top of the other gunner. Mace took two short lengths of scrap wire from the litter on the floor and bound their hands thumb-to-thumb, then unhurriedly stepped over them and walked back to the cockpit just as the gunship settled on the broad corpse-littered killing zone about ten meters in front of the ankkox.

Outside, the other two gunships from the flight were heeling around, turrets sparking as their laser cannons racked toward him. Depa and Kar crouched in front of the head of the ankkox, battering away a flood of blaster fire; Chalk and Nick lay flat in the shadow of one of the ankkox's massive side-curved legs, returning fire with chattering assault rifles.

Mace hit the release for the troop bay doors, and as they fell open, he poked his head out the hole left by the missing windscreen. When the others saw him, their mouths fell about as far open as the doors.

"What are you waiting for?" Mace's deadpan was flawless. "Flowers and a box of candy?"

Depa sprang into the open, blade flashing faster than the eye could follow, making herself a standing target to draw fire that she splashed back at their attackers while the others scrambled to their feet. Nick sprinted past her, assault rifle chattering from the hip. Kar dived under the ankkox and rolled up and ran with Chalk cradled like a child in his massive arms. Fire from the surrounding trees tracked away from Depa, clawing for the bounding *lor pelek*.

Mace frowned. "That's about enough of *that*," he muttered as he reached into the Force to flip a bank of switches and key an initiation sequence that ganged the targeting servomotors for the ball turrets through the nav console, and gave him fire control.

Twin Taim & Bak quad laser cannons roared to life, hammering thunder into the jungle. Trees exploded like bombs, filling the air with a cloud of flying splinters and wood dust that made an impromptu smoke screen to cover Kar and Chalk's run to the gunship with Depa sprinting hard behind them.

Nick appeared in the cockpit door behind Mace. "We're in!"

"Good. The gunners?"

"The tied-up guys?" The younger man shrugged. "They're out."

Mace nodded. "Hang on."

This was the only warning they got before the gunship leaped straight up, rising like a volcano bomb on screaming overdriven repulsorlifts. Cannonfire from the other two gunships blasted the ground where it had been and tracked upward to pound the gunship sideways, dents popping up like boils in the side armor.

Mace slewed the gunship through a rising turn, but the other gunships had him bracketed, closing in from either side. Through the roar of impacts and shrieking near-misses, he heard Nick shouting, "The door! Close the *door!*"

He twisted to look over his shoulder. He saw Depa on her feet in the middle of the troop bay, swaying, eyes squeezed shut as though the battle had brought on one of her headaches. Nick huddled in the doorway, arms around his head; Kar had Chalk tucked into a corner, and he crouched in front of her, shields raised to catch stray bolts that shot in through the open bay door and zinged in hot splintering ricochets around the compartment.

Mace said, "Depa."

Her eyes opened.

His lightsaber leaped from its pocket within his vest and shot toward her like a bullet.

Her empty hand met it in midair; her pain-glazed eyes lost focus. He felt her in the Force: a sinking surrender like an exhausted swimmer drowning in a rising tide.

Slipping into Vaapad.

Eyes closed once more, she gave one slight nod.

Mace keyed a sequence on the pilot console. The open door stayed open. The troop door on the opposite side dropped open as well.

Particle beams streaked into the troop bay.

Both blades flashed.

The gunships outside bucked under the impact of their own cannonfire. On one, a turbojet engine blasted loose of its mount and tumbled away, bouncing down the mountainside trailing smoke and white-hot shreds of its cowling, and the gunship spun half out of control. The other gunship took its cannon blasts directly in the cockpit.

The transparisteel windscreen of a Sienar Turbostorm was thick and very durable; most kinds of shrapnel or fragments wouldn't scratch it. Even heavy-caliber bullets would leave only dents. A quad laser bolt could make a hole. One did.

The next five went *through* that hole.

The gunship spiralled into the jungle, its cockpit full of shredded flesh.

Depa opened her eyes.

They smoked with darkness.

19

SHIP TO SHIP

Muscle bunched along Mace's jaw as he forced himself to turn away and focus on his flying. A glance at the short-range sensors showed him gunships all over the place: the computer counted fifty-three in the zone of engagement, with more curving toward them over the horizon. He keyed the troop bay doors shut and cut in the turbojets. "Nick. Take nav."

"Sure. Er—yes, sir." Nick glanced at the empty sockets left behind by the ejected chairs. "Um . . . where do I sit?"

"Monitor sensors. We should be seeing the *Halleck*'s landers any second. Kar! Chalk! The emergency repulsor-packs are next to the turret hatches. You have thirty seconds."

Nick wedged his feet under the chair-socket struts and gripped the nav console's split-yoke controls, squinting against the stiffening wind that whistled through the empty gap in front of him. The gunship's aerodynamics shaped the wind blast past the cockpit instead of into it, but even the minimal back-eddy leakage was enough to stagger him. His eyes lit up as he took in the array of screens on the console—especially the twin screens with targeting reticules displayed at their centers.

"Hey, what's this do?" He twisted the split-yoke in opposite directions, and the images on the screens spun wildly to match.

"Don't touch those."

Nick hit the thumb switches on both controllers. The screens filled with parallel bursts of cannonfire as the quad lasers roared. "Yow! Fire control? For *me*? Oh, General, you *shouldn't* have!"

"I realize that."

"It's not even my name-day . . ."

"Nick."

"Yeah, I know: sensors."

"And—"

"—shut *up*, Nick. Yeah, whatever. Hrr." The wind whipped wisps of breath-fog from his mouth. "Starting to get cold in here. Out here. Are we inside or outside?"

"We're approaching seven thousand meters. Check those sensors: red hits are friendlies, blue are hostiles."

"Well, shee," Nick said. "What are you so worried about, then? There's like fifty-some friendlies already here, and another *hundred and ninety-two* on the way—I mean, they're like *everywhere*—and there are only thirteen hostiles, and the friendlies are all *over* them—whoa. Now there are twelve . . . oh, wait. I get it. Whoops."

"Whoops is one word for it."

"Sorry. I'm a little dopey."

"Yes."

"Uh—there's a flight of our *friendlies* trying right now to climb our butts—*whoa*, what's that?" A lock-on alert flashed; the accompanying buzzer was half-buried in the wind noise. "They lit us up! Missiles incoming! *Six* count, closing, dead astern!"

"Back-trace the missile lock and feed it to the computers for counter-fire."

"Great idea! I'll get right on that *first thing* as soon as I *graduate* from *gunnery school*!"

"Fine then," Mace said through his teeth. "You said you can shoot. Let's see it."

"Woo-hoo! Now you're *talking*!" The ball-turrets rotated and the quads blazed to life; the gunship was now climbing straight up, shrieking for space like the starship it once had been. "*Yes* indeed! Come and *get* it!" One of the missiles intersected a stream of cannon bolts and detonated in a burst of black smoke and white fire. "How was *that?*"

"Not bad," Mace said. "Try not to shoot our tail off."

"Some people are never satisfied—"

"Nick. The other five."

"Yeah, yeah. If you wanna be *that* way about it—" He flipped the arming levers on all four aft missile-tubes. "One two three *four!*" he shouted, triggering them in order, and the gunship bucked as a staggered flight of four concussion missiles kicked to life and spun twisting white ropes of rocket-smoke down to meet the five missiles behind.

The first impact-burst drew the next missile, and the next, expanding into an immense fireball fed by all nine.

"Shee," Nick snorted disgustedly. "That was hardly any fun at all."

"It's not supposed to be fun. Save those missiles."

"What for?"

"Depa!" Mace called, shouting over the wind shriek. "Are you ready?"

She appeared in the doorway, leaning on it for support as though the gunship's artificial gravity were too strong for her. "Ready enough," she said. "I can fight. I can always fight. Take your blade."

Mace shook his head. "You'll need it," he said, and cut all power to the gunship's engines.

Its momentum kept it climbing, but slowing now with a lazy twisting barrel-roll as the pursuing ships shot past. It hung poised at its apex for a stretching instant.

The pursuers peeled away from each other in matching ellipses, two of them curving down to dive toward them once again while the third held back for high cover.

Mace worked the controls grimly to hold the ship nose-up as it slid backward toward the ground. "Right or left?"

Depa said, "Left," and then she dived straight up into the sky through the cockpit's open front, tucking into a ball to tumble through the falling gunship's slipstream turbulence.

"Yow!" Nick said. "Why doesn't somebody *warn* me about this stuff?"

"Lock cannons on the right-hand ship. Continuous fire. No missiles."

"I'm on it." The right side quad turret tracked briefly, then roared a chain of energy into the clouds.

Mace twisted the control yoke to angle the falling gunship's nose to the right so that the portside turret could join the fun, then reignited the repulsorlifts at full power and kicked on the turbojets' afterburners. "Hang on."

"I'm on that too."

The ship jounced and fought the controls, and the gunship diving toward it suddenly bloomed with fire that pounded them like giant particle-beam fists. Mace got a glimpse of Depa, straightening her tumble into feet-first plummet with both lightsabers flaming at full extension above her head.

Mace slammed the control yoke sideways and the gunship shrieked into a rising corkscrew that lit up stress-warning indicators all over his console; it got them out from under the rain of cannonfire, but their targeting computers couldn't process the constantly changing vectors, and their own fire went wild as well. Nick looked over the indicators and his eyes went huge. "Hey, is this bucket designed to *do* this?"

"I hope not," Mace said through his teeth as he fought the controls. "Put fire back on that ship."

"Who, me? The *computer's* not fast enough—"

"The computer," said Mace, "can't use the Force."

"Uh, yeah. Okay. Sure."

Just before he overtook them, Mace saw the left-hand gunship spearing downward against the thrust of reversed engines, twisting into a spiral evasive action to avoid colliding with Depa—

And he felt the surge in the Force that drove her directly into its path.

Her blades took it just below the windscreen and drove in to the handgrips, and the rushing airstream around the gunship's nose flipped her over and whipped her up across the cockpit, dragging her blades through the transparisteel to slice free a huge gaping arc.

"Woo!" Nick shouted from beside him. "*Love* them easy-openin' *cans!*"

"Kar! Chalk! Time to go!"

The Korun girl climbed into the cockpit between Mace and Nick; she looked pale and in pain, but still fierce. The *lor pelek* shouldered in behind her. They both wore emergency repulsor-packs strapped across their backs. "You know how these work?"

Chalk nodded silently in reply; Vastor slapped the graphic instruction card sewn onto his harness and snarled at him. *I can read.*

"Um, are we bailing out?" Nick said. "Because, y'know, somebody forgot to get *me* one of those—"

"Nick."

"What?"

"Shoot."

"Right. Right. Sorry. Here, watch this." Nick let the port turret go silent, while the starboard quad clawed at the militia ship; the battered ship jinked aside to evade the pounding—directly into a stream of fresh fire from the port turret. "See? *That's* shooting—"

"With *real* shooting," Chalk told him, "wouldn't be shooting *back*, him."

"Shee. What does it take to *please* you people?"

Mace nodded to Vastor and Chalk. "Ready?"

Without waiting for an answer he cut power to the turbojets and flicked the repulsorlifts into reverse; overstressed metal squealed in the gunship's every joint as it blasted down toward stall speed. Mace wrenched the yoke and flipped the gunship upside down. Kar Vastor wrapped one arm around Chalk's shoulders and with the other grabbed the empty rim of the windscreen gap, then pulled them both smoothly out onto the roof. With one explosive kick to clear the gunship's artificial gravity, he and Chalk fell away, tumbling toward the jungle thousands of meters below.

"On second thought," Nick said, "I guess I don't *mind* staying with the ship . . ."

Hammers pounded the gunship into a bucking spin as the militia ship that had stayed back on high cover finally joined the dogfight, and the one they had left behind rose beneath them. Mace worked the controls savagely, whirling the gunship through evasive gyrations more suitable for a starfighter than for an antique blastboat; the port turbojet took a pair of cannon-blasts, and Mace's next whirl proved too much for its damaged mounting. It tore free in a scream of tortured metal. The ship roared through an uncontrolled spin.

"Take it easy!" Nick shouted.

Mace muttered, "I don't do *easy*."

"What?"

"I said, *shoot back!*"

"How? I can't even *see* them!"

"You don't have to," Mace said as he pulled the crippled gunship into another corkscrew climb, trailing smoke and shredded durasteel. "Forget about aiming. Just *decide*."

"Decide *what?*"

Mace reached into the Force and sent a wave of calm down his connection with Nick. "Don't aim," he said. "Decide what you want to hit. Fire where you *know* it is *about to be*."

Nick frowned thoughtfully. He turned deliberately away from his screens, and looked Mace in the eye. Bemusedly, absently, casually, he nodded, sighed, and triggered the gunship's cannons.

He was still wearing that same thoughtful frown when his cannon blasts shattered the starboard turret of the gunship below, then penetrated the inner hatch and blew the ship in half.

He said, "Wow." His calm vanished as quickly as it had come. "I mean, *wow!* Did you *see* that?"

Mace kicked the limping gunship out of its climb and into a steep power-dive away from the last one. Slowed by their missing turbojet, they swiftly lost their lead as it dived to pursue them, and cannonfire raked their stern. Mace worked the repulsorlifts madly, making the ship jerk, leap, and spring in random directions like a monkey-lizard on raw thyssel. Fire from above pounded them, but Mace's wild maneuvers were preventing it from laying in the multiple precision hits needed to blast through the Turbostorm's heavy armor.

The lock-on alert screamed, and Nick's voice almost matched it. "Missiles incoming!"

Mace didn't even bother to look. "Take care of them."

The perfect confidence in his tone steadied Nick instantly. He flashed his brilliant grin. "Don't mind if I do . . ."

As the turrets rotated to the rear and roared back to life, Mace scanned the jungle toward which his limping ship dived. It was hard to get a sense of scale—he might have been only hundreds of meters above it, or as many dozens of kilometers. Then the swarming gun-metal specks of the balance of the militia fleet that swarmed above the canopy snapped the scene into perspective.

There—a thousand meters below, maybe more, the distress strobes flashed on the repulsor-packs that Kar and Chalk wore. A single gun-ship streaked to intercept them, then slowed. And stopped, hovering.

And the minuscule figures of Chalk and Kar landed lightly on its roof.

A moment later its nose came up, angling straight for him. Mace nodded to himself and let the Force guide his dive into an intercep-tion course. He checked his screens. "Missiles?"

"Handled." Nick's tone was so like the Jedi Master's that it might have been deliberate mockery.

Mace didn't mind. "There won't be more. He won't endanger that friend of his coming at us."

"Um, shouldn't *we* endanger that friend of his?"

"No need."

"How come?"

"That's not *his* friend."

Turret quads on the rising gunship blazed to life, and Mace gave the repulsorlifts a kick that jerked the Turbostorm a dozen meters above the line of dive so that the twin streams of particle-beam packets passed harmlessly beneath him to take the pursuing gunship full in the cockpit.

The explosion was impressive.

The rear two-thirds of the gunship trailed smoke on its way down to the jungle. The front third was the smoke the rear two-thirds trailed.

"That," said Mace Windu, "was shooting."

Nick made a face. "Oh, sure. Chalk. I told you she can handle the heavy stuff. But you should see her in a gun fight. Pathetic. Just pathetic."

"Get Depa's transponder code off your widescan, then get her on comm. We need to coordinate our next move."

"I'm just glad to hear you *have* a next move."

"How many friendlies do you count?"

"Scan count on the droid starfighters . . . Woo. Sure you really want to know?"

"Nick."

"Two hundred twenty-eight."

"Good."

"Good? *Good?*"

"To the lower left of your widescan, you'll find a joystick the size of your thumb. That's your designator control. Start designating droid starfighters as targets for our missiles. One missile per starfighter, and don't save any. Do not—repeat: DO NOT—light them up until I give the order. And do *not* designate anything *other* than a droid starfighter."

"Not even, say, one of those *sixty-seven gunships* in our zone of *engagement?*" Nick pointed to the swarm of "friendlies" in a different part of the screen. "Because *they* seem to be taking a little interest in *us*, if you know what I mean. They are coming *at* us. In a *hurry*."

"Sixty-seven? How many are on intercept vectors?"

"Was I not clear on that? Maybe I should have said: By the way, have I mentioned that we're about to get our butts shot off?"

"How *many?*"

Nick gave a weak, half-hysterical giggle. "*All* of them."

Mace Windu said, "Perfect."

The regimental commander was designated CRC-09/571. Haruun Kal was his third action in combat, and his first as regimental commander. At Geonosis, he had taken part as a battalion commander in the airborne infantry; his group had led the frontal assault on the Trade Federation battle globes. He had served, again as battalion commander, at the disastrous skirmish on Teyr. On board the

Halleck, as the days awaiting action stretched toward weeks, he had drilled his brother troopers relentlessly, sharpening their considerable skills to the highest perfection that could be achieved, absent blooding his regiment in actual combat.

There had been blooding enough today, as a hornet cloud of droid starfighters swirled around his tiny fleet.

He had watched a third of his regiment die.

Some of the landers had been disabled rather than instantly destroyed, and they had been able to eject survivors: meteor swarms of space-armored troopers floating into low orbit, repulsorpacks sparking as they slowed and angled their minutes-long fall toward Haruun Kal's atmosphere. The surviving landers had not been able to keep all the droid starfighters engaged; there were plenty of starfighters left over to slaughter the men, as well.

They had flashed among the falling troopers with cannons blasting: silent streaks of scarlet lancing the black void with robotic precision, each hit leaving a broken corpse floating in the middle of an expanding globe of twinkling crystals, white and pink and blue-green: breath and blood and body fluids flash-frozen in the vacuum, shimmering and lovely in Al'har's light.

But the other troopers had not panicked; with polished fire discipline and plain raw courage, the falling troopers had turned upon the starfighters the weapons they carried upon their persons, coordinating their fire for greater effect. Three light repeaters, when turned upon the same starfighter, could break down its shields so that a single shot from a blaster rifle might disable an engine; groups of grenadiers scattered proximity-fused proton grenades in improvised mini-minefields; and when their weapons were exhausted, in desperation, men used their own bodies as weapons, manipulating their repulsor-packs to shove themselves into the path of starfighters whipping past at dogfight speeds. In such collisions, neither could hope to survive.

The troopers had not been fighting to defend themselves; they knew their lives were over. But they had never stopped.

They were fighting for the *regiment*.

Every starfighter they took down was one less that might attack their brothers. CRC-09/571 was not particularly emotional, even for a clone, but he had watched their sacrifice with a hot swell in his chest. Men such as those made him proud to be one of them. His only drive was to discharge his duty; but he also nursed a secret desire to *do* something, to *achieve* something, that would be worthy of his men's astonishing heroism.

To hit *back*.

Which is why he felt a sting in his guts—what an ordinary man might call anger and frustration, but which CRC-09/571 only barely noticed, and immediately dismissed—when his comm lit up with orders from General Windu.

Orders that his ships were to immediately cease fire.

Cease fire despite close pursuit by DSFs.

Despite three additional droid starfighter wings—192 units—closing on them from beyond the planetary horizon.

Despite sixty-nine Sienar Turbostorm gunships streaking up from the surface to intercept them.

His anger and frustration showed only in a certain hopeful tone when he demanded General Windu's verification code—perhaps this was an enemy, impersonating the general—and in the slight reluctance he felt to confirm, when the general's code came through correct.

General Windu, as far as CRC-09/571 could determine, was ordering the clones to die. But CRC-09/571 could no more disobey a lawful order than he could walk through armor plate.

As they hurtled down from the stratosphere above the Korunnal Highland, the guns on all the Republic ships fell silent.

Droid starfighters swarmed over them, weapons blazing.

As his lander was pounded from all sides by multiple cannon hits, CRC-09/571 noticed an odd thing on his command-scan screen: some of the gunships below seemed to be firing on other gunships.

To be precise: sixty-seven of the gunships below seemed to be firing on the two that were in the lead.

These two did not return fire. They streaked at full power in a steep climb, scissoring side-to-side, heading straight for the mass dogfight so that the cannonfire which missed them—nearly all of it—blasted upward into the cloud of DSFs. Most of it passed harmlessly through, of course, not being aimed at the small agile craft, but several DSFs took blasts squarely, and exploded.

CRC-09/571 frowned. He had a good feeling about this.

Not far below, in the open cockpit of one of the two gunships that were the targets of those behind, Mace Windu said, "All right, Nick. Light them up."

"Yes, *sir!*"

Nick Rostu flipped a single switch, and the droid brains of twenty-six different droid starfighters—one for each of the missiles remaining in the Turbostorm's launchers—felt the sudden internal alarm-buzz of sensors detecting a missile lock.

Coming from a *friendly* ship.

The droid brains found this puzzling, but not overly distressing; they were still focused on their primary mission, which was to destroy any and all Republic craft attempting to orbit or land on Haruun Kal. But they were programmed to monitor possible hazards, and each of them set some of their spare capacity to searching memory banks for any response programs that might be indicated in the event of missile-locks from friendly craft.

There weren't any.

This, the droid brains did find distressing.

And there *was* the issue of those laser blasts . . .

Only one second later, thirty-two additional droid brains among the swarm of starfighters had exactly the same experience.

Because all four of the Krupx MG3 mini missile launchers on Depa's gunship were fully loaded.

As the two gunships penetrated the perimeter of the sprawling dogfight, Mace said, "Fire."

A Krupx MG3 tube could fire one missile every standard second; each MG3 had two tubes, which carried magazines of four mini-missiles apiece. The Sienar Turbostorm close-assault gunship had four Krupx MG3s: two forward and two aft. On Mace's command, both ships emptied their magazines. The gunships blossomed with fire and rocket exhaust.

Sixteen missiles per second roared twisting through the sky.

The dogfight became a tangled web of vapor trails.

In the gunship's open cockpit, Nick watched his widescan, whistling. "Wow. Those starfighters are *quick*."

Mace said, "Yes."

"Two thirds of our missiles are gonna miss altogether. No: three quarters. More. *Damn*, they're fast."

"It doesn't matter."

"What do you mean, it doesn't matter? It's just our *butts*, that's all! Not to mention those poor ruskakks in the landers."

Mace Windu said, "Watch."

Nick's estimate proved to be overly optimistic: of the fifty-nine missiles fired, only six found their targets. Three more were accidentally intercepted by DSFs which they were not locked onto. The rest were destroyed by the droids' inhumanly precise counterfire, or were simply evaded by the nimble craft; dozens flashed away into the sky until their propellant was exhausted and they began the long slow tumble to the surface.

However—as Mace had pointed out, down in the battered cavern base—droids were stupid.

That was not to say that they could not adapt to changing circumstances. They could, and did: often with a speed and decisiveness that no organic brain could match. These droids had comprehended they were under attack by "friendly" vessels before the initial flight of sixteen missiles had fully engaged their engines. An attack from a single friendly vessel might be a mistake, an accident, no more. But *two* vessels, both of whose transponder codes identified as friendly, had opened fire on them in a coordinated attack.

Without warning.

The droids would not wait for further attacks. They adapted with lightning speed, and remorseless droid logic.

And Nick Rostu, staring down into his widescan screen, didn't even notice his own jaw dropping farther and farther as first one, then a dozen, then a hundred and more, red scan-hits changed to blue.

"They're going hostile," Nick murmured in awe.

"Yes."

"*All* of them."

"Yes."

Two hundred and twenty-seven DSFs peeled off from the land-ers—whose silent guns had dropped them below the droid brains' threat horizon—and fell upon the sixty-nine Turbostorms in a tornado of destruction.

Gunships began to burn, and fall.

"You *planned* this?"

"There's more."

"Yeah? What do we do now?"

A dozen starfighters converged on them.

"Now," said Mace Windu, "we bail out."

He took hold of Nick's belt. Nick stared at him in open horror. "Don't tell me."

"All right."

A Force-pushed leap yanked them both out of the cockpit a full second before the gunship began to crumple under hundreds of cannon-hits; two seconds later it exploded, but by then Mace and Nick were already fifty-eight meters below and gaining speed, hurtling without benefit of repulsor-packs down through the dog-fight's flame and smoke and airbursts.

Nick's shriek sank unheard under the windrush and explosions.

Mace mouthed, *You told me not to tell you.*

Nick spent much of the ensuing fall complaining in a loud—though inaudible—voice about having to end his young life as "some fraggin' nikkle nut–brained Jedi Master's *straight* man."

Free-falling, one hand keeping a tight grip on Nick's belt, Mace reached into the Force and felt for his lightsaber.

He found its familiar resonance far below. Nick stayed locked in a fetal ball, hugging his thighs to his chest in a white-knuckled death grip and shouting obscenities between his knees. Though he had a tendency to tumble, his tight "cannonball" made him close enough to aerodynamically neutral that Mace could direct their fall by angling his own body.

They soared toward a target he could barely see: two kilometers below and a quarter-klick to the west, a gunship whirled toward the jungle in a flat spin, spewing thick black smoke. The DSFs were ignoring it, concentrating instead on the gunships that still fired and twisted and dodged in frantic attempts to evade them.

Depa was doing a fine job of appearing crippled and helpless.

Now and again some chunks of smoking durasteel or a hunk of repulsorlift would overtake Mace and Nick on their long, long fall, seeming to drift down past them at variously leisurely paces, according to their individual quotients of wind-resistance. No bodies passed them, though; Mace and Nick fell already at close to the terminal velocity of the human form.

On Haruun Kal, that was slightly less than three hundred kilometers per hour.

The gunship's rate of fall was considerably slower; it only *looked* like it was going in out of control. Which was why, when Mace had towed Nick to within a few hundred meters above the gunship, a considerable exertion of his Force-strength was required to slow them enough to avoid a catastrophic splatter.

Nick had lifted his eyes only once, as they plummeted toward the roof armor of the gunship: just long enough to recall vividly what Mace had said about leaving a red smear on a windscreen. His head was tucked back securely between his knees when Mace brought them to a thumpingly unceremonious landing that sent them bruised and bouncing along the top of the spinning ship.

Mace's free hand lashed out with effortless accuracy and latched around the widescan sensor dish-mount; his other, still locked on Nick's belt, brought the young Korun to a stop facedown over what was still nearly a kilometer drop to the jungle.

"You . . . remember . . . back when we met?" Nick gasped breathlessly into the swirling winds. "When you . . . just about broke my arm . . . with that fraggin' docking claw you use for a hand?"

"Yes?"

"I . . . *forgive* you."

"Thank you." Mace hauled him up onto the gunship's roof. Nick wrapped both arms around the sensor dish mount. "You go on ahead," Nick told him. "I think I'll just lie here and shudder."

Using the Force to steady himself on the spinning ship, Mace worked his way forward on hands and knees until he could peer into the cockpit over the rim of the wide lightsaber-cut that opened it to the air.

Chalk sat in nav; she looked up and swore. Vastor stood behind the cockpit chairs: his stare was cleanly fierce. Depa reached up to him from the pilot's chair with a warm welcoming hand on his. Her eyes were glazed with exhaustion and pain, but no surprise. "I thought you told me I'd only have to save your life *once* more."

He said, "Excuse me."

He rolled onto his back and reached behind his shoulders to grab the rim of the cut with both hands, then jackknifed and swung himself smoothly inside feet-first, without waiting to see if Vastor had gotten out of the way.

He had.

"Nick is on the roof," Mace said. "Open one of the bay doors for him."

The troop bay doors of a Turbostorm swing out and down so they could be used as landing ramps. Depa keyed the starboard door to open halfway, making it into a kind of chute down which Nick could slide, then worked the controls to cancel the gunship's spin.

Mace nodded to the *lor pelek*, who now filled the cockpit doorway. "Kar: help him in."

Why should I?

Mace was not interested in debate. He gave his head an irritated shake and waved Vastor aside. "I'll do it my . . ."

His voice trailed away, because Vastor had stepped aside, and Mace had moved to the doorway, and now he could see into the troop bay.

It was crammed with dead bodies.

Mace sagged sideways; only his shoulder against the jamb seal held him upright.

Depa had chosen a full ship.

*   *   *

His numbed brain couldn't count them properly, but he guessed there must have been twenty corpses in the bay: an infantry platoon. The pilot must have been young, excited, confident, sure of a glorious kill—so eager to get into the fight that he had sailed into battle without discharging his passengers. He had paid the price for that confidence; his corpse lay crumpled on top of what must have been the navigator's, just inside the cockpit door.

Mace's jaw hardened. He found his balance again, and stepped over their tangled lifeless legs to move deeper into the bay.

All of the corpses in the troop bay wore the militia Graylite body armor; most of the armor had been burned through in several places by close-range blaster bolts. Mace could too easily imagine inexperienced militia men—boys—turning their weapons on Depa as she moved from the cockpit into the bay. The effect of opening fire with energy weapons, point-blank upon a master of Vaapad, was mutely testified to by every charred ring around a finger-sized hole in the armor, and by the burned and lifeless flesh beneath.

Between surprise, panic, and cramped quarters, half of them had probably shot each other.

Several of the bodies bore the characteristic blackened gapes of lightsaber wounds, instantly cauterized by the blade that had opened them. Depa's handling of the ball-turret gunners had been more elegant than Mace's; brutally efficient, she had simply stabbed directly through the durasteel of the hatches, killing the men in their chairs.

The corpses still sat there, dead hands locked around the dual grips of their quads.

And, of course, the smell: seared flesh and ozone.

There was no blood. No blood at all.

Every single one of these men had been dead before she'd ever picked up Chalk and Kar Vastor. Twenty-four men.

In less than a minute.

Mace turned around, and found Kar Vastor staring at him, fiercely triumphant.

He growled simply: *She belongs here.*

Mace silently turned away and climbed the half-open door to help Nick into the troop bay.

Sliding down the door into that compartment full of dead men struck Nick speechless. He could only crouch with his back against the slant of the door, trembling.

Mace left him there. He brushed past Vastor and reentered the cockpit. "Chalk. Give me your seat."

The Korun girl frowned at Depa. Depa nodded. "It's okay, Chalk. Do it."

As soon as he could settle into the seat, he leaned over the sensor screens, studying them intently. He felt Depa's eyes upon him, but he did not lift his head.

"You can say it, if you like," she said after a moment. "I don't mind."

Keeping half his attention on the widescan to watch the droid starfighters shoot down gunship after gunship, Mace turned the other half of his attention to the gunship's data logs, calling up flight plans. Control codes.

Recognition codes.

"Really, Mace, it's all right," she said sadly. Half-blind with migraine, her breath coming a little short, she blinked dizzily through the remainder of the windscreen. "I know what you're thinking."

Mace said quietly, "I don't believe you do."

"It's not that my way is the right way. I know it isn't." A soft, bitter laugh. "I do know it. But it's the *only* way."

"The only way to what?"

"To *win*, Mace."

"Is that what you call what you have done? Winning?"

She nodded exhaustedly out toward the dogfight that still raged above them. "This battle is a masterpiece. Even after everything I have seen you accomplish, I could never have believed something like this if I hadn't seen it myself. You have done a great thing, today."

"Today's not over yet."

"And yet it's all for nothing. At this day's end, what will you have done? Destroyed most of the militia's airpower? So what?" Her voice was going hoarse, and her words became labored, as though she could not bear the effort to push them out through her pain. "You have bought us days. Perhaps weeks. No more. When you're gone, we'll still be here. We'll still be dying in the jungle. The Balawai will get more gunships. As many as they need. And we'll go back to killing them. We have to make them *fear the jungle*. Because that fear is our only real weapon."

"Not today."

"What? I—what do you mean?"

"I have decided," Mace said, still studying the sensor screens, "that you have been right all along."

Depa blinked in disbelief. "I have?"

"Yes. We used these people for our purposes; to abandon them now, when their only choice is to suffer genocide, or to commit it?" Mace shook his head grimly. "That would be as dark as any night in this jungle. Darker. That is no innocent savagery. It would be active evil: the way of the Sith. There is fighting to be done. The Jedi cannot walk away."

"You—you're serious? You really mean it?" Disbelief struggled with hope in her pain-wracked eyes. "You're going to walk away from the Clone War? You're going to stay here and fight?"

Mace shrugged, still watching the scan. "I will stay here and fight. That doesn't mean walking away from the Clone War."

"Mace, the Summertime War isn't something that can be resolved in weeks—or months—"

"I know that," he murmured distractedly. "I don't have weeks or months to spare. The Summertime War won't last that long."

"What? How can you say that? How long do you *think* it will last?"

"My best guess? About twelve hours. Maybe less."

She could only stare.

And finally, he saw on the widescan screen what he'd been waiting for: the droid starfighters peeling away from the dogfight and streaking back toward space, and the handful of surviving gunships turning to limp home.

"See that?" he said, opening his hand toward the screen. "Do you know what that means?"

Depa nodded. "It means that someone figured out what we did."

"Yes—and that this someone has the control codes for those starfighters." He turned toward her now, and in his eye was a spark that on another man would have been a wide fierce grin. "I told you: I don't have weeks or months to spare."

"I don't *understand*—What are you doing to *do*?"

Mace said, "Win."

He keyed the command frequency for the Republic landers. "General Windu for CRC-09/571. Stand by for verification and orders. Initiate simultaneous data link. Tightbeam."

The comm crackled. "*Seven-One here. Go ahead, General.*"

Depa was so astonished by the orders she heard Mace issue that she nearly crashed the Turbostorm into a mountain. When she had finally wrestled the craft back to stability, she flipped on the autopilot and faced her former Master breathlessly. "Are you *insane*?"

"Just the opposite," Mace said. "Haven't you heard? There's nothing more dangerous than a Jedi who has finally gone sane."

She sputtered like a droid with a shorted-out motivator.

"And if you don't mind, I'd like my lightsaber back," he added apologetically. "I think I'll need it."

"But—but—but—" Finally the words burst out of her. "We're going to *take Pelek Baw*?"

"No," said Mace Windu. "We are going to take the whole *system*. All of it. Right now."

20

DEJARIK

The key to the Gevarno Loop was the Al'har system. The key to Al'har was control of the droid starfighter fleet. The fleet was controlled from a secure transmitter below the command bunker of the Pelek Baw spaceport.

The spaceport did have a chance. But only one.

Two of the landers and their complements of troopers had been grounded at the Lorshan Pass, to establish a defensive perimeter around the lone open grasser tunnel, and to provide light artillery support. The other ten hopped over the mountains and kept going at their top atmospheric speed, which was not particularly impressive, but was still somewhat better than could be done by the few battered Turbostorms that were limping back to their various bases, scattered among the larger towns close by on the Highland.

Only one of the gunships went as far as Pelek Baw.

It crept over Grandfather's Shoulder on one-quarter repulsorlift power, leaking smoke and radiation. The tower officers at the spaceport listened in horror to the pilot's gasping message: a reactor breach. Imminent catastrophic failure. The pilot had heroically kept his craft in the air, making for Pelek Baw, because only the spaceport itself was fully equipped for containment and decontamination—to have landed anywhere else might have meant the sacrifice of his crew, and of the infantry platoon on board . . .

The news leaped like lightning from the tower to the ground staff, from the anti-rad techs to the bored garrison crews working the spaceport's Confederacy-provided array of modern turbolasers and ion cannons; this was the most exciting thing that had happened since the Separatist pullback. The battle at the Lorshan Pass had been astonishing, even tragic, but that was all the way on the other side of the Highland, and so didn't really count.

Every eye in the spaceport watched the Turbostorm, either in person or on screen, rooting for it, praising the crew's selfless courage as it swung wide around the city so as not to endanger civilians below, some praying aloud that they would make it, many more secretly hoping to witness a spectacular crash—

Instead of tending to their duties, such as monitoring their sensor screens.

After all, why should they? The spaceport was linked in realtime with the network of detector satellites in orbit around the planet; nothing was in the air right now except the twenty-odd surviving gunships. The last of the droid starfighters had returned to space hours ago, and the Republic landing craft which had caused so much excitement had vanished shortly thereafter.

No one was worried about those landers. After the staggering 40 percent losses they had suffered, the Republic ships surely would seek no further battle. Without a doubt, they were hiding in the "soup"— the thick oceanic swirl of toxic gases that surrounds the Highland plateau—until a cruiser could sneak in-system to extract them.

Without a doubt.

This was a considerable display of confidence on their part, because those same detector satellites on which they depended were as out of date as the rest of the local government's planetary equipage. Their IR and visual-light detectors were useless to penetrate the thick hot swirl of the "soup," and the satellites' more subtle sensors were defeated by the extremely high metals content of the gases. Once the landers went deep enough, they effectively vanished from the face of the planet.

Which is why any sensor tech at the Pelek Baw spaceport with the discipline to keep his eyes on his short-range screen might have seen indications of something extraordinary.

Pelek Baw spread along the western shore of the Great Downrush, the mightiest river on Haruun Kal. The Downrush was fed by tributaries from across the Highland—from as far east as the Lorshan Pass, and as far north as the lands above the impassable cliffs called the Trundur Wall. By the time the great river reached the capital, it was a full kilometer wide. Its dramatic roaring spray-clouded plunge from the terminal cliffs that formed the southern boundary of the city was one of the great natural wonders of the sector: it foamed and misted and spread as it fell kilometer after kilometer, becoming a snowy fan that stirred the roiling "soup" below into wild fractal whirls and blooms of colorfully immiscible gases.

What the sensor tech would have seen, had he been disciplined and duty-conscious enough to still be looking into his short-range screen, was ten *Jadthu*-class Republic landers climbing, straight up, *within* the Downrush Falls—single file, battered by the thundering water, but perfectly cloaked from long-range detection. If the sensor tech had seen that, the outcome might have been different.

That was the only chance they would have had.

But the sensor techs' attention was caught up in the drama of waiting to see if the crippled gunship could possibly struggle in for a landing before it blew up.

Not to mention the fact that a second or two before it would have touched down, it opened fire on the guardhouses surrounding the spaceport's control center, and an instant later seven immense half-naked Korunnai with shaven heads leaped from it, landing on the permacrete like pouncing vine cats, and charged toward the control center with their hands full of blaster rifles spitting fire.

And that these unexpected Korunnai were followed by a man and a woman bearing what was unquestionably the single most conspicuous and instantly recognizable type of personal weapon in the entire galaxy, and the type least welcome when it appeared on the opposing side.

The Jedi lightsaber.

So flustered were the spaceport's crew, that not a being among them even bothered to look up until the very moment the light of Al'har upon their positions was eclipsed by the shadows of hovering *Jadthu*-class landers.

Then they *did* look up: in time to see ten durasteel clouds burst in a rain of armored clone soldiers of the Grand Army of the Republic, whose arrival was so swift, efficient, and disciplined—and in such overwhelming force—that the antiship emplacements were taken without the loss of a single trooper.

The same, however, could not be said of the militia crewmen.

The clone troopers, being unsentimental about such things, did not even bother to wipe the blood off the walls and floors before replacing the crews with their own men.

The fighting at the control center was hotter, and lasted a few seconds longer, but the outcome was the same—because the attackers were Akk Guards and Jedi, and the defenders were, after all, only ordinary beings.

The capture of the Pelek Baw spaceport took less than seven minutes from the instant the gunship opened fire, and resulted in the capture of 286 military personnel, of whom thirty-five were seriously wounded. Forty-eight were killed. Sixty-one civilian employees of the spaceport were detained unharmed. All of the spaceport's aerospace defense units were captured intact, as were all spacecraft then on site.

Taken together with the Battle of Lorshan Pass, the capture of the Pelek Baw spaceport would have been considered one of the masterstrokes of General Windu's distinguished career, if only the rest of the operation had gone as planned.

But it is a truism that no battle plan long survives contact with the enemy.

This one was no exception.

Mace didn't even have to leave the command bunker to watch everything start to go wrong.

The command bunker was a large, heavily armored hexagon in the middle of the spaceport's control center, filled with angled banks of consoles. The only illumination in the room was spill from the console monitors and the huge rectangular holoprojector views that dominated each of the six walls; the general gloom thickened below console-height so that everyone inside waded hip-deep in shadow. Dead space below the wall screens was currently serving as a holding area for prisoners, as well as a makeshift aid station where wounded men and women sat or lay while clone troopers dispassionately tended their injuries.

Kar Vastor and his Akk Guards paced the perimeter of the room, restless as the wild animals they so nearly were. The Force swirled around them as they stalked among the terrified prisoners; Mace could feel them drawing on the prisoners' fear and pain and anguish, gathering it into themselves, storing it like living power cells.

Mace hadn't asked what Kar was planning to do with that power. He had a more pressing problem.

In the darkest corner of the room stood an armored console, separated from the rest; it wore a codelocked cowl of durasteel to prevent tampering. This console was a late addition to the command center, having been installed by specialists from the Techno Union at the same time they had modernized the spaceport defenses. It was called the mutiny box, and contained individual triggers for each of the destruct charges built into every turbolaser and ion cannon, every strongpoint and anti-starfighter turret.

It seemed the Confederacy did not trust that the justice of its cause was sufficient to ensure the loyalty of its troops.

In the shadow of this console, on a makeshift pallet made of seat cushions ripped from nearby chairs, lay Depa Billaba, nearly blind with pain. She had been weakening ever since the seizure of the command center, and now she lay with one arm covering her eyes. Blood trickled from one side of her mouth, where she had gnawed her lip raw.

Troopers controlled all the essential stations in the command center. Several of them had removed their helmets to accommodate earpieces or goggles; Mace avoided looking in their direction. Empty helmets sitting on the consoles too closely resembled the full one he had left on the arena sand at Geonosis.

Mace stood at the satellite console. At one shoulder stood Nick, breathing out a continuous whisper of obscenities. At his other was the stolidly motionless presence of CRC-09/571.

CRC-09/571 was still wearing his helmet. This made it easier for Mace to talk to him. He didn't particularly want to see the commander's face.

He remembered too well the first time he had seen it.

Just knowing that face was there, under the smoked mask of the helmet, was like a mocking finger tapping on the back of his head to remind him of Geonosis. Of everything that had happened there.

Of everything his failure had begun.

He did not want to be reminded of Geonosis. Especially not now.

He couldn't take his eyes from the monitor. Onscreen was the realtime display from the detector satellites in geosynchronous orbit.

"Seven-One."

The clone commander's voice crackled through his helmet speaker. "Sir."

"Get the landers' engines hot. All of them."

"We never shut them down, sir."

"All right." Mace's habitual frown deepened. "If we go, we'll need to give them plenty of targets. Initiate start-up on every ship in the port. Every one that's armed gets a gunner. How many of your men are qualified pilots?"

"All of them, sir."

Mace nodded. "Detail your best—no." He scowled at himself. Though many of the craft in the spaceport carried some armament, only the landers themselves were actual warships. This would be virtually a suicide mission. "Ask for volunteers."

"It would be the same, sir."

"I'm sorry?"

"We always volunteer, sir. All of us. It's who we are."

"Your best, then."

"Yes, sir." CRC-09/571 turned aside to issue crisp orders on his helmet's command-comm.

Nick stopped cursing long enough to ask, "Are we leaving?"

"No time," Mace said, still staring into the screen.

It showed the airspace over Pelek Baw.

"It's that bad?" Nick spread his hands. "I mean, you've got a plan, right? You've got some trick to get us out of here?"

"No more tricks," Mace said.

The sky was full of droid starfighters.

Incoming.

"How long do we have?"

Mace shook his head again. "Seven-One. We hold the ranking militia officer, yes?"

"Yes, sir. Major Stempel."

"Get him."

CRC-09/571 saluted stiffly. Mace acknowledged his salute with a wave of dismissal, and the clone commander strode away toward the huddle of prisoners.

"What good is *he* gonna do us?"

Mace pointed to a console a few meters away. "You see that? That is linked by landline to a secure transmitter beneath this bunker. Which is the only one on this planet that can send orders to those starfighters; that's the reason this bunker *is* a bunker. Whoever called them in had to *be* here."

Nick nodded, understanding. "The control code."

CRC-09/571 returned, accompanied by two troopers who held between them an ashen-faced trembling man in the sweat-stained uniform of a militia major. "Major Stempel, I am Mace Windu," Mace began, but the shaking man cut him off.

"I—I know what you want. But I can't help you. I don't *know* it! I swear. I *never* knew it. The codes are on a *datapad*—it's just a big personal datapad in an armored shell. He carries it *with* him. I didn't even know what he was *doing*—he just ordered me to relay his signal through the control console—"

Mace closed his eyes, and put his hand to his forehead.

He felt a headache coming on.

"Of course. I should have expected this," he muttered to himself. "I keep forgetting that he's smarter than I am."

"He? He who?" Nick demanded. "Who is this *he* you keep talking about?"

"Priority signal incoming," the trooper at the comm board announced. His helmet rested on the console at his elbow; a cybernetic headset hung across his brow and down one side of his jaw, but even so, when he looked back it was Jango Fett that Mace saw.

"He says his name is Colonel Geptun," said this stranger with the face of a dead man. "He's asking for you, General. He's calling to accept your surrender."

An immense, bluishly-translucent Lorz Geptun smiled his well-fed lizard smile down into the command bunker from the main holoprojector view. His khaki uniform shirt was again impeccably starched, and his aluminum-colored hair was swept back from his forehead.

"General Windu." He spoke with the same cheery lilt. "When last we met, I had no idea I was entertaining such a *distinguished* Jedi Master. Not to mention famous. It's an honor, sir. How was your trip upcountry?"

Depa was sitting up now, leaning on a desk, staring dazedly up at the screen. The light cast by Geptun's image threw black shadows that swallowed her eyes.

Kar and his Akks still paced. The clones stood motionless.

"I take it," said Mace Windu, "that you did not get my message."

"Message? Oh, the *message*. Yes, yes, quite. My Jedi Problem and all. Very thoughtful. Most appreciated."

"Then you didn't believe it."

"Should I have?"

"You had the word of a Jedi Master."

"Ah, yes. Honor, duty, justice. The flavor of the month. I can't *imagine* why I wouldn't simply take the word of a Jedi Master. Really, what could I have been thinking? Mmm—*by* the way, how *is* Master

Billaba? Hasn't found the mass murders of our citizens to be a strain on her health, has she?"

"You," said Mace Windu, "said something about surrender."

Geptun's lips pressed together as though he tasted something sour. "Really, Master Windu, it's not every day a man in my position achieves such a resounding victory. In any civilized society, I should be permitted a moment to savor it."

"Take all the time you want. Call back when you're finished."

"Ah. Quite. After all, I didn't call to gloat. Well, not entirely. So. This is your situation.

"There are several hundred droid starfighters over your position. Anything that takes off from the spaceport will be shot down without warning. Anything airborne throughout the capital district, in fact. Meanwhile—oh, by the way, have I complimented you on your maneuver at the Lorshan Pass? Brilliant, Master Windu. Truly a work of art. You must be quite the dejarik player." His pale eyes sparkled gleefully. "I have been known to indulge in the game myself. Perhaps—should our discussion today end profitably for us both—we might have a match some time."

"Isn't that what we've been doing?" Without a sideways glance or change of expression, Mace sent a pulse in the Force down the connection he had forged with Nick Rostu. The young Korun's eyes widened, then narrowed; his face went blank, and he turned away to speak softly to a nearby trooper.

"In a way, Master Windu. In a way. So. Where was I? Yes: Meanwhile, back at the Pass . . . I have fifteen thousand regulars on the ground. And while your clever bit of droid-baffling cost me almost fifty gunships, I have some left. Several, in fact. Of which twenty or so are already at the Lorshan Pass, and have already made a bloody mess of your landers and your defensive perimeter. I'm told your surviving troopers still hold the mouth of the tunnel, but of course they won't for long. I imagine their next move will be to mine the tunnel, and collapse it like you did the others. Which works for me; I have sappers clearing the other tunnels already. We'll be inside within the hour. Which is exactly how long you have to save your people."

"An hour."

"Ah, no: you misunderstand. I am plagued by unreliable subordinates; perhaps you can sympathize. My troops are not so disciplined as yours. They are young men, after all, and their blood is up. It may take them an hour to get inside. It may take them ten minutes. Once they enter those caves, I should be very much surprised if any Korun leaves that place alive."

"Geptun—"

"*Colonel* Geptun."

"—there are over two thousand *civilians* in there. The old, and the very young. Would you have your men slaughter children?"

"There is only one way to stop them," Geptun said regretfully. "I must give them the order to stand down before they breach those caves."

"And for that, you want our surrender."

"Yes."

"There are," Mace said slowly, "civilians in *here*, as well."

"Of course there are." Geptun's smile broadened. "Civilians that you, Mace Windu, would give your life to *protect*. I cannot be bluffed. Not by *you*."

Mace lowered his head.

"Don't take it too hard, General. In dejarik, part of true mastery is recognizing when a game is lost." Geptun cleared his throat delicately. "You have, sad to say, only one move left: to resign."

"Give us a a little time." Defeat had leaked into Mace's voice. "We—we'll have to talk it over—"

"Ah, time. Of course. Take as long as you like. It's not actually up to *me*, is it? My sappers are quite, shall we say, *gifted*? They could break through at any moment. It would be—mmmm, *ironic*—if your surrender were to come too late to save all those innocent lives . . ."

"Yes." Mace's voice was subdued. "I'll call back on the same frequency."

"I look forward to it. It's been a pleasure playing against you, Master Windu. Geptun out."

The image on the huge wallscreen faded. Silence shrouded the room.

Depa tottered to her feet. "Mace . . ." Her voice trickled off into a whimper of pain; she lowered her head and clenched her jaw, pulling herself together by sheer willpower. "Mace, we can't let the militia kill those people. *Your* people—"

"My people," said Mace Windu, "are Jedi."

He lifted his head, and he didn't look beaten at all. "Nick."

Nick Rostu looked up from the console where he was huddled with a pair of troopers, and his eyes sparkled. "*Got* him. The Ministry of Justice. Pegged him with his own bloody satellites!"

Depa looked stunned; Kar Vastor's face birthed a predatory grin.

Mace nodded. "Depa. Time to fight. Are you strong enough?"

She passed a hand before her face, and her gaze sharpened for a moment, but then she sagged, holding herself up with one hand while the other pressed against her temple. "I—I think so, Mace— but it's too, too—there's so much . . ."

The ragged exhaustion in her voice twisted in his stomach like a knife. "All right. Stay here."

"No—no, I can fight—"

"Perhaps you can. But I can't, while I know that you're about to collapse. You're staying. That's an order."

He turned away. "Nick: you're with me. Get Chalk and meet me at the gunship."

Nick jumped for the door, then jerked to a stop, whirled, and made a credible attempt at a salute that he ruined with a smirk and a one-armed shrug. "Sorry: forgot." Mace acknowledged his salute, and Nick vanished through the bunker's doorway.

"Mace—" Depa struggled toward him, and reached out as though to take his hand from across the room. Kar Vastor strode up behind her, arms out to catch her if she fell. "You can't—you won't have a chance . . . They'll shoot you down before you clear the landing field."

"They won't shoot me down. I'm not going up. That gunship is about to become Haruun Kal's largest landspeeder. Nick knows the streets. He can get us where we need to go."

She half-fell toward the nearest chair; Vastor caught her and lowered her gently into it. She winced a rueful thanks up at him, and placed her hand on his before turning back to Mace. "You're going after the Colonel—?"

"I don't need him. I need that datapad."

"What will you . . ." Her eyes drifted closed, and she had to force the words out. Kar squeezed her hand, and a half a smile flowed across her lips before draining into the burn scar at the corner of her mouth. "What will you do . . . with Geptun?"

Mace stared at them: Depa Billaba and Kar Vastor.

He had to go. He had to leave her behind. Let her stay. With *him*.

He might never see her again.

He couldn't make himself say good-bye.

In the end, all he could do was answer her question. "Colonel Geptun is a dangerous man," he said. "Exceedingly dangerous. I'll probably have to kill him."

He frowned, and tipped his head in a Korun shrug. "Or, possibly, offer him a job."

T wilight.

Turbolaser batteries cast building-sized shadows across the darkening plain of permacrete. Silent clones sat behind the plated shields of antistarfighter duals and quads; the only sound was a soft whine of servomotors as computer-tracked cannons traced the motion of droid starfighters still too high to be more than bright specks in the setting sun.

A tiny noise—a half-swallowed whine of pain and frustration—brought Mace's attention up from the gunship's preflight checklist. Chalk was struggling with the nav chair's seat straps; her tightly bandaged wounds wouldn't let her twist far enough to reach the length control. Her face had gone so pale that her freckles stood out like grease-splatters, and a streak of blood reddened the sheath of bandages around her chest.

"Here, let me." Mace adjusted the strap length and buckled her in. He frowned at the blood on her bandages. "When did this happen?"

Chalk shrugged, avoiding his eyes. "On the jump, maybe. At the Pass."

"You should have said something."

She pushed his hands away and busied herself with weapons checks. " 'M okay. Tough girl, me—"

"I know you are, Chalk. But your wounds—"

"Don't have time to be hurt, me." She nodded up through the oval lightsaber-cut gap in the windscreen. Far above the city, the setting sun struck sparks from the impossibly complex shimmerfly dance of the droid starfighters. "Are in danger, people. People I love. Can hurt *later*, me."

The fierce conviction in her voice gave Mace pause. An inventory of his own wounds flickered through his mind: his concussion that was giving him this headache, his cracked ribs, his sprained ankle that had him limping, the infected blaster-burn on his thigh, the spray-bandaged bite wound that Vastor had given him, not to mention all his minor cuts and the bruises that covered so much of his body it was hard to tell one from the next.

And yet he fought on, and would fight on. Wounds? Right now he could barely feel them.

Because someone he loved was in danger.

"When this is over," he said, nodding his understanding, "you and I will check into a med center. Together."

The smile she gave him showed only a trace of pain.

Nick poked his head through the cockpit doorway. "Looks like we're a go—hey, look at *this*," he said with a sudden frown, staring out through the windscreen.

Through the shadows slashing the landing field loped Kar Vastor. His shields flashed eye-stinging highlights from the glowpanel dayfloods that now, with sunset passing, shone upon the ships. He waved as he ran, clearly asking Mace to wait for him.

"What, does he want to fight again or something?" Nick brightened. "Y'know, we *could* just shoot him—*accidentally*, like. One of those senseless weapons-check tragedies—"

"Nick."

"Yeah, yeah."

Without expression, Mace watched Vastor approach. Only moments ago—just before he left the command bunker to come out here—he had pulled aside CRC-09/571 for a private conversation.

"Your orders come only from *me*, do you understand?" he had told the clone commander. "I want you to be absolutely clear on that."

CRC-09/571's helmet had tilted to a quizzical angle. "But Master Billaba—"

"Has been relieved of her duties. As has Kar Vastor."

"And his men, sir?"

"They have no military rank or authority."

"Would the general like them disarmed and restrained?"

Mace had grimly surveyed the cramped quarters of the command bunker, crowded with troopers and prisoners. In his mind, he saw twenty corpses in a gunship's troop bay. "No. I'm not sure you can. But watch them. They are not to be trusted. They may become violent without warning. They may try to harm the prisoners. Or possibly even you."

"Yes, sir."

"And get the prisoners out of here. Away from them. Not all at once. Make up some pretext, and start moving them out as efficiently as possible."

"And if there is a confrontation, sir?" CRC-09/571's dry voice had slowed, as though the commander were reluctant to even consider the possibility. "If they attack?"

"Defend yourself, your men, and the prisoners," Mace had told him. "Use all necessary force."

"Lethal force, sir?"

Mace had stared at his own reflection in the commander's smoked eyeshield. He had to swallow once, hard, before he could reply.

"Yes." He'd had to look away; he'd found that reflection too dark for what he knew he had to say. "You are authorized to use lethal force."

Out on the landing field, Vastor didn't bother to come around toward the troop bay doors; without breaking stride he burst into a Force leap that carried him up to the Turbostorm's nose below the cockpit with a clank that must have been his deactivated vibroshields getting in the way of his grab for the nose armor. He climbed up into view, settling himself into a crouch on the nose armor outside the windscreen.

He squatted there for a moment, forearms resting on his bent knees, staring gravely at Mace through the opening.

Mace, Jedi of the Windu. Even his growl was reluctant. Almost contemplative.

"Kar."

We have not been friends, you and I. If we both survive this day, I suspect that again we will not be friends.

Mace only nodded.

We may not meet again. I would have you know that I am glad I did not kill you this afternoon. No one else could have done what you have done today. No one else could have brought us so far.

This, also, did not call for a reply. Mace waited.

Vastor's mouth compressed as though sharing this caused him pain, and his growl became almost a purr, low in his throat.

I would have you know that I am proud to be your dôshalo. You are a credit to the Windu.

Mace took a deep breath. "You," he said, slow, coldly deliberate, "aren't."

It was Vastor's turn to silently stare.

"I am not Mace, Jedi of the Windu. Windu is my name, not my ghôsh. You and I are not dôshallai. The Windu are no more, and what you have done disgraces their memory. My ghôsh," said Mace Windu, "is the Jedi."

He went back to his preflight checklist. "It would be good," he said distantly, "if you were to be gone when I get back."

Vastor had turned his face toward the spiral dance of the starfighters as Mace spoke; he did not seem to hear. He stared upward as though listening to the stars. He passed a second or two in silence and stillness, then he nodded gravely and looked back at Mace.

Until we meet again, dôshalo. He spun like a startled branch leopard and sprang down from the Turbostorm's nose to sprint away across the floodlit permacrete.

Mace flicked the last ten switches into flight sequence, and the Turbostorm rocked gently as its repulsorlifts brought it up to an altitude of just under a meter.

"Let's go."

*   *   *

By the time the Turbostorm roared through the spaceport gates into the warehouse district of Pelek Baw, it was already doing over two hundred kilometers an hour. The lightsaber gap in the windscreen shrieked like a bad wailhorn in a third-rate smazzo band. Immense night-blackened blocks of warehouses crowded the right-of-ways for a kilometer or more north of the spaceport, but the streets themselves were empty. Mace intended to take advantage while he could.

Nick held on to the backs of Mace's and Chalk's chairs, squinting doubtfully up through the windscreen's gap. "Uh, y'know, if you don't mind my asking, are you *sure* those droid starfighters won't come down for ground vehicles as well?"

"I'm sure."

"But, I mean, how do you *know*?"

"I'll show you." Mace heeled the Turbostorm over, using its thrusters to help negotiate a tight corner; it bounced jarringly off a warehouse hard enough to dent its armor and knock a steamcrawler-sized hole in the building's wall. He fought the controls and steadied the ship, then nodded forward along the long straight stretch of street.

Half a klick ahead, the gigantic slope-armored hulk of a ground assault vehicle clanked out from a side street.

Mace said, "That's how."

Its turret was already rotated the quarter turn to bear on the Turbostorm and Mace said, "Chalk," but she was ahead of him: the quad turrets on both sides of the gunship burst to life and filled the street with streaking packets of energy—

Which crashed into the GAV without even scratching it.

Nick was shouting, "You'll never breach that armor!" while Chalk was letting her gaze defocus and her hands relax on the split yoke. "Not shooting at his *armor*, me," she murmured and she held down the triggers as the GAV's cannon bucked with the launch of an armor-piercing shell—

That met a laser blast nose-first while still inside the barrel.

The explosion was gratifying.

It left the cannon's barrel peeled back on itself in a spray of blackened durasteel twists, making the GAV look like a droid smoking an exploding cigar.

"Okay," Nick said. "*Now* I'm impressed."

The GAV's gunners opened up with its heavy slug-repeater, making riding in the Turbostorm resemble having one's head inside a durasteel trash barrel that's being clubbed by a pack of drunken squibs. Slug impacts pounded prismatic dents across the transparisteel windscreen. Mace said, "Time to get off the street."

"You can't!" Nick shouted. "They'll shoot us down!"

"Off, not up. Open fire."

Chalk held down the quad triggers. Mace yanked the control yoke to slew the Turbostorm sideways and sent full power of both quads against the warehouse beside them. A huge mouth, teeth of duracrete dangling from reinforcing bars, suddenly gaped in the wall, and Mace rammed the gunship through the gap.

Inside the building.

"Yow!"

"Know what you're *doing*, you?"

"Keep firing."

Cargo containers flashed by them to either side, lit red by the blaze of fire from their guns, then another cannon-blasted mouth opened in the opposite wall and they broke out into the next street over—

Which was also full of militia.

At least a company of heavy infantry, with a couple of mobile artillery pieces and possibly more out there that Mace didn't have time to identify because he just kept the gunship roaring straight on through the middle of them and into the warehouse across the street before any of the astonished Balawai could so much as charge their weapons.

Blasting through buildings when they had to, zooming along open streets when they could, zigzagging and backtracking to find gaps in the tightening net of heavy armor that was rolling through the warehouse district, they fought their way out into the city, leaving a wake of astonished Balawai and an immense connect-the-dots trail of burning warehouses.

*   *   *

Sometimes, when things go wrong, they go wrong one at a time: a chain of misfortune that must be dealt with link by link. Those are the easy times.

Sometimes troubles come in a starburst.

When they had finally broken free from the warehouse district, Mace brought the gunship down to a walking pace. The evening thoroughfares of Pelek Baw were crowded as always, but beings of all species hastily stepped aside for the idling gunship cruising through the city at street level.

At least, whenever they stopped staring long enough to move.

"Nick. Do you know where we are?"

The young Korun leaned around him to stare out the windscreen; off to their port side, the sky was red with the light of the fires they'd left behind. "So much for the element of surprise . . ."

"Nick."

Nick shook his head dejectedly. "Don't you get it? They *know we're coming* now. The Ministry of Justice is like a *fortress*. Hell, it *is* a fortress. Not even *you* can get in there. Not now. Now they'll be *ready* for us."

Mace said, "They always were. That's all right: we're not going there."

"Huh?"

"Geptun is smart. Possibly too smart for his own good. He knows we'll come for him; it's the only move we have. That's why we tracked his signal so easily: he *wants* us to hit the Ministry of Justice. If he were really in the Ministry, he could have found a way to mask his signal. There won't be anything there except a very large number of troops. Or possibly only a very large bomb."

"Then what are we fraggin' *doing* out here? Where *is* he?"

"A place with electronics sophisticated enough to fake the origination data of a comm signal," Mace said. "I may not be the dejarik player our colonel is, but there's nothing wrong with my memory. The one time we met, it was on the occasion of the death of someone he described as an *old friend*."

Nick's eyes narrowed. "Tenk . . ." he breathed. "You think he's at the *Washeteria.*"

"Can you get us there?"

"Sure. Simple. All you gotta do is bear northeast—"

He was interrupted by Chalk's hand on his arm.

She gave him a sickly smile, and her throat worked as though she were struggling not to retch. "Maybe . . . maybe better—" She coughed wetly.

Blood spattered from her lips.

"Chalk!"

Her fingers dug into his arm: a spasm. Her other hand was pressed to her side. Her face was gray, and her eyes looked foggy. "Maybe better take nav, you," she said, and slumped.

Her hand fell away from her ribs, revealing a ragged hole below her breast. She crumpled forward against the nav chair's safety straps. In her back was an exit wound Nick could have put his fist into. The chair-back had an even bigger hole, and the cockpit wall behind bore a splash of blood and tissue and shreds of black synth-leather.

Nick threw his arms around her, holding her head up, pleading with her empty eyes. "Chalk, no, not you, come on, not you *too*, come on, Chalk, *please*—"

Mace looked at the windscreen: at the line of rainbow-ringed slug dents from that first GAV: a line punctuated by the lightsaber-cut gap.

She had taken that slug minutes ago. Without a word. Without a *sound.* She had held on—had *fought* on—

Because people she loved were in danger.

"The *medical* center—" Nick's voice had gone thick. "The medical center's only a klick or two from here—"

Mace's decision did not take even a full second. General or not, he was still a Jedi. "Just tell me which way to go."

"Okay. Okay." Nick tore himself away from Chalk and pointed toward an intersection ahead. "Okay, go left at the corner, then—"

The street in front of them erupted like a chain of volcanos: explosions at the terminal points of scarlet particle beams that rained upon them from the night sky: aimed not at the street but at a hurtling dark shape that twisted through a barrel roll over the buildings before it took a direct hit and tumbled into a ball of debris-spewing fire that slammed an apartment block only a few dozen meters short of the Turbostorm.

The blast picked up the gunship and spun it down the street.

Of the unarmored groundcars, and the pedestrians, the taxicarts and street vendors, the elderly on their stoops and the children who had darted playfully around the tall lightpoles—

Nothing was left but smoking rubble and twisted metal.

"What in the—" Nick reeled off an impressive string of obscenities. "—was *that?*"

Mace wrestled the Turbostorm out of its spin and cut the engines; the ship skidded down the street trailing a fountaining tail of sparks. He leaned forward, his knuckles pale on the control yoke, and stared up through the windscreen.

"May the Force give me strength . . ." he whispered: as close to a curse as he had ever come.

That hurtling dark shape had been one of the Incom Skyhoppers from the spaceport. The cannonfire that had rained on the street and brought down the skyhopper had come from droid starfighters.

The night sky was full of ships.

Above the *city.*

"Oh, Depa . . ." Mace breathed.

More than four hundred thousand people lived in Pelek Baw. Drawing fire from the starfighters down upon it could put the entire capital to the torch.

No: not *could.*

Had.

The skyhopper wasn't the first ship to crash into the crowded streets of the capital tonight. And there were over a hundred more, from tiny racing yachts to immense freighters.

He felt the city in the Force: a holocaust of flame and darkness.

Panic. Rage. Grief.

Horror.

There was nothing else left.

But the spaceport had a different feel entirely.

"Depa, what have you *done?*"

The comm panel chimed to announce an incoming voice-and-visual. Numbly, Mace reached past Nick and Chalk to hit the receive key. Scanning lasers in the comm unit traced a blue-lined image shadow on the windscreen: an electronic pre-echo of the larger-than-life holo-image projected into the burning night outside.

An image of a huge Korun with a shaven head and a smile like a mouthful of bone needles.

He growled, and Mace wondered how Vastor could expect to be understood—his Force-powered semi-telepathy wouldn't modulate a comm signal—but this little mystery instantly solved itself.

When the *lor pelek* growled, the dark storm that had swallowed Pelek Baw growled with him.

Thank you for giving us the city, dôshalo. His smile spread like flames on oil. *We have decided to redecorate.*

Mace opened his mouth to ask for CRC-09/571—and closed it again. The commander had been warned not to take orders from them.

They must have killed him.

"Kar, where's Depa?" Mace held his desperate horror locked deep inside his chest. "Let me talk to her."

She doesn't want to talk to you. She doesn't want to see you. Ever. I have arranged matters so she won't have to.

"Kar, stop this. You have to *stop* this!"

And I will. Vastor's lips pulled back from those needle teeth, and there was no longer even the pretense of a smile. *When everyone is dead.*

"You don't understand what you're doing—"

Yes, I do. And so do you.

Mace's stare burned like the city around him.

He did understand. Finally. Too late.

He had no words for what he felt. Perhaps there were no words.

I called to say good-bye, dôshalo. Depa will remember you fondly. As will we all. It is a hero's death you go to, Mace of the Windu.

Mace showed his own teeth. "I'm not dead yet."

Vastor's blue-imaged head tilted a centimeter to the right. *What time is it?*

Mace froze.

A metallic *clank* echoed in his memory.

A clank that might have been deactivated vibroshields hitting the nose armor of a Sienar Turbostorm.

Or—

Not.

"*Nick!*" Mace's sudden shout shocked the young Korun like a shot from a stun baton. "*Hang on!*"

"Hang on to *what?*" The arming levers on the seat ejectors flipped up; Nick swore and threw his arms around Chalk half a second before the triggers pressed themselves and explosive bolts blew the windscreen up and out and her chair shot toward the rooftops, out of balance and tumbling into the night sky as the time fuse on the proton grenade Vastor had mag-clamped to the Turbostorm's nose precisely where its shaped charge would blow a dozen kilos of shredded armor plate through the cockpit sideways—

Detonated.

Mace found them by following his Force-link with Nick.

Double-loaded and out of balance, Chalk's ejector chair had carried them only as far as a black rooftop, flat and sticky with tar, before crashing to spill them across it. Flames from other buildings around lit its walls and cast its square shadow toward the stars.

Nick's silent silhouette knelt with bowed head beside her. His hand gently stroked bloody tangles of hair away from her face; tears from his eyes fell to her cheeks, as though death had finally allowed this tough girl to weep.

Mace stood at the roof's rim and looked out across the city.

His chair had carried him a dozen blocks away. He had come here on foot.

The streets were a nightmare.

Cannonfire rained at random. Missiles that had lost their targets blasted groundcars and streets vendor stalls. People ran and screamed. Many were armed. More carried bundles of valuables saved—more often looted—from burning buildings. Bodies lay sprawled on the pavement, ignored except for the curse they would get when someone tripped over them in blind panic.

He'd seen a little girl clutching the bloody tatters of a corpse's dress while she tried to scream life back into its body.

He'd seen a Wookiee and a Yuzzem locked together, clawing and biting and shredding each other, howls of terrified rage muffled by mouthfuls of each other's flesh and fur.

He'd seen a man not two meters in front of him chopped in half by a blasted-free hull plate that had fallen from the sky like a tabletop-sized cleaver.

From the rooftop, the capital of Haruun Kal looked like a night-shrouded volcanic plain: a vast dark field pocked with calderae that opened on hell. Clone-piloted ships streaked and spun and rolled, desperately dodging starfighters that swooped and dived and spat flame. In those contests it didn't matter who won; the city lost.

Pelek Baw had always been a jungle, but only in a metaphoric sense. Vastor had brought the real one.

He *was* the real one.

And he was eating this city alive.

"I always used to . . ." Nick's voice was soft. Almost expressionless. Just slow, and faintly puzzled. He still knelt over her. "I used to, y'know, kind of think . . . y'know, maybe someday, when I leave this fraggin' planet . . ."

He shook his head helplessly. "I always kind of thought she'd be coming *with* me."

"Nick—"

"Not that I asked her, you understand. No. Not that I ever had the guts to *say* anything to her. About that. About—" He lifted his face to the cold distant stars. "About *us*. It just . . . it was just, y'know, just never the right *time*. And I kind of thought she knew. I hope she knew."

"Nick, I'm sorry. I cannot tell you how sorry I am."

"Yeah." Nick nodded slowly, pensively, as though each motion of his head welded another layer of armor around his grief. Then he sucked air through his teeth and shoved himself to his feet. "Lots of people are sorry tonight."

He had her gunbelt in his hands.

He moved to the roof rim to stand beside Mace and look out across the burning city. "They're all against us now," he said softly. "Not just the militia and the droids."

"Yes."

He buckled Chalk's gunbelt around his waist, and tied her holster down to his left thigh, to match his own on his right. "They've turned on us. All of them. Kar and his Akks. Depa. Even the clones."

"The clones," Mace said distantly, "are only following orders."

"Orders from our enemies."

Now it was Mace's turn to lower his head: Mace's turn to nod layers of armor around his own grief. "Yes."

"And on our side—it's us. You and me. Nobody else." He drew her gun, smooth and fast, checking its heft and balance. He popped the clip and snapped it back in. "Y'know, Kar saved her life."

He spun the pistol forward, then reversed it so that its own spin slipped it snugly into the holster. "Temporarily."

Mace murmured, "It's always temporary."

He stared down into the pandemonium on the street. An armored groundcar filled with militia swung around a corner. The gunner on the roof-mounted EWHB-10 fired short bursts into the air to clear the road; some of the armed looters returned fire.

Nick said softly, "You got any idea what we're gonna do?"

Before Mace could speak, Nick smiled tiredly and raised a hand. "Don't bother. I know what you're about to say."

"I don't think you do."

Mace gave the militia vehicle below a speculative frown.

"We're going to surrender."

22

SURRENDER

The Highland Green Washeteria was an imposing verdigris-domed edifice of gleaming white tile set off by obsidian grout. When the groundcar pulled up to it, its sign was dark and its elaborate array of arched windows were sealed by durasteel blast shutters.

A block away, the streets were choked with burning wreckage; here, all was dark and still.

The squad's noncom peered dimly through the groundcar's windscreen. "Dunno why the colonel'd be *here*," he said doubtfully.

"Maybe he wants a bath," Nick said dryly from the rear compartment, where he sat among the other four sweaty, tired-looking regulars. "Which wouldn't do any of *you* guys any harm either, I mean, *shee . . .*"

"He's here," Mace said from the front seat next to the noncom. "Let's get out."

"I guess he *could* be here," the noncom admitted reluctantly. "Okay, everybody out."

As the squad piled out onto the walkway, the noncom muttered, "I *still* think we shoulda tried the Ministry. And I probably oughta put binders on you, too."

"There's no reason to go to the Ministry," Mace said. "And you don't need the binders."

"Ahh, frag the binders anyway. Okay, let's go." The noncom tried the blast-shuttered door. "Locked."

Purple energy flared. Durasteel sizzled. White-hot edges dulled to red, then darkened entirely. Mace said, "No, it isn't."

The noncom used the barrel of his blaster rifle as a pry bar to swing open the door. "Hey, what are *you* guys doing here?"

The broad sculpted lobby of the Washeteria had been turned into a heavy-weapons nest. A platoon of militia crouched, squatted, or lay behind temporary barriers of expanded permacrete. Tripod-mounted repeaters were levelled at the open door. The men's faces were drawn, their eyes round and haunted; here and there a rifle muzzle trembled.

An oddly familiar voice replied, "A guy might want to ask you the same question."

"Well, I captured that Jedi everybody's looking for, didn't I," the noncom said. "Here, come on in."

Mace stepped around the open door.

"*You!*"

It was the big man from the spaceport pro-bi showers, and he didn't look frightened at all.

Mace said, "How's your nose?"

The big man went for his sidearm with an impressively swift draw.

Mace's was faster.

By the time the big man's blaster cleared his holster, Mace was staring at him past the sizzling purple fountain of his blade. "Don't."

Nick said, "You guys know each other?"

The big man held the blaster steady, aimed at Mace's upper lip. He said sourly, "*Captured* him, did you?"

"Uh, sure, Lieutenant—" The noncom blinked uncertainly. "Well, okay, they surrendered, but it's the same thing, right? I mean, he's *here*, ain't he?"

"Stand away from them. All of you. Right now."

The squad scattered.

Mace said, "I need to see Colonel Geptun."

"Y'know, that's a funny thing." The big lieutenant squinted past his blaster's sights. "Because he don't want to see *you*. He told me *specifically*. About you. He said you might show up here. He said you're supposed to be shot on sight."

"Shooting at Jedi," Mace said, "is a losing proposition."

"Yeah, I've heard that."

"Lieutenant, do you have a family?"

The officer scowled. "None of your business."

"Have you looked *outside* recently?"

The big man's jaw tightened. He didn't answer. He didn't have to.

Mace said, "I can *stop* it. Those ships your droids are chasing are piloted by men under my command. But if something were to happen to *me* . . ."

The big man's chin drew down stubbornly. His men frowned at each other; some bit their lips or shifted their weight. One of them said doubtfully, "Hey, Lou, y'know—I got two kids, and Gemmy's up with another—"

"Shut it."

"Your choice is straightforward," Mace said. "You can follow orders and open fire. Most of you will die. And your families will be left out *there*. *Without* you. And without any hope other than that their deaths might be quick.

"Or you can bring me to Colonel Geptun. Save hundreds of thousands of lives. Including your own.

"Do your duty. Or do what's *right*. It's up to you."

The big man ground out his words between clenched teeth. "You know the last time I could *breathe* okay?" he growled, pointing at his nose. "Guess. Go on. Guess."

"Yours is not the only nose I've broken on this planet," Mace said evenly. "And you deserved it more than he did."

The big man's knuckles whitened on the blaster.

Mace lowered his lightsaber but kept its blade humming. "Why don't you call the colonel and ask? It is possible," he said with half a nod back toward the bloody chaos outside, "that he has changed his mind."

The lieutenant's scowl thickened until it broke under its own weight. He shook his head disgustedly and let his gun arm fall to his side. "They don't pay me enough for this."

He came out from behind the permacrete barrier and went to the house comm at the hostess desk. A brief conversation went on in undertones. When it was over, he looked even more disgusted. He returned his blaster to its holster and waved his empty hand at his men. "Awright, stand down, everybody. Put 'em away."

While his men complied, he walked over to Mace. "I'll need your weapons."

From behind Mace's shoulder, Nick said, "You don't have to take our weapons."

"Don't quit your day job, kid." The lieutenant held out his hand. "Come on: I can't bring you down there armed."

Mace silently handed over his lightsaber. Nick flushed while he dangled his pistols from one finger through each trigger guard.

The lieutenant took both pistols in one hand, and weighed Mace's lightsaber in the palm of the other. He gave it a thoughtful frown. "The colonel said you're Mace Windu."

"Did he?"

The officer looked the Jedi Master in the eye. "Is it true? You're really him? Mace Windu?"

Mace admitted it.

"Then maybe I don't mind the nose so much." The big man shook his head ruefully. "I guess I'm lucky to be alive at all, huh?"

"You," Mace said, "should consider a new line of work."

The entrance to the Republic Intelligence station was a waterproof hatch; it was disguised as part of the checkered tile pattern on the bottom of a steaming mineral bath fed by the natural hot springs below the Washeteria. The lieutenant led Mace and Nick to a wading-stair from the deck down into the shallow end. Two sweating regulars brought up the rear, rifles slanted across their chests.

Nick made a face. "Stinks in here. People really want to go *in* that?"

"Not many, I bet," the big man said. "If they did, it wouldn't make a real good secret entrance, would it?"

A concealed latch opened a code panel that swung down from the stair rail. The lieutenant tucked Mace's lightsaber under his arm so he could punch some keys, and the field generator built into the stairs and the pool floor hummed to life. An electric crackle heralded the opening of a channel; walls of sizzling energy held back the sulfurously steaming water. Toward the deep end the channel became a tunnel. Another code panel opened the waterproof hatch, and openwork stairs with drains beneath them led down into a dry, brightly lit room filled with the very latest electronic surveillance, codebreaking, and communications equipment.

A handful of people in civilian clothes monitored the various stations like they knew what they were doing. There was an undertone of insistent muttering, and many of the console monitors showed only snow.

The lieutenant showed them to a small gloomy chamber with holoviewer walls and a heavy lammas table in the center. The only light in the chamber came from the holoviewers: they showed real-time images of the city. The ceiling sparkled with swooping droid starfighters and the hurtling ships they pursued. Burning buildings cast a dull flickering rose-colored glow that silhouetted a small plump man seated at the far end of the table.

"Master Windu. Please come in." Geptun's voice was thin, and the self-deprecating chuckle he offered had a fragile edge. "It appears that I miscalculated."

Mace said, "We both did."

"I never suspected that Jedi could be capable of such . . . *savagery*."

"Neither did I."

"People are *dying* out there, Windu! Civilians. *Children*."

"If your concern for children had included Korunnai, we wouldn't be here right now."

"Is that what this is? *Revenge?*" The colonel sprang jerkily to his feet. "Do Jedi *take* revenge? How can you do this? *How can you do this?*"

"You are not the only one," Mace said evenly, "with unreliable subordinates."

"Ah—" Geptun sank slowly back into his chair and lowered his head into his hands. A weak, sickly laugh shook his shoulders. "I understand. I didn't misjudge you. *You* misjudged your *people*. This is all your mistake, not mine."

"There will be plenty of guilt to go around. All that is important right now is the power to make it *stop*."

"And you have this power?"

"No," Mace said. "You do."

"You think I haven't *tried*? You think I don't have every person in this *station* working to deactivate those starfighters? *Look* at this— you see all this?" Geptun's voice was going shrill. A shadow-wave of a trembling hand swept the images on the walls and ceiling. "These are *land-line* sensors. Hard-wired. Want to see our *remotes*?"

He stabbed a control on the tabletop. All four walls and the ceiling fuzzed to eye-stinging white snow.

"See? Don't you *see*? All our signal-jamming controls are at the spaceport, too! Even if you *wanted* to order your pilots to stand down, you *can't*. We can't get through—it's out of our hands . . . We are helpless. Helpless."

In the white light from the screens, Geptun looked pale and disheveled. His eyes were red and puffy. His lips were swollen as if he'd been chewing them. Black sweat stained his blouse from his armpits to his belt.

Mace said, "There is one more thing you can try."

"Enlighten me."

"Surrender."

Geptun's laugh was bitter. "Oh, *certainly*. Why didn't *I* think of that?" He shook his head. "Surrender to whom?"

"To the Republic," Mace said. "To me."

"To *you*? You're my *prisoner*. And you're wasting my time." His hand shook when he waved at the lieutenant. "Take them away."

The big man shrugged. "You heard him—" the lieutenant began, but he finished the statement with a sudden yelp of surprise and pain when the lightsaber he held ignited in his hand, the blade stabbing downward to drive a smoking hole through his thigh.

His hands opened; the pistols clattered to the floor and the lightsaber flipped into Mace's palm. "You hold it like this," Mace said, sizzling blade poised a centimeter from the end of the big man's nose.

The two regulars behind them cursed and fumbled with their rifles. Nick spun to face them and brought up his arms as both his pistol yanked themselves through the air to smack into his hands. "Let's just not, okay?"

The two militiamen, blinking and cross-eyed as they tried to focus on one muzzle apiece, settled on the better part of valor. Pale and grimacing, the lieutenant sagged against the holoviewer at his back, clutching his thigh.

"These are my terms," Mace said evenly. "The planetary militia will immediately cease all operations in the Lorshan Pass. You will turn over to me the starfighter control codes. And, as the ranking military official—and the ranking officer of the Confederacy—you will sign a formal surrender ceding Haruun Kal, and the Al'har system itself, to the Republic."

"Colonel—" The lieutenant's growl was thin with pain. "Maybe you oughta think about it. Y'know? Think about it. I mean, all the guys—we got *families* here—"

Geptun clutched the edge of the table, livid. "If I don't?"

Mace shrugged. "Then I won't save your city."

"How am I supposed to trust that you will? That you even *can*?"

"You know who I am."

Geptun trembled, and not from fear. "This is extortion!"

"No," Mace said. "It's war."

The formal surrender had been drafted, witnessed, and signed right there in the Intel station.

"You know this has no legal standing," Geptun said as he affixed his signature and retinal print. "I sign this surrender only under duress—"

"Surrender is always made under duress," Mace observed dryly. "That's why they call it *surrender*."

Mace set the comm gear to automatically make a number of trans-

missions the instant signal-jamming abated enough that communications could resume. Many of the transmissions would be simple
orders to the various battalions of militia to lay down their arms.
More significant would be a HoloNet report to Coruscant with a
copy of the surrender agreement, along with an emergency summons
for a Republic task force. If the Republic could get here in force before the Confederacy did, their landing would be unopposed. By the
time signal-jamming would end, he'd have control of the starfighters; even if the Separatists got here first, Mace would be in a position to make the Al'har system uncomfortably hot for them.

And if they tried to land, the spaceport controlled the planetary
defenses as well.

Now all he had to do was control the spaceport.

They had the whole platoon plus the armored groundcar squad for
escort through the chaos of Pelek Baw.

Geptun got them through the militia perimeter that stretched in
a thick arc among the burning warehouses, then Mace stepped out
of the groundcar. "Nick. You drive."

He shooed away the rest of the militiamen. Geptun started to follow them. "Not you, Colonel. Get in the car."

"Me?" The ride to the spaceport had given Geptun time to recover
his composure; he looked almost his old self again. "You can't be serious! What do you expect *me* to do?"

"You'll transmit the deactivation codes. To make sure nothing goes
wrong."

"Why should I have to do *anything*? What will *you* two be doing?"

Nick stared through the windshield at the spaceport gates.
"Killing people."

Geptun looked at him, blinking as though he were expecting a
punchline.

Mace said, "Get in the car."

"Really—I mean, please—I don't know what kind of man you
think I *am*—"

"I think," Mace said, "that you are a very brilliant man. I think that
you have more courage than you have ever guessed. I think that you

truly care about this city, and the people in it. I think your cynicism is a fraud."

"What—what—really, this is *astonishing*—"

"I think that if you were truly as corrupt and venal as you pretend," said Mace Windu, "you would be in the Senate."

Geptun's blank gape hung on for one silent second, then gave way to an abrupt guffaw. Shaking his head, still chuckling, he walked around to the other side of the groundcar. "Here, young man, shove over. I'll drive."

"You will?"

"You might have to shoot people, yes?"

Nick looked at Mace; Mace shrugged, and Nick slid over to the passenger side. Geptun adjusted the pilot's seat to make himself comfortable behind the control yoke. "I suppose," he said with a vast theatrical sigh, "I am as ready as I will ever be."

Mace ignited his lightsaber.

He lifted its blade, and stood for a moment, staring into its blaze as though he could read his future there.

Perhaps he could.

That killing flame might be the only future he had.

He let it drop to his side but held it alight, and walked toward the spaceport gates.

"Follow me."

Geptun engaged the groundcar's drive system and let the armored vehicle roll along behind the Jedi Master's deliberate stride.

Turbolaser towers loomed to either side. From the city at his back came the shriek of fighting ships cutting the air, the hammer of weapons and the rolling booms of exploding buildings, but beyond the durasteel bars of the gate, all was silence and stillness.

He reached the gate, and looked across the bare landing field toward the control center.

Empty. Silent. Vast. The dayfloods threw stark white glare.

His blade flashed. Durasteel clanged on permacrete.

Mace walked into the spaceport.

The groundcar rolled in after him.

He had no idea what to expect here. He thought he was ready for anything. He was almost right.

One thing he didn't expect was the crackle of a helmet speaker from the ground-level hatch of the turbolaser tower to his left.

"General Windu! General Windu, is that you?"

Three troopers crouched in the doorway.

Mace called, "Yes."

"Permission to approach, sir!"

He waved them over, and they came at a run. They snapped to attention in perfect file. "With the general's permission—the sergeant sent us out to see if it was you, sir!"

"And it is," Mace said. "Me."

"They said your ship blew up."

"Did they?"

"Yes, sir! They told us you were dead!"

Mace Windu said, "Not yet."

Mace stared at the bleak durasteel of the blast door while the trooper captain filled him in.

The blast door was a full meter thick, and locked with internal bolts of neutronium. Its surface was smooth. Dull matte gray. From the outside, it was controlled by a code panel. The inside had a manual wheel. When the wheel was engaged, the code panel was useless.

The command bunker was more secure than most treasure vaults. Only the swiftness of their assault had allowed Mace, Depa, and the Akk Guards to capture it in the first place; the defenders had not had time to swing it shut.

The brightly lit corridor seemed unreal. A full platoon of heavy assault troopers crouched in a tight arc on the white tile around the blast door, bolting tripods into the floor and charging weapons. Four more platoons waited in reserve, two down either direction of the corridor. Mace stood in front of the door. Geptun sat on a heavy repeater's fusion pack, white-knuckled hands clutching his armored datapad. Nick sat on the floor with his back against the wall beside the door, eyes closed. He might have been asleep.

The trooper captain was designated CC-8/349. He told Mace that the regiment had had no communication from the bunker since the news that the general had been killed; that was shortly after Master Billaba had ordered them to use the spaceport's ships to draw the droid starfighters down upon the city. The rest of the clone troopers had been ordered to stand ready to repel a militia infantry assault.

Since then, there had been no communication from the bunker. No one had entered. No one had left.

Mace had a good idea how the inside of the bunker looked right now. Too good an idea.

A surge of dark power spread across the city like the shock-front of a fusion bomb.

Behind that door was ground zero.

"Makes you wonder," Nick said slowly, eyes still closed, "just what they're doing in there."

Mace said, "They're waiting."

"For what?"

He looked down at the lightsaber in his hand. "To see if I come back."

Nick seemed to chew this over. He opened his eyes and pulled himself to his feet. He shook his arms loose and hooked his thumbs over his gunbelts. "Then I guess we shouldn't disappoint them."

Mace frowned at the slug pistols holstered on Nick's thighs. "You should borrow a blaster."

"Fine with these."

"Blasters are more accurate. More stopping power." Mace's voice was grim. "More shots."

Nick drew his right hand gun, turning it over as though admiring it for the first time. "Thing about slugs is, they only go one way," he said lazily. "Blasters are all well and good, but I don't particularly care to eat my own shot. Slugs don't bounce."

"Off a vibroshield they will."

Nick shrugged. "Not off a lightsaber."

Mace lowered his head. He had no answer.

The sick weight that had gathered in his chest for so long now threatened to crush him altogether.

"Captain Four-Nine," he said slowly. "No one comes out of there but us. Do you understand? No one."

"General, we should go in first—"

"No."

"With the general's pardon: That's what we are for."

"Your purpose is to fight. Not to die uselessly. Master Yoda knew better than to send troopers against a single enemy Force-user on Geonosis; in that bunker may be as many as *seven*."

"Eight."

Mace glared at Nick. Nick shrugged. "You know it's true."

The Jedi Master set his jaw.

"Eight."

He turned again to CC-8/349. "I will go in first. Your men will enter on my command. Two platoons. Come in shooting: blast anything that moves. But this is *not* search and destroy. You're there solely to cover Colonel Geptun. You will take all available measures to protect him, and to ensure that he completes his mission. *His* mission is the objective of this operation, understood? If he fails, nothing else matters."

"Yes, sir. Understood, sir."

"The rest of you will remain out here to hold the doorway. If you have to. And if you can."

"Um, if I might interrupt—?" Geptun coughed delicately. "Has anyone considered just how we are going to get *in*?"

"Just like we do everything else," Nick said. "The hard way."

"Pardon?"

"Shaped charges," Mace told him. He turned to the trooper captain. "Proton grenades. Blow the door."

"General—!" CC-8/349 stiffened to attention. "With the general's pardon, sir, Commander Seven-One's still in there! With more than twenty men. And there are prisoners to consider, sir. Including civilians. If we use proton grenades, the casualties—"

"There is no one in that room except the dead," Mace said heavily. "And the people who killed them."

He nodded to Nick. "Cover my back from the doorway."

The young Korun drew Chalk's pistol from his left holster. He held both guns low and loose, and nodded back.

"Colonel Geptun."

The plump little Balawai pushed himself to his feet. He clamped the armored datapad under one arm but still held it with both white-knuckled hands. One of his kneecaps jumped and shuddered, but his voice was light and steady as ever. "Ready when you are, Master Jedi."

"I can't protect you in there."

"Lovely."

"You won't be using the console. The transceiver unit itself is in a chamber below the bunker. I will provide access. Stay out here until I call for the troopers."

"Certainly. I am in no, ah, *hurry*, if you take my meaning. I have never been anything remotely resembling a hero."

"People," Mace said with tragic conviction, "change."

He ignited his blade. He held it with both hands.

"May the Force be with us."

He looked at CC-8/349.

"All right, Captain. Blow the door."

23

THE HARD WAY

Greasy smoke curled from the shattered blast door. It reeked of blood and flesh and human waste.

The smell of death.

Mace stood next to the door, waiting for the smoke to thin.

The command bunker was dark as a cave. The only light was the white shaft that spilled in through the opening that used to be the door. The interior materialized as though it slowly drew substance from the haze itself.

Bodies were everywhere.

Piled along the walls. Draped over the banks of monitor consoles. Facedown on the floor in black pools.

Some wore combat armor. Some wore militia khakis. Some wore no uniform at all.

Some were missing pieces.

Mace's blade hissed in the smoke as he went inside.

As a weapon, a lightsaber was uniquely tidy. Even, in a sense, merciful. Its powerful cascade of energy instantly seared and cauterized any wound it inflicted. The wounds rarely bled at all. It was a *clean* weapon.

A vibroshield was not.

The floor in the command bunker was treacherously slippery.

Mace trod with care. Behind him, Nick slipped through the doorway and put his back to the wall.

All was silence and death. A whole different world from the madness outside. Inside was a darker madness.

So dark he might as well be blind.

"Depa," he said softly. "Kar. Come out. I know you're watching me."

His answer was a low, silky predator's growl that seemed to come from everywhere at once.

We don't have to be enemies.

Mace brought up his blade. He moved cautiously around the ruins of the monitor bank closest to the doorway.

Aren't we on the same side? We've won the planet for you, haven't we?

Mace reached into the Force, feeling for the emptiness below that would contain the transceiver. With each step, he worked his feet down, seeking solid footing on the floor before taking the next.

Do you really want to fight us? We are kin, you and I.

We are your own people.

"You were never my people." Mace spoke without emotion. "A man like you will always be my enemy, no matter whose side you're on. And I will always fight you."

Why do they name you a Master? You have mastered only futility. You cannot possibly win.

"I don't have to win," Mace said. "All I have to do is fight."

A low snarl was the only warning he got.

Nick's guns roared flame at a hurtling dark shape that leaped from nowhere. Sparks clanged in the gloom as Mace whirled instinctively and slashed at the shape and it vanished in a dive that carried it over the console bank. Before he'd even seen what it was.

He'd never felt it coming.

Dark power swirled around him.

He let his blade shrink away and crouched between two console banks, his heart hammering. "Nick!" he called. "Did you get him?"

"Don't think so." Nick's voice came out thin and tight. "Sounded like he took both on the shields. You?"

Mace smelled smoke: charred flesh. "Perhaps. A piece of him, anyway."

"See where he came from?"

"No. I think—" Mace's breath hissed through his teeth. "I think they're hiding among the bodies. Stay ready."

"You better believe it."

The low snarling growl became mocking. *Your Force can't help you here. Here there is only* pelekotan. *And we are only* pelekotan's *dream.*

Mace crept his way silently along the console bank.

You didn't feel me coming at you. You can't.

"That wasn't you," Mace said, low.

But it was. One-seventh of me.

Your pardon: one-eighth.

He could feel the transceiver chamber now: two meters away on the far side of this console bank. Its ceiling began a meter and a half below the floor.

You have lost her. Lost her to pelekotan. *Lost her to* pelekotan's *dream: a world free from Balawai.*

Mace muttered, "We are all Balawai here."

He triggered his blade just long enough to stab into the leg well of the console under which he crouched, and carve an arch out of its back just large enough to crawl through. He pulled the cutaway piece free and laid it flat.

On the far side lay a knot of dead clones. Four. He had to crawl over them.

Someone had taken off their helmets. Their eyes were open.

Jango Fett's dead face stared at him four times over.

Dead eyes looked into him and saw nothing but his guilt.

He kept moving.

The spot he needed was just ahead. Mace finally tore his attention away from the dead clones, and froze.

Someone had been carving the floor there already. Blackened hunks of the command bunker's armor plating lay strewn around a human-sized pit already nearly a meter deep. Beside them, a slim form in tattered brown robes lay crumpled on the floor.

Her lightsaber was still in her hand.

For one giddy instant, his heart sang: she had anticipated him. She *hadn't* fallen to the dark—it had been an act, all an *act*! She had been cutting through the floor to *help* him—

But it was only one instant. He knew better.

Of course she had anticipated him: she knew all there was to know about his style. She'd known exactly what his target had to be, and she hadn't been cutting into the chamber below in order to help activate the transceiver.

She'd been going there to destroy it.

Looked like the proton grenade blast had caught her just in time. She didn't seem to be breathing. In the blinding swirl of dark power that filled the bunker, he could not feel if she still lived.

You have gone very quiet, dôshalo. Do you think silence can save you? Do you think that because you cannot feel me, the reverse is also true?

Too much fatigue; too much pain. He had no room left in his heart for more.

He would grieve later. Now, looking at her corpse, he felt only a vague, melancholy relief that he hadn't had to kill her himself.

Do you think there is anything about you I don't know?

"I think," Mace said, "that if you were all you claim, I'd already be dead."

He pushed himself into a forward roll that brought him up to a crouch, and looked down into the hole. She'd done most of his work for him already. He could cut through with a single stroke.

You are not yet my kill.

"No? Whose kill am I, then?"

The answer to his question was a lightsaber's emitter jammed against his belly.

Mace had time to think blankly: Oh. Not dead. Faking.

"Depa—?"

She screamed as she triggered her blade. And kept screaming as its green fire chewed a tunnel through Mace's guts and speared out his back. His hand seized hers instinctively, locking her blade against his body so that she could not kill him by slashing it free. His own blade ignited—

But he could not strike her. Even now. Not here, so close he could kiss her instead; not while her scream spiraled up into a shriek; not while he had to look into her wide staring eyes and see no hate or rage but only stark agony.

He was going to have to do this the hard way.

He struck downward into the pit beside them, his blade slicing out a lopsided ellipse of armor plate that dropped into darkness below and clanged to an unseen floor.

"*Geptun!*" he roared. "*NOW!*"

Flashes of battle:

—shadows fleeing the bunker as swarms of screaming electric blue blaster bolts rebounding off walls shoot them to rags—

—a flood of troopers spreading into a wave through the doorway, weapons gouting lightning-colored energy, Geptun in the middle of them, head down and running, datapad cradled like a baby in his arms—

—a buzzing shield of silver flame that sliced through a blaster rifle so that it exploded and took with it the trooper's hands—

These images burned in Mace's brain as he fought for his life against the woman who should have been his daughter.

He brought his blade back up from the pit and turned his wrist on the forehand so that his recovery stroke took her in the temple with his lightsaber's butt. Her fingers slipped off the blade's activation plate and it shrank back down through his body. She howled and punched his eyesocket with her free hand, but Mace got his foot wedged between them and he shoved her away with a powerful thrust.

At the same instant both of them backflipped into the air, landing on their feet poised in perfect mirror images, their blades whipping in identically curving slashes almost too fast to see.

Blaster bolts howled around them. The air crackled with streaks and splatters of energy. Their blades flickered and whipped and no bolt touched their flesh.

Their eyes never left each other's.

Something had torn in his guts when he did the backflip. Smoke trickled upward from the hole in his belly. He could smell it, but he felt no pain. Not yet. His blade whirred through the air.

Hers whirred faster. She advanced.

The slashes never stopped. They would never stop. They flowed one into the next with liquid precision.

This constant near-invisible weave of lethal energy is the ready-stance of Vaapad.

"Depa," Mace said desperately. "I don't want to fight you. Depa, *please*—"

She sprang at him, screaming without words; he couldn't know if she'd heard him. He couldn't know if language still had meaning for her.

Then she was on him. His whole world turned to green fire.

Twenty-four troopers entered the bunker in a wedge around Colonel Geptun. Nick Rostu kept his back against the wall while he watched them die.

Akk Guards leaped over and past them, and with every leap another clone fell. The clones never stopped, never faltered, firing blaster carbines from the hip, forcing their way forward over the bodies of their comrades.

And it wasn't only clones who died.

The Force nudged Nick, and he swung a pistol and fired without thinking. A leaping Akk Guard whirled and the slug banged sparks off his shield, but in the instant his attention was diverted he fell against the muzzle of a trooper's DC-15 and blue energy exploded out his back.

This Akk Guard had been a man Nick knew, as he knew them all. This one's name had been Prouk. He'd liked to gamble, and he once lost sixty credits to Nick on a bet, and he'd paid it.

Another nudge from the Force and another shot took out the knee of an Akk Guard. He crumpled on top of a dying trooper, who still had enough life left in him to hold down the trigger of his carbine and blow the akk to rags.

This was the Guard whose nose Mace had broken. His name was Thaffal.

Nick was waiting for his next shot when a massive shadow rose up right in front of him; intent on the Force, Nick hadn't seen him coming. He said, "Whoops."

This one's name was Iolu. He had saved Nick's life during a firefight, once. A long time ago.

"Hello, Nick," Iolu said, and drove his shield's sizzling edge toward Nick's neck.

Depa's blade was everywhere.

Mace backpedaled, parrying frantically, absorbing the shock of her attacks with bent arms and a two-handed grip. He was taller than she, with more reach and weight, and vastly more muscle in his upper body, but she drove him backward as though he were a child. Green flame struck through his guard, and only a frantic jerk of his head turned what would have been a brain-burning thrust into a line of char along his cheekbone.

Still he did not strike back.

"I will not kill you," he said. "Death is not the answer to your pain."

Her reply was a scream louder and more savage and an onslaught to match. She broke through his guard again and scorched his wrist. Another stroke burned a slice through his pants leg just above the knee.

Power roared around her, a rising storm of darkness.

Mace got it now: as each Akk Guard died, his share of *pelekotan* backflowed through the bonds Vastor had forged among them.

She was getting stronger.

And with each stroke of her blade, he could feel himself slipping into the shadows. He had to. She was too strong, too fast, too everything. The only way he could survive was to give more of himself to Vaapad. To give all of himself.

To sink into *pelekotan*'s dream.

He felt it: he had reached his own shatterpoint. And he was breaking.

The vibroshield flashed toward his neck.

Nick's knees buckled and he bent backward like a drawn bow. Iolu's fist grazed Nick's nose as the horizontal vibroshield passed over the young Korun's upturned face and bit into the wall so smoothly that the Akk Guard's knuckles hit as well; the unexpected shock loosened his grip on the vibroshield's activator and its hum died, leaving it stuck fast in the wall.

Before Iolu could pull it back out, Nick flipped his pistol's muzzle up against the Akk Guard's extended elbow.

The slug didn't quite blow his arm off.

Iolu swayed, stunned.

Chalk's gun in Nick's other hand came up under Iolu's chin. "Never liked you anyway," Nick said, and pulled the trigger.

The corpse fell against him. Its shattered arm slipped free of the shield's retaining straps. Nick pushed himself sideways out from under, looking for another target, and the dead Guard slid down the wall.

Geptun was nowhere to be seen. He was either dead or down with the transceiver. Either way, there was nothing left to do but fight.

A knot of clone troopers stood back-to-back, firing desperately at one lone Akk Guard who leaped and spun and slaughtered with demonic precision.

No: not an Akk Guard.

It was Kar Vastor.

Nick leveled Chalk's gun. "This is for *her*, scum-packer," he muttered. "Never liked you either."

But her pistol was too heavy for him to hold steady. His own seemed to have gained a dozen kilos as well. "What the frag—?"

His knees turned to cloth.

He looked over at Iolu's corpse. The other shield, one that still hung silent along his dead arm, was stained bright red. Dripping.

Nick said, "Oh."

He looked down. A huge diagonal gash opened his tunic across his abdomen, and his legs were soaked with blood. He sagged back against the wall.

"Oh," he said again. "Oh, nuts."

And, in the end, he was just too tired. Too old.

Too wounded.

Through the trace of Force connection he had with Nick, Mace felt the young Korun collapse. Something broke inside his head, and all his own wounds crashed upon him.

Every cut and bruise, every cracked bone and sprained joint, the man-bite on his shoulder and the hole through his guts: all of them blossomed into silent screams.

His lightsaber went heavy, and his arms went slow. She burned a stripe across his chest, and he staggered.

His fighting spirit wasn't destroyed. It wasn't even far away. He could feel where it had gone. He could reach out and touch it.

It was waiting for him in the dark.

Lorz Geptun quivered uncontrollably. Crouched in the cramped chamber that was filled with the refresher-sized tranceiver, he tried not to listen to the steady diminuendo of the blaster fire above. Each gun that fell silent was one less man up there to protect his life.

His hands trembled so badly he could barely punch the keys on the codelock that sealed his datapad's armored shell. When he finally got it open, he had to fumble in the inky shadows for the linkport on the transceiver. His shaking hands made inserting his pad's datalink resemble threading a needle with his feet, but he got it done.

With a gasp of triumph, he keyed the droid starfighter recall sequence.

Nothing happened.

A moment later, his datapad's screen announced:

ECM FAULT. UNABLE TO EXECUTE. ECM FAULT.
ECM: Electronic Counter-Measure.
The signal-jamming was still on.

In the Force, Mace felt Geptun's despair. It felt like a gift.
Another man might even have smiled.
He took one last look at the darkness that called to him—
Darkness within mirroring darkness without—
And turned away.
He let his blade vanish. His arms dropped to his sides.
Depa moved in for the kill.
Mace backed away.
She leaped for him, slashing, and he slipped aside. She pressed her attack and he retreated, over bodies and through blaster-riddled wreckage of console banks, until he came hard up against a console that still had power: indicator lights flashed like droid eyes in the gloom.

The blade of green fire whirled up, poised, and struck.

He let himself collapse.

He fell to the floor at her feet, and instead of cleaving his skull, her blade slashed the console behind him in half. Cables spat blue sparks across the burned gap.

This was the console that controlled the spaceport's signal-jamming equipment.

Down in the transceiver chamber, Geptun stared at his datapad's screen with astonished reverence, conscious of having been unexpectedly granted undeserved grace.

It read: COMMAND EXECUTED.

In the skies over Pelek Baw, as the snowcap on Grandfather's Shoulder kindled with the first red rays of dawn, droid starfighters disengaged from clone-piloted ships and streaked back into the depths of space.

In the command bunker, the swirl of dark power crested, paused, and began to recede.

Mace lay on the floor. He didn't think he could get up.

Depa stared down at him, her face lit jungle-green by the glow of her blade, and a single needle of light seemed to pierce the dark madness in her eyes.

"Oh, Mace . . ."

Her voice was a moan of astonished pain. Her blade vanished, and her arms fell limp and helpless to her sides. "Mace, I'm sorry—I'm so *sorry* . . ."

He managed to lift a hand to reach up to her. "Depa—"

"Mace, I'm sorry," she repeated, and brought her lightsaber up to put its emitter to her own temple. "We shouldn't have come."

"Depa, *no!*"

Mace found he did have the strength to rise, to stand, even to leap for her, but he was exhausted, and wounded, and far, far too slow.

She squeezed the activator plate.

A single sharp report—like a handclap—rang out behind him, and a spark flew from the metal of her blade as it was smacked spinning from her hand.

It twisted lazily through the air and clattered among the wreckage.

She blinked dizzily, as though she couldn't quite understand why she was still alive, then crumpled to the floor.

Mace turned toward where the sound had come from.

Sitting next to the corpse of a dead Akk Guard, his back propped against the wall, one hand pressed to his chest to hold closed a horrible wound, Nick Rostu grinned past the smoking barrel of the pistol in his other hand. "Told you . . ."

"Nick—"

"Told you I can shoot . . ." he said. His fingers opened and the gun fell to the floor; his hand dropped on top of it and his eyes drifted shut.

"Nick, I—"

The young Korun was beyond hearing.

Mace said softly, "Thank you."

He swayed. He had to put out a hand to the wrecked comm console to steady himself.

The bunker had once again gone quiet and dark and full of death. Quiet except for a low growl.

The growl came from a black shape that rose like corpse-fungus from among the bodies.

So, dôshalo. Here we are. For the last time.

"Perhaps."

The shape smoked with power. More power than Mace had ever felt.

And he was so tired. So hurt. The lightsaber wound in his belly radiated pain that scraped away his strength.

The shadow beckoned. *Come on, then: jungle rules.*

"On the contrary," Mace said slowly. "Jedi rules."

What are Jedi rules?

"You don't need to know," Mace told him. "You're not a Jedi."

Vibroshields whined to life. *I am waiting for you, Jedi of the Windu.*

Mace extended a hand, and his lightsaber found it.

He stood, waiting.

You fear to attack me.

"Jedi do not fear," Mace said. "And we do not attack. As long as you stand in peace, so do I. You have just learned two of the Jedi rules. For what little good they will do you. You haven't been paying very close attention, Kar. And it's too late to start now. It's over."

Nothing is over! NOTHING. Not while we both live.

"This is another Jedi rule." Mace took a couple of steps to one side, to find a space of floor where he didn't have to fear tripping over a body. "If you fight a Jedi, you've already lost."

The dark shape came closer. *Fine words from a man I've beaten before.*

"The starfighters have been ordered off. The city will stand. They've surrendered to the Republic. We have no reason to fight."

Men like us are our own reason.

Mace shook his head. "This isn't a big dog thing. If I must, I will hurt you. Badly."

You can't bluff me.

"No, but I can kill you. Though I would rather not."

More Jedi rules?

Mace sagged. "Do you have a move to make? I'm too tired for this."

Sleep when you're dead, Vastor snarled, and leaped.

Ultrachrome flashed. Mace could have met him, blade to shields, but instead he slipped aside.

He had no intention of fighting this man. Not here and now. Not anywhere. Not ever.

Vastor was younger, stronger, faster, and immensely more powerful, and he wielded weapons that could not be harmed by the Jedi blade. Mace couldn't win such a battle on his best day, and this day was far from his best: he was exhausted, badly wounded, and heartsick.

But the fact that his lightsaber couldn't hurt those shields didn't make them invulnerable.

As Vastor gathered himself to spring again, Mace reached into the Force. The vibroshield stuck into the wall above Nick's head squealed against the bunker's armor as it came to life and pulled itself free and streaked like a missile toward Vastor's back.

Vastor's incredible reflexes whirled him, and those same reflexes snapped his shields in front of his chest in plenty of time to block—

But they didn't actually *block* anything . . .

There was a reason why, when Vastor's shields met to make that metallic howl, he always brought them together back-to-back, instead of edge-to-edge.

The flying shield's vibrating edge sheared through both Vastor's shields, through both his wrists, and buried itself in the bone of his chest, stopping less than a centimeter short of his heart.

Vastor blinked astonishment at Mace as though the Jedi Master had betrayed him.

Mace said, "You were warned."

Vastor's head shook weakly, suddenly palsied. He dropped to his knees. *You've killed me.*

He sounded like he couldn't make himself believe it.

"No," Mace said. "That's another of the Jedi rules. Killing you is not the answer for your crimes. You're going back to Coruscant. You're going to stand trial."

Vastor swayed. His gaze went blank and blind.

"Kar Vastor," said Mace Windu, "you are under arrest."

Vastor pitched forward. Mace caught him and turned him face-up before lowering the unconscious *lor pelek* to the floor.

Then he pulled himself back to his feet, leaning on the console.

His vision grayed and lost focus; for a moment he wasn't sure where he was. This might have been Palpatine's office. Or the interrogation room at the Ministry of Justice. The Intel station, or the dead room at the Lorshan Pass.

Perhaps even the Jedi Temple . . . but the Jedi Temple wouldn't ever *smell* like this.

Would it?

"Master Windu?"

He remembered the voice, and it brought him back to the command bunker.

"Is it over?" Geptun called tentatively from the transceiver chamber. He sounded very old, and more than a little lost. "Can I come out now?"

Mace looked down at Kar Vastor, and the spreading pool of blood in which he lay. He looked at the scattered corpses of clone troopers and militia techs. He looked at Nick Rostu, crumpled against the wall.

"Master Windu?" Geptun's head appeared slowly over the rim of the hole in the floor. "Did we win?"

Mace looked at the sad, shrunken form of Depa Billaba, and thought about his victory conditions.

"I seem to be," Mace Windu said slowly, "the last one standing."

It was the only answer he had.

THE JEDI'S WAR

FROM THE PRIVATE JOURNALS OF MACE WINDU:

I still dream of Geonosis.

But my dreams are different, now.

A Republic task force arrived to take possession of Haruun Kal and the Al'har system within forty-eight standard hours of my arrest of Kar Vastor; it seems they had already been dispatched to answer a distress call from the acting commander of the *Halleck*.

Their landing was unopposed.

The Republic will not occupy Haruun Kal; acting under my authority as General of the Grand Army of the Republic, I redesignated the Korunnal Highland. It is no longer enemy territory, and Haruun Kal is no longer officially a war zone. On my recommendation, the Senate has declared the combat operations on Haruun Kal to be a police action.

Because I have decided to treat the Summertime War as a law enforcement problem.

Which it would have always been, had the financial interests behind the thyssel bark trade not been able to buy off certain Senators and Judicial sector coordinators.

We are in the process of disarming the jungle prospectors and the remaining bands of Korunnai guerrillas. It's going surprisingly well; the jups are terrified of Republic soldiers, and the Korunnai bands are mostly exhausted and sick. As they come to understand that they will not be mistreated, many simply surrender altogether. All charges of atrocities are being investigated. If those responsible can be identified, they will be tried, and they will be punished.

The planetary militia remains, though at greatly reduced strength. The militia regulars will now become what they should always have been.

Keepers of the peace. Not soldiers.

Many of them have volunteered to be inducted into the Republic Army.

Including, unexpectedly, Colonel Geptun.

He has not been charged with any crime. The vast bulk of the atrocities committed against the Korunnai were done by jungle prospectors, not the militia. Even his threat of a massacre at the Lorshan Pass turns out to have been a bluff. He never ordered any such thing; in fact, the militia's written rules of engagement specifically prohibit the targeting of civilians.

Not only have I recommended he be accepted into the Grand Army of the Republic, I have already written out his transfer to Republic Intelligence.

We will need him.

Nick—I should say, Major Rostu—continues to convalesce in a medical center here on Coruscant. I do not know if I can keep my promise of a job teaching unconventional warfare, but I have no doubt we can find something for him. I have submitted a recommendation to the Senate that his brevet rank be confirmed.

And that he be awarded the Medal of Valor for conspicuous gallantry under fire, and actions above and beyond the call of duty.

I have also assigned to Chalk a posthumous commission. Her real name, I have learned only now, was Liane Trevval, and that name will appear in the Senate record. I gave her the commission to render her eligible for the same medal.

I have no other way to express my respect for who she was.

Her great akk, Galthra, has vanished. If an akk's Force-bonded partner dies, it is customary to put the beast down, for it is not uncommon for akks who have lost their person to go insane, and vicious.

Galthra went into the jungle. I can only hope she stays there.

Pelek Baw will be rebuilt. There is too much money in the thyssel trade for its epicenter to lie in ruins for long. The casualties—

Are recorded elsewhere. It is a staggering number.

No one on Haruun Kal will ever forget that night.

Kar Vastor also continues to recover from his wounds. His hands were saved, and he is under detention here in the Jedi Temple, where his power cannot sway his jailers.

He will not be immediately tried for the murder of Terrel Nakay; that will only be filed against him in the event of his acquittal on his initial charge. For the trial of Kar Vastor, we have revived a category of crime under which no one has been prosecuted in four thousand years: since the days of the Sith Wars.

Kar Vastor has been charged with crimes against civilization.

And Depa—

Depa will face the same charge.

Someday.

If she's ever declared competent to stand trial.

After reading my report on Haruun Kal, Supreme Chancellor Palpatine—in his characteristically warm and compassionate way— took time from his more pressing duties to come to the Temple and look in on Depa personally.

He was accompanied by Yoda and myself; the three of us stood alone in a darkened observation room, watching through a holoviewer as three Jedi healers attended to poor Depa. She hung suspended in a bacta tank. Her eyes were open—submerged in bacta one has no need to blink—and they stared fixedly through the transparisteel at something only she could see.

Depa has not spoken—has not *moved*—since her collapse. The greatest Jedi healers of the Temple can find nothing organically wrong with her. Bacta has cured her physical wounds; it cannot touch the rest.

When the healers touch her through the Force, all they find is darkness. Vast and featureless.

She is lost in infinite night.

The Supreme Chancellor watched only for a moment or two before he sighed and shook his head sadly. "Still no progress, I take it?"

Yoda watched me gravely while I struggled to find words to answer. Finally he sighed and took pity on me.

"To end her life, she tried," he said. "Most tragic this is: to have sunk so deeply into despair that she can no longer see light. Yet we must not follow her there; hold on to hope, we must. Recover she may. Someday."

Though perhaps I should not have admitted it, the truth pushed its way out of me. "I would almost have preferred to lose the planet, if I could have saved Depa."

"And do you know what caused her breakdown?" Palpatine pressed his hand against the holoviewer, as though he could reach through it and stroke her hair. "I recall that learning this was one of the stated purposes of your mission to Haruun Kal, and yet your report offers no definite conclusion."

Slowly, I admitted, "Yes. I do know."

"And?"

"It's difficult to explain. Especially to a non-Jedi."

"Does it have anything to do with that scar on her forehead? Where her—what did you call it?"

"The Greater Mark of Illumination."

"Yes. Where her Mark of Illumination once was. I recognize that this is painful for you, Master Windu, but please. The Jedi are vital to the survival of the Republic, and Master Billaba is not the only Jedi we have lost to the darkness. Anything we can learn about what might cause one to fall is *incredibly* important."

I nodded. "But I cannot offer a specific answer."

"Well, the scar, then. Was she tortured?"

"I do not know. Possibly. It is also possible that the wound was self-inflicted. We may never know."

"It is a pity," Palpatine murmured, "that we cannot ask her."

Some few seconds passed before I was able to respond. "I can only speculate in general terms, based upon what she told me, and upon my own experiences."

Palpatine's eyebrows twitched upward. "Your own?"

I could not meet his gaze; when I lowered my head, I found Yoda staring up at me. His wise wrinkled face was filled with ancient compassion. "Fall you did not," he said softly. "From this, strength you can take."

I nodded, and found myself once again able to face the Supreme Chancellor. "It's war," I said. "Not just *that* war, but war itself. When every choice you make means death. When saving *these* innocents means that *those* innocents must die. I'm not sure that any Jedi can survive such choices for long."

Palpatine looked from Yoda to me, his face a mask of compassionate concern. "Who would have thought that fighting a war could have such a terrible effect on a Jedi? Even when we win," he murmured. "Who would ever have *thought* such a thing?"

"Yes," I could only agree. "Who would have thought it, indeed?"

"Wonder, one must," Yoda said slowly, "if *that* might be the most important question of all . . ."

There followed a long, uncomfortable silence, which Palpatine finally broke. "Ah, sadly, questions of philosophy must wait for peacetime. We must focus on winning this war."

"That's what Depa did," I said. "And look what it did to her."

"Ah, but such a thing could never happen to—say, for example—*you*," Palpatine said warmly. His lips wore an enigmatic smile. "Could it?"

I didn't tell him that it could. That it nearly had.

I think about that a lot, these days. I think about Depa. About everything she said to me.

And did to me.

I think about the jungle.

She was right about so many things.

She was right about her Jedi of the Future. To win this war against the Separatists, we must abandon the very thing that *makes* us Jedi. Yes, we won on Haruun Kal—because our enemy broke under the club of Kar Vastor's monstrous ruthlessness.

Jedi are keepers of the peace. We are not soldiers.

If we become soldiers, we will be Jedi no more.

Yet I do not despair.

She was wrong about some things, too.

You see, she got lost fighting someone else's war. She was fighting the wrong enemy.

The Separatists are not the true enemies of the Jedi. They are enemies of the *Republic*. It is the Republic which will stand or fall in the battles of the Clone War.

Even the reborn Sith are not our enemy. Not really.

Our enemy is power mistaken for justice.

Our enemy is the desperation that justifies atrocity.

The Jedi's true enemy is the *jungle*.

Our enemy is the darkness itself: the strangling cloud of fear and despair and anguish that this war brings with it. That is poisoning our galaxy. This is why my dreams of Geonosis are different now.

In my dreams, I still do everything right.

But I do in my dreams exactly what I did in that arena.

If the prophecies are true—if Anakin Skywalker is truly the Chosen One, who will bring balance to the Force—then he is the most important being alive today. And he is alive today because my Jedi instincts were working just fine.

Because my mistake on Geonosis wasn't a mistake at all.

If I had done as Depa said I should have—if I had won the Clone War with a baradium bomb on Geonosis—I would have lost the *real* war. The Jedi's war.

Anakin Skywalker may be the shatterpoint of our war against the jungle.

If he is—if Anakin is the being born to win that war—it does not matter if every other Jedi in the galaxy dies.

As long as Anakin lives, we have hope. No matter how dark it gets, or how lost our cause may seem.

He is our new hope for a Jedi future.

May the Force be with us all.

CLONE WARS
TIMELINE

With the Battle of Geonosis (EP II), the Republic is plunged into an emerging, galaxy-wide conflict. On one side, the Confederacy of Independent Systems (the Separatists), led by the charismatic Count Dooku and backed by a number of powerful guilds and trade organizations and their droid armies.

On the other side, the Republic loyalists and their newly-created clone army, led by the Jedi. It is a war fought on a thousand fronts, with heroism and sacrifices on both sides. Below is a partial list of some of the important events of the Clone Wars and a guide to where these events are chronicled.

MONTHS
(after *Attack of the Clones*)

---

0   **THE BATTLE OF GEONOSIS**
Star Wars: Episode II – *The Attack of the Clones* (LFL, May '02)

0   **THE SEARCH FOR COUNT DOOKU**
Boba Fett #1: *The Fight to Survive* (SB, April '02)

+1   **THE BATTLE OF RAXUS PRIME**
Boba Fett #2: *Crossfire* (SB, November '02)

+1   **THE DARK REAPER PROJECT**
The Clone Wars (LEC, May '02)

+1.5   **CONSPIRACY ON AARGAU**
Boba Fett #3: *Maze of Deception* (SB, April '03)